D1508615

SPECTRUM

SPECTRUM

BOOK 1 OF THE F.O.K. SERIES

SHEILA SULLIVAN

Spectrum Book 1 of the F.O.K. Series is a work of fiction. Names, characters, places, and incidents are the products of the author's imagination or are used fictitiously. Any resemblance to actual events, locales, or persons, living or dead, is entirely coincidental.

I greatly appreciate the heavy lifting done by my editor, Kristen Tate. Kristen used her exceptional editing skills and humor to help refine this story. You may contact her through her website at www.thebluegarret.com. Thanks to Christie Lee Duffy for her most careful proofreading. Christie Lee may be contacted at www.EvenFlowEditing.com.

Earlier drafts of this book were read by Emily Robinson, Shanna Crawford, and Martha Shumaker. I thank them all for wading through the weeds of this story before Kristen got a hold of it and trimmed. All of you provided helpful insights and encouragement to continue writing.

All errors, issues, and things that cause the writing to be less than perfect are the mistake made by the author. Yes. The wonderful people involved in editing, proofreading, and typesetting are not responsible for those mistakes. Quite possibly those mistakes are planted in the book to see if you are reading closely. I, the author, am kidding. No one likes mistakes. Least of all me. I want you to enjoy the book and not be hindered by mistakes. If you find grammar or spelling mistakes my advice is to let it go and keep reading.

You can reach out to me through my website, www.sheilamsullivan.com .

Drop me a note at info@sheilamsullivan.com

Copyright © 2017 by Sheila M. Sullivan
All rights reserved.

ISBN 978 -0-9989648-0-5

Book Layout and Cover Design by Phillip Gessert www.gessertbooks.com

For Janine
Infinity and beyond raised to infinity

CHAPTER ONE
BUENA VISTA IRISH COFFEE CLUB

F RANCES relapsed into her Catholic muscle memory as she dipped her finger into the holy water held in a small marble bowl set to the right of the church entrance. Her mother said that being Catholic was in their Irish DNA. Did that mean that they had a mutant gene? She made the sign of the cross as she walked up the center aisle of the Saints Peter and Paul Church, focused on the ceiling in search of a sign that god was indeed going to strike her with lightning if she tried to approach the main altar. Not ready to test the theory, Frances saw the confessional cubbies off to the side of the main mass area and took a short cut through the empty pews.

The ornate, walnut-colored confessional rooms in this church were old school. They were the size of a phone booth with a small red light over the top of the door to indicate if another sinner was inside seeking penance to absolve them of whatever crimes they felt needed to be forgiven. Frances paused over her thought—were confessions crimes or sins? Due to a mishap one Saturday where she waited for three hours in a confessional booth, she quietly knocked on the center door with the giant cross.

"Hearing a confession. Please pay attention to the lights," a deep male voice said.

"Sorry. Just checking to make sure someone was in there," Frances said.

As Frances was deciding if she should enter the empty confessional booth, an elderly woman exited from the left side of the confessional cubby. She stopped and smiled at Frances and held the confessional door open for Frances. Shoot. Frances felt obligated to follow through now. The woman's dark-gray hair was covered with a delicate white lace scarf, reaching far back in the church's history of austere dress codes. Frances remembered her mother and grandmother wearing something similar long after the Vatican reforms made the head scarf optional. A swoosh followed by a loud click caused her to jump as the priest opened the small screened window that joined his cubicle to Frances's. This really was old school. When she left Catholic school, confessions were done face-to-face in the rectory in St. Louis.

Frances placed a finger on her forehead, heart, and across her chest, and said, "In the name of the father, son, and holy ghost, bless me, Father. It has been…fifteen…no, seventeen…more likely…quite possibly twenty years since my last confession." Frances knelt next to the screened panel, noticing that the priest on the other side was bald.

"May god the father of all mercies help you make a good and much awaited confession."

"I don't know where to start, Father."

"How about just one or two highlights of the sins you wish to confess. I have a mass to prepare for this afternoon."

Frances giggled, as this priest had a point. A listing of every sin committed over the past two decades could take a while. An excel spreadsheet of sin would be needed. Who keeps track of their sins like that anyway? Frances took a deep breath.

"I'm lost. My marriage ended in divorce. I left my job that ultimately left people without jobs. I'm not honest with my parents about being an artist. I'm scared there really is a heaven and hell. And I am going straight to hell. Father, why is the address of this church 666?"

"Well," the priest began, ignoring her last question. "You have strayed from the teachings of the church. Did you have your wedding annulled?"

"No. I wasn't married in a Catholic church. I didn't think I had to get it annulled. I'm more concerned about lying to my parents," Frances said.

"Concern is a start. It shows you might be capable of performing your acts of contrition."

"I'm afraid of who I really might be and I am—"

"Afraid of who you really might be is not a confession. What is it you're trying to ask god to forgive?"

"I'm sorry, Father. This was a mistake." Frances closed her eyes. As the tears fell, she couldn't identify why.

"I don't think I can help you. You must ask god, the father of mercies through the death and resurrection of his son, for forgiveness and strength. Say ten Our Fathers and five Hail Marys."

The wooden window shut, and Frances was alone in the dark confessional box. Her heart jumped into her throat as she pushed her way out of the confessional. She stifled a sneeze as she tried to control her tears and noticed that there was no red light over the other confessional booth. In an act of strange directness and a desire for some sort of answer, Frances went into the other booth. This time she was ready for the sound of the wood panel opening.

"In the name of the father, son, and holy ghost. It has been thirty...no maybe only fifteen seconds since my last confession."

"What in heaven's name?" the priest said.

"Father, I need to know what god will think of me," Frances said.

"Think of you about what?"

Frances scratched her head and wondered if the priest was suffering from short-term memory loss. "Father, I told you I was divorced and never married in the church, and I am struggling with who or what I am."

"You sound like a woman. Say ten Our Fathers and five Hail Marys."

"That is what you told me to do a minute ago. Does that mean I now say twenty Our Fathers and ten Hail Marys? How does that help?"

The wood panel shut, leaving Frances alone in the second confessional booth, more confused than when she had entered. She rose slowly and pushed the door open. An empty church greeted her return from a second failed attempt to get clarity. Frances ran toward the closest exit door of the church. Out on the sidewalk, she wiped away her tears and decided to walk to the Buena Vista from North Beach. It would give her time to try and settle her thoughts. The priests in a progressive city should open their arms to anything. I thought they were supposed to help herd the lost sheep back into the flock. Who am I kidding? I have always been the black sheep of the family. How do I know I am not already in hell? That church's address might be a sign.

"Let's rip this Band-Aid off quickly," Frances said as she clasped the cold brass door handle and walked into the Buena Vista. It had been far too long since she had enjoyed this ritual with her friends.

"Welcome back, Frances Olar Kavanagh. We missed you when you were playing survivor on married island. Nice shirt. When do we get ours? You know the boys are going to say that shirt is wonderfully gay," Winter said.

"Are you done? That was quite the barrage. Now I know what your victims feel like in cross-examinations," Frances said and settled herself into a chair between Cheryl and Winter. From her messenger bag, she pulled out a stack of five T-shirts. It was not lost on Frances that they both had already ordered and were halfway through Irish coffees.

"They are not victims; they are witnesses. And I rarely go to court; I do transactional law," Winter said.

"I have a peace offering for each one of you. I designed these T-shirts to mark the F.O.K. reboot of the Buena Vista Irish Coffee Club," Frances said.

"Gifts are not going to stop us from holding you accountable for deserting us when you met and married that dickhead," Winter said.

"These are awesome. I love the happy leprechaun sliding down a rainbow drinking an Irish Coffee," Cheryl said. "These are so gay. I hope you got the boys extra smalls because they wear T-shirts like they are painted on their bodies. Why are all the hot men gay?"

"Winter, it is understood, and I do deserve some scolding. Take a shirt. Honest, I give it with no strings attached because a club needs a logo and a T-shirt." Frances handed Winter a shirt. She knew Cheryl was right about the sizes and she was going to hear it from the boys about calling them fat indirectly by giving them adult larges.

"Frances, have I not taught you anything? V-necks are much more flattering for women." Cheryl took out a Swiss army knife and started to cut the high collar out of her T-shirt.

"Who carries scissors in their purse? Hey morning glory, what's the story?" Frances asked, trying to ignore the fact that Cheryl was cutting up the T-shirt.

"What are you not telling us, Frances? There is a very odd look about you this morning. It looks like you have been crying and don't you dare blame it on allergies," Cheryl said.

"I will tell you later. Did you know there is a Catholic church in town that has 666 as its street address?"

"That sounds like a joke. Visit satan recently?" Winter asked. "I've got it. You are now officially back in the dating pool and thought a satanic cult was a place to find a date? That could be totally kinky."

Frances shot Winter a scathing look.

"I didn't tell her about anything other than that you are thinking about dating. And quite possibly you went out on a date or two. Really, I said nothing." Cheryl held up the T-shirt and smiled. "Much sexier. Now I don't mind wearing a little leprechaun on my chest."

Frances said nothing as she turned to search for their waitress, ready to get her own Irish coffee. "I'm more than ready to order some food and don't really want to wait. I can see you two didn't."

"Hey. No judgment. I got here and saved us this table. I've got some news to share this morning." Winter took the last sip from her Irish coffee. "You know, Frances, there are some great dating websites that can help you get back into the world of dating. You don't have to join a cult."

"Slow down. Now that my personal life is fodder for gossip, and you know I'm attempting to be back on the market again, I think…I'm wanting to meet a person the old-fashioned way, face-to-face."

"You mean most likely drunk and in a bar. That's the old-fashioned way. I think whiskey goggles are worse than beer goggles," Cheryl said.

"When have you ever seen me drunk?" Frances asked.

"Not my point, Frances. You know we did continue the club when you ditched us over those few years you were playing trophy wife in Marin," Winter said.

"Ouch. I worked. Where is the love?" Frances asked.

Frances, suddenly distracted, waved both her arms like she was expecting someone to pass a ball in her direction. "Hey, Mary—"

"Settle down. Already have your order placed. A little birdie told me you were back. I saw you come in and tried to avoid that T-shirt you are wearing. You got the hungry look this morning, so you are getting the potatoes with your eggs." Mary deposited a round of Irish coffees on the table and was gone.

"She is efficient. Guess I will be eating eggs and potatoes this morning. Where to start with new business? I went to a speed dating rodeo Tuesday night."

"What?" Winter practically snorted her sip of coffee through her nose.

"A rodeo? Is that where you all sit on cows or horses or hay bales?" Cheryl asked.

"Not exactly. I call it a rodeo because I felt like a cowboy climbing on the back of a crazy bull—those three-minute rounds were intense."

"I would have gone with you," Winter said, smiling in a way that made Frances think of a cat ready to pounce on a bird.

"Didn't need the competition. The women in attendance were far more interesting than the men who showed up. How to describe the differences…the majority of the women looked like they were on a casting call for a show on the CW and the men were rejects from *The Muppet Show*. It was crazy. This one guy sat down and asked me if I knew if Jesus Christ was the son of god? Who does that?"

"I love Muppets. How did you respond to the bible thumper? Do you think he was a spy for your mother?" Cheryl asked, trying hard not to laugh.

"I channeled someone other than myself because I said, 'Did you know that Satan is his brother?'"

"Saint Frances, who are you trying to fool? That is totally how you would handle that type of freak, not to mention you went to the 666 church this morning," Winter said.

"He got up and left. We still had a full two minutes and forty-five seconds left on that round." Frances laughed and let her finger play in the cream collar on her Irish coffee.

"Did you match anyone?" Cheryl asked.

"I put in a couple of numbers. I really hate this though, because I haven't been contacted with anyone's information."

"Give it time, F.O.K. It takes those organizers at least a day to get everything done," Winter said.

"But those speed dating organizers said we would know in an hour. How did I not match with any of the twenty-two men I spent three minutes chatting up? I'm not ugly."

Mary set down the breakfast plates on the table. "Not that I was listening, but you're so cute with your red hair and freckles. You are the American poster child for a fine Irish lass. Now, do you need ketchup or hot sauce?" Mary winked as she set both bottles on the table, not waiting for an answer.

Frances dug into her eggs and was glad her carb-counting neighbors had not shown up to make her feel guilty about eating potatoes. She breathed in the scent of rosemary and garlic on the home fries and thanked her Midwestern upbringing for teaching her to love potatoes. Her second bite full of potatoes was almost swallowed when the carb-counting duo, Russell and Simon, sat down at the table.

"Good morning, all. Looks like we are throwing all caution to the wind," Russell said, pointing to Frances's plate.

"Be nice, Russell. She went on a speed dating rodeo circuit and wasn't matched. Got zip, zero, nada," Winter said quickly as she swallowed her own bite of carbs.

"Ouch. I'd eat myself numb too," Simon said. "I'm off to the bar to get our cups of liquid happiness. Anyone else need a refill? These are on us as the new bartender is a friend."

"I swear you two know everyone in the City," Frances said.

"Only the fun people." Russell winked.

"Now that the boys are here, I'm announcing that I'm officially off the market for now. And to prove I am growing up, I bought a condo in Laurel Heights about two blocks off Presidio Avenue." Winter said the words with such force it almost caused Simon to spill the Irish coffees he was attempting to place on the table.

"You did it? You pulled the trigger on two huge commitment decisions at the same time? What is happening in this world?" Frances asked.

"I think that the little old lady in Pasadena crossed that center line," Russell said.

"What? You? But you're the one we depend on to fill our minds with brilliant stories of the 'straight' men you mine in the City." Simon loved using air quotes and Frances found his whole argument that there were no straight men in the City curious. How could that be when so many of the men she knew were married to women?

"Serious? Are you all serious? You make me sound like I'm nothing more than a bitch in heat looking for her next victim, incapable of building anything lasting." Winter looked at the gang and drank down the last of her Irish coffee.

"Did I say that, Russell?" Simon asked.

"No. Did I say that, Simon?"

"No. Not what I heard," Frances answered. "Winter, with you out of the dating scene, how am I going to survive? You had promised we could go out together. You were going to teach me how to date in this crazy world. Where is this make-believe man that took you out of the dating pool?" Frances asked.

"First, Jason is working, and he is very much real. Second, Frances, you and I talked about your dating last week. You even said you had to focus more on your art if you are going to make a real go at it as a career. Then you come in and tell us you went to a speed dating nightmare. We are on different levels of the spectrum. Let's go out, just the two of us so we can tackle some of this. Oh…I know, you can help me move into my new place and we can solve your dating faux pas then." Winter smiled.

"Dating faux pas?" Frances asked.

"I suspect that you lead with your recent divorce, your job change, or you did one of your off-in-outer-space stares," Winter answered.

"Ouch. Some friend you are and quite scary because you might possibly be a psychic," Frances said.

The group erupted into laughter and started to sing with the music playing in the background, which happened to be the Irish Rovers' rendition of "The Unicorn." Soon the regulars familiar with the music were raising their glasses and voices were singing:

"… some cats and rats and elephants, /…but sure as you're born, Don't you forget my Unicorn …"

FRANCES looked around and realized how much she loved this place as she watched her friends and the strangers join in song and laughter. This was what the Buena Vista Irish Coffee Club was all about. She found it hard to believe that Winter was no longer playing the field. It was Winter who had made them all promise to check her into a mental hospital if she ever mentioned the word "serious" and "one man" in the same sentence. And to top off the shock, she bought her first house. Frances was most curious to find out more about this real man who got her to agree to an exclusive arrangement. This was a very rare happening—almost as rare as seeing a unicorn in downtown San Francisco. The morning took away the pain that she was not matched with anyone from the speed dating rodeo.

"Frances, I'm serious. Please help me move. Consider it a down payment on my helping you navigate the dating world," Winter said.

The table was in full conversation as Frances looked at Winter who was giving her the softest eyes she could. This woman could manipulate a toddler to turn over their favorite toy and a jar of candy. What the heck? Frances knew the main reason Winter was asking her to help move, and it had to do with Frances's truck. It was always about what helped Winter save money and exploit her friend's good nature. Frances noticed Winter did not ask anyone else at the table to help her move.

"Sure. You know that I love helping people move." Frances tried hard not to choke over her words.

"Perfect, Frances. I will get you back on the dating horse and this one won't buck you off," Winter said.

CHAPTER TWO

FRANCES

6:00 a.m. Her iPhone chirped nonstop with an avalanche of texts. Frances, now awake, knew sleep was out of the question; the only time her smartphone produced such a sing-song patter was when her family took to their electronic devices. Sometimes Frances wished her family still had only the one phone per household incapable of texting and conference calls. That was a very different time. As she lay in bed listening to the repeated chirps of the phone, she contemplated committing a Kavanagh family cardinal sin by not responding to the family text-a-thon. Why had she not turned the damn thing off? You know why, Frances Olar Kavanagh. Your mother would have your head served on a silver platter with a placard reading "This is what happens when one of my kids ignores me." Frances pulled the covers over her head and wondered if she was doomed to live in a world where her family would never let her sleep past six in the morning. Was there cell phone service in Antarctica? Would the family noise invasion continue if she moved there?

Frances pulled back her comforter and studied the rough-cut wood beams of the loft ceiling as she tried to emerge from her drowsy fog. The unevenness of the beams, wet-sealed concrete floors, and exposed brick sold the space. What artist doesn't want a raw open space with tons of natural light to feed into the story of it all? One difference played out in this loft space and that of the 'starving artist': this one had a gourmet kitchen, spa-like bathroom, and a price tag out of reach of most artists. Frances surveyed her new home and worried about keeping the lifestyle she developed as a business and health care consultant to the C-suite executives on an unknown painter's budget. When people asked what she did for a living, her answer was slow to change. It did not take her long to stop saying 'painter.' For some reason, people equated 'painter' with houses and walls. The term 'artist' defined her in the eyes of others as 'poor' and 'unemployable.' She shook her head to stop the crazy thinking of titles and work.

Frances stayed nestled under her down comforter as the iPhone songbird changed its tune to the first few notes from *The Addams Family*. She couldn't help herself and double snapped her fingers along with the song. As a fan of anything remotely related to Charles Addams and his darkly humorous and macabre cartoons, she had assigned that iconic television theme song to her parental unit's phone number. Granted, her family would consider themselves the direct antithesis of the Addams family, but Frances could count multiple ways her Kavanagh family were weirdly kooky. The main support was how ghostly pale they all were. When they were young, she and her siblings were teased because they were so pale that the blue tint of their blood veins showed through their translucent skin.

She rolled over and contemplated what form of torture she might need to unleash on her nieces and nephews. After all, they were the responsible smarty pants who showed Nanna and Pappy Kavanagh how to send texts—such fun for the grandkids and a new form of control over Frances and her siblings. Once the Kavanagh rulers embraced texting, Snapchat, and Twitter, the whole landscape of social media changed for Frances and her seven siblings. God forbid you were busy with work or life. The demand for immediate response was now 24/7; it was like you were working for a start-up tech company. Only, this demand from the Kavanagh Irish Mafia wasn't softened by a potential IPO payout. Frances dropped Facebook the day she got poked by both her parents. She stretched her arms and legs, removing herself from her warm cocoon as she thought about a rumor that Facebook had taken the so-called "poking" feature away as someone at Facebook also found "poking" from one's parents creepy. To unplug and keep something private in her life, Frances had wiped her electronic fingerprints from any form of social media.

Frances yawned, cracking her jaw joint, which caused her to grimace. One of these days would her jaw just hang open forever? She raised herself up enough to reach her phone on the reclaimed cafe table she used as her nightstand and glanced at the cascade of messages on the screen. It was now 6:35 in the morning. Thirty-five minutes of texting from the family. Frances flopped back on her pillow and screamed out into the empty loft, "Time zones, people! Remember your time zones." It was after 8:30 a.m. in St. Louis, Missouri, hometown to most of the Kavanagh clan.

Her parents had instilled their own Kavanagh rule of law when they were young: "To be productive you must wake before the early bird and get that worm first." Frances had escaped both early morning worm eating and the winters of Missouri more than twelve years ago, never looking back. She scrolled to the top of the text conversation, one so long she was grateful for her unlimited data plan. Otherwise she would be in some serious debt for their modern concept of a family dialogue. A glance out the long east-facing wall of windows showed San Francisco living up to its weather reputation. Fog bounced softly against the buildings, cloaking any view beyond ten feet. It kept the industrial-turned-artsy enclave around 3rd Street tucked in for the morning.

Frances fished for the furry sheepskin slippers under her bed. How they ended up under her bed every night was a mystery. Did she sleepwalk and kick them out of reach in the middle of the night? Was it a slipper house elf up to no good? Now her body was chilled from lying on the cold concrete floor while retrieving her slippers. She shivered in her thin T-shirt and boxer shorts, thinking about the flannel nightgowns she and her clan were forced to wear when growing up. They were torture. Flannel nightgowns combined with flannel sheets were a secret combination parents used to Velcro their children into bed. Frances remembered that once she was tucked in bed, it was almost impossible to get out of this bed prison. It often required a fellow inmate, otherwise known as a sympathetic brother or sister, to help her escape the sticky bonds of flannel on flannel.

Part of her new world order, Frances was actively trying to override the instant twitch response the smartphone age had brainwashed into her. Such dependence often made her feel like she was gasping for air if she was separated from her phone. Now that instant response programming was in her family, and it felt like it was extrapolating into faster and faster response-time requirements. Her addiction was worse.

She often called her phone the base camp of her operations. It had fed her everything she felt she needed, from news to the electronic chains that kept her held fast into the family. When her phone had sounded, it was hard for her to avoid that instant need to know exactly who or what was communicating. God forbid one second pass between a message sent and received. She went through withdrawals when she attempted to unplug herself from her phone umbilical cord. The withdrawals were tame compared to the lectures she had received from her mother. Her friends and ex-husband found her devotion to her family almost cultish. She never could explain what it meant to be a cadet raised Irish Catholic under the rule of Bridgette and Patrick Kavanagh.

The serious pronouncements of punishment from her mother, Bridgette, an Irish force of one, enforced the message that you did not mess with Mom and expect to win. Her mother's brogue accent was strong enough to stand disembodied, as her dictates ran on continual loops in the minds of her children. Frances sighed as she saw she had a new voicemail. That meant she would need to listen to the message and lecture left by her mother. Even though Frances had excelled on her college debate teams, her mother always managed to come up with a better argument, one that systematically dismantled any logical explanation Frances attempted. It was easier to leave the phone on than endure the aftermath. It amazed Frances how quickly her mother became an expert on all things voicemail. If her phone failed to ring and went directly to voicemail, it was not good. Mama Kavanagh always came up with several horrid end-of-the-world scenarios as to why you did not pick up the phone.

Frances jumped when her phone vibrated in her hand, simultaneously singing out *The Addams Family* theme song again. That was unusual. That meant only one of two people could be calling her at 6:42

a.m., and Dad never called. Frances knew she had to answer. Mom's usual modus operandi was to leave a message and then log how long it took for a return call. The longer it took, the harsher the lecture.

"Hi, Mom."

"Oh, hello honey. I'm sorry, did I wake you? Patrick, can you click the stove off? Hang on Franny. Pat, turn the stove off and don't forget to take the garbage out."

In lightning fashion, Frances contemplated a number of responses but did not feel like a word jousting with her mother this early. It always happened this way. Mom would call and then carry on a conversation with someone else. It was crazy.

"Nope. My voice has changed as I am approaching another birthday and quite possibly going through adult-onset puberty." Frances walked over to her kitchen, reaching across the counter for the magic button on her Nespresso coffee machine while balancing the phone between her shoulder and ear. Coffee was a must to keep her focus and learn about what was sending her phone into constant agitation.

"If you were up, why weren't you responding to the conversation?"

"Mom. Texting is not a conversation. This is a conversation. Remember when you used to call and talk?"

"Pat, don't forget we are going to lunch with the Seavers today. I need to stop at the drug store—"

"Mom, why are you calling? If you are going to have a conversation with Dad I am going to say good-bye."

"Frances, there was an earthquake in California. Are you okay?"

"Yes, Mom. I'm fine. The earthquake was down in San Diego, more than five hundred miles away."

"No need to be snippy. Are you rolling your eyes? Stop it. Your father worries about you out there. San Francisco gets earthquakes too. Are you coming to our party?"

How did her mom know when she is making faces? Did she have video surveillance equipment installed in her apartment? Her first sip of coffee sparked her brain flint burning up the last of the cobwebs that slowed her thinking. Party? Had she missed something? She quickly scrolled through the thirty or so texts that had been her alarm clock.

"Frances, did you hear me?" Bridgette asked.

"Your party is still six months away. Why do you need to know if I am coming right this minute?"

"Well. We don't know what to think about you. You quit your job. You divorced Richard. You live in California. What happened to our happy little Franny?"

"Mom, you haven't called me Franny since I was ten. My neighbors like to call me Franny because they think I'm adorable. But in answer to your question. Yes, I am coming to your fortieth wedding anniversary. California is part of this country the last time I checked. Jesus—"

"Frances, you don't use the lord's name in any context with that tone of voice. We love you, Franny. I need to hear it from you."

"Hear what, Mom?"

"Frances Olar Kavanagh, don't you play dumb with me. You know exactly what I need to hear. Your sisters and brothers are worried about you too."

"Did someone say something to you? Stop worrying…I went to confession this weekend." Frances hoped this statement would distract her mother and get her talking about church.

"Now you need to start going to weekly mass. Frances, I am not playing around here. Knock it off."

"Did Edna tell you?" Frances asked. She sat down on her piano bench gripping the phone, wanting to crush it in her hands. Frances was still attempting to work through her own questions and fears about leaving the business world and starting to date again without attracting the judgement of her mother. Frances knew that she had only shared her leaving her job with Edna and Agatha. They had promised that they would not say anything.

"Frances, are you still there? I'm waiting. You owe your father and I more respect than what you are showing us now. You think that because you live so far away that you no longer need to get our permission?"

The tremor in her mother's voice let Frances know that her mother was borderline close to her plate-throwing anger phase. The loft started to spin as Frances's stomach lurched first up and then to the side as the tilt-a-whirl questioning her mother was throwing at her felt like it propelled time backwards and she was six years old again. Most of the choices Frances was making in her life now were off the conservative Catholic path her parents had plotted out for her.

"Mom...I—"

"Frances Olar Kavanagh, are you telling people that you are now—"

"Listen, Mom—"

Frances pulled her phone away from her ear as she listened to her mother shout something about church to her father. Then she heard her telling her brother Bernard to open the dishwasher so the dishes could dry. Bernard spent more time at their parents' home than his own. Did he really move out when he became a doctor? The list of directions continued as Bridgette Kavanagh continued to engage in conversation with whomever walked into the kitchen. It always amazed Frances how her mother would start a conversation only to ignore the person she held hostage on the phone line. To hang up was nothing less than a sin against the mother, and the Kavanagh children quickly learned never to hang up or talk back to their parents.

"Frances, what do you mean that you are now calling yourself an artist? How could you do that to your father? And after all the graduate schooling you've done."

"Yes, Mom. I am an artist," Frances said. She breathed a sigh of relief. It was out and she had said the words.

Her mother ended the call with no good-bye, only a click of the phone. It was not lost on Frances that her dad was worried yet never called. Why was her mom using her toddler nickname? It didn't really matter; Frances was not ready to chat up Mama Bridgette about her career change or the other issues causing her stomach to tie itself in knots most recently. Frances walked back to her overly inviting bed, wanting to curl up in the softness and reclaim the lost early morning sleep. She watched the fog as it filtered the sun and created one of those days that supported a good, deep sleep.

Before she could enjoy a return to the luxury of sleep, her actual phone alarm sounded. Ah, the dependence on this little monster, she thought to herself. With a swipe of her thumb, she silenced the barking dog. Crap. She read her calendar reminder and wanted to hide. Frances had completely forgotten that she was going to help Winter move today. Off-kilter after that strange phone call with her mother, Frances was not in the mood to be schooled on dating while moving heavy boxes and furniture for Winter.

Winter collected heavy antique furniture and books and was moving into her new condo today. Frances flopped down into her cold leather chair and greatly missed the warmth a roaring fire or a bathrobe could provide as her body shivered, forcing her to hop up and grab a blanket before settling back down. While she waited for her body temperature to heat up enough to stop her teeth from chattering, she debated the pros and cons of bailing out of Winter's move today.

She had been guilty of bailing on responsibilities promised to friends before. The consequences were not dire and friendships survived, although she was coming off of dumping her friends during her marriage and self-exiled life in Tiburon only a few miles north of San Francisco. One time that she should have bailed but didn't proved to be rather disastrous. She was the maid of honor for a childhood friend. The night before her friend's wedding, Frances had watched her nephews for her sister. The three boys had the stomach flu and she was sick with it that next morning. Frances arrived a few minutes before the ceremony believing the worst of the flu was over. She was very wrong as she spewed the contents of her stomach all over four of the groomsmen who were waiting to escort the bridesmaids. The wedding photographer had captured the moment in full color. That was ten years ago and the bride only started talking to her again recently.

The Kavanagh parents had instilled a sense of service to others since they were all in utero. Frances felt that she responded with great charity to her friends. Winter wanting her help to move from a fourth-floor walk-up to her new condo was extreme. That was a different kind of ask. It held in it a sort of physical danger in dragging boxes and crap down four stories.

Well, that was mostly true. Lately, she was very responsive to the needs of her friends and tried to help most of the time. What to do? Frances chewed on her thumbnail as her gaze stopped on two black-and-white photos she had framed and hung on the giant wooden column that helped support the rooftop. The developer had left some of the old ropes and metal plates on the crossbeams. What stories could those relics of the old building share? Frances loved to let her mind wander, especially when she was searching for an excuse. This excuse had to be worthy of getting her out of a promise to Winter. The photos raised a summer full of memories and quite possibly the planting of the seed that brought Frances out west.

Frances had taken the photos on her first walk in the redwoods when she was only nine. Her family had come west for an educational summer vacation. Frances was thoroughly educated that summer about being the middle child in the Kavanagh clan. Sometimes Frances described herself as the bridge between the older and younger Kavanagh kids. Bernard, one of her older brothers, said she was more pond scum than human.

The torture she endured on that summer trip was unjust. Her mother claimed it had nothing to do with Frances having brought a stray skunk into the house the day before they left on the six-week summer adventure. It was a mistake any young animal lover could make. It looked like a little bushy-tailed kitty. The family's real cat went after the skunk, and the sofa and Frances suffered complete fumigation due to the spraying. Frances knew that was why they shoved her way in the back of the station wagon. No amount of tomato juice was going to get that smell out of her. The result was that eight out of ten times she got carsick.

Funny how the mind works, she thought, as she felt the slightest wave of nausea come over her from that awful memory. To this day, Frances still could not eat a fast-food cheeseburger. One would think that after the first time she got sick, they would have moved her to another location in the car, maybe one with circulating air. Nope. After the sixth time she threw up, she had plead her case that Bernard was shorter than her and could read in any position and not get sick. But Bernard—being a boy, and one with a Napoleon complex—was given the choice and had said no. Frances still remembered the way he stuck his tongue out at her after he sealed her torture in the barfing section of the station wagon.

She was told to be tough because she was part of the Kavanagh clan. Her dad told her some story of having been run so hard in the army that he learned to swallow his puke. The drill sergeants made the soldiers eat their own puke right off the ground. She had never really been sure if that story was true. Frances did not challenge her dad. He handed her a bucket and told her not to miss, spill, or let the dog eat it.

Due to the memories brought up from that summer, Frances pondered if it was time for the two photos to go. She had snapped the one photo when she seriously considered running away from her family and the cruel punishment of being carsick for the rest of July and August. St. Louis was so far away from California, and those roads in California were exceptionally winding, clearly engineered by civil engineers schooled in making children carsick. She had wandered deep into the redwood forest looking for a hobbit family to adopt her. The grove of redwoods she came upon had formed a perfect circle. After she ran around the inside of the circle touching each one of the trees, she stood in the center of them and captured the rays of sunlight etching each branch, trunk, and treetop in the most magical gold light.

The second image was taken when she hiked slowly back toward the vomit wagon. Two people were standing next to a redwood tree and Frances raised her camera, thinking the shot would show how giant the trees were compared to the people. Looking through the viewfinder, Frances snapped the picture just as the two people leaned in for a kiss. Frances stood completely still as she realized they were both girls. They kissed on the lips like people in love do in the movies. Frances ran all the way back to the vomit wagon and did not say a word.

When the images came back from Walgreens drugstore photo shop, her dad only looked at the photo on top—the snapshot of the redwood trees—and said Frances had channeled the spirit of Ansel Adams before handing her the packet. Frances remembered her heart beating out of her chest as she carefully looked through the rest of the pictures. She took out the one of the two girls kissing and hid it. Her dad had asked her for the first picture he saw and said it was artistic. At the time, she didn't know who Ansel was, but her dad seemed proud. After that trip, cameras became a part of her. She had entered the photo in the Missouri State Fair junior division for eight- to fourteen-year-olds and won a blue ribbon for the circle of redwoods. Edna, the first born, ruined it when she announced that all junior division entries got blue ribbons. Gall, her favorite brother, told her that Edna was jealous because Dad liked the photo. A smile settled on Frances's lips as she felt the rumblings deep inside.

Another sip of coffee allowed the rumblings to fully percolate into a brilliant idea. In the last few moments, this day had transformed from forced, free, moving labor to a play day. A shadow of guilt started to invade her brain, and she quickly pushed it back with the knowledge that Winter had plenty of resources. Plus, shame on Winter for attempting to save a few dollars by breaking the backs of her friends by schlepping her law books, heavy furniture, and random crap out of a four-story walk-up.

Before her guilt reached levels that would force her to change her mind, Frances skipped taking a shower and threw on a pair of jeans, a long sleeve T-shirt, and her favorite cowboy boots. She brewed another dose of coffee into her to-go cup while she quickly brushed her long, naturally red curls. Her hair was something she gave up trying to control years ago. It was a blessing and a curse having thick curls cascading down her back. A baseball cap sporting the logo of her new favorite team, the SF Giants, helped keep her mane under some control. It took two meetings of the crew at the Buena Vista to get her to consider supporting the hometown major league baseball team. Sometimes she wore her Cardinals baseball hat and watched their games in secret. Today, she sported the hometown team's World Championship hat as she bolted out the door on her way to a day of freedom. It did not bother her that the orange hat did not provide the best complement to her red hair and pale complexion. She was not out to impress anyone today.

CHAPTER THREE
LISTENING TO THE REDWOODS OF MUIR WOODS

FRANCES drove her white four-wheel drive king crew-cab truck north through the damp fog-shrouded San Francisco streets. People were starting to venture out into the City, and she loved the simple way these city streets awoke. The action on the streets started out with the lonely sounds of a delivery truck or two. Then, as the dawn skies brightened into day, the streets filled with people commuting, dogs walking, and children playing. It all blended into the lively city yawning awake to the morning. The accumulation of buses and cars cascaded everything into a full-blown symphony.

With her truck window open, she breathed in the crisp air. This morning the City smelled of mist, salt water, and wet concrete, confirming for Frances that she was driving closer to the San Francisco Bay. She took a right turn, quickly followed with a left, onto Marina Boulevard. It was not the most direct way to the Golden Gate Bridge; it was her way. The fog was so thick it held the Golden Gate Bridge hostage behind its gray folds. Usually, the bright-orange spires of the bridge were visible from this section of the drive along Marina Green, but this morning she drove forward on faith—faith that the bridge was there and she soon would be across it and headed to the redwood trees within Muir Woods.

She felt a surge of power while driving her truck compared to the other cars idling at the red light with her. On her left, she looked down on a Vespa, a MINI Cooper, and some other small hatchback. Her F250 could fit all three of those 'meep-meep' cars into the back and still have room for more. The purchase of this truck was the first thing she did for herself after her divorce from Richard was finalized. She took the Mercedes into the Ford dealership and drove out with her truck. The truck's engine purred as she drove it across the Golden Gate Bridge. After some serious teasing from Russell and Simon, Frances named her truck "Snow White." The name represented that the truck was badass and strong, like the latest rendition of the Snow White story put out by Hollywood.

Cheryl and Winter told her she would never be able to find parking in the City, that no one in a city needed a truck, and it was a waste of resources. Words were used in conversations about her being crazy, an oil hog, and quite possibly a climate killer. All the comments about the climate and waste aside, she seemed to become very popular very quickly after buying the truck. It was amazing how many people started to move big things when a friend bought a truck and made the mistake of offering to help. Yes, I'm crazy, she thought to herself, but not over the parking issue—it was the fact that she became a free moving service. What was that about? Why could she not say no? This morning she had promised her friend that she would be there but was now pulling a flakey friend move by not showing up and not calling.

Frances's phone sounded, and she saw Winter's face appear on the screen. Focused on the traffic on the bridge, Frances let the call roll over to her voicemail. She took a deep breath as the open window let the fog, wind, and cold ocean air into her truck cab. Frances told herself that her choice to duck out on Winter would not be a big deal. As she entered the tunnel on the Marin side of the bridge, Frances knew the call with her mother had undertones that had the ability to break her determination. Frances gripped her steering wheel as the cold of the morning air penetrated through her clothing, mingling with the judgment from her family, and she shivered.

Her mother had a way of delivering disappointment in her life choices that caused Frances to swallow so hard she felt the tears start to rise. She knew Winter would think her no-show had to do specifically with the four flights of stairs and no elevator at Winter's old apartment building. That would be ninety percent correct. Frances would have to figure out how to explain that the call with her mother caused all her bones to liquefy. How does one continue to exist with no skeletal support? Jellyfish seemed to do fine without bones. Frances needed to figure out how to keep her backbone in place when talking with her mother.

Her brain was starting to get angry with herself for not at least phoning Winter. Frances focused on the emotions around the photos of the redwoods, which her consciousness mashed with the call from her mother. Frances shook her head. Something had shifted. The remodel she was conducting on her insides was major. She was tearing out walls, building new strengths, and questioning whether the walls concerning how she fit into her family needed to be removed. They were supporting foundation walls holding up some deeply set rules of family.

It wasn't until she drove herself out west, so many years ago, that she started to realize the distance did not change. Whether she lived in the home or not, the reality of being part of a family unit with any autonomy was a hoax. The call with her mom reinforced her distance and the fact that her family traveled around one another in parallel orbits that never really touched. Frances knew she was out of place and she needed space alone. It was the lack of honestly interacting that caused Frances to know that she could not share everything she was thinking with her family. When she asked too many questions, her parents became frustrated. It did not take her long to learn to stop.

That second picture that Frances had taken during that long-ago summer morning foretold more about hidden secrets in this family. Before she had pulled it out of a dusty old box, she had shared it with only two other people in her life. It was a picture that she was starting to understand more, along with her love of the story, "Fried Green Tomatoes." What caused her to contemplate the paths in life she traveled was how that photo would come to life in college. Maybe life was not random. She carried the photo with her but always kept it hidden until she moved into this space. It was her secret. It had always confused her because she knew something about the picture, if she allowed herself to explore, would unlock a part of herself she was scared to face. She had worked hard to always be proper and pleasing to others; it was time for her to please herself. Although the call with her mother pushed her back into another reality—the reality that her life, to be her own, might mean the loss of her place in the family.

The devil sitting on her foot pressing the gas pedal helped her accelerate past her worry about Winter. The Irish Catholic guilt that was sitting on her shoulder told her to call her friend and apologize when she arrived safely at Muir Woods. Frances checked her dashboard clock and figured she had about twenty minutes left to come up with some excuse.

Her dashboard clock read 7:33 a.m. when Frances pulled into a rock-star parking spot in the first lot leading into the main entrance, near the gift shop and ranger station for Muir Woods National Park. She shut off her engine and listened to her truck settling into place. Frances picked up her phone and her heart sank with the help of her guilt as the words *No Service* announced that technology had not made it to this spot in Muir Woods yet. It was both a blessing and a curse. This was not good. She would not be in contact with Winter for a couple of hours at least. Frances grabbed a light jacket out of the back seat of her truck and tied it around her waist. She started walking through the parking lot with her phone out in front of her as she searched for any signs of service.

A giggle escaped her lips; she realized she was wearing a long sleeve red shirt. She had learned from her truly geeky friends who religiously followed *Star Trek* about the bad karma of the red shirt. No one wanted to be the red shirt on the away team. They were the first to get killed, although Frances had spotted the problem with this argument, pointing out that Scotty wore a red shirt but always came back to the Enterprise.

Frances continued to search for a phone signal on her way toward the start of her hike. With each step, Frances felt the pressure build up in her chest. When her phone suddenly lit up with half a bar, Frances jumped for joy and promptly lost the signal. "Found life for the technology, Captain, but it is elusive." No one was around, so she had to laugh at her own joke. One jump forward was too much, so she took a slow step back. She recaptured the half bar and quickly texted:

I am hiking in Muir Woods. Sorry. I'll explain later. Xoxo F.O.K.

SHE reviewed her message and quickly pressed send. When she got confirmation that her message had leapt into the data world and was on its way, she shoved the phone in her front jean pocket and headed into her adventure for the morning: the redwoods.

A smile spread across her face as she walked under the huge wood sign framing the entrance to the walking paths in the park. The wonder of the redwoods always presented new and exciting beauty with each visit. It was too early for the ranger station to be open, so Frances grabbed a paper envelope and paid her admission to the park. She knew she probably could have gotten into the park without paying, but her conscience, combined with the early programming of her Catholic guilt circuitry, would not let her. Plus, she wanted to keep this beautiful place protected. It wasn't like she believed her tiny admission fee would make a difference, but she did not want to add any more negative drops into her karmic bucket. She might be in enough trouble with god or whoever ran the karma accumulators without adding to her already heavy karmic debt.

The grumbling coming from her gut made the smile on her face flatline. The first tremors through her body came and went, and Frances lengthened her stride past the first few placards explaining the redwoods, the history of the area, and the foliage. She knew them all well. Truth be known, she came here as often as she could. As she was deciding what path to follow, the grumbling rumbling in her gut happened again. Her gut sent a most urgent message to her brain. Frances, you idiot, you only had coffee this morning. Coffee with no form of food was a magic formula for flushing out her system. Her gut overrode the brains desire to hike deep into the redwoods. The gut-mandated detour led her to the public restrooms. Would they be open this early in the morning? Her body was letting her know that she was close to the point of explosion. She was almost in a full trot toward the door of the women's restroom, praying that it was open. No one was around to see her lose her dignified public persona.

Relief flushed throughout her body as the bathroom door gave way easily and she successfully landed her targets. Her body was now trying to calm the adrenaline it pumped out over the sudden intestinal distress from coffee. Frances pondered her rather strange thankfulness at having an open restroom. The relief she felt of being able to use a toilet in such a situation was at least number four on her top-ten gratitude list. It was above sex. "Great, Frances!" she said to herself. "No wonder no one picked you as a match. You are more grateful for plumbing in the woods than sex."

Why did thinking about sex bring her thoughts back to Winter? Was it because Winter had no problem getting men to do whatever she wanted? Or was it that Winter wanted to help Frances get immersed into the dating world? Frances shook her head and realized that to get the most out of her day, she had to let go of any sort of guilt over not showing up for Winter. It was not like this one choice was going to damage their friendship. Really, she needed this day not to cart furniture and book boxes, but to think about her choice to turn her back on a lucrative consulting job for a career as a painter. When she was young, she had spent her days painting with anything that worked: pudding, mud, paint, ink, and her mother's makeup. Her parents responded to her use of her mother's makeup by grounding her and making her go to mass every morning before school for two weeks. Because of that, Frances became a closeted painter. They had no problem with her getting into photography, but for some reason painting was off limits. She never asked why because she did not want to go to early morning mass any longer than the initial punishment made her. Frances washed her hands and headed back out to the redwoods and the forest. She was hoping for some insights into her abrupt decision to become a professional artist, along with her internal stirrings to get back into the dating game.

The fog was starting to lift, and focused lines of sunlight were highlighting parts of the path in front of her. This morning, it was all quiet: the fog, the trees, and the empty path before her. This precious silence would not last for long as the tourists and locals wanting to hike through the beauty of the trees would descend and fill the park. Tourist season lasted the whole year in San Francisco, which made it both special and, at times, a little claustrophobic. Frances walked deeper into the woods, letting her thoughts out to be free, to roam like little puppies sniffing out squirrels. The woods provided a place for her to walk, acting like a soothing, mind-calming meditation. Maybe meditation was not the correct word; Frances was actively thinking about her life direction and what that meant.

CHAPTER FOUR
A PECULIAR CONVERSATION

F RANCES had lost track of time in what she decided was her own private redwood grove. The trees started to doff the fog, revealing their grand stature against the sky-blue backdrop as it finally made its presence known. She looked left and then right before hopping across the well-marked path, then she hiked up toward the center of another small grove of redwoods. She stood tall and turned in a circle, watching the crown of the trees reaching into the sky. With arms outstretched, she opened her chest wide and inhaled fully. The smell of the Pacific Ocean mixing with the wet dirt of the forest gave her a comfort that was difficult for her to explain. Frances quieted the chattering in her mind.

She walked the inner perimeter of the circle of trees and said hello to each tree. Ever since she was little, she had always believed in the feelings of trees. She closely studied how the above ground roots of one tree hooked into the roots of the tree standing next to it. Each detail gave her a deepening gratitude for her friends. Redwoods were referred to as the friendship trees because of their need to have the stabilization of another tree's roots in the grove to stay standing. It made her think of her band of faithful friends, her chosen family, she had developed in San Francisco. Did this mean that she was ready to let go of her Kavanagh role? She felt the depth of her fear of losing her family in the call with her mother. Frances took a few more deep breaths into her lungs and held each one of them for as long as she could before she exhaled.

The crisp air, cool against her face and hands, continued to energize her as she stopped next to one of the shortest trees in the grove. She estimated its height at only thirty feet. It was the runt of this little grove. She threw her arms as far around the trunk of the tree as she could manage. She pulled her face close into the furry, rough, red bark of the tree and closed her eyes as she tightened her arms around the trunk of the tree. When she opened her eyes, she noticed a blooming pink rhododendron and giant green sword ferns. Somehow hugging this tree made her feel so good that she decided not to let go. Her eyes closed and she lost track of time.

Voices tore through her peaceful silence and hug fest with the tree. Frances realized that she had miscalculated how far off the trail she was. She tried not to move much as she turned and realized that she had run parallel to the path and was basically a few feet from it. Her hands kept a strong grip on the tree trunk as she and the trees watched and listened for the intruders on the trail. The sound had traveled faster than the people. A group of tourists rounded the curve on the trail, spewing noise pollution into the silence of the forest as several members argued for returning to the gift shop. What were they doing this far out on a trail this early in the day? Frances had hiked a good forty-five minutes to give herself a buffer from the crowds. Usually the loud tourists lingered around the ranger station, the cafe, and the little fifty-yard loop through the beginning of the park. Most thought this small expanse of walking path was the extent of the forest and the hiking.

Frances so wished she had the power of a chameleon so she could morph her body to match the deep red brown of the bark. Before she could stop it, her body betrayed her location by creating one of the loudest farts she had ever heard.

"What the hell?" Frances said and slapped her hand over her own mouth. Would they confuse that deafening sound with that of a bear? She peeked to her left and saw that the group had stopped. To make matters worse, her stomach started adding its own sounds. She shut her eyes, pushing herself into the tree even further in complete mortification. Was this karma paying her back already? Who farts like that? She had not remembered adding a bullhorn to her pants.

Frances thought about sliding down to the base of the tree and crawling through the ferns to try and exit before anyone could really figure out that they heard a fart in the woods. It was too late. Frances froze when she noticed that a young boy (of course it was a boy) had stopped and was looking right at her. She decided that she had better get this over with, so she kissed the tree she had hugged and hopped back onto the trail, brushing the bark and dirt off her pants. The boy continued to watch her, and she turned to face him and smiled.

"Hey lady, why were you holding that tree? Was it because you were afraid your fart was going to blow you away?" the boy asked. For the second time that morning Frances froze. When she regained her composure, she faced the boy directly and bent down a little to match his height. She had to bite her tongue so as not to laugh at his Alcatraz sweatshirt. Why people dressed their children in such ware was lost on her because nothing says "I love my kid" more than putting them in prison garb.

"You saw me hugging the tree? Trees need hugs and love from us," Frances said, trying to completely ignore the fart comment. She watched as he tilted his head first to the right and then to the left. He rolled his eyes and looked up at the sky as he crossed his arms. His reaction made her realize she had been busted by a fart expert.

"I heard you fart. Trust me, I know farts. Were you talking to the tree? I'm supposed to say excuse me when I fart out loud." He took a couple steps closer to her.

"Well—" But before she could answer, her little interviewer was rattling off a story about farts.

"Lady, I know you farted and it was loud but it wasn't as loud as the fart I did in school."

"What?" was all Frances could muster. This was now one of the more peculiar conversations she could ever remember having had with anyone, and that included the freaks at speed dating.

"In my school, we don't sit on chairs. We sit on these big, red, bouncy balls. My fart was so loud and so strong it broke the bouncy ball."

Frances squinted as she heard this and wondered if it was true. But then, why would he make this up? They were having a fart-to-fart moment here.

"I was hoping no one heard my fart since I was out in the woods and not in a classroom. But yours couldn't have broken the ball!"

"It did!…Well, I was jumping up and down on it like it was a butt trampoline and then the fart came out. Everyone in class was laughing and then I was lying flat on my back. I killed the ball. My fart was so loud."

"It wasn't that bad."

"It shook the walls." He laughed a little and his cheeks turned red. "I understand the force of a fart. Did your fart blow you into that tree?"

"No. The tree kept me planted on the earth. You're right, it was a real ripper and it might have launched me into space."

Frances was thinking of how to get this kid off the fart topic. This brave little four-foot-tall human dressed as a convict, with blonde curls peeking out under a black and gray striped Alcatraz hat, did not seem in a hurry to catch up with his family. He was getting bored with her silence and started to bounce from one foot to the other.

"I learned how to hip-hop dance at school."

"Looks like you are really good." She was glad he had the attention span of a gnat and had moved past the fart conversation. Before the discussion could continue, both the young boy and Frances froze when a thundering voice reached back along the path.

"Greggory Carlos VanMeter! Get over here right now. What did I tell you about talking to strangers?"

"Uh-oh—big trouble. Mom used my whole name."

"You'll be okay. Nice talking with you, Greggory Carlos VanMeter. My name is Frances Olar Kavanagh, F.O.K. to my friends."

"Your friends call you…Fuck? That's not very nice." Greggory said.

A square-shaped woman wearing a gray-green sweatshirt sporting a scene of a cat holding a frying pan full of mice grabbed him by his upper arm and started to pull him back toward the stopped, waiting group. The boy's eyes were stuck on Frances as the square woman (most likely his mother) continued thundering at him. Her use of his whole name meant he was going to be in some sort of serious trouble.

Poor kid. He was trying to turn his little feet over fast enough to stay walking so he wouldn't be dragged along the path.

Frances stood and sheepishly waved at the boy, then she turned away in the opposite direction. The last thing she wanted was to see that chef cat sweatshirt again. Upon turning, the little crowd had erupted in obnoxiously loud laughter. But was it obnoxious? They were in the outdoors, not a library. She thought about a line her sister Agatha had used with Frances and now with her own kids: "Use your inside voice!" It had earned Agatha the nickname of "The Voice Volume Enforcer."

The laughter of Greggory and his family trailed off behind her and she was on her way back toward the front entrance to the park. Frances figured that little Greggory had told them that she, the lady, had farted so loud it blew her into a tree. She thought about continuing her play day at Stinson Beach. She could be there within the hour. But before she ventured too close to the park entrance, she decided she needed to hug one more tree and made her way off the trail to a huge giant of a redwood. Frances realized that pondering the stupidity of this life could cloud the surrounding brilliance. She thought about her little questioner, Greggory, and hoped he would try hugging a tree.

Around the bend in the trail, Frances walked directly into a little fog bank that clung low against the trees and ground. The moisture was collecting on the leaves, ferns, and bark surrounding her. The cool wetness felt nourishing against her face as she pressed it to the trunk of the tree towering at least sixty feet above her. With the wet fog seeping into her jeans and the smells of the forest mixing with the salt air of the ocean, Frances felt alive and happy. One more deep breath let her drink in the beauty around her, and she felt her mind clear of the questions about family, career, and her ability to date post-divorce. This place was like no other place; it brought peace to her. It was still as mystical as it was when she snapped those two photos when she was that young girl seeking refuge from the back of the station wagon.

More voices were heard coming up the trail, and Frances left her tree and started to stroll back toward the cafe and civilization. The ocean was going to be her next place to visit on her play day. She figured a bus must have arrived, as the path up ahead was now heavily infested with tourists wearing the latest in cameras and San Francisco landmark fashions. She now became the fish swimming upstream against the current. Every few feet someone would tap her and speak to her in an unknown language. They would simultaneously mime the motion to take her picture. She was not sure what language they were speaking but it all ended in laughter and pointing. Each time, she smiled toward them standing next to a giant tree as they would go through physical antics to cross the language barrier to get her to turn around, at which point causing the laughter to start again. Odd as it was, Frances really did not think about it. The fourth or fifth time this happened, her face flushed red as her irritation was mounting. What the heck was going on? She knew that she wasn't model pretty but she was not ugly either. Often people used other people in pictures to show some perspective to the giant trees. She did notice that none of the tourists had red hair and maybe that was the interest.

Frances shook her head and doubled her steps to get out of the mob of tourists now clogging the entrance into the woods. The laughter continued to follow her along with strange words and finger pointing in her direction. "Rude" was the word that kept coming to her mind. People always said Americans were rude when traveling abroad, but this group was going to be nominated by Frances. She stopped to catch her breath by a carved black bear that pointed tourists in the direction of the gift shop. There was a new group of tourists. These ones spoke English. She figured they had to be from the Midwest because they all wanted to stop and get a "pop," which meant "soda," not "dad" in other parts of the country. Now the English speakers started to laugh, and Frances turned around quickly to see what they were laughing about. When her eyes met theirs, they looked away smirking. That was it. Frances looked down at herself and did not see anything amiss. Sure, her pants were a little soaked down by her boots and she did have some dirt on one knee, but it was nothing to write home about.

She pulled her phone out to use it as a mirror to check her face. She was intently studying her reflection when a woman tapped her on her shoulder.

"What the—" Frances screamed as she jumped up in the air, practically hurdling over the five-foot-tall bear sculpture.

"I'm sorry. Didn't want to scare you. You've got something stuck to the back of your pants."

Frances's face flushed instantly red as her hand reached behind her to find the offending hitchhikers stowed away in her belt. She quickly crumpled the toilet seat cover and toilet paper tail into a tight ball, circling to see if she had anything else hanging off her backside. Frances's little spin-in-a-circle dance caused more chuckles from the crowd.

"You got it. You're good," the woman said, muffling a laugh.

It no longer mattered; Frances realized that more than thirty people had seen her bathroom faux pas and not one of them had felt the need to help her. Nope, not one, not even the little fart expert, Greggory. Was it karma working already? Was that it? Frances felt her face as it flashed through at least thirty different shades of red. Would she become a viral video? She threw her hands up in the air and walked back to her truck.

"Okay. I get it," she said out loud, not caring who watched her now, arms outstretched to the heavens. "This is what I get for running out on helping Winter move her heavy-ass books to her new condo. I'm sorry, universe."

A smile turned up the left corner of her mouth as she opened the door to her truck. This was going to make a great story when some time went by—maybe thirty years. The remedy to such humiliation would be the laughter from her neighbors, Russell and Simon, collectively known as "The Gays." Not to mention the jokes that the girls would come up with over this one. Well, Winter would agree that the universe was getting even with her, but Cheryl and Dana would laugh. Frances swung herself up behind the steering wheel and savored the initial deep turnover bursts of the diesel engine as it roared its power.

Frances took her time exiting her parking space and caught her eyes in the rearview mirror. What were you thinking when you married Richard Peter Enos? The transmission clicked into reverse, and she knew the part of her that had her go through with that marriage had ignored most of her instincts about love, life, and her dreams. Now, her choice was to head west to Stinson Beach and the ocean or take a left back to 101 South and the City.

CHAPTER FIVE
WINTER'S MOVE

WINTER Renee Keller huffed her way back up four flights of stairs, rethinking her miserly way to save money. What was she doing? Well, she sighed, as she leaned against the stair railing, the tribe she worked with at the law firm had rubbed off on her. She pushed off the wall, leaving a rather large sweat mark on the faded grayish paint as she rounded the landing and started on the last twelve steps that led to her fourth-floor apartment. Had she really understood and thought about the whole time-is-money argument? Real movers would be schlepping her through this move. She had made such a rookie mistake to save some money. Instead, she could be at her desk billing clients for her legal mind to cover her new mortgage.

Winter checked her Fitbit and saw that she had already reached six thousand steps by 9:00 a.m. Sure, this was exercise but with each passing step her body let her know that it was close to a total shut down. When she reached her apartment, she was going to call and find out why Frances and her truck failed to show at the set time and date. It was not like Frances to be AWOL when she was trying so hard to make things right after disappearing for a couple of years.

"Winter, where did you put the screwdriver?" Jason asked from her bedroom. Winter tried to hide the fact that she was seriously sucking in some air as she huffed and puffed through her front door. Why had she thought it was cool to smoke in law school? Her mind was a mess of stress from the move and the fact that she failed to fully appreciate the four fucking flights of stairs.

"On the dresser." Winter took the first place available to sit and leaned back, wiping the sweat off her face with her already soaked T-shirt. She listened as Jason, her man-squeeze and the reason she had taken herself off the market, attacked her wrought-iron bed frame. It didn't sound like he was using the screwdriver in the correct way; the sharp banging of metal on metal pierced her eardrums.

Thankfully, Jason had borrowed a friend's truck with a trailer to help haul her belongings to her new condo in Laurel Heights. She felt she needed to pinch herself because this condo was her dream come true, one she had established for herself six years ago. She caught and landed a client so rich that she could dictate her promotion to partner in the firm. The founding partners were going to promise her anything to keep this client in the firm. Now a newly minted law partner, she was pulling in the big bucks. The condo was a trophy of sorts for her. When she was young and rather wild, her father told her she would not amount to anything. He said this to her right before he left them all. Her mother was left to raise four kids on her own. Winter was the youngest and in many ways the scrappiest.

"Hey, where's your friend?" Jason asked as he carried part of the iron bed frame out of the apartment.

"I'm going to give her a call now."

Winter blew a kiss toward Jason, craving the chance to lay her hands on his chiseled chest. His muscles were showing through his sweat-soaked white T-shirt and his pair of basketball shorts. God, she loved his body. He was the most muscular man she had ever dated and she loved it. Right now, her apartment smelled of his musky sweat and soap. It fed her inner lust beast to be in his arms. Winter thought about the bets that had been taken by the motley crew over Irish coffees on how long she would be with him.

Frances could be such a devilish ringleader. Though Frances ranked first on her bitch list for skipping out on moving day. She chalked it up to the fact that Frances was not in the best of shape to climb four flights of stairs once. That could be enough to make anyone grumpy.

Winter smiled because currently she was beating the predictions of her friends claiming Jason would not last beyond three weeks.

Winter's body winced as loud clanging noises rang through the building while Jason maneuvered the iron bed frame down four flights of the tight stairs. When she had first located this apartment, she told herself the stairs would keep her in shape. These same steps on her last climb up seemed to be growing in height and number, no longer a welcome daily routine. An argument formed in her mind on how to get money back from her Pilates and spin classes; they were not giving her the cardio conditioning she thought she should have after such strict adherence to the classes.

She turned her attention back to her front room, currently filled floor to ceiling with boxes of books. Why had she been so in love with books? There was something to be said for the digital age and paperless books. Who knew that paper could be so freakin' heavy? She shut her eyes, blocking out the boxes, the mess, and the fact that she was already over the moving part after having only been at it for two hours.

"God damn it, Frances needs this workout more than I do," Winter said as she dialed Frances's number.

"What?" Jason asked as he leaned against the door jamb, sweat dripping off his chin and making a puddle on the floor. He must have taken the stairs two or three at a time to be back up there so quickly. Winter couldn't resist the urge to go kiss her man.

"I was calling my soon-to-be-ex-friend, Frances. This is so much harder than I thought it would be, and I think my book boxes are breeding. I swear, this place gets fuller with each trip down." Winter watched as her fingers traced the tight pectoral muscles of Jason's chest.

"No playing until the job is done. I've got the guys coming over. Unlike your friends, mine will show up and actually be able to help." Jason gently pushed past her and grabbed three book boxes, taking the journey down the mountain of stairs.

Winter sighed as she watched her ultra-fit man take her heavy crap down the stairway from hell. That was it, Winter was going to splurge for movers to schlep all her crap into the new condo; there was no way she was going to do it. She wanted to play and did not want to exhaust her man past the point of being able to get her body going later tonight.

It took her less than five minutes to schedule a crew of movers and order drinks, food, and dessert for the beautiful Neanderthals that made up Jason's circle of guys. A nice group, but their deepest pursuits were reading protein powder containers and watching YouTube videos of impossible basketball shots. Jason had a deeper side that he did not share with his band of brothers. There was nothing wrong with the cave-dwelling grunts and spurts of laughter he shared with his little group of boys; however, it was part of the reason she was ready to get off the merry-go-round of men for a while. This one had a mind.

In a quieter moment, Winter had caught him reading her dog-eared copy of *Jane Eyre* and felt a stirring in her soul. He was the first man that could she could ever remember reading Brontë's work, let alone a book that had more than pictures. It made her heart skip a couple of beats with desire. If the gang had only known that he was a closeted bookworm. They only judged him by his appearance. "Gym rat" was used more than once to describe him. Simon and Russell warned her that men who looked like Jason really did play on both teams. Frances had warned her about falling for such a guy. It was not fair for Frances to give her judgment when Winter recalled her own cautions to Frances concerning Richard went unheard. Frances had married Mr. Richard P. Enos anyway. His name should have been enough to run. But when Frances married, she had dropped the crew like yesterday's fad and left them staring at an empty stage where a friendship had once existed.

San Francisco was such a different time and place for Winter when she lost Frances to the "marriage years." Winter had more time than she knew what to do with and started to collect men. It was easy for her. She had become an expert at spotting the truly straight man. Russell and Simon often argued that there is no such thing. They claimed straight men were like unicorns and honest politicians. Winter found many of her single female friends shared a common complaint that San Francisco was a desert for the straight woman because men appeared to be so confused in this city, not knowing for themselves if they were gay, straight, bi, or whatever. Winter found the straight boys became very easy to spot once she cracked the straight man's dress code. Her code was to look at a man's socks and shoes. If their socks matched their outfit or they wore nice shoes, you must stay away. This worked most of the time. There were a few mistakes but those were usually men who had recently moved to the City from a landlocked state and had not been shopping yet.

Winter looked at her phone and decided to send a text to Frances since her call had landed directly in voicemail. What to say? Should she be worried or pissed in her text? Frances wears big girl pants, she can take the truth. *Hey F.O.K. You better be dead or I will kill you for not showing up to help me move. Winter Keller with an "I".*

CHAPTER SIX
ETHAN'S COLLECTION

ETHAN Charna stood on top of the wide concrete wall that kept most of the sand separated from the sidewalk and road along Ocean Beach in San Francisco. His gaze locked on the surfers bobbing on the surface of the gray ocean as they waited for the next set of waves. The wind brought the brisk cold air from the north, causing Ethan to turn his leather jacket collar up to protect his neck from the chill. His tall thin body ached to be in the water; the wave sets were worth riding this morning. Ethan remembered how it had taken him a while to get used to surfing in a full wetsuit. The cold waters off the Northern California coast presented a challenge that at first intimidated him, but once he had conquered his own fears, he fell in love with the rugged toughness that cold-water surfing had given him.

He looked down at his paint-stained shoes and was heading into thoughts of regret over pawning his surfboard and wetsuit. He told himself he needed to let it go to free up his time and so he could complete his painting, sculpture, and film projects. A hit off his pipe calmed him down as he watched a surfer drop into the trough of a beautiful wave. Ethan curled his hand around the pipe and controlled his urge to punch the wall he was leaning against. The surfboard pawn was all part of a role he felt he had to play.

"Hey, ya punk. You better not be smoking dope this time of morning." Emily leaned against the wall and grabbed Ethan's legs, causing him to almost fall off the wall.

"Watch it." Ethan hopped down and sat on the wall with his back to the ocean and the surfers. It was good to be out and about before the beach got busy.

"Coffee?" Ethan asked while pointing at the thermos in Emily's hand.

"And a good morning to you, Master Ethan. Help me up." Ethan stretched out a hand and Emily climbed up the wall to sit facing the ocean. She handed him her thermos cup. Emily Alexander was a stark contrast to Ethan's pasty white skin, his dark wavy hair, and neck tattoos. She was clad in neon-green running tights and a bright-orange running jacket that matched her bright-orange running shoes. Her face sported a gold tan that was so perfect it almost didn't look real. Her light-blonde hair was pulled back neatly into a ponytail, enhancing her sharp jawline and blue eyes.

Ethan stood on the wall ignoring Emily's attempts to take her coffee back. He laughed as Emily tried to jump for her coffee that he held high over her head.

"Not fair, ya twiggy giant. Give me back my coffee. You have some explaining to do. What do I owe this early morning meeting to? I never see you anymore. You can't blame it on my new computer lab, either. You know, Ethan, when you were doing your graduate work, I brought you food and good cheer. And I never made you jump for it."

Ethan handed her back the coffee with a sigh. His eyes focused back on the gray waves pounding the beach. He blinked a couple times, processing what he was going to say as he realized that he had no one to share what he was thinking. He turned and faced Emily.

"She's been divorced long enough now. I helped move her out of the artist studio to her own artist space and loft down on Second," Ethan said as he turned away from Emily. He did not wait for a response and started to walk along the top of the wall away from Emily.

"Hold it right there, Mr. Charna. You can't drop a bomb like that and take off. Who are we talking about? Which *she* are you referring to? I know we are twins separated at birth, but sometimes you over credit my ESP." Emily hopped off the wall and started trotting to keep up with Ethan's long strides.

"Frances. The woman who used to have the studio space next to mine—you commented on her more than once."

"Oh yeah. The red-haired one. She's hot. If she's divorced, you can legally ask her out."

Ethan stopped, turned, and flipped Emily the bird with both hands. His eyes were cold and hard. This was not a joke and Emily was not listening to him. Ethan swallowed hard to keep himself from yelling at Emily over her unknown stupidity.

"I haven't seen her in weeks. She no longer comes into my studio since she has her own live-work space in an overly priced condo loft conversion." Ethan hopped off the wall and leaned against it with a choppy ease. He dug around in the pocket of his leather jacket. He pulled out a well-packed glass pipe. A half smile crossed his lips as he admired his own packing job then inhaled another drag.

"Shit. Ethan, why are guys such—" Emily smacked him on his arm. "What are you going to do about this? And how come you never ask me about my work? I brought it up. I got my computer lab. I think you might be smoking a little too much. Do I need to do an intervention?" Emily asked as she danced around him practicing her boxing steps.

"I see you started the boxing classes," Ethan said.

"Oh man, you're not changing the subject. You didn't offer me a hit?"

"You don't smoke," Ethan said has he took another long inhale off the smoldering pipe. The wind blew the smoke away quickly. "You are safe where you are—you won't smell like a skunk." Ethan laughed as he watched Emily dodge the heavy smoke of the pot he was using to dull his edges this morning. He wondered how much to play on Emily's emotions this morning. This pastime of getting Emily to do what he wanted started back when they had met in high school.

"Does this hot redhead even know you are crushing on her?" Emily punched him playfully in the gut. In one motion, Ethan stood and captured Emily in a headlock. Emily started to lightly punch at Ethan's back.

"Hey, watch the kidneys. I only have two and you're stronger than you look," Ethan said as he laughed and kept his hold on Emily.

"Tap out. Tap out! I need more coffee before we start wrestling," Emily said.

Ethan released his headlock, allowing her to retrieve her coffee.

"There's the Ethan I know and love. Do you remember the game we used to play all the time? The one we started our senior year in high school?"

Ethan turned to watch the surfers. His focus distant, he worked hard to hide his true thoughts from the probing stare that Emily was laying on him now.

"What game?" he asked. "You mean smear the queer? We were so wrong according to today's standards." Ethan coughed as he took another hit from his pipe.

"No. Interesting though, as I was the only queer in the group and you guys could never catch me." Emily followed Ethan's gaze, watching the surfers and the ocean.

"Can a lesbian be a queer?" Ethan asked.

"Sure. I don't really subscribe to the labels, but I've been called queer, gay, lesbian, carpet muncher, muff diver, bean flicker, butch, dyke, bull dyke, gold star, femme, stud, and my personal favorite, not-normal." Emily laughed. "Well, are you going to ask her out?"

"I don't know."

"Ethan, are you sure you're a straight guy? I think your dating radar needs a swift kick. Not only do you match your tie to your socks, your belt matches your shoes. Who does that? Oh, and you have great kicks for a guy. Minus those on your feet right now. If you don't ask Frances out, my friend, you leave me no choice—I will. You can be such an idiot. I'm thinking she plays for my team anyway and you know I have excellent gaydar."

"Not an idiot! You think everyone is gay or lesbian like all the other queers I know. Not original." Ethan turned and started to walk away.

"Seriously? Ethan, are you a complete asswipe? Ask her out. What is the worst thing that can happen?"

"She's out of my league. You know what happened the last time I went for a woman out of my league."

"Hey dude. That was different. She had graduated and took a job across country. It was a natural point to end the relationship. Except for you, ya dumb-ass. You followed her like a little puppy." Emily said.

"You know they never found Annette?"

"What? No. Why would I know that? You never talked about her. I do remember how hurt you were when I helped you move back home. The East Coast was not right for you, man, and you know it. That woman was a bitch. She had no clue what a wonderful person she had in you. Man, she was too old for you."

"Shucks. You make me feel like I spit glitter and make rainbow unicorn face paintings. I'm not that good," Ethan said.

"Hmm...let me see, I have known you since you started defacing state property with those awesome pieces of twisted art. I'm an excellent judge of character and you are, my friend."

"Aren't you curious about Annette?" Ethan took a clove cigarette out, cupping his hands trying to light it in the wind. "You actually never asked me about her when you came back and helped me pack things up." Ethan watched Emily and knew that he was in control of information and Emily was not going to figure out this puzzle.

"What was there to talk about? You told me she dumped you. I wasn't going to rub salt in your open broken heart. Shit. You left art school and moved across the country for her. I couldn't care about her. When you two got together, you basically disappeared on me. I was happy to have my best friend back and moving home."

"You are strange," Ethan said and played with the growing ash on the end of his cigarette.

"I'm strange? I am not boring you with tales of all the girls I loved before. What is up with you? If you are going to get maudlin on me, I am going to finish my run and get myself to work."

"I've got something to show you." Ethan pulled out his phone and located a picture of a billboard.

"What the fuck, Ethan? What does this mean?" Emily continued to look at the photo that showed a picture of Annette and a hotline number. "The date on this billboard said she went missing a week before you moved back home."

"I was back in New York visiting some friends a week ago and had to stop to take this picture. I was shocked too." Ethan took his time snuffing his cigarette out on the side of the cement wall. He slowly exhaled the smoke as he watched Emily study the photo.

"Ethan, she has been missing for six years. What the fuck?"

"I didn't do it," Ethan said as he sat up straight and stretched.

"I didn't say you did anything—"

"She is obviously dead. Who goes missing for six years?" Ethan hopped off the wall and started walking toward his car.

"Ethan…I…what do you want me to do with this information? This is fucking weird. You were in love with this woman. Now you act like it is no big deal she is most likely dead? What is going on with you? You didn't tell me she had gone missing after she broke up with you."

"Emily, you can be such a drama queen. I showed it to you because it freaked me out. The police had asked me some questions right before we left but no one had said anything about her missing. I had no clue until I saw that billboard."

Ethan took his phone back from Emily and hid his smile. Annette had hurt him when she told him to leave her life. There were so many ways one could leave a life. He debated continuing this conversation with Emily since she was not handling it well. Sometimes he wished Emily was a guy and not a girl who fucked other girls. They used to have so much fun going out. They had an ongoing competition to see who could get a girl's number in the bar. It never mattered if the woman was gay or straight. They were equals. Ethan remembered why he did not hang around other guys. He had nothing to say to them. In art school, he started watching snuff films, and his roommate turned him in to the resident assistant. The only other person he ever shared his fascination of snuff films with was his younger brother, Gabriel. Gabriel and Ethan had parted ways after their grandmother died a few years ago.

"Ethan Charna, your mother and grandmother are turning over in their graves. What type of shit are you trying to tell me? I trust you that you did not have anything to do with her disappearing."

"Emily. You know me. I could never hurt another person. You know that to your core."

"Sorry. How did this conversation get so fucked? You are an amazing artist and person. I love you more than my own brothers. You are my chosen brother, one who smokes too much pot, and I still love you. Wake up, man, and get back into the world today. I'm sorry. Now you know why she never called you. Remember all those times you came crying to me about Annette not calling you?"

"You have a point. It wasn't her fault if she was dead. God, I miss surfing. That guy just dropped into a perfect wave." Ethan pointed out to the water and knew that he had Emily back into a better frame of mind.

"I've got to help you get back into a relationship. I challenge you—no, I dare you to ask that red-haired fox out. That's it. Ask her. If you get a date, I will buy back your wetsuit and board from the pawn shop." Emily stood in front of Ethan, stopping his forward progress. "That whole motivation-through-reward concept."

"Not going to happen." Ethan turned away from Emily.

"You owe me. No way you can refuse this dare." Emily's eyes twinkled.

"I am not going to do it. I don't care about the board and wetsuit enough," Ethan said.

"Such a liar. Didn't you just swear to god that you wanted to be out there surfing? Fine. We have a competition then. The competition is the first one to go on a date with the red-haired fox."

"You can't. I like her. She doesn't even play for your team. She was married to a man. Shit, she and all the other women in the studios talked about George Clooney and fucking Ryan Gosling," Ethan said.

"I am. You forced my hand. The competition is on and the loser has to post a nude selfie on the social media outlet of the winner's choosing."

"Fine. But she isn't a lesbian."

"Well, I might be getting another toaster and a lesbian troop beaver badge for flipping one to my team since you claim she is a straight girl."

CHAPTER SEVEN

CAREFUL: NEPHEWS HAVE BIG EARS

FRANCES decided she needed to give her sister Edna a call. It had been about a week since she had last checked in with the Kavanagh family ground control. Edna had earned the "ground control" nickname the year she wore out her tape of David Bowie's *Space Oddity*, playing the title track until the whole family, including the dog, had the darn song memorized. The ongoing text messages about the parental unit's upcoming anniversary party had encroached on Frances's freedom. That bizarre early morning call from her mother had her wondering exactly what information Edna had been feeding their mother. Art was a nice hobby in the Kavanagh clan but not a serious profession sought by smart, sensible people.

How to get Edna to talk without giving out any more information? The challenge was on as Frances took her phone and went and sat on a makeshift bench in the corner of her loft, where she watched the northeast portion of the City from her windows. The sky was overcast and the light was easy on the eyes as she dialed her sister's number. Why would the family mind so much that she now called herself an artist? Yes, she had gone all the way through college and graduate school, gaining a PhD in economics with an emphasis on public health. Through it all, she painted. When she had worked ridiculous long hours as a business consultant, she had figured out how to paint almost daily. Most of the time her painting time was well after midnight.

Every Kavanagh knew that when talking with Edna, it was important to keep the conversation short because otherwise she had them volunteering for something she wanted done. Frances figured that her sister must have picked up her conversation skills from watching all those television crime shows. Sometimes it felt like Edna was grilling her straight from a TV script. Edna always managed to get the best secrets out of all the Kavanaghs.

Frances decided it was better to call and see if she could help with the party and not to bring up anything about her life. She knew there was a lot of planning going into their parents' anniversary party, and it was all falling downhill to Edna. Edna was attempting to follow the path to family sainthood; she did pretty much whatever Mom wanted her to do. Plus, she was always the one put in charge. Or was she a control freak and true genetic reproduction of their mother?

It wasn't that Frances was not excited about the whole affair; it was how her family did not understand why she divorced Richard. This was the same family where the majority boycotted the wedding based on the fact he was not Catholic. The only people to attend her wedding from her giant Irish family were her great-grandmother, Grangran, and her sisters Agatha and Theresa.

Frances let out a deep sigh as she called Edna. Each ring of the phone made Frances wonder if she should hang up again. Now she was committed because Edna hated seeing a number she knew without a message. Frances realized that phones and messages were some of the number of quirks her conservative family shared. Another one was how they followed the direction of the Bishop in how they voted. There was no such thing as separation of church and state in the Kavanagh household. A framed painting of each one of the popes since Vatican II hung in the Kavanagh living room. One year, Frances had given her dad a Secret Santa gift that got the whole family in trouble. It was a pope-on-a-rope soap. When he opened it in the living room, their mother gasped and tried to cover the eyes of the popes staring at them. Those paintings gave Frances night terrors as the popes' eyes would follow you around the room.

Frances was not looking forward to inheriting her painting of a pope. Their mother had said that when she died, each one of her children would get a pope painting. Maybe I should hang up and call Brice. Brice was so chill and nothing ever seemed to rattle him. He would know the scuttlebutt on the party but due to his gender he would not be responsible for anything. Brice's youngest son, Desmond, had a special place in her heart. In his last birthday card he had written a joke especially for her.

Happy Bornday Ant Franny. A b-day joke for you. What do you call a redhead who loses her temper? A Ginger Snap. I love you Ant Ginger Snap.

Xxoxxoo Desmond.

It never bothered her that Desmond continued to use "ant" for her. It made her laugh and at the same time wonder if the little guy really did think she was an insect. Chances are it was a direct result from a story Brice had fed his kids, Spencer and Desmond. At least they both received names outside the catholic naming scheme.

The phone clicked and brought Frances back to her task at hand.

"Hey, Sis," Frances said as brightly and loudly as she could.

"Who is this?" Edna asked.

"Frances. Remember me? I'm the black sheep of the family. Baaaa baaaa."

"Seriously. You picked a fine time to call. I'm putting the twins to bed. Don't you ever think before you dial?" Frances felt the bite of the Kavanagh mother tongue sting as she glanced at the clock, which read 6:00 p.m. She realized it was 8:00 p.m. in the holy land of St. Louis.

Frances held her phone out, wondering if she should hang up. Why do people answer the damn phone if it isn't a good time? The last time she checked, she was not a mind reader. Edna had to blame someone for her getting off schedule even though she had answered the phone. Tonight, Frances would be the issue.

"Oh shit. I'm sorry—"

"Mommy, your phone said shit!"

"Max said shit, Mommy. You said we can't say shit."

"Mommy. Eric said shit after I said shit."

"Ma, Max said shit again." This statement was followed by laughter as the boys continued to say the word over and over. Frances smiled as she listened to the conversation of shit she had started more than a thousand miles away.

"See what you did? Mom was right. I'll call you later."

Her sister was not happy. That was the angry mom voice. What did Edna mean that "Mom was right"? Right about what? Frances looked at the clock again and then remembered she had to meet Winter downtown for a make-up dinner. "Shit!" Frances started laughing as she knew Winter was going to hate her for being late again. No time to worry about the latest family drama. Frances splurged and used Uber to get herself a car quickly in the City. Moments later, a shiny black car pulled up in front of her building. Frances was not going to mess this meeting up because all it required was eating some scrumptious food at Isa in the Marina District. Frances loved the French fusion food they served.

The black car pulled up to the restaurant and Frances could see Winter sitting in the window seat sipping a drink. Hopefully it was her first drink, or if it wasn't, she prayed that she had drunk multiples and was numb to the time.

"I'm so sorry." Frances kissed Winter on the cheek as she sat down next to her in the cozy window seat.

"You're late. I ordered." Winter took another sip of her cocktail.

"Perfect. I'm sure it will be fantastic."

A waiter dressed in black with a crisply starched white apron appeared with a dirty martini, garnished with four olives, and a basket of the restaurant's famous bread.

Frances kissed her friend on the cheek again and took a quick sip of her drink. "You are too perfect to be my friend. Am I forgiven? How's your new place?"

"One question at a time. You owe me some explanations. Start with whatever possessed you not to show up on my moving day. You can follow with the dating stories I know you have but don't share. And I've never heard what finally caused you to go ballistic in your divorce. Spill the beans."

"Do we have to talk about me? I want to celebrate your new home."

"Start talking. I see your lips moving but not with the story I want to hear yet. We've got all night."

"You already know most of the story concerning the divorce."

Frances looked at Winter, who gave her a hard blink back. Frances figured Winter was not going to say another word until she got what she wanted. They both took another long sip from their martinis.

"I really do want to hear about your new place, and I feel like lately the world has been focused on me when we've gotten together."

"Frances, you are always the center of attention. It might be your red hair. It's just you and me. No judgment. Wait. Moderate judgment allowed because of the jokes you made about Jason."

"How did you know?" Frances asked.

"Know what?"

"Know that Jason was worth you pulling yourself off the market?" Frances said.

"That's none of your business and I resent you for asking the question. Now back to you answering my questions."

It took Frances a moment to compose her thoughts and think of the fastest CliffsNotes version of her divorce because it was in the past and Frances wanted to keep it there. She had ditched her friends when she thought she was in love and knew now she was a fool for dropping them for Dickhead.

"You also have to promise no more *Saving Silvermans*," Winter said, looking almost hurt. Frances and Winter had watched the movie at the same time in different cities, texting one another throughout the whole movie. Frances recalled that most of the texts were digs at her for dropping her friends once she had married Richard. Frances took another sip and tore off a piece of the warm crusty French bread as she thought about her friendship to Winter; she had finally found her voice again.

"Our lives are better than the Hollywood ending of *Silverman*. I promise that I will not abandon my closest friends for a relationship ever again. How long would you say that we have been friends?"

"Good friends, I would say eight years."

"But we met working as consultants, and so I would say that we actually are celebrating a dozen years," Frances said and shoved a soft bite of warm French bread with a nice dab of whipped butter into her mouth.

"What is the gift for the twelfth anniversary year? I'm going to look that up." Winter took out her phone. "Silk. You can get me silk pj's," Winter said smiling.

"Now that's a special gift. How about a silk scarf instead?" Frances knew her cheeks were blushing. Was Winter hitting on her? Oh my god, this is so hard. Here they were sitting in an intimate nook in a romantic restaurant sharing food. Would other people jump to the conclusion that she was on a date? This was San Francisco after all. Frances got into questions in her mind and figured now or never.

"Winter...I...well, there is something I am thinking about—"

"Frances, knock it off already. I know you're a reluctant artist. So what if you have a PhD in economics? You need to stop worrying about what people think."

"Easy for you to say as you are not getting grilled with questions about your sanity from every member of your family." Frances sat back in the booth and started to create a small butter sculpture on her bread plate with her butter knife.

"True. How many Kavanaghs are there? Sixty-two? You Catholics are the poster families for why the rhythm method is not a form of birth control."

"Funny. I am actually thinking I would like to expand my dating pool."

"Now you're talking. Garçon, two more drinks here, please."

"How is it you always make it look so easy. Wait staff responds to you instantly. Even when you are a demanding little one."

"What are you talking about?"

"You had asked me about the pivotal moment I knew that I was over Richard and the divorce was final. It was at the Hops & Hog over by 9th and Irving. Richard had used his mother to manipulate me and get me there. It got me to violate the number one rule my attorney drilled into my head: 'don't ever meet or talk to your ex outside of the meetings we establish.' That night at the Hops & Hog was the only time I did, and it was good I did because it showed me what a complete asshole he really was."

"Why do you always hold out on the good stuff?" Winter took a sip of the newly delivered martini poured tableside into a chilled glass.

"Trust me, this wasn't good. He showed up with a sales contract for the house. It basically signed over all the money from the house to him."

"That rat bastard. Did he think you were not going to read it? I read everything before I sign it, but then I'm a trained professional."

"Would you handle your own divorce? So much cheaper."

"Frances, you know what they say about attorneys who represent themselves? A fool. What'd you do?"

"I picked up the contract, shoved it in my purse, got up, poured two glasses of water over his head, and left."

"No. Really? Oh my god, I wish I could have seen that—"

"He totally deserved it because he brought my replacement with him that night."

"You mean he brought a date to your meeting? That is …"

"Fucked up. But you know I had realized deep down that the marriage really had fully fractured the day we took Riley to the vet and they could do nothing more for that wonderful dog. He was so awesome, all two hundred and fifty pounds of him."

"That's not a dog; that's a pony. What was he again?"

"He was the love in the marriage."

"Christ, Frances, you are so dramatic sometimes. What breed weighs two hundred and fifty pounds?"

"Sorry. If you open the Pandora's box of my divorce you are going to get the bad, the ugly, and the downright melodramatic." Frances smiled at a couple who had stopped to read the menu in the window. She pointed to the bread and mouthed the word "yummy." Winter got into the action as the waiter delivered a steaming pot of open clamshells in a white wine and butter sauce. Frances and Winter both bent over the bowl and deeply inhaled the aroma of white wine, shallots, and garlic.

"Do I have to talk? Can't we enjoy the food and talk about fantastical unicorns? What about your latest man? He's made it past the three-month mark. Are you getting serious? And again, I am asking you how do you know?" Frances said as she took a tiny fork and started in on the bowl full of clams. If she was doing a documentary on why one would want to live in this city, she would start with the clams at Isa's. San Francisco was special and so different from St. Louis. Her hometown had many cutting-edge restaurants, but the main difference was the location. San Francisco had the ocean, the bay, the Golden Gate Bridge, and Chinatown, not to mention that the climate was so easy and beautiful to live in year-round.

"Earth to Frances. Hello?" Winter and the waiter were both staring at her.

"Sorry. I was lost in the food and thinking about St. Louis."

"Yes. She needs another drink." The waiter took the order and was gone in a flash.

"You know, you have always checked out for as long as I've known you. It's so bizarre. It's also one of the many quirks that makes me curious to keep on knowing you. I could start telling people that you are body jumping or something—I told the waiter that it was a low alcohol level."

"Isn't it strange how we ended up here at this moment? The two of us in the same city at the same time? You're now a property owner with the rest of us." Frances held her water glass up for a toast, and Winter clinked with her martini glass.

"What are you talking about? You are finally turning into a real adult. Life is about to realize what it means to have Frances growing up. It amazes me that you could grow up at all and escape the Catholic clutches of the Kavanagh clan. I heard nine out of ten people born in Missouri stay and die there. The odds were not in your favor."

"I'm the one that got away. Or quite possibly was the one forced out. Not quite sure sometimes," Frances said.

"You mean your family cast you out to the heathens? Now back to me. Jason is fine for now. He's sweet. His friends really saved my ass on the move, with which I seem to remember one F.O.K. promising to help with, Ms. I have a big truck and love to move big-ass furniture and boxes of stupidly heavy books."

"I am so sorry. I really am, which is why dinner is on me."

"I'm thinking about forgiving you, but I need more than 'sorry.'" Winter crossed her arms over her chest and gave Frances a good strong look.

"My mom called that morning and was upset about me telling people that I am now an artist. I guess someone had mentioned something to her at Sunday mass a week ago. I really do not understand her sometimes. It was like I was out here sacrificing chickens in my bathroom and using their blood for paint. I think she was going to tell me I am going to hell for painting." Frances cringed. She was completely guilty of bailing on her friend and was glad that Winter had no problem ordering whatever she wanted off the menu. But her excuse did seem rather flimsy.

"Okay. I think you should play with your ultra-conservative Catholic parents and tell them you are dating women." Winter laughed as she drove her fork into a plate of roasted red potatoes with rosemary and garlic. "I love this food. It makes me so happy."

"Some might call you a mind reader," Frances almost whispered. Her hand shook as she reached for her water glass. This was moving into a new territory for her and she wondered if she could talk with Winter about her curiosity. "I am curious about it. You know, it seems like it is the thing to do in Hollywood these days."

"Frances, are you trying to tell me you want to see what it is like to date a woman?" Winter set down her fork and turned a little so she could face her friend.

"I...well...could it be any worse than dating a man? You should have seen the real winners at the speed dating thing I went to." Frances picked up her drink and gulped down about half of it.

"Well, did anyone ever call you from the speed rodeo round-up dating circus you went to?"

"Nope. It so totally sucks. But I did go on a date with this guy Cheryl hooked me up with from her work."

"Oh, that must have been entertaining. Is he a *Star Trek* fan or a *Star Wars* nerd?"

"Winter, that is so not nice. Cheryl does work with some real—"

"They're IT guys. An average description for the unmarried IT male is: lives in his mommy's basement and is generally pasty white. Oh my gosh, was he warm mocha? Or worse—a fake orange tan?"

"Stop it. His name is Mark, and he was pasty white like me. No freckles, though."

"Why didn't you set up a rescue call with me?"

"It really didn't last that long. We had no chemistry and dinner was only twenty-five minutes because he inhaled his burrito in, like, seconds."

"You went for Mexican food on a first date?"

"I love Mexican food, and it was actually quite good. We went Dutch, of course."

"I know you are saving the good part. Does he live with his mother?"

"Honestly, I don't know the answer to that. When I arrived, he was waiting for me outside the restaurant and was clearly nervous."

"Duh. Then what happened?"

Frances sat up as straight as she could, tucked her chin into her chest, and looked at Winter without turning her head, which forced her to turn her whole torso to see her.

"I don't know if I can get my voice to his nasally low octave, but he said: 'Cheryl told me you were pretty. Apparently, she and I have very different perspectives on what constitutes pretty.'"

"No."

"Yes. He turned and walked into the restaurant. I didn't know if I should follow or not. I wanted to kill Cheryl—trust me, he was no looker. Maybe we're the only two single people she knows, and she figured she would throw us together because it was evil and fun."

"What did you do?"

"I ordered a shot of tequila and a burrito with a nacho plate and beer chaser."

The two erupted into laughter.

"He didn't say anything the rest of the time. He inhaled his burrito and water and left after he paid for his order and 1.9 percent of the tip, based upon the quantity of what I ordered. I think he estimated that the beer and tequila shot with 98 percent of the total."

Winter couldn't stop laughing and the waiter approached with a look of some concern. The couple sitting next to them filled the waiter in on the conversation and then he left, returning with two more martinis. The evening turned into nirvana for Frances; through all their laughter she knew that she and Winter were back on track again. As the conversation ebbed and flowed, Frances let Winter explain uninterrupted how important it was to understand that no man comes trained.

"After all you have been through, you must let me help you out. I know you. Trust me, Frances. I can get you a super date. One that will erase the IT floppy disk date that Cheryl set up for you."

Frances took a sip and a bite of her crème brûlée and decided she had nothing more to lose.

"I accept your help. I don't know that I trust you or anyone right now."

"Ouch. That is harsh. Maybe you aren't ready to date again because if you can't even trust your friends who love you—"

"Sorry. Not what I meant. You know what I mean. Don't you?" Frances took Winter's hands in hers and squeezed them tightly. "I don't want another Richard, and I don't know if I trust myself as I was the one who went through with it, ignoring all the warnings."

"Frances, you know that I care about you and know that you are an exceptional and weird person. Use some of my self-confidence until you find your own. To be part of the adult world, you are going to have to trust again. You can start by trusting me to find you a great date."

"Show me some mercy and don't make the first date hang gliding or rock climbing," Frances said.

"Understood. You promise to follow through if I put my energy into helping you? No bailing on this. Raise your right hand and swear over this most sacred bread basket."

Frances followed through and looked around the small restaurant to see if anyone was watching her make a promise using a bread basket.

"I, Frances Olar Kavanagh, do promise to go out on the date that Winter sets up for me. I will not bail because I really cannot afford any more make-up dinners with you."

CHAPTER EIGHT
MINI BURNING MAN

A couple months after her divorce finalized, Frances decided to invite her friends over for a last hoorah to her whole married life. She collected the items that Richard had never bothered to pick up after they had sold their home. Angry with herself for having paid her movers to move his items along with her own, she threw the last of the letters, cards, pictures, and mementos into a garbage bag to make it easier to carry up the stairs to the patio. She looked at his possessions, lumping herself into the pile, as items so easily cast off it was salt rubbed into her stupidity. It stung more than she wanted to admit to herself. Her friends had told her, and rightfully, that she was indeed insane and way too nice in holding onto his items thinking that he might want to come and collect them. In some strange way, she knew it was her own self-imposed punishment. Richard had broken her spirit down to the point where she believed she was lucky to be with him. He reminded her on a daily basis how handsome and sought after he was. The absurdity of his emotional brainwashing came crashing down when she finally discovered he had lied, cheated, and pilfered her life and her money.

Frances sat on the first step leading up to the roof of her building, staring at the last hefty bag of Dickhead's items. She checked to make sure she had her phone in her pocket and then stood to carry the last of his trash up to the mini Burning Man fire sculpture. She wasn't sure that what she had built in the fire pit was exactly legal for a rooftop patio, but she wasn't going to go ask the powers that be for a burning permit either.

Out of breath, she leaned on the door handle for stability and took stock of her work. The base of her mini Burning Man was built from a pair of Sperry topsiders, a couple of rolled-up magazines, his squash racket, and some other miscellaneous man items. The body was framed out with scraps of wood she found in the fire bin. Her creation looked a little like a scarecrow from a Brooks Brothers store. The main body was layered with a couple of Oxford shirts, a baby-blue and white sweatshirt from his college, a couple of silk ties, and some skinny jeans that made her wonder if they were his as she never saw him wear anything like them. She glanced through the items left in the bag. These old letters and photographs would be used to stoke the fire.

Her friends may not have understood her marriage, but they did indeed understand her concept and need to hold her mini Burning Man party. The whole lot of them were practically giddy when she suggested it over dinner last week. Dana had shared that she wished she had done something similar after both of her divorces. Cheryl added that hitting a couple thousand tennis balls helped her get through her aggressions resulting from relationship breakups. The comment explained why Cheryl had such great arms and why she wore so many sleeveless shirts and dresses. Then there was Winter; she had profited handsomely from her divorce—the advantage of her being a good attorney who knew exactly who to hire to represent her. Winter shared that her favorite pastime was watching divorce proceedings in family court. It made her feel elated over what she wrangled out of her ex-husband.

Winter, Cheryl, and Dana were going to join her around 8:00 that night to help her light up the night sky with a burning of the old bad energies of her ex-husband. It had taken Frances more hours than she wanted to admit getting everything collected and sculpted into the fire pit. In a period of both panic and need, Frances did a few laps around the rooftop, wondering if she was going to get a couple of million drops of bad karma deposited in her karmic account for burning

Richard's crap in a crudely made effigy. The point to ponder was how he couldn't have really broken her heart because she had never known if she was ever in love with him in the first place. When Frances comprehended that she was in a loveless marriage, it caused her more sadness than she anticipated.

The sun was going down, giving softness to the light that cast the sky in beautiful shades of pink and orange. Frances, done with her preparations, sat down in one of the pink metal chairs the gays had refurbished for the enjoyment of the building. She uncorked the bottle of red wine she had brought up for her celebration and poured it into a mason jar. The jar contrasted sharply with the cost of the aged burgundy liquid being poured. The three-hundred-dollar bottle of wine tasted all the sweeter on this night, no matter the delivery device. This bottle had been rescued from the wine cellar that Richard tried to exit the marriage with in the divorce. Much of the wine had been carefully collected by Frances even before she had met him. She had been planning to open a series of small-plate eateries across the Bay Area, another dream that was smashed to smithereens through her marriage. He knew exactly what he was doing through his calculated marriage to Frances. Now, thankfully, she was one hundred percent divorced.

Frances let her head rest on the back of the chair and took another slow sip of wine. Rolling the dark-red liquid around her mouth, she savored the calming, smooth richness of this heavy cabernet with the velvety finish. She slowly swallowed the flavors of dark cherries mixed with pepper and earthy richness.

"Here's to being free from Richard Peter Enos." Frances raised her glass to the sky in a toast and then took another sip. "Oh Riley, I do miss you, my furry friend. I know you are out in doggie heaven playing with a great gang of pups and having a grand ole time."

"Hey woman, whose ghost are you talking to?" Russell asked as he walked over to study the peculiar sculpture in the fire ring. "What is going on here?"

"Did you ever have a love that was so pure, so unconditional that your soul broke into a thousand pieces when that love died?" Frances asked and kept her tears back as she offered to pour a mason jar for Russell.

"No time for a drink, Simon and I have a couple we are trying to talk out of adopting a baby. I'll take a rain check though." Russell studied the bottle. "Duckhorn Cabernet Estate Special—very nice, and from the Howell Mountain region, no less…this must have put you back a pretty penny."

"A few pennies. I was thinking about Riley, my Swiss mountain dog. How could Richard, a real asshole of a person, find such an amazing dog?"

"Frances. Isn't that the same dog that would chew up his shoes, leave brown deposits on his side of the bed, and basically scare the crap out of him with his bark?" Russell sat down, still studying the scarecrow sort of thing standing in the fire pit.

"Yes. He never destroyed anything of mine, and we had such wonderful conversations. When Riley passed, I finally awoke to the power inside of me and knew I had to do something different."

"Didn't Richard serve you with divorce papers? And can you please explain what all of this is up here? I was planning on having our little intervention 'don't adopt' dinner party on the patio tonight." He stood and walked around the pit.

"Oh shit. I am so sorry—I didn't check the calendar to see if anyone had reserved the rooftop. This is my Burning Man. The gang is coming over, and I thought I sent an invitation to you and Simon. Oh…maybe I didn't because I wasn't sure how you boys would respond to me burning a man. Well, not a real man. Did you say intervention adoption dinner party?"

"You do listen. Friends of ours think a baby will save their relationship, but between you and me, separate houses and lives is the only thing that will save that relationship," Russell said. He took the mason jar of wine from Frances's hands and took a sip. "That is yummy. Enough. If this means you are moving on past your divorce, Richard, and all the drama, I sprinkle my fairy party dust and bless the affair. My party will be so much easier downstairs anyway." Before exiting, Russell kissed Frances on her forehead and took another sip of wine out of the mason jar. "That is smooth—very nice, F.O.K."

Frances checked the time and saw that the crew should be arriving any minute. Was this really going to work for her? So many things had been traveling around her brain about her life, marriage, and the thought of dating again. It all felt so heavy. She was no longer twenty-something, and dating seemed like a foreign world. Had she wasted her time? It was her own fault because she was so unsure. She followed the order of expected events. Go to school, get a graduate degree, get married, buy the house, and give mom and dad grandchildren. Was she that horrid that her life went way off the tracks? Frances covered her face with her hands as she tried to rationalize that she cared more about Riley than she ever did for Richard. What did that say about her? She cried for herself and the pain of her failure.

Frances wondered if Winter had remembered their conversation from the make-up dinner. Winter could be so obtuse sometimes and take things as a joke. Why had she told Winter that she was thinking about going on a date with a woman? Frances looked around the rooftop and picked up her phone, scrolling through her emails. What had she sent to Dana? She kept scrolling through her sent emails looking for the one she had sent to her close and wise friend, Dana Rainer. It was an email she wished she could recall because she wrote it after one too many glasses of wine. Maybe she really did have the Irish drinking gene. Why was she drinking so much now?

Could she ask Winter to keep her revelation about dating women private without raising any issues? Frances chewed on her pinky finger and decided she would try to figure out if Winter could even recall the conversation after the food coma they were in when they left Isa's that night. She could tell Winter that she was not going to be dating as she needed to focus on her painting and new art career. That was it—she had no time to date anyone or anything.

Frances turned up the music and sang along to Creed's song "Are You Ready?", yelling the lyrics "life has just begun!" at the top of her lungs. She loved the fact that she could play super DJ from her phone; she remembered all too well her stacks and stacks of poorly mixed tapes. Today's world let her plan her mixed music play in minutes. Frances shook her head, thinking about her nieces and nephews never having to go through the hours of making mixed tapes the old-fashioned way.

She had never been to the real Burning Man event in the desert, but stories of it had always piqued her curiosity. She stopped checking the time after 8:15 and thought about starting the fire promptly at

8:30, with or without her girls. Her playlist was loaded up with essentials from Metallica, Soundgarden, and of course, Led Zeppelin. "Good Times Bad Times" blasted out of the speakers and rolled into a remix house version of "This Is My Fight Song." Frances let the energy of the music get her up and out of the chair.

"Where's the fire?" Cheryl yelled as she popped through the rooftop door. She was quickly followed by Winter and Dana. All three were bearing bags filled with tempting treats for the celebration. Dana came over and dumped two bags of food from the deli down the street on the picnic table. The table was decked out with a nice cloth that Russell had neglected to take with him. Frances felt a little twinge of guilt but was glad he had left it; the top of that thing was nasty looking no matter how many times the boys had tried to clean it. Stains that should be studied were living on the surface of that rooftop furniture.

"You guys are right on time. The man is to burn promptly at 8:30. I've got the music worked out for the whole thing." Frances grabbed some empty mason jars and passed them out to her chosen family. "This is a nice Cabernet."

"Too much for me. Stop." Dana pulled the glass jar away. Winter rushed her mason jar over to catch the pouring stream of wine with lightning-fast reflexes. She caught the wine midway to the rooftop.

"Fill me up—I'll drink for Dana too," Winter said.

"Holy crap, Winter, I had no clue your reflexes were that quick," Cheryl said.

"Can't let wine like this go to waste. It would be a sin." Winter winked at Frances as she walked away with her jar-o-wine. "Feels like I'm back on the farm. See you broke out the good crystal and paper plate china for this lil' party." Winter said.

Frances stopped and stared at her friends and wiped some tears away. What she saw were her friends supporting her saying good-bye to a part of her life that held so many regrets. Would she be able to snap out of it? The plan in doing this whole activity was to cast off the regrets, the hate, and the blame.

"Now, Dana, you know you can spend the night. I already have an air mattress bed made for you," Frances said. This took her mind away from the feelings that were making her cry. She quickly dodged the look of "no way" from Dana and turned up the music. The party was fully started as Cheryl was busy getting some food arranged on the table. Winter was over at the fire pit and studied Frances's handiwork. Frances caught her smiling.

"What do you call this design, Frances?"

"Dickhead burning at the stake," Frances said. With a long wooden match, she lit the sparklers and handed one to each of the women as they gathered around the fire pit. Frances poured some lighter fluid on the pile of Richard's shit, then took her own sparkler and flung it in a high arc toward the center of the pit. A light trail traced the path of the sparkler as it landed on the left loafer and sparked the lighter fluid into flame.

Dana was waving her sparkler around in the air making different light designs. Winter held hers and took a sip of wine, waiting to see how quickly the flames moved up the effigy of Richard. Cheryl took her sparkler and jabbed it into the center of the sweatshirt body and stamped her feet with glee as the flames shot out horizontally from the center. Frances turned the music up and sang along with the Talking Heads' "Burning Down the House." Her off-key sing-along caused both Winter and Dana to throw their sparklers into the roaring fire so they could cover their ears. The sight of the flames and the random items burning had them all hypnotized.

Frances watched the fire and the dancing light that the flames cast across the rooftop. Her friends' faces were hard for her to read in the odd light. They had never understood her marriage, and she could never exactly explain why she had basically fallen off the face of the earth for those few years. Each person there, including herself, had suggested she might be insane. Right now, she looked around at her little tribe and let her feelings of sisterhood fill her up. She felt so good standing there with her friends. She approached Dana, who was standing closest to her, and took her hand.

"Thank you," Frances mouthed the words silently to her friends.

Cheryl and Winter came over and the four women stood hand in hand, watching the flames devour the figure. "Everybody Dance Now" came roaring out of the speakers, and the group started to dance around the fire pit. The flames continued to grow, and Frances was starting to feel real heat. She danced around the ring and checked over her shoulder to make sure the two fire extinguishers were at the ready. Three more songs played and the tribe kept right on dancing.

Dana was the first to sit. Winter and Cheryl were not far behind her. A surge of energy overtook Frances, and she continued to yell at the top of her vocal range. She swallowed the freedom of it all. A wicked, crooked smile crossed her face as she dug into the garbage bag and pulled out several pictures of Richard showing his dimpled, smiling face. Then she threw them into the kinetic freedom of energy the flames had created. The red, yellow, and blue licked hungrily around the edges of the photos and made short work of the images. Frances let the energy of the flames transfer into her. She started chanting the colors of the flames: "Orange, blue, red, purple."

Cheryl brought over a water bottle and gave it to a hoarse-voiced Frances. The flames continued to circle the pit, dancing and mixing up into the smoke that swirled high into the night sky. Her heart pounded so hard that she had to clasp her hands over her chest. Through the release of it all, she let her tears loose. She cried like she had never cried before. The rapid-fire beating of her heart made her wonder if she was breaking all over again. Her heart was breaking over the failure to protect and know herself. She had known that the marriage was wrong from the start. She cried over her lost dreams. The fire was now consuming the lying that had happened between the two of them.

"Fuck you, Richard!" Frances screamed at the top of her lungs. "Fuck you, Frances, for being too afraid of your own shadow and allowing yourself to marry Richard. He didn't deserve you." Frances clenched her hands into fists and shadowboxed the flames. After a few minutes, she stopped and stood completely still. No one moved on the roof. The crackling of the flames was the only sound to be heard as the music playlist had played itself out. Dana came and wrapped a blanket around Frances, who then took the blanket like a great cape and sat down to watch the fire. Winter, Cheryl, and Dana moved seats in a circle around the last of the mini Burning Man.

"You know, I wasn't the only failure in this marriage," Frances said quietly.

"We know," Winter responded for the group.

Frances picked up her almost empty mason jar of wine and swirled the red-black liquid around in the bottom of the jar.

"You don't think I have drinking problem, do you?" Frances asked as she downed the last of her wine and reached for another bottle.

The group erupted into laughter. "Nope. But you might be a wild pyromaniac. I'm shocked no one has called the fire department—those flames got pretty darn high and this smoke looks and smells toxic," Winter added.

"You know, my brother Bernard thinks I have a drinking problem," Frances joked as she gladly accepted more wine into her jar.

"Isn't he the one you had believing he was actually a puppy because your parents had taken him to a witch?" Cheryl asked.

"Frances, you did not do that," Dana said.

"I never did. He's older than me, but not by much. It was the older kids. Lucky I wasn't named after Saint Bernard of Clairvaux like Bernard was. You know, I think he became a doctor because of his namesake. Saint Bernard was known as the 'Doctor of the Church.' Trust me, the stories he was told convincing him that he came to the family as a Saint Bernard puppy were priceless. They continue with the nieces and nephews, who think he is actually some sort of werewolf or weredog."

"And you wonder why people think Catholics are crazy?" Winter shook her head and poked at the collapsing fire with a piece of wood.

Frances stood and went to the bag and the last of Richard's crap and saw that it still contained some letters and cards, as well as their wedding album. The letters and handwritten cards were sprinkled onto the flames without hesitation. She watched them reignite the flames, forcing them higher into the darkness of the night. Frances clutched the wedding album under her left arm and stared into the center of the deep-orange flames, the white coals, and the few wood logs that supported the base of the fire.

"You might want to rethink throwing that wedding album into the fire," Cheryl said quietly as she came and stood next to Frances. "It's part of your history and how you got to this point. There might be pictures of people you do love captured in that album."

Frances sat down and started flipping through the wedding album. With each glance, her heart punched her throat as she stared at herself and Richard in poses that were so staged. She could not tell from her own expressions if she was happy. The woman in the white dress was unknown to her. Frances flipped through the pages faster and faster but stopped on one that showed the five bridesmaids. It was an action shot where they were spread out behind her, all jumping up in the air. They looked like they had come straight from a CW Network soap opera casting call because they were all so perfect looking. Frances did not know one of her bridesmaids. Richard and his mother chose each one. How utterly strange, Frances realized in hindsight.

"I've got to let you guys know why I basically disappeared when I met and married Dickhead." Frances sat back and closed the photo album.

"Are you sure you want to share that with us? You know you don't have to. We are so glad you are back with us now." Dana blew a kiss over to Frances sitting on the other side of what was left of her Burning Man creation.

"I do. I realize that I allowed him to dictate my days. He would make me feel like I was less than anyone else. The whole time we were together, he never celebrated my birthday. What the heck was I thinking when I let him erase my phone? That was it—I wasn't thinking. His mother gave me this lecture about how I was here to support her son in this life. That his happiness was my responsibility now."

"Holy crap, Frances. I thought I had it bad when I married the only son of a Jewish mother. That is rough. You married into the 1950s version of *Leave it to Beaver*," Winter said as she took a long slow sip of her wine.

"One day passed and then another and then it was a year. I had not talked to any of you. I should have picked up the phone or driven over to see you guys. There were so many excuses, and I was ashamed. I deferred everything to him." Frances stood and started to jump around in circles. The heavy wedding album still in her hands, she felt the tears burn as she was feeling her freedom and strength breaking apart the fear and pain from those years she allowed herself to disappear.

She stopped her list of excuses and opened the photo album and used her strength as she ripped out the first several pages and flung them into the fire. The flames shot up around the heavy photo pages with a new hunger for items to consume and devour. The smiles and faces in the photos turned to black ash, and it struck Frances that the transition from burning to ash made her feel better. These weren't her friends or her family.

Frances stood up, stretching her legs and releasing the pressure on her knees. A slight wind came in from the west and swirled around the roof, dancing between the fire and the table. Wind fingers turned the pages of the wedding album to a picture Frances had forgotten. There, looking stronger than ever, was her great-grandmother, Kathryn Mary Kavanagh, her beloved Grangran. Frances traced her finger along the smiling image of Grangran's face. Grangran was next to Frances, standing as tall as she could in her purple gown and hat, her fingers laced through Frances's.

She did not wipe the tears away from her face as she recalled that this was the last picture taken of her Grangran. She passed away in her sleep peacefully a week later. The family had withheld that information from Frances because she was on her honeymoon with a man that her parents had refused to meet. Frances ripped the page from the wedding album and held the picture close to her chest. The fire, her friends—all of it faded away as Frances talked to her Grangran.

"I'm out," Frances said aloud.

"She has finally lost her marbles. I think Frances is talking to the smoke?" Winter whispered to Dana.

"Grangran, I'm sorry I was so blind and did not take your advice," Frances said, and the tears started rolling down her face. Cheryl went over to her iPhone and scrolled through some playlists, settling on a Celtic mix. She then walked over and put her arms around Frances and led her back to the pink deck chair.

"Cheryl, I am not going crazy. When my Grangran died, she visited me in my hotel room in Maui. Richard was passed out from drinking too much, and I was unable to sleep. She looked so young and so happy when she came to me that night. I didn't tell anyone because I wasn't sure it was real. I can still hear her voice. She said as plainly as I am talking to you now: "Everything will be fine once you find your way out." Then, she evaporated like an early morning mist. Tonight, the flames touched the silence of her power in the smoke and I saw her."

"Now that is a story. Ghost of your great-grandmother in your honeymoon suite," Winter said as she handed Frances a bottle of water and a couple of napkins. A wave of comfort washed over Frances as she smiled through her tears at her friends and the happy, dancing flames of the fire. She stood and took the box holding the last few papers and threw the whole thing on the flames. Still holding tight to the picture of her Grangran, Frances walked over to the now-closed wedding album and tossed it on top of the renewed flames. The smoke turned a heavy gray black as the flames sported the colors of the light spectrum. Frances noticed that the gang, including herself, took a couple steps back from the toxic green-black smoke.

Frances dropped the photograph into her chair and walked to the edge of the fire ring as the flames of the fire gobbled the last of the items up. A deep guttural scream erupted from the most primal center of Frances's core as the fire fully obliterated the last of Richard's crap. Her scream grew in volume and power as the fire continued to burn. It took Frances to the edge of her vocal and lung capabilities; she pulled in a deep full breath and let the loaded gun of a scream unleash itself.

Dana, Winter, and Cheryl surrounded Frances, and they all looked at one another, unsure exactly what to do with a friend who may have fallen off the edge of any sort of reality. Dana raised a hand to stop Cheryl from touching her and gave Frances the room to scream. Winter was starting to look toward the direction of the rooftop door, wondering when the SWAT team was going to bust through. It might look as bad as it sounded, like they were torturing a person.

"Oh, shit," Frances said quite calmly and sprang over the chair to grab the bucket of water she had filled as her first defense against a runaway fire. A big piece of burning paper had risen high up into the air, broke free of the fire ring, and flew low and fast across the roof, landing on the faded gray outdoor carpet. It started to burn brighter as the dry carpet appeared to want to join the flames. Frances threw the entire bucket on the burning paper and watched as it sizzled and fizzled, fighting against the water. She bent over the dark puddle of ash and burnt paper, catching her reflection in the mess of it all. It was okay. She was okay. Despite the smear of ash across her face, she was okay and had not burned the building down.

"I look like a character out of a Dickens novel," she said as she returned to the silent group. "I'm finally free of it all." Frances threw her hands into the air and took a victory lap around the fire pit. When she stopped, she caught the look of concern simultaneously broadcasting across her friends' faces. She flopped down on the picnic table bench and focused on the fire, motioning to her wide-eyed friends that they needed to sit as well. She took a new bottle of wine and poured it into a mason jar that someone had left on the bench. As she watched the fire and followed the tips of the flames up to the smoke, she blinked hard a few times. In the flames, she thought she saw her Grangran dancing. Frances smiled a broad, deep smile and helped herself to the feast her friends had brought to the celebration.

CHAPTER NINE
DANA

Dana Rainer sat in her favorite wooden garden chair, which she had placed facing east to catch the rising sun as it cleared over the hills of Oakland. The San Francisco Bay was still dark gray as the early morning light had not found the water's surface yet. Cars on the Richmond–San Rafael Bridge still used headlights as they headed west, giving her a ribbon of light to watch. The morning paper lay unopened on the overturned clay pot standing in as a table. This time of the morning allowed Dana the luxury of listening to the natural life waking around her. The bees were up and busy, already collecting for their bustling hives. Flight paths of the worker bees appeared well established as they flew from flower to flower in the lavish garden. The lavender, lemon tree, and honeysuckle were in beautiful full bloom this time of year.

"Keep up the good work, my little pollen haulers," Dana said.

Some scratching of dirt close to her chair distracted her attention away from the bees and the view. "Hello, Doris. You're up early." Dana reached down and Doris, her chicken, bobbed her head as she slowly walked toward Dana's outstretched hand. The chicken was one of the few things left from Dana's classroom days. Dana had spent more than thirty years as a biology teacher, a career which had left her with lots of stories.

The stories she loved the most were how her chickens, first Margaret Miller and then Doris Day, turned teenage high school students into respectable real people. Dana reached down and stroked the back of Doris's soft red feathers. Doris went back to scratching the dirt and picking up seeds and small bugs. Dana watched the chicken and then surveyed the garden for her dog, Lulu. She figured Lulu, a true creature of comfort, had climbed up into her bed inside the house and was fast asleep. Early mornings were not Lulu's thing.

Throughout her morning chores, Dana spent her time thinking about how to answer Winter. It irritated Dana to lose her mindful meditation in pulling weeds and checking her bees to worry about pushing Frances back into the world of dating. Winter had come up with a great idea for helping Frances. It was more than Dana wanted to do, but she could see the logic and the fun in the plan. Cheryl was already on board with Winter's idea. The three of them had gone to lunch two days ago to discuss the situation of Frances. The Saturday morning Buena Vista Irish Coffee Club had been peppered with some rather sad stories of her dating escapades. Dana loved Frances and her quirky outlook on life. Frances could make her believe that unicorns do exist. Still, a divorce could play havoc on a woman, and getting back into the dating pool wasn't easy. After all, Dana reasoned that she had taken her own years to heal after both of her divorces.

Dana, Cheryl, and Winter had compared notes on conversations and emails shared with Frances over the past few months. Then, they discussed bringing up the fact that they were trolling dating websites for Frances at her Burning Man party. They had decided not to tell her at the time to keep the new away from the old, and let her move past it all. Cheryl thought the party was awesome and not the place to bring up dating. Winter had said she thought the whole fire thing was being a little melodramatic but long overdue. Dana had not shared what she thought.

"Doris, get out of my Swiss chard." Dana clapped her hands toward Doris, who was attempting to nest herself in for a nap in the Swiss chard planter box. This current chicken came to her through a group of big, tough high school senior boys who bought her the fuzzy little baby chick a few days after Margaret Miller, the class hen, died. She didn't want another chicken. None could replace the beautiful Margaret; she was truly a mother hen to those students, as she somehow knew which student needed her most in each class period. The thought had occurred to her that Margret Miller was a psychic chicken, due to her uncanny ability to calm teenagers. She was a rather amazing chicken and acted more like a well-trained dog, doing tricks for blueberries and cheese. Those senior boys had become so attached to Margaret that they cried over her passing and decided to get Dana a new baby chick. Now, this baby chick was a full-grown, ten-year-old Rhode Island hen trying to nest in her garden, specifically in the beautiful Swiss chard.

Dana knew that Winter and Cheryl needed her to protect them from Frances should their plan go south. That was reason enough to stay out of the fray. The scientist in Dana was curious about the experiment and she loved Frances, so she had to stay on the team to find Frances a person to date. The sun finally cleared the top of the Oakland hills and was in full view for Dana in her North Bay haven. She closed her eyes and lay back, pulling in the beauty of the sun's rays. The thought of helping Frances by pushing her off the metaphorical cliff gave Dana a wicked little smile. Dana knew that if her own mother were still alive, she would be saying, "Jesus H. Christ in the mountains, Dana Hope Rainer, what are you dunderheads up to now?" Take a risk, Dana thought to herself, and she knew that it was worth it to help the gang and have some out-of-the-ordinary fun for herself.

Dana picked up her phone while she kept an eye on Doris, who was still clucking around the Swiss chard, and dialed Winter's number.

"Good morning. I want a cup of coffee. Oh yeah, and count me in on your diabolical plan. You guys come over here and we'll get it done tonight." Dana didn't wait for a response and hung up. She knew Winter understood her short, curt phone calls, so she never worried. Dana rose and pulled some ripe lemons off her decades-old lemon tree and headed upstairs to bake something for the three of them to enjoy while they assumed their roles as yentas for Frances.

The view from Dana's main floor was spectacular. She stopped to watch the Larkspur ferry on its way to the City. A slight breeze was coming in through the open window, and Dana thought about the way

Frances finally let out all her tears at her Burning Man. It was time to write a note to Frances. Dana sat down at her desk and booted up her laptop.

She waited for the screen to come up and wondered how she could best help Frances ease back into the dating world. Winter's plan was to throw her into the deep end of the pool without any life jacket. Could Frances swim? Dana sighed and decided there was only one way to find out, and that was to get it done.

CHAPTER TEN

BORROWED TIME

T HE San Bruno Mountains looked purple in the early morning light. Ethan's mother had prepaid for herself and her two sons to all be buried in a traditional burial ground at Hills of Eternity Memorial Park when she first learned about her diagnosis. She had said the doctors told her that with the current drug therapies, she wouldn't need to have her breasts removed. Ethan stopped and started to count the headstones. When they buried his mother, he counted the headstones instead of listening to Rabbi Shuler and the people gathered graveside who told him and his younger brother, Ian, how wonderful their mother was and that she was in a better place. How did they know?

There were so many things he never got to say to his mother when she died. She was only forty. Who dies at age forty? It wasn't fair. Ethan hated his mother for dying. It took him years for his heart to figure out that she did not cause her own breast cancer. He blamed her for not getting the surgery, for listening to the doctors, and for not letting their father gain custody after her death, leaving them stuck under the care of her mother with all those rules.

Ethan walked down the row of gravestones, glancing at the names and seeing how many other graves had stones placed upon them. He turned the small round granite stone over and over in his pocket. His grandmother would drag him and Ian to the grave once a week. She would say a couple of words under her breath and then, using her left hand, place a stone on her daughter's gravestone. She called it an act of Shiva and that it is their tradition, their responsibility. Ethan rebelled and stopped going. He spent most of his high school years living at Emily's house. Her parents were cool and knew nothing was going on between them because Emily declared she was a lesbian at age five.

Twenty headstones from the curb, Ethan stopped and lowered his head. He felt the tears coming to the surface.

"I miss you, Mom. I'm so afraid."

Ethan looked around the cemetery, relieved that he was the only early morning visitor. He sat on the wet grass and let the cold wetness soak into his jeans. He kept the stone in his hand and dug the other hand into the grass. An urge to dig his mother up and free her from the dirt overwhelmed him.

"I need to know what to do, Mom. Last night I watched something that made me realize that she is lost to me. She will never say my name or touch my head the way you did when I was little."

Ethan took the stone and placed it in his left hand and got to his knees to place the stone on the top of his mother's grave. There was another stone on the grave, and Ethan knew that his brother had to have come by at some point—they were the last two left in the family.

"Mom, I know you are no longer around but sometimes I wish you were. I don't want to do anything to her, but it is getting harder and harder. She is my muse."

Ethan lay down with his face pressed against the grass. He cried out and sunk his teeth into the grass, pulling it up and chewing it in his mouth. The taste of the earth quieted him as he settled his face against the grass. Images of the video he watched went through his mind. He stretched his arms out and knew that someday he would rest above his mother in this place. It was all arranged. When she told him that she had gotten him a gift, he had thought it was a new skateboard.

At eleven, learning that his mother purchased a family grave for herself and her two sons sent him into a tantrum. He told her that he hated her and that she was stupid. Ethan shut his eyes and remembered the tears in his mother's eyes. He never apologized to her. Why?

Ethan turned onto his back and stared at the sky, watching its hue change from a dark steel blue to a pale blue. He wondered what it would be like to lie in a box several feet below where he was right now.

"I'm so sorry, mom," Ethan said. His tears were streaming down into his ears.

He gripped the grass in his hands and ripped up roots and dirt. Ethan sat up and shoved the handfuls of earth into his jacket pockets. Was there some way to get Frances to understand how much he cared for her? Cold from lying in the wet grass, Ethan stood and started to walk back toward his car. His crying fit over, he turned and looked at the small holes he had left in the perfectly manicured grass over his mother's grave. He fingered the grass and dirt in his pockets and felt like he was carrying a part of his mom with him. His phone rang. He tried to wipe some of the mud from his hands to answer his phone.

"Good morning," Ethan said. A surge of energy pulsed through his body.

"I hope I didn't call you too early. Would you want to go see that new exhibit at the de Young with me today?" Frances asked.

Ethan turned around in a circle with his hands raised in the air. He had done it. Frances was calling him.

"What time? I can pick you up."

"How about we meet in the sculpture garden at the giant safety pin—say, around 11:00? I've got to run some errands this morning and will be over on that side of town."

"Sounds good. See you there."

Ethan ran the last thirty yards to his car. He needed to go home and take a shower. The last forty-eight hours he had been out collecting items for his own masterpiece. This invitation gave him a renewed energy to fully think out his plan with Frances. He needed to call Emily. Ethan got into his car and dialed Emily's number.

"Hey Em," Ethan said when she answered.

"Morning to you, my friend. What's up?" Emily asked.

"Frances called and we are going to the latest exhibit at the de Young. Looks like I win."

"You simple man. I said date. That is not a date. A date is getting some sort of carnal knowledge. I thought we made that clear years ago. It was you that came up with the date definition," Emily said.

"Fine. I will. It is all borrowed time anyway."

"What does that mean? Ethan, are you at your mother's grave again?"

"No."

"You know you are only lying to yourself. I've got to go—I am teaching a class at eight this morning," Emily said.

Ethan slid into his car and glanced at the laptop computer sitting on the passenger seat. He needed to get home and clean his car out. He was never directly taught to lie—it came naturally. Maybe Emily was placed on this earth to keep helping him perfect his lying. The morning traffic would slow him down, but he had plenty of time to review what he recorded last night. The key with Emily and probably Frances was to tell the truth every now and then. Maybe he needed to bring Frances out to visit his mother.

CHAPTER ELEVEN
F.O.K.!

THE proof that she was once again officially Frances Olar Kavanagh came with the delivery of her new driver's license. Thank god she had talked the grumpy man controlling the DMV counter, who had to have been channeling the speed of a snail, into letting her retake her picture rather than reissuing the horrid picture of ten years before when she had first arrived in the Golden State. The frizzy-hair look was not particularly flattering. Granted, driver's license pictures are meant to be awful. That's a fact of life. Her Costco membership picture was running neck and neck with her high school graduation portrait in the race for most embarrassing photo ever taken of her.

It was an issue, her name, mostly due to her initials. Frances collided a lot with the nuns who ran her formative years from elementary through high school. She loved her name. It was not hard to get her friends to call her F.O.K. for short. Somehow, though, the nuns would get themselves worked up over kids calling her by her initials. It was never really an issue for her. They were her initials, F.O.K. When she hit middle school, she learned that her initials had some comedic power. What had her parents been thinking when they named her? She was so glad to be reunited once again with her birth name after her divorce that she seriously contemplated putting her monogram on everything she owned, from her truck to her toothbrush.

Excited to announce the return of her maiden name, Frances texted out *F.O.K. is BACK!* to her entire address book. She knew that she might get some strange questions about the text, but she didn't mind. It felt good. Before she got too carried away, her phone rang.

"Hey, Agatha," Frances said and sat down on her leather couch, surveying her messy loft and thinking that if she had Agatha's self-control, this place would be spotless.

"What do you mean, F.O.K. is back? Where did you go?"

"It means my name is officially mine again. I am no longer Mrs. Richard P. Enos." Frances laughed into her phone. "Note to self: never will I marry again, but should I consider it…check the name first. What's up in your neck of the woods?"

"If you would take some time and call your parental units occasionally, you would know. Mom and Dad are trying to get Bernard set up with some single woman from the parish."

"Oh, I'm sure that's going over well. Not." Frances was always curious about Bernard's lack of social graces because the rest of the clan was darn funny and outgoing. They all had ordinary high school years with first loves, heartbreaks, and fun. Bernard was the odd exception. He was not friendly. He felt people were below his intellectual level and were a waste of time. Ironically, he was a pediatrician.

"Frances, you don't remember why? Bernard had that hard crush on Sister Mary Michael. She was your teacher in seventh grade."

"Not triggering anything?" Frances said.

"Bernard lost his virginity to Sister Mary Michael. I guess you were on a different planet. I can't believe you don't remember. Dad was ready to kill Bernard because Bernard carried on about how Sister Mary Michael was going to leave the order and marry him when he was eighteen."

"That memory is getting less fuzzy. Geez, I must be getting older because you think I would remember this."

"The drama of Bernard's first love resurfaced last year. You are not going to believe this, but Sister Mary Michael did leave the order, but not for Bernard," Agatha said.

"Really. I had no clue a nun could leave. Who did she marry?"

"She married that priest from St. Patrick's Parrish and they brought their kid to Bernard with an ear problem."

"Holy shit. How did you hear about it?" Frances asked.

"You know mom's golden boy. He was crying to her about it in the kitchen when Edna and I were trying to get everything done for the Sunday family dinner. Mom stopped the conversation when Bernard said he hated all women."

"Bernard is such a bastard."

"Frances, don't let Mom or Dad hear you say that. Next to the Christ child, Bernard is more than likely their favorite. On to other news…Dad is ready to fire Beatrice."

Frances pulled her phone away for a moment. How could Dad fire one his other favorites? That would be impossible. Unless he finally saw the Beatrice that the rest of the Kavanagh clan witnessed. Nice was not the word one used to describe Beatrice.

"No. I thought he was going to leave everything to her when he stated she was the only one with a brain in the family."

"Beatrice has decided she is not going to church anymore. The last big scandal on hiding some priest from the police in Boston did it for her."

"Agatha, do you think Mom and Dad thought they were going to have a bunch of devout kids ready for sainthood if they named us after the saints on their respective feast days? Really, it was a rather bad crapshoot for us."

"You got off lucky. At least the new pope chose your name. You would have thought they had made you pope when he chose that name. Mom was going on and on about how special your name is, reserved only for special people. Yup. You are 'special.'"

"Not nice. My numbers have dropped in the family polls greatly since then. I promise that if I ever name a human, I will make sure it is one heck of a cool name. And I will triple check to make sure the initials do not spell something stupid."

"Are you pregnant?" Agatha asked.

"No. Only through immaculate conception. How would I be pregnant? I am not dating anyone and don't plan to be anytime soon. What kind of question is that?"

"Thought I could shake you enough with such a wild question that you would tell me what is really going on with you."

"Nothing is going on that isn't normal. I am finding my voice. Divorce is—"

"Frances, I know what divorce is, and you make life so much harder than it needs to be."

"How do you know what I'm feeling? You have been married for almost, what, twelve—"

"Sixteen years. I've been married sixteen years and trust me, I have thought about divorce too."

"Agatha, nothing is wrong with me. I am figuring out who I want to be and who I am." Frances said.

"Shit. I mean shoot. I must go, Frances. Your favorite nephew, Matthew, came in carrying a snake and I need to go. Mark, stop rolling Luke across the floor. He's a baby, not a watermelon." Agatha hung up and didn't give Frances time to inquire about what type of snake her nephew had brought into the house.

How she missed her nephews. The antics of those boys served Agatha right for all the pranks she pulled when they were kids. Karma is a bitch that can pay one back in spades. Those blessed three rough-and-tumble boys were giving her a good run for her money. The naming mechanics Agatha and her husband used made no sense either. Why would anyone name their sons after apostles? If the Irish did indeed save civilization, it would be a good idea to start naming our kids something new and powerful. Frances then realized that her sister had never gotten to the reason she called. That was odd. Agatha did not call out of the blue to chit chat. Was she on a mission for their mother? Did she really think she would admit if she was pregnant and unwed? Frances covered her face with her hands and screamed.

"Well, it looks like it's another quiet night for us. I had thought going to the museum would inspire my creativity and I could paint. No one told me about the number one disease hitting artists. Procrastination." Frances said this to her handmade crowd of needle-felted animals. The herd she had created over the last several months now numbered around a hundred and ranged from sharks, flying pigs, rabbits, and hedgehogs, to cartoon characters she loved. Granted, the felting needles were sharp and sometimes drew blood, but she still loved the whole process of the folk art, which gave her little felted wool buddies. They had migrated all over her loft.

Frances turned on her "get into the mood to create paintings" playlist. Jennifer Paige's song "The Devil's in the Details" blasted through her loft. "How appropriate," Frances said to herself. She had to get her story straight for herself first before she tried to explain it to anyone in her family. What the heck is she doing and why does she make her life so difficult?

The temptation of diving into her European feather-top bed, covered in the softest, coziest sheets, was becoming stronger and stronger. Since her mini Burning Man party, Frances had started to isolate herself again as she dealt with some of those shadow emotions. She did not have to compromise with anyone, nor did she need anyone to save her.

Frances read her nerdy math clock. It was a source of great fun because only the true nerds knew how to read the red colored digital squares. When she moved to the land of Silicon Valley, her brother Brice had sent her the clock to weed out the fake nerds. The fact she could read it meant that she was a real nerd. Was it too early to go to bed? Was she depressed? She last spoke to Cheryl over a week ago and was given some important message about getting back on the horse of civilization or something like that.

Frances took stock of her canvases leaning against the window wall. She had managed to land a couple color studies that could lead to some real painting commissions. The color studies came through a friend who was redesigning a local bank's satellite branches in Santa Rosa. For Frances, she felt like the universe was starting to open her channels to sell her paintings. She had to keep telling herself that this was real work. Her brain was yelling at top volume to treat this work as real as when she helped a company reimagine its brand or products. The creative work of art for some reason was not seen as "real" work by her tribe, family, and the society at large. Frances almost gagged thinking about the number of hours she had spent over Excel spreadsheets, PowerPoint presentations, and killing trees for presentations that no one ever really read anyway.

People wanted to take her joy when she started to talk about her art and the number of hours she put into the paintings she created.

When she said the word "artist" to describe the type of work she did, people would roll their eyes, wanting to know what her husband did to support her. Were they jealous of her ability to pursue her creative talents? That was what she told herself when dealing with the mortified shock that she wasn't using her PhD anymore. Now that Frances thought back to the strange phone conversation with Agatha, she realized the question about work had not been asked. That was a first. She felt her parents had sent all the Kavanagh clan a list of questions to ask Frances. The calls from her siblings and aunts and uncles were becoming a little too rote and similar. Frances thought about telling her Aunt Kelly, a true leader in the Daughters of the American Revolution, that the reason she no longer worked was because work schedules got in the way of her cult responsibilities. It was hard work living in a yurt and teaching goats sign language. Her Aunt would believe her.

Frances sat down on her bed, wondering if all families were like secret undercover spy organizations. She did have it a little bit easier because she was in the lower end of the birth order. This meant there were other siblings with more time served, and the parents usually focused on them. Even though Frances and all her siblings were named after Catholic saints, none of them resembled a saint in any form. Frances hypothesized that part of the naming scheme settled on the slim reality that people would say, "Yeah. Those Kavanaghs, a family full of saints." That never happened, but she knew her mother could daydream about it.

To make herself feel better about not doing the color studies she had promised to have done in the next week, she decided to call Winter. After the third ring, Frances decided she would follow through to voicemail and leave a message. She hated leaving messages.

"Hey, Winter Keller, guess what? Ethan is single and I know you are off the market, but you keep asking about him. I saw him today. We went to that exhibit you said would bore you to tears. Call me."

The phone was no longer going to be a distraction, and so she put it under a stack of books on her nightstand. She returned to her stack of canvases. Her mind went back to her name and her family's naming scheme again, Frances was so grateful that she was born on the day they celebrated Saint Francis of Assisi. As a kid, she knew it was the day she could bring her turtle, bird, two dogs, a cat, and a picture of a skunk to church to be blessed by Father Nick. It was the one day in the Catholic church calendar that made sense to her, and Saint Francis loved animals and children, not people.

Frances laughed as she remembered the year Kenny Barbellious brought a garter snake he caught in the schoolyard to mass. He felt the snake needed to be blessed. Father Nick had screamed when Kenny brought the snake up to bless it and told him to let it go. Kenny did exactly what he was told to do: he let the snake go right there at the front of the church. That was fun because everyone got out of mass early. Stories about that snake still living in the church were alive with the kids today at Our Mother of the Immaculate Conception, otherwise known as "Our School of Holy Torture."

Frances had also been told that Saint Francis of Assisi was their Dad's favorite saint. Their Dad had taken a baby pool out for that date and everyone had said she was going to be a boy. When Frances came out a girl, Dad said, "Hell, Francis can be a girl's name too." Mom got after him for saying the "h-word" in the same sentence as a saint's name. Frances laughed out of relief, thankful they gave her the feminine spelling of the name but failed to think about what word her initials spelled out. Who names their daughter Olar? When Frances confronted her mom over the fact that her middle name was ugly, she got quite the lecture. She learned to not say a word about being named after some old great-great-great-aunt. Her parents felt some big responsibility to keep the old bizarre names alive to cement the Irish connection. Agatha loved to point out that Frances would always be a walking curse word.

To further fuel her procrastination, the thought to call her younger sister Theresa flew through her brain. Theresa was probably the nicest one of the lot of them. She never judged any of them or spread family gossip. What was wrong with her? At one point, their mother had said that Theresa had to have been switched at the hospital because she was the only one born without flaming red hair. Theresa's hair was still red, only it was the color of a beautiful red sunset, not the orange-red of a clown's wig. Theresa helped Frances make the choice to see a therapist to help her through the divorce. Funny thing about Theresa—she had moved to New York City and no one ever said she had lost her moral compass like Frances.

She was working as a set designer for a theatre company, which seemed completely logical to Frances. However, it did not meet the bar for accomplishments and standards required by Kavanagh tradition. Theresa had left Notre Dame halfway through her junior year—who does that in an Irish Catholic family? The sun still rose and the world still turned, and the Kavanagh clan still loved their Theresa. Frances had some twinges of jealously over the ease and apparent freedom at which Theresa could live her life.

Families had favorites, and F.O.K. knew she was not even in the running to be nominated. In this case, the holy children in the Kavanagh clan award rested on Bernard, Beatrice, and Theresa. Frances couldn't hate them for it, though, because Theresa was completely sweet. Everyone in the family cursed up a storm, but she had never heard a nasty word come from Theresa. Not one. Something was up. Even though they named her after Mother Theresa before she was made a saint, there had to be some explanation. No Kavanagh was that squeaky clean.

"What the heck, Frances?" Was she trying to find dirt on Theresa to jump up a couple levels on the rungs of the Kavanagh approval ladder? It was not like she needed any cover for anything from the family. Frances had already fallen from mediocre level to the lower rungs with the divorce. The "I told you so" message arrived from her mother a day after she announced her situation.

Frances had given into the temptation of her bed and rolled over onto her stomach and buried her face into her pillow, letting out a howl. If she had howled aloud in her loft, it would have sent Winston, the giant dog next door, into hysterical howling. "Someone save me from trying to find dirt on Theresa and my own putrid boring existence of memories," Frances said out loud to the emptiness of the loft and night around her. "This is not a struggle I need right now. I shall go to a movie," she announced to her brood of wool buddies as she channeled a sloth for energy to get off her bed and headed for her laptop to check movie times.

"Oh. You are so correct, Mr. Shark. If I decide to go out to the movies, I will have to shower and change out of my paint-stained University of Washington purple sweatpants and T-shirt." Frances scowled at her own appearance as she caught herself reflected in the window and tried to cover the fact that she did not just agree with a needle-felted shark. Or could she go out like this? It was, after all, San Francisco, and she was now playing the role of a—what did Agatha call it?—an eccentric trust fund baby without the trust fund.

There was that theater on Van Ness that had reports of rats running through it. What would be worse? A fashion "don't" of a woman dressed in purple? The rats had to be in the rafters. Those floors were stickier than the glue traps meant to capture rodents. The last time Frances had dared to see a movie there, her shoe got stuck to the floor and she walked right out of it.

Frances decided to check herself out and stopped to look at her current state in her full-length mirror. Headlines will read, "Homeless grape walks into movie theatre and dries up because she got stuck to the seat," she thought.

Frances flopped back down onto the chaise lounge chair that had most recently become her favorite place to curl up in the late afternoons. It could be the fact that she had upholstered the thing in something that resembled shaggy blue fur. The chair could double as a Muppet; add the eyes and Cookie Monster would have a cousin. The idea had crossed her mind to make blanket arms out of the shaggy blue fur material so she could be hugged by the Cookie Monster chaise lounge. With her luck, some kid would come over and scream uncontrollably that she had butchered Cookie Monster and made a chair out of him.

She glanced once again at the stack of newly stretched and prepped canvases waiting for her. Was it possible to have painter's block? Art was so fickle. One minute she felt like she was on top of the world as the creative images flowed so easily out of her and landed on the canvas. Then, in less time than it took to say her full name, the images were gone and she was left standing at a canvas with no memory of how she got there. Her thoughts were bouncing all over the place. She thought that her sister, Theresa, was in fact living with the same roommate she had moved to New York with from school. What was her name?

Movies. That was what she was going to do with her time. She didn't care if she looked like a homeless purple grape. Grapes make wine and wine is wonderful. She did have a color study to paint for the bank, and she was running out of time to get that completed.

Was she procrastinating because she needed the pressure to produce something a bank would want to hang in their lobby? "Shut up. Other painters would kill for this commission."

She noticed she had new email and was easily distracted from finding a movie. She clicked on a new email from Cheryl.

Hey Lady,

Are you up for the Saturday Buena Vista run? You missed the last one and I was hoping you would be there. It is always so much more fun with you.

Later,
C

FRANCES felt a twinge of guilt for less than a second. How could she forget to go to her own fun coffee group? Time to get your shit together woman. Frances closed her computer and stared at the plain canvases.

CHAPTER TWELVE
ETHAN'S SHADOW

E THAN was parked down the street, away from any streetlights outside Frances's loft in his resurrected junkyard masterpiece, a rebuilt 1975 Cadillac sedan. No one in Frances's group had seen this latest reclaimed working creation. He took out a clean glass pipe and packed the bowl with some well-shredded weed. The smell was sweet and he felt his body anticipate the hit. Ethan lifted the pipe, the flame from his lighter flashing bright as he pulled the smoke deep into his lungs. "Smooth" was all that crossed his mind as he closed his eyes and held the smoke captive in his expanded lungs. Ethan's head fell back against the headrest and he opened his eyes to the lush thick smoke exhaled from his lungs.

His left hand started to pick at a hole in the door panel large enough to show off the inner workings of the door handle. This current wreck held a huge 454 Chevy truck engine. When he found the almost pristine engine on the lot of Frank's Car Corral on El Camino down in San Carlos, he had to pinch himself. Usually, an engine like this was sold for big money when it came into a yard. It was an overlooked treasure, and he bought the smashed truck for a hundred bucks and a bag of weed. The thought of selling the engine for what it was worth crossed his mind a few times, but then another idea hit him when he came across the old Cadillac. It was from an era when a six-foot back seat meant one really could stretch out and have some fun. Not to mention the size of the trunk. It took him less than three months to piece this car back to life. He called his junkyard creations his zombie cars. For Ethan, scavenging through a car junkyard gave him a place of refuge when he failed to generate any of his other artwork.

He often told people that when art first entered his life, it had saved him. He had been failing out of high school and started spray-painting the hallways of his school. It was a mystery to the school. A couple of black kids got expelled over it. He never said a word. Sometimes he wondered if he had no courage when he thought about those boys who took the fall for his teenage rebellion.

When he branched out and started to paint over the chalkboards in the classrooms, the teachers knew they had made a mistake, but no one fixed the injustice. The administration and rumor mill at school continued to blame the expelled kids. Ethan learned a valuable lesson from all that harmless mischief: he could get away with whatever he wanted. He was part of the privileged class known as the white male. Ethan thought about Emily and how he had used her over the years. She was the one who had caught him all those years ago. She had the skill to catch him in the act of defacing the property. The art teacher suspected but saw Ethan as a kid who needed to be encouraged and not punished. That teacher could have set the rest of the high school administration straight.

The night Emily finally caught him it was only due to his own misstep. Angry over Ethan standing her up again, she had hacked into his phone to figure out where he was. How could he have forgotten they were going to go to an all-night showing of the *Rocky Horror* movie sing-along fund-raiser. She had followed the signal from his phone straight to him. He tried to deny he was the graffiti artist while holding a can of spray paint—she practically socked him unconscious because he could be so condescending toward her. He knew though that if he could fool Emily, he would be able to fool anyone. It soon became his game.

The spray-painted mural work he had done in the school was beautiful and usually based on some well-known great work of art with a slight twist. In the history room, he had repainted Leonardo da Vinci's

The Last Supper across multiple blackboards. Only, his *Last Supper* had each of the disciples sporting automatic weapons and the faces of well-known mass murderers from Hitler and Stalin to Charles Manson. It was disturbing and beautiful at the same time. That all of it was created with spray paint made it even more impressive. Emily had made him go to the art teacher at the school and confess to his works of art.

Ethan shook his head as he thought about that stupid hippie schmuck of an art teacher. He encouraged Ethan to leave school. Man, his grandmother was so angry she had actually called his dad over it. Ethan and his brother had lived with their grandmother. Their father had turned over all his parental rights for thirty thousand dollars. Ethan saw him once or twice a year. When he got in trouble over leaving high school, his father showed up. His dad told him that it was his fault. His mother's death was a direct result of Ethan being a real shit that he caused her to give up and let the cancer kill her. He finally did leave high school, got his GED, and got accepted into art school. He knew he had Emily and Mr. Deaver to thank for not sending him to the authorities. In the last painting he did at the school, he painted himself into his version of Pablo Picasso's *Guernica*. No one ever figured out the clue and his guilty admission. He knew he could basically hide out in the open.

Art school opened parts of his mind that he had no clue were there. He had jumped back and forth from painting to sculpture with a passion. He would find objects cast away on the side of the road and scour junkyards for pieces. The excitement he felt in creating a piece from his found treasures was unlike anything he felt until he had met Annette. She was in his figure-drawing class, a required class for everyone in the school. Ethan had felt it was all a waste of time and existed only to give a boring, uninspired artist a teaching job. It sucked. The only reason he went was to draw Annette. She sat across the room from where he sat. Ethan also hated the fact that this class only seemed to have male models. It was hard to cover up what he was doing when he had to be drawing a dick. One day, he told the instructor that he was drawing the feminine essence of the model in his sketches. That worked once.

Outside of class, Ethan had started to follow Annette around the campus. He spent hours sketching different ideas of what he wanted to do with her. He felt like he was standing still in time as he realized that he was invisible to her. To test this theory, he started to sketch her openly. Sometimes he would sit right next to her in a coffee house and openly sketch her. She never looked his direction. Annette had so many friends that she was always distracted by them. How could he get her to notice him? Ethan started to leave his drawings where he knew she would be and there was no question that those drawings were of her. Ethan had perfected a hyper-realist skill in pencil drawing.

It took Ethan four months to get up the nerve to ask Annette out. He had left the question on a drawing of her sitting at a table in the coffee house she frequented with her friends. She said yes. He fell for her so hard and so fast that he had no clue what had happened to him. Art no longer satisfied his emotional passions. Ethan lost himself in her like she was his whole world. They dated for two years. Then, she graduated with her Master's in fine arts and left. Ethan was so devastated that he followed her across the country to upstate New York. There, the world collapsed around him. She didn't want to see him anymore. Once again, Emily fished him out of his strange vortex and brought him back home to Oakland. He finished art school and went back to seeing what he could do without detection by Emily.

He had missed Emily, his partner in junkyard salvage. Ever since she had started her graduate program at Stanford, their relationship had changed. Ethan picked off a large piece of the door panel. He studied the piece of fake wood closely. It had come off in the shape of a sickle blade. A slight smile crossed his face as he took another sip of the smoke off his pipe. He looked up at the corner of the building where Frances's loft was and noticed the loft was dark.

Ethan thought about how many times he had started to talk to Frances about how he really felt about her. There was always some reason for him to avoid asking her out on a real date. Frances would start talking about someone else or ask him a question about his work. Ethan had helped her move all her painting supplies into the studio space next to his. He built her shelving and spent hours and hours talking about art and sometimes life, and then she talked about her divorce.

Ethan turned on his computer in the car to watch Frances. He had spent time gaining her trust and becoming her go-to handyman. That afforded him the ability to install a very extensive monitoring system in Frances's loft. People were so easy to manipulate when they were sad. Annette had been easy because she had no self-esteem about herself or her art. Frances was different in some ways. The challenge made Ethan excited. He typed in a couple of commands and moved the video camera installed in the top corner of a kitchen cabinet to focus on Frances's bed and main living area. These video cameras were top notch and made no sound as he remotely moved them, searching for the best angle. Then anger started to rise as he realized that she never asked him about himself. All that time that he had helped her as that dickhead tortured her through the divorce, Ethan had been invisible to her. He wanted to be her rock. All he wanted was to hold her, to kiss her, to feel himself inside her. But she never looked at him that way. What made him think that she would find a reason to love him now? She was worse than Annette. The cameras were not picking up any activity. But he was sure she was there.

The glow of the laptop pulled Ethan's attention back to viewing the dark loft. Nights were frustrating because Frances often sat in the dark of her loft. What was wrong with that woman? Was she trying to save on her electric bill? Cripes, he thought, he should start paying it for her. The way her place was set up, the streetlights cast shadows that hid her from him. Sometimes she was in there, but the lack of light made the loft appear empty. His left hand gripped the steering wheel, forcing the blood out of his hand, and he sank down below the level of his car window. At some point in time, Frances would come back into his view and he would get his fix. He needed his fix. It was one of the only things that was keeping him from doing something more. "Frances, don't make me force you to fight for your life," Ethan whispered to himself. He undid the buttons on his jeans and thought about some of the women he had made into his art pieces. His favorite work had been Annette. But as Ethan worked his hand and saw images of what he could create with Frances, he knew he had a new masterpiece. Ethan closed his eyes and let his body explode into his vision.

CHAPTER THIRTEEN
HOW TO GET HUNG

I N need of some reassurance about her professional stability, Frances called Nathan, who managed one of her favorite art galleries in the City. He provided the kind of shot-in-the-arm enthusiasm that kept her going. It was no wonder she loved spending time with him. The artists featured in the gallery were people who managed to make a living doing this creative thing, art, or what her parents called a silly hobby. Frances stopped as she caught her reflection in the window.

She turned a couple of times from front to back and decided her blue pressed slacks and white button-down shirt were respectable enough for her to walk through the doors of the gallery, which was close to the fancy pants region of San Francisco. With all the infusion of tech money, most of San Francisco was out of reach for the average laborer. It was getting harder to find a grungy part of the City with great cheap eats and people wearing sweatpants.

Nathan had told her to bring down a painting or two to the gallery because he had some extra room to fill on the wall. Frances knew he was being kind to her as the gallery he worked for carried only the well-known named artists. The artists shown in the gallery were the modern-day masters with their art-world pedigrees to justify getting thousands of dollars for their work. Not wanting to pass up such a generous opportunity, Frances went to her painted canvases. Upon examining them, her heart fell into the pit of her stomach. Not one painting struck her as anything that deserved hanging. Most artists would kill to be hung, and here she was with nothing to hang except quite possibly herself. Maybe her parents were right and she needed to give up on her stupid dream of being a professional artist.

She was her own worst critic. Well, maybe that wasn't entirely true since she had heard people say "my dog could paint better than that" about one of her works. She reached inside her brain and shut off her families' voices to find those paintings that looked like a dog or cat had created the darn thing. This allowed Frances to separate her work into two categories. From there she knew she was getting closer to pulling a couple of canvases out to show Nathan. "This is a business," she told herself repeatedly. Before she had even started painting seriously, she had started networking in the art world.

The process was not difficult for Frances because she saw the gatekeepers as the gallery owners and gallery managers. She made it a priority to go out and meet them one-on-one. Even though she had detached herself from the business world, she had not fully exited. She was selling a different commodity now—art rather than organizational and strategy planning. In some respects, she felt this was easier. Now, she held a tangible product in her hands as she chose three finalists from her pile. Not able to narrow it down any further, she still felt some trepidation at showing anything to Nathan. Would she tell him her criteria for the pieces she chose? She knew he would be honest and not hang any if they were not up to par for the gallery. Nathan was a friend during her marriage because Richard and Frances had purchased a couple pieces from the gallery. Richard had tried to hide the paintings during the divorce, but Nathan helped Frances with providing both the invoices and copies of the payments. It was his wonderful record keeping and pictures of the checks that Frances wrote out of her own banking account that allowed her to win those paintings in the divorce. After everything was final, she had brought the paintings to Nathan and he sold them for her. Richard had threatened to sue but never did. Nathan Steiner was the first gallery manager she contacted when she decided to paint professionally.

Frances thought about taking Uber to avoid the pain of parking downtown but decided she was getting to be too extravagant in constantly using the car service. Money easily went out of her account at a much faster and greater rate than it was being put into her account. Arguments of having a steady paycheck deposited at regular intervals were dancing with concrete boots in her brain. That point on money spending settled, she decided to take the bus. Frances had to continue to convince herself that the bus was so much easier; the stop was less than a block from the gallery. She bit her lower lip as she looked at the size of the paintings. The task of carrying those paintings was going to create a challenge that would most certainly justify using Uber or finding another solution.

Frances sat cross-legged on her floor staring at the giant paintings and knew it was going to be quite the battle to get those on and off a metro bus. She looked around her place for something that could make carrying them a little bit easier. When she found some twine, she was in business. She placed butcher paper between the canvases and fashioned a way for her to grip the four-foot-by-five-foot canvases without too many issues. "Now or never," she said to herself and was good to go wait for the bus. "The awkward walk will be worth it," she told herself as she angled the canvases through her loft door. It was going to be a three-step-and-rest process. As the elevator door opened, Frances hoped that there was no wind outside because she could see herself going airborne. Now that is a thought—a personal flying device to get around the City. That would look totally cool; just think of the art. Lost in her thoughts of fantastical designs, Frances loaded her canvases into the elevator and was on her way.

Frances made it to the bus stop on the corner across from her loft just as a bus pulled away. She was fine with waiting for the next bus. The fresh air and sun felt good. Another person, plugged into his smartphone, joined Frances for the wait. When another plugged-in person almost ran into Frances's paintings, it gave her an idea for a painting. The irony was not lost on her when she pulled her own phone out of her pocket to quickly capture her creative inspiration. She got it down and started scrolling through the notes she had been recording on her phone for a while.

When the bus pulled up, Frances was more than ready to get her paintings to Nathan. She hesitated as she saw the three steps to get on the bus and the tight turn required at the top of the steps. No help was coming from anyone on the bus, and the driver made sure to look away as she calculated the best way to navigate. The paintings were awkward and gave her some logistical problems maneuvering around the first seat to make it into the bus. The driver was off before Frances could sit and secure herself or the paintings. The acceleration of the bus forced her to fall against the window, losing any grip on her paintings. As her face stopped her fall against the somewhat greasy bus window, Frances thought she saw someone ducking behind a car parked across from the front door of her loft. When she righted herself, and had control over her paintings, she looked back down the street and thought she saw Ethan getting into a huge Cadillac. Odd. The guy had the tall thin body dimensions of Ethan. The long, dark, unkempt hair also matched his.

Frances felt an odd twinge in her stomach. Why would Ethan be outside her loft and not let her know he was there? It felt like forever since she had visited him and the other artists she befriended when she was in that first studio space. Maybe he had come over to see her and then saw her getting on the bus. Some voices started to echo in her mind, telling her that story was not right. She decided to phone Cheryl.

"Hello, crazy painter lady."

"Hmmm. Should I say, you and I have a different definition of crazy." Frances responded.

"Okay. I will edit myself. Hello, may I please speak with Insanity?"

"Funny. I'm calling about Ethan. I think he was outside my building but didn't ring me."

"Odd? Now this sounds interesting. And to think I was going to let your call roll over to voicemail."

"I'm headed to see Nathan at the gallery with some paintings, and I know I saw Ethan duck behind a car across the street."

"You are on the bus with your giant-ass paintings? How many people did you wipe out? Of course, you fell. Grace is not your middle name."

"Cheryl, I am serious. You know when you get a weird feeling about someone."

"Really? Are you sure? He would've said hi, don't ya think? When that guy is around you, he only seems to have eyes for you," Cheryl said.

"What are you talking about? I think he's gay. He has never once mentioned women in a dating sort of way. I never really asked him. I was thinking that he must have seen me get on the bus. But then why would he act like he was trying not to be seen? Then he jumped into a car that quite possibly was manufactured from parts of thirty other cars. It was a mess." Frances said. She dropped her phone as the bus lurched and her paintings started to slide out of her hand.

"Stop creating drama. You are hanging around Simon too much."

"I am serious, this freaks me out. I know it was him." Frances looked over her shoulder and tried to peer through the windows of the bus to see if that crazy car was behind the bus.

"But you aren't sure? Frances, you're turning into a paranoid personality. Do you think Ethan likes you?"

"Oh my god, no. I really do think he is gay or maybe asexual. He never talks about people in a sexual way."

"That does not negate a person's sexuality or interest. Maybe he didn't talk about them because he likes you."

"I never—at least, I don't think I ever—flirted with him."

"Frances, you have no clue when you are or are not flirting. Although, you do flirt with Simon and Russell a lot."

"That's okay because they're gay and happily married. Besides, they flirt back with me and none of it is sexual. Maybe it isn't flirting then, because I am—well, they are very cute."

"You are a walking contradiction."

"Maybe," Frances said as she chewed on lower lip.

"Call Ethan and ask him if he was at your place today. Then you can stop all this mind game crap."

"Good idea. I will after I get done at the gallery. T.T.F.N."

"Later."

Frances felt a little better. Cheryl had a way of sounding like one would expect the voice of reason to sound. Although Dana was usually her go-to sounding board. The past couple of months Frances felt she had talked Dana's ear off with all her questions about life after divorce, biology, attraction, and the stupidity of most men. She knew she was being a little more paranoid than her life really warranted. The flirty thing, though, might be a problem. Did she give Ethan the wrong signs? She really thought he was gay, and anyway, he was totally not her type. When she had brought him up to the Buena Vista Irish Coffee Club huddle shortly after moving into the studios, no one agreed with her gay assessment. Winter thought Ethan was gorgeous, but then again, the tall, lanky, brooding dude, who maybe showered once a week, was her thing. Frances preferred men who had regular hygiene habits—at least a shower a day. A man with dirty hair was something Frances could not tolerate.

The bus was pulling up to her spot and she carefully stood, balancing her paintings using the strength of her whole body. It was a fight to get out of the bus due to a couple of other passengers trying to get around her as she maneuvered the three large canvases out the middle door of the bus. Once free on the sidewalk, Frances breathed in deeply and, taking control of her paintings, penguin-walked the half-block to the gallery. Nathan saw her and came running to open the double glass doors.

Frances blinked her eyes hard, trying to get them to adjust from the bright sunlight outside to the darkened world of the gallery with its matte-black walls and dark-gray carpet. Light was focused on the art and each piece sparkled like a jewel. Frances was silent as she took in the beauty of the pieces currently hanging. They were breathtakingly beautiful. She started to regret bringing anything so rough into the gallery.

"Hello, my darling." Nathan flamboyantly held out his arms and kissed Frances once on each cheek.

"Wow."

"What have you brought me?"

"I am scared to show you what I thought was done."

"Nonsense. I will have none of that from you. Show them to me and then I will tell you if it is art or if it is shit that I can still sell." Nathan went to a wall and removed a painting, opening a space that Frances wished was a black hole that would swallow her piece up forever. This waiting for Nathan to give her thumbs up or down was causing her to regret eating salsa and chips for breakfast. "You know, the only way to view a painting is under proper lighting, so let me see these up here."

Frances let go of the first of her three canvases and wondered where she could ditch the other two giant canvases she was left holding. Why did she feel like she was selling off her children? These were her creations, and now they were going to be judged as worthy or not. What the heck was she thinking when she decided to paint? This was more traumatic than she had anticipated. The world slowed down while Nathan looked as if he was working under a strobe light as his motions slowed and became robotic. He came back to Frances and pried the other two canvases away from her. Nathan took each one separately and looked them over closely. After what felt like hours, he chose one to hang.

Nathan stood back with his right hand rubbing his chin. Frances stood stone still, afraid to move for fear that she might get a second go at the salsa and chips at any moment. If this is what it felt like to get hung in a class A gallery, she did not like it much. To date, her art sales came through her friends from the business world and an interior decorator who probably upsold her work to the clients.

"Nathan, that is so amazing." A woman's voice came from behind Frances. This caused Frances to spin around so quickly that she ran into a ladder, causing both the ladder and herself to crash to the floor.

"Great Scott! Frances, are you okay?" Nathan came running, but Frances had accepted the outstretched hand of the woman who had startled her. She looked like an angel with a halo of light from the bright outside streaming in around her. Nathan was there brushing off Frances and asking her if she was okay, but it was all lost as Frances had tunnel vision focused on the face of this woman.

"Might I have my hand back?" the woman asked.

"Olivia Porter-Stevens, allow me to introduce you to our next great painter, Frances Kavanagh."

"Frances, your painting is exceptional." Olivia took her hand out of Frances's and walked over to the painting.

"I told Frances to bring down some work so we could hang it on the space that opened up in the back."

"Nathan, that painting will stay right here. People will come into the gallery because this is inspiration captured in paint. What is this work's title?" Olivia asked, not taking her eyes off the painting.

"*Sounds of Breaking Glass,*" Frances whispered.

"Olivia and her family own this gallery and a few others in New York and Chicago," Nathan said.

"We will be opening a couple more this year. I am working on one in Seattle, and my sister is pulling one together for the Big Island of Hawaii."

"Wow." Frances knew her ghost-white complexion now flashed bright red with the words "complete idiot" cycling through her brain. She could not get her brain to function, nor could she pull her eyes off Olivia. She had felt a surge of energy run through her body when their hands met. What was going on? Why hadn't she done more to her hair and put on a little makeup? Right now, she was feeling like a miserable tragedy, a dispensable cast member from a James Joyce novel.

"Nathan, take the other two and hang them over here." Olivia had started to remove work that was priced at over fifty thousand dollars from the wall to hang Frances's unframed canvases.

"I do not know what to say. I—" Frances stuttered.

"Frances, you do not need to say anything except that you will join me for a late lunch. Nathan will take care of getting this hung while we are out."

Frances quickly looked to Nathan and felt strange. It almost felt like Olivia was dismissing him. This gallery was always one of the most profitable galleries in the City due to Nathan and his ability to nurture his high-end clients. He could get them to buy anything. One exhibit that he sold out was literally garbage. The artist had gone out to the trash cans of hotels and used his finds to put together his "Seven Sins" sculptures. The art stunk. Each piece boasted the rotting food left over from expensive meals, spoiled milk, decaying meat, and other items that were no longer recognizable. A dump smelled better than that art. Yet every piece sold for more than the price of a smart car.

Olivia had retrieved her purse and put her hand out to Frances. Frances gave a slight smile to Nathan, who had an odd look on his face. Frances walked past Olivia's outstretched hand and feigned that she did not see it as she opened the door to the gallery. All of this was such a surprise to her. She would follow up with him later. She mouthed the words "thank you" in his direction and hoped he had seen them.

"Where shall we go to lunch? This is your city, so you direct us," Olivia said.

Frances stood mute as Olivia opened the back door to a sleek, black Bentley sedan, exposing the cream-colored leather interior and blonde wood accents. Soft music could be heard coming out of the car, and it took Frances a moment to realize that Olivia was waiting for her.

"Unicorns," Frances whispered.

"What was that? Is there a place called Unicorns?" Olivia asked.

Frances settled into the back seat of the car and was worried that she was going to scuff the perfect soft leather. What was she thinking when she accepted the invitation to lunch? Their eyes met, and this time Frances saw the flecks of green in the darker blue irises of Olivia's eyes. Her smile was effortless and full.

"No. Sorry. I use the term when I see rare beauty in the City."

"Are you talking about me or the car?" Olivia asked and took Frances's hand in hers. The driver waited motionless behind the wheel as the two women were distracted by one another. "I have another option? I could make you something to eat at my place, and we could talk art and where you want to go with your painting without interruption. Honestly, your work is so raw and expressive…it is truly inspired. People will pay for work like yours."

Frances wanted to curl up into the softness of the leather seats and listen to Olivia's voice. The smell of jasmine flowers mixed with the smell of the leather, and it was all so intoxicating. Frances tried to come up with a restaurant, but her mind was drawing a blank. How could there be a completely empty white board in her brain? She loved food and knew all the best places for whatever style of food one wanted. Right now, her brain was empty and all the animals were not only out of the barn, they had vacated the farm completely.

"Is your place far?" Frances asked.

"Does it matter? I have a car that will take us anywhere."

"Do you eat meat?"

"Yes—among other things. I do enjoy eating meat."

"Feel like a little jaunt south to San Carolos? Trust me, it is worth it. They make an amazing mater challaw, plus kebabs and pumpkin kadu with a meat sauce that is addictive." Frances whipped her phone out to get the address and tried not to look at Olivia to see her reaction.

"Sounds fun. I've never been, and a drive down the peninsula would be nice. I've got a house in Los Altos Hills I haven't seen in a while. Do you have any time constraints?"

"There was nothing written in pen on my calendar. Oh shoot—I left my messenger bag in the gallery. Do you mind?" Frances started to open the door, which was on the traffic side, and Olivia quickly pulled Frances's hand away.

"Relax. My driver will go in and get it for you."

The driver, without another word from either of the women, was out of the car and walking into the gallery before Frances could take a full breath. What was going on and why was she tripping over her words in her brain? This woman was crashing into her with an intensity she had never felt before. Is this what money did for a person? Frances could not take her eyes off Olivia. Her complexion was flawless. The gentle slope of her nose stopped the perfect distance above the most kissable lips Frances could ever remember seeing. Wait. This is a woman. What the heck, Frances Olar Kavanagh? She asked you to lunch, nothing more. She is going to be talking art. Relax.

"Maybe Nathan can't find my bag. I probably dropped it behind a desk or something. I should go in and help them try to find it."

"It is okay. You don't need it. I invited you to lunch. They'll find it." Olivia gently placed her hand on Frances's forearm. The touch electrified Frances, and she felt like she had put a fork into a live socket.

"They found it." Frances giggled and wished she could shut that stupid nervous button off for good. The driver climbed into the car with the ease of a panther stalking its prey and handed Frances her very well-used purple and gold Timbuk2 messenger bag. Frances tried to quickly tuck the paint and dirt-stained bag under her legs. Words were not forming for her now, and she handed her overly smudged-up phone with the address to the restaurant to the driver. He nodded and put the car into gear. A smoked glass divider rose, providing a level of privacy that Frances had not anticipated.

Frances wondered if Olivia would be able to see her heart jumping out of her chest. All Frances could think about was kissing those beautiful soft lips. A power overcame Frances as she felt the softness of Olivia's hand moving her red curls back so Olivia could touch Frances's neck. Shivers of surprise and fear raced through Frances's body as Olivia pulled her close and Frances tasted the slightest hint of vanilla, strawberries, and coffee when their lips met.

"I …"

"Shhh." Olivia placed her lips back on Frances's and placed her other hand on her thigh.

"Olivia." Frances pushed Olivia back and removed her hand from her thigh. "I have never kissed a woman like this before." Something was wrong as Frances no longer saw the lips as kissable. What was she thinking? This woman could make her art career. Relax. You are an adult.

"You are doing a great job. Practice makes perfect." Olivia smiled and pulled Frances toward her again.

"Wait. I…I really don't know what to say. You are…I'm feeling …"

"Frances. It is okay. You are beautiful, and there is something so special about you. Let me show what a beautiful thing an avalanche of exploration in this new world can be for you and for the promotion of your art."

CHAPTER FOURTEEN
OPERATION HOT DATE

DANA paced back and forth in front of the giant picture window in her living room as she waited for the girls, Cheryl and Winter, to arrive. The screw-up had occurred because they were playing with someone else's life. What were they thinking? Dana was wringing her hands, worried that they had really screwed everything and the pooch to boot. No one saw the setback she did. Why did they have to change the settings? They were doing such a good job at screening the possible suitors. They were so close to implementing the plan. But now it was all about to explode. Dana missed the world that existed before email.

It was now time for them to implement the full plan—operation date finder for Frances. Were they all fools to think they could pull this off and have something good come out of it? Right or wrong, they were tired of listening to Frances talk about the hypotheticals and fig-ured it was time to push her off the freakin' cliff. She would either fly or crash. With Frances's latest attempts at speed dating, cooking class-es, and whatever else to meet a possible date failing miserably, it was time to help. Dana's pacing was starting to wear on Lulu, who decid-ed to remove herself from the commotion of people; she stretched her legs carefully so as not to upset the resting Doris Day. Doris Day of-ten slept on top of Lulu with her beak tucked into her wing. It was a unique friendship between the dog and the chicken; strangely, that odd friendship gave Dana hope that what they were going to do for Frances might work.

"Hello. Anyone home?" Winter's voice broke through Dana's worried pacing as she walked through the front door, closely followed by Cheryl.

"Come in, come in, no engraved invitations or announcements needed." Dana went toward the door, followed by both Lulu and Doris Day.

"Dana, it is so strange you have a chicken living in your house," Cheryl said as she set her computer down on Dana's dining room table.

"Doris Day and Lulu think it rather odd that you two have been here for a minute and have not offered them a treat."

Both Cheryl and Winter went over to the cookie jar and got out a couple of treats for the girls, who happily danced around them.

"Have either of you said anything to Frances?" Winter asked, eyeing the response of both Dana and Cheryl.

"Not I," Dana said, holding up three fingers and mouthing the Girl Scout Oath.

"Don't look at me. I basically have not had any conversations with her since we hatched this plan because I didn't trust myself. Winter, have you said anything to her?" Cheryl stood with her hands on her hips challenging the attorney to a comeback.

"I have you both beat. Not only have I not talked to her about what we are up to, I even got more confirmation that what we are about to do is what she wants. We went to dinner at Isa, and I led her down the path of talking about Richard. That always disarms her. She tries to find ways to avoid talking about that guy. Frances is so over the whole divorce thing. What got interesting was she started pointing out who she thought was attractive, and we saw a lot of people in the Marina district."

"That doesn't mean she is ready to start dating," Dana said as she prepared a plate of snacks for the crew.

"We have the power to change her world and give her something else to focus on for a while," Winter said as she helped herself to a Nespresso coffee.

"Make me one too," Cheryl chimed in as she sat down and booted her computer up.

"There is whipped cream in the fridge. We might as well splurge since we are about to Frankenstein a date," Dana said over the hiss of her Nespresso machine.

"Does anyone know if she got the emails from the dating site? We changed it back so quickly—I am hoping those few hours were not enough to send her anything. Based on her speed dating fiascos, this girl needs our help," Winter said.

"Time to come up with a date for her then, before she knows what hit her," Cheryl said as her hands flew over the keyboard answering the email.

"Perfect. Who's the winner out of the five we limited the list to?" Dana asked. "Or should I call them the date marks? I'm still so un-nerved that we are playing with people's lives. I guess my vote is for the one who likes that same damn book she does. What are the odds on that one?" As Dana said this, Cheryl and Winter burst into laughter. "Crap. It makes her sound almost like a nerd—it could be endearing."

"I think we need to run with that one. It's perfect for a date match-up; they have something weird in common." Winter took a sip of her coffee and snorted it up her nose as she started laughing all over again. "This is going to be so much fun. We all might need to register in a witness protection program when Frances finds out about this, but it is fun."

"It won't be that bad. I love answering these emails like I'm Frances." Cheryl said and got to work on composing the email inviting the winner out on a date.

Lulu came over and lay down next to Dana's feet. Colors from the setting sun were now visible on the buildings across the bay. The setting sunlight lit the living room with a warm orange glow, giving Dana a boost of energy as she watched Cheryl typing away faster than a hamster on a wheel. What was the worst thing that could happen? They would read the responses and filter through them, saving Frances the heartache of it all.

"What would you have done if no one responded to your post?" Dana asked. "That would be devastating. Do you think she'll want to know how many responses she got?"

"We need to include another picture because this one specifically asked for one to prove the picture with her ad was really her," Winter said, breaking the hypnotic sounds of Cheryl's typing.

"Good point. But which one?" Cheryl asked.

"I'm all over this part of the plan." Winter started searching through her phone, looking for the perfect picture. "We need something that says I'm fun and sweet like *Irish Coffee with a kicker at the end.*"

The three spent the evening going back over the email they constructed. They had to be sure they were echoing what they thought Frances would write. Dana corrected the spelling and grammar. It was the high school teacher in her that wanted to make sure they were one hundred percent correct in those two departments. As to what Frances might be seeking, the group agreed to stay positive and not write anything about dickheads or men who grunt. Lulu kept their spirits up by switching from person to person for attention and successfully begging for nibbles from the snacks on the table.

"This is a masterpiece. I want to date her after reading this," Winter stated as she read through the latest version of the email date request they had created for Frances.

"The picture of her hiking at Crater Lake works perfectly. That deep blue of the lake makes her red hair and green eyes pop."

"You're right, Dana. Why is she so photogenic? When I'm with her I don't see it. What am I missing?"

"Winter, not nice." Dana put her hands on her hips, the teacher's disapproval stance that came so naturally to her.

"Now, why did we send out the email to five different people? Was it because the one who likes the same book might not answer?" Winter asked.

"Jesus H. Christ in the mountains! You knuckleheads were only supposed to send the date request to the first one we decided on—this is not going to be good." Dana sat down and held her face in her hands.

"Dana, it's going to be okay. It will all work out," Winter said.

CHAPTER FIFTEEN
ONCE BORN INTO THE IRISH MAFIA...

"FRANCES, have you fallen off the face of the earth?" A rather terse voice greeted Frances from her voicemail. She flopped back onto her bed and covered her face with her hands. How was it that her mother always had the most amazing timing? No time to decompress from her time with Olivia, getting her paintings hung in a real gallery, and noticing that the sun was shining in San Francisco. Frances figured one of her siblings had paraded to their parents with the juicy news that their problem child had fallen even further into the pits of hell. It wasn't that Frances was the most unfavorable one of the family; it was just that she didn't come close to doing anything they thought was exceptional or valuable.

When she got calls like this, she would mentally remind herself that she moved two thousand miles away for both physical and emotional distance from the family code of conduct. That code had her in church every Sunday from the time she could toddle until she bolted for college at eighteen. Never had she made her mind up so completely as she did when she announced at age four that she was going to move to California and live with Snow White and the Seven Dwarfs. Oh Jesus!—Frances thought to herself—she was already a lesbian at age four. She realized now that she had crushed hard on Snow White. Her brain, for better or worse, kept that little nugget of knowledge hidden from her until just now. Her parents had packed up the kids for the first of many cross-country torture trips. That year, the trip happened to have been to Disney. She spent most of that trip being carsick too while sitting on Agatha's lap.

Disney was real to her at that age. When they first entered the park, she ran up to Snow White. The princess was so beautiful, and the dwarfs, who were huge compared to her, were funny. The memories were vague and probably mostly made up. Frances smiled at this little walk down memory lane. Her phone rang again, and she could see that her Mom was at it once more. She knew that someone had talked to her.

"Hi, Mom," Frances said as she walked over to the latest painting she was working on and picked up a brush.

"Don't 'hi Mom' me. Do you have something you want to tell me, Frances Olar Kavanagh?" Her mother had used her full name. The Catholic guilt buttons were being firmly pushed. It made sense to her after her parents had installed all those buttons at birth. It usually worked. However, Frances was feeling a shift in her family button department.

"Guess the sibling spy network talked with you," Frances said without emotion or fanfare.

"I want to hear it from you. Is it true? You know the Catholic church does not approve of such, such …" Frances could hear her mother trying to choke back tears. This time, though, she did not fall for the manipulation.

"Mom, I don't understand how you still support an institution that harbors sex offenders."

"Patrick, did you stop and pick up the flowers I asked you to? Agatha wants you to come over tonight. I forgot to tell you that she needs some help with invitations for your side of the family."

It was happening, like it always does. Frances gets a call from her mother, only to hear her carry on a conversation with someone else. "Mom, you sound busy. Call back when you aren't so busy," Frances said.

"Frances Olar Kavanagh, you have no right to talk about the church, and that's not what we are talking about. Answer me. Are you really telling people you are an artist?" Her mother practically choked on the word. Frances couldn't help but laugh. That righteous Midwestern accent added to the Irish brogue made the whole conversation seem like a parody. They had covered this not too long ago—was her mother losing her memory?

"You know, Mom, I don't know. An artist? Hmm. But I do think I am bisexual. Do you really want to discuss my sex life?" Frances knew this was pushing the conversation.

"How dare you speak to me that way? Well, I don't think you are whatever you called yourself. You're reacting to losing your husband. If you would lose some weight, get your hair done into a nice controlled style, and wear some makeup, you might find another man who would—"

"Mom. Seriously? I didn't lose Richard. He cheated on me and stole money from my account. What about Richard was so great? You didn't even come to our wedding."

"We didn't attend your wedding because it was against the church. Patrick, don't forget to bring in some firewood for the fireplace."

Frances did something she had never done before and hung up on her mother. She shut her phone off. The anger, confusion, and years of all those buttons being pushed exploded onto the canvas in front of her. Frances grabbed for paint, brushes, and didn't slow down until late into the evening. When she finally ran the family anger out of her, she saw what she had painted and signed her name in the lower right corner. This was a new one for her, a painting finished in anger. Under her signature, she painted the title of this work, *Freedom in Trouble*.

Frances knew that her mom was scared and unsure. Who knows what her siblings had relayed to the parental unit? At this point, she was too tired to worry about it. The first thought was someone had told her she closed her financial account with the firm in St. Louis that the whole family had used. She thought about writing her mom an email, but then decided it would be better to let the whole conversation be exactly what it was and nothing more. Frances didn't really know for herself what she was at this point. She had been sexually involved with both men and women. At one point, she thought she had been in love. Christ, she thought, she had even married the man. One thing Frances knew deep down was that she was not going to let anyone take away her freedom to figure this out.

The awakening, as she referred to it, had been unleashed by Olivia. That marathon lunch date took her into the stratosphere. Frances let her hand trace her breast as she thought about how Olivia had caressed her body. It was something she was not going to forget. Those feelings of hot passion were forming deep inside her as she replayed the way they made love and talked all night and into the next day. They fed each other waffles with Nutella and strawberries brought up by room service. It was like a movie. She had shared so much with Olivia. Frances paused over this—Olivia had more than one residence in the area. Why did they stay at a hotel?

Frances needed to calm herself down. She sat down at her piano and lifted the keyboard cover and removed the red felt she used to protect the ivory keys. Her hands now resting on the cool ivory keys of her Steinway grand piano, she recalled how Richard had wanted to sell it because it had cost more than buying a small car to move. She fought to keep it and was glad she had. Her parents had gifted the piano to her when she turned sixteen. Out of the Kavanagh's massive clan, she was the only one who played the piano. All of them had been tortured with lessons and, despite that torture, Frances had fallen in love with the piano.

Her right hand started to push the keys in a new formation of notes, a new melody coming to her fingers. Her left hand picked up a major chord progression and the notes floated out of the piano. She had wished she had turned her iPad on to record what she was playing. Sometimes she played new music and note combinations and thought she would find them again, only to have them disappear as quickly as they had come. The music produced images and colors in her mind as she played. Sometimes, when she closed her eyes, she would feel as if she was traveling through the world on the notes as they escaped out of the body of the piano. To Frances, this piano was an intimacy in creativity and life that she had not found in any other form, or with anyone else, for that matter. It was hard sometimes for her to know where she started and stopped in relation to the music.

CHAPTER SIXTEEN
VISIONS OF A HAPPY MATCH

F RANCES was restless as she scanned her loft. The last couple of days she had painted with a passionate rage. Sleepless nights were catching up and now she was unable to focus—she kept coming back to her piano. Playing often calmed her down. The few steps from the couch to the piano unleashed another bout of fear. What had happened with Olivia? Why had Frances felt so relaxed after Olivia kept chiseling away at her? When her fingers touched the ivory keys, she usually relaxed. But not today. Frances tried to let the music free her from her fears. The music was fast, chaotic, and jarring. Frances did not edit her strength and pounded the keys harder than she intended. It was unlike her to play with this fear, this anger and unknown energy pouring into her fingers. With the energy surging through her as she thought about Olivia, she realized that she could probably handle a run of staccato notes unequaled in their pace. It was a race of triplets that would make professional formula racecar drivers jealous.

The notes placed a new hunger inside her for passion and possibilities. Olivia opened her to a suspended reality in the way she touched her. Frances felt like she was falling into memory sensations in her body caused by the way Olivia had so gently touched her. It was an unknown dream and then she was gone, back into her world. Frances let the music transport her to another world where she imagined what Olivia was doing. Visions of seeing her beautiful naked body resting in her bed were the highlights of Frances's fantasies. Frances let her fingers poke around the keys until the melody came to life. It had been years since she played the song "Wicked Game."

Frances played hard for the next forty-five minutes and felt the sweat dripping down her back from the effort of her direct, forceful playing. It was a mash-up of classical, with velocity exercises morphed into current music. Maybe this could be a good way to burn calories? Frances screamed out with frustration. The music opened her mind to think about the possibilities of risk; she wanted to take risks in so many ways, but she had never voiced exactly what she wanted to herself—let alone to anyone else. Sure, she danced around it, but it was all talk and no action. Did she really know what she wanted?

Hungry from her exertion at the piano, Frances stood, staring at her red enamel gourmet stove. From the twelve oversized burners to the two giant ovens, the kitchen appliance was a piece of art, one where she could create her masterpieces of culinary delight. The fact that she had not done any real cooking in months was not lost to her or her health as she reached for a can of soup and a can opener. That was the extent of her cooking tonight. The creamy tomato soup with mashed-up soda crackers was her go-to comfort food when she was overwhelmed. Would the gourmet stove gremlins come and take this beautiful kitchen away from her for the violations of failure to cook anything resembling real food?

Frances warmed the soup over a low gas flame and leaned against the oversized farmhouse sink that she had discovered at an estate sale in Sebastopol. The sink was found before she had decided on buying her own place. Isn't that how most people do it? Find the kitchen sink and then find the place that works with the sink. It was one of those days with no agenda, so she had driven north on Highway 101, exploring the world. Luck rode with her when she had stopped at the estate sale for directions back to the highway. It took two guys to wrestle the sink into her truck. They expressed some truck envy and questioned why a city girl would own such a beast. It made her smile as she returned to the City with her treasure.

"Such a shame that I haven't cooked any real food—" Before Frances could finish her thought, her front door burst open, causing Frances to grab the first thing she had within reach. The fear of an unwanted intruder also had her wishing she kept her mobile phone attached to her. Her right hand was raised high overhead with her weapon. The commotion of several voices, packages, and laughter made it appear that Frances was being invaded by a shopping bag monster.

"Put down the can opener," Winter said as she dropped her bundle of packages on the table. Behind her came Cheryl and Dana, also toting armfuls of curious bags and a couple of shoeboxes. "What's for cooking?"

"You might not want to eat what I am making. It comes from a can," Frances said as she went to her wine cabinet and searched for the right bottle.

"Frances, were you talking to yourself? Girls, we are too late," Dana said as she came over and threw her arms around a very stiff and un-friendly Frances. "When was the last time you spent time in a shower with soap?" Dana asked and withdrew her arms.

Frances went over to the pile of bags and boxes on her table, unsure of what to say or do next. It was clear that clothing, makeup, and shoes were part of the loot piled high on her table. Frances slowly turned to face the three women now standing almost completely still. The only sound to be heard was that of wine being poured by Winter, who had set out four glasses on the giant butcher block kitchen island.

"What is going on here?" Frances asked. The can opener had been placed on the counter.

"No one make any sudden movements. Frances is already spooked enough," Dana said.

"What was that?" Winter asked. "Frances, you swore over the most sacred warm crusty French bread in the City that I could help you find a great person to date. I have done that, and we are here to make sure you don't go out dressed like you. What I think you were doing was saying 'thank you, my dearest friends, for finding me a great date.'"

"Remind me to move the hide-a-key," Frances said as she walked over and picked up a glass of red wine.

"All for one and one for all!" Dana said with gusto. Frances was the first one to take a sip of the wine and, within less than a second of the wine hitting her tongue, she spat the wine out across her kitchen island. Before she could say anything to stop the others from getting a mouthful of muddy vinegar, Winter spat a stream of red wine back into her glass. Dana had taken such a small sip that she really did not know what to do with the taste of vinegar that hit her tongue. Frances took the glass out of Cheryl's hand and poured the wine down the drain.

"That's nasty. Did you make this wine yourself?" Winter coughed through the small amount of wine that was stuck in her mouth.

Frances's laughter was loud and deep. "I promise that was not planned." The giggles came fast, and she was having a hard time controlling her body as she reached for the bottle of wine. "Seriously, this Cab goes for a couple hundred bucks. Clearly something went wrong with this bottle. I promise it was not planned." Her laughter building with each labored breath, she struggled to inhale. The room was spinning as her oxygen levels were getting lower. Frances gripped the side of the counter before she completely lost control and fell to the ground in uncontrolled laughter.

"The madness has set in from all the paint sniffing. I think we are too late," Dana said.

Winter narrowed her eyes at her friend. Her cynical lawyer mind had her pick up the cork and study it closely. Seeing that the strong smell of vinegar was recorded in the history of the dark cork, she told Frances, "You are safe. This cork speaks your truth. But that outfit of yours speaks of a thin line between you being lost to the world of many lonely nights and thinking Christmas sweaters are high fashion."

"I had no clue I was having company."

"Defensive, are we? Not only do you have company—you have a date. We found it through the World Wide Web," Dana said as she placed herself between Frances and the door of the loft before she unleashed the news. The trio had decided it was best to let Dana reveal the course of this night's events.

"I have a what? You matched me with someone online?" Frances's voice reached an octave that was most likely heard only by dolphins.

"Relax. We took care of everything and, as you can see, you are going to have a makeover. Not that you need one—" Dana used her serious teacher voice to try and calm down Frances.

"Despicable. You are all despicable." Frances crossed her arms and sat down on her couch, not moving a muscle.

"No. You are, and we are your minions. Here to get you ready," Winter said.

"Jesus H. Christ in the mountains. Woman, you need some air in here. You know, you really might just cut an ear off smelling all these oil paints and thinner fumes." Dana quickly took herself out of the tension and opened all the windows that worked. The fresh air from the San Francisco Bay flooded into the loft, replacing the heavy paint fumes with cool, salty air. Dana walked around the new stack of stretched canvases and spotted the paintings that had kept Frances hostage for the past few days. Winter and Cheryl both noticed Dana's focus and came over to see what she was looking at on the floor of the loft.

"Wow. These paintings are exceptional. You really are an artist. What are all these little paintings? Did your big painting have a litter?" Winter asked, breaking the silence.

Frances grabbed the purple cashmere throw from the back of her couch and pulled it over her to ignore the crowd. She was not in a mood to answer questions about this sequence of paintings, as she was not sure about it herself. Frances stared at her fingers and tried to rub some of the dried paint off her left index finger. Sometimes Winter could rub her the wrong way, and now, Winter's safety hung by a thread that was spider-web thin. It made Frances seriously think about this strange friendship.

"Okay, little lady, enough discussion. Time to go hop in the shower," Dana said, sitting down next to Frances. "Please, for your fellow humans, get in that shower."

"Not so fast. You all forgot to ask me if I wanted to go out with a murderer." Frances pulled her blanket a little tighter around herself.

Cheryl and Winter came and sat down on her coffee table directly in front of her.

"You are so melodramatic. This is what people do in the age of the internet. Come on, we found a great one for you. Let this be an experiment where you are the head of the lab, and we are your minions who do all the fucking work while you get all the headlines and the glory," Cheryl said, trying to lighten up the mood.

"Yeah. I even bedazzled the criminal with more pictures of you from Halloween last year. The perp we picked wrote back in complete sentences and listed *Hitchhiker's Guide to the Galaxy* as a favorite book too. What are the odds? It is a cosmic collision," Winter said.

"Or we can call this the comedic science-fiction literate serial killer," Cheryl said.

"Not helping, Cheryl. To the shower. I am not going to ask again. Chop-chop," Dana said.

"Okay. Okay. Okay." Frances stood and addressed each "okay" to her crew and stomped off to the bathroom.

"That was easier than I thought," Dana said and sat back down on the couch. "But did you see her hair? What are we going to do about that? She's got dried paint in her hair."

"Relax, Dana. I'm on it and I am calling Russell right now. I know they're home—I heard Winston bark when we broke into her place." Cheryl, cell phone in hand, walked over to the fridge and opened it, looking for something to eat.

"In all the years I taught teenagers, I was never as scared as I was coming in here tonight, and we aren't even halfway through the night. It wasn't like I was at a country club, either. I taught in inner city schools in Oakland." Dana went and poured herself wine from a new bottle that Winter had opened. They had all learned from the vinegar wine, so she performed the sniff test before taking a sip.

"Dana, how did you meet Frances? I don't think I ever heard the story," Russell asked. He had let himself in and walked in on the women standing in the kitchen. His stealth manner never failed to make Dana jump, and this night was no exception. Dana took her fist and playfully hit Russell on his arm.

"Stop it. You always scare me. What is this? Are you keeping track of how many times you can make me jump out of my skin? I hope you have a defibrillator close at hand."

"Sorry." Russell lightly pecked Dana on her cheek as he took a glass of wine from Cheryl. "Where's our victim?"

"I heard that. I'm drying off. Were you in on the plot too?" Frances shouted through an almost closed bathroom door.

"I know nothing. *Not one thing*," Russell said, putting his arm out in a mock salute.

"You are dating yourself, Shultz. You need to eat some more donuts. You look more like a handsome Colonel Klink with hair to me, and the only reason I can say that is you two forced me to binge watch Hogan's Heroes," Frances said as she wrapped her hair in a towel and joined the crew freshly scrubbed. "For the record, I was going to shower."

"Sometime this year?"

"Cheryl, you can be so—"

"Listen, we have about one hour to get you from this to fab to the restaurant. No more sauntering, questioning, or joking around." Dana was using her teacher voice and the crew fell in behind her.

It was a hustle of people, packages, and blow dryers. Frances caved in and let the crew go to work. They finally decided, without her input, on a beautiful light-gray suit with a subtle lavender pinstripe, a lavender silk blouse, and charcoal-colored two-and-half-inch heels with a cool pattern. It suggested a sophisticated, subtly sexy woman. The skirt had a great side slit that showed her rather well-defined muscular legs without being overly revealing.

Russell put Frances on one of her bar stools and went to work on the mop of red snakes. Dana stepped back and let the younger ones work their magic as they transformed the hermit, Frances, into a very dateable woman. Cheryl and Winter took turns with the makeup.

"Now, you aren't giving me a cat face or painting a butterfly or something stupid on my face, are you?" Frances asked as Winter applied eyeliner to her upper left lid. "I can see it now. Suit by Brooks Brothers, hair by Russell of Modern Design, makeup by...the Toddlers."

Cheryl and Winter burst into laughter, and the whole crew lost control for a few moments. Russell struggled to keep his focus and not lose his composure. He had done a French twist around the right side of Frances's head, giving her a beautiful profile and a sophisticated look. It was all he could do to hold on to what he had created.

"Don't move," he mumbled through a mouthful of hairpins.

"Ladies, we must move it now. We don't want to be late," Dana said, bringing focus back to the minions. Frances felt butterflies come to life in her stomach. Was she really going to go through with this? Frances took a deep breath and stood when Russell held his hands in hers. She walked over to the full-length mirror that made up one of the walls to her bathroom and gasped at her own reflection.

CHAPTER SEVENTEEN
HIGH-STAKES DINNER

"Shocked we made it here in time," Winter whispered to Cheryl as the crew took up prime viewing seats at the large U-shaped bar that claimed most of the real estate in Meadows Bistro, the latest restaurant to boast farm-to-table sustainable gourmet vegetarian food in San Francisco. When the well-known Millennium restaurant pulled out of the City and went to the East Bay, it created a bloody feeding frenzy in the upscale highbrow vegetarian restaurant scene.

"Should we have left her standing at the hostess station? It's very close to the front door," Dana said as she glanced back at the strangest cocktail menu she had ever seen.

"I don't think she is going to bolt. Granted, she's always a flight risk even when she's completely comfortable; however, she is also very curious, so she's staying." Winter turned to the bartender. "I'll have a Trolley Tam Tumbler, please. Put it all on my check." Winter pointed to Dana and Cheryl who were still unsure of what exactly Meadows Bistro was supposed to be selling.

"I'll have what she's having and make it a triple." Cheryl turned back to make sure Frances was still there.

Dana didn't like the pressure and the bartender was staring at her, so she finally pointed to a drink and prayed to god it tasted good and not like tree bark or composted tea bags.

"What is wrong with a good steak house? Don't people eat meat anymore?" Dana asked.

Frances studied the decor of the restaurant as the hostess walked her through the beautifully set tables. Many tables were set with two place settings on light-gold tablecloths. The lighting in the place was subdued and pleasant, casting soft shadows that added a level of privacy for the diners. It was hard to tell if the walls were a dark blue or eggplant purple. The off-white, faux leather cushions covering the dark wood chairs made them look almost comfortable. The smells of roasted garlic, grilled onion, and juiced ginger coming from the open kitchen were intoxicating. Frances spied an appetizer on a table that looked both beautiful and tasty. The butterflies in her stomach were now in full flight, performing an air show routine complete with smoke and cannon fire. She took her seat and let the hostess replace the purple napkin with a silver one. It had been a while since Frances had eaten in a restaurant that paid attention to the color of the clothing you were wearing and matched your napkin to it.

"Can I start you with a drink while you are waiting?" the hostess asked.

"I would love a dirty martini with Grey Goose Vodka."

"Might I suggest one of our signature drinks? We use only liquor distilled locally and humanely. Perhaps you would like the Fog Horn. It's made with olive juice from our farm in Marin and a rye made in Santa Rosa."

"That sounds peculiar. Can I have the rye with a couple of ice cubes without the olive juice?"

Frances watched as the hostess slightly bowed, backing up with her drink request. This gave her time to give a half smile to the three musketeers seated at the bar watching her every move. She thought it would help her to keep them close at hand. It was all a little unsettling to her, and she tilted her head first to the left and then to the right, trying to let out some of the tension. She had hoped the butterflies would calm down with a few sips of water, but it only seemed to give them more fuel. Her ears finally let her hear the music that was softly playing in the background. It was a jazzy mix, and it suited the atmosphere of the place. Hushed conversations were circling around her as she waited.

A young waiter delivered her drink in a crystal tumbler. The glass and the table settings struck her as a place trying too hard to recapture the posh look of mid-century America meets modern day huppie. A huppie in Frances's world was a businessperson who capitalized on the hippie craze. These vegetarian gourmet bistros had no issue charging thirty dollars for a couple of oyster mushrooms doused in kale highlights. Although, the aroma of the food being made had her excited to try the fare of this five-star vegetarian restaurant. She knew that Winter loved this place and was glad it had the street fight to outlast the critics of San Francisco. Frances took a sip of her drink. She quickly reached for her water. The taste of the drink was horrid; Frances hoped that it was not a sign of things to come. How could a place with such a rich menu serve a drink like that? If pond water and salty Hawaiian Punch got together, this drink would be their baby.

Fumbling for her phone, Frances dialed Winter. "That is the worst drink I think I have ever had—you couldn't pick a place that had a decent bar?" Frances hung up and smiled at the crew with her best beauty queen wave. She was also a little irritated that they told her she normally dressed like a preppy Boy Scout or, worse, a Mormon on a mission. That was why they had gone shopping for her. It was uncanny that they had found a suit that fit her so well. There was nothing wrong with her usual crisp, white, button-down shirt and simple pair of trousers. But it had been a while since she had gone shopping for anything other than athletic wear, which included sweatpants, sweatshirts, and hats with sport team logos. Then again, they really were not around during the Richard years and all the parties when she wore beautiful dresses and makeup, and looked all the part of a Marin county wife.

"What is she thinking about over there? She hasn't looked at us since she took one sip of that drink. Where is her date? It's ten after." Winter was starting to get nervous. "Maybe we have a no show?"

"Winter, that is crazy talk. Frances looks stunning. Traffic is a mess out there. I'm going to put five down on Frances bolting in the next ten minutes." Dana said.

"Dana, that is—I'll put five down on fifteen. Cheryl, do you want in on the action?" Winter asked, smiling as she took another sip of her drink. "Who could resist the email invitation we sent?" Winter started laughing when Cheryl almost knocked her off the barstool. The other half of the computer-found date walked in, dressed in an off-white suit that had the look of expensive Italian tailoring written all over it.

"Looks like Frances is caught in our trap, and the games are about to begin," Cheryl said, taking her cash bet off the bar.

"Put that back. The bet is still on—she could still bolt in the time increments we put out." Winter grabbed Cheryl's arm by the wrist to stop her from taking the very small pot of cash.

"Holy crap, that profile picture does not represent well. What a catch…That is one hot specimen," Winter said.

"What about Jason?" Cheryl asked.

"I'm with Winter on this one. Oh, I so want to see Frances's reaction," Dana said. The three gathered their drinks and relocated to a better vantage point so they could see Frances's face without obstruction.

"Do you think we did the right thing?" Dana whispered.

"Dana, you can't start backtracking now. The hostess is about ten steps from Frances's table." Cheryl was watching Dana, ready to clamp her hand over her mouth should she start to shout "Fire!" to clear the restaurant.

"Maybe we should have prepared her for this date a little more," Winter said.

"Well—what if we did set her up with a serial killer?"

"Seriously? Dana, you are forbidden from watching any more news. I met Sean online, and he's still alive." Cheryl let her smile slowly rise across her face as she waited for the full effect of her words to sink in.

"F.O.K. is going to kill us. You know that, don't you."

"Winter, give it a rest. I think this is why she has been in so much turmoil. How many more months are we going to listen to her latest summary of what she's read about, watched, or researched—her taste in music has always been suspect. Besides, I know I'm a little curious myself after seeing what walked in the door and is now standing in front of Frances." Cheryl said.

CHAPTER EIGHTEEN
CURIOSITY KILLS MORE THAN CATS

"HELLO. It is so wonderful to finally meet you. You pulled off a feat getting us into Meadows. I've been trying to get in here for a couple of months."

It took her eyes a moment to adjust in the light. Or maybe it took longer for her brain to interpret exactly what her vision reported through her optic nerves. Frances blinked her eyes hard a couple times, trying to get her brain to work. The awkward silence was getting deeper by the millisecond from her inability to utter a word of greeting to the tall, beautiful, and exquisitely dressed person who had spoken to her—a person who was, in fact, a woman.

"Hmm—Frances, it is a pleasure to meet you." The female stranger spoke again. Frances blinked hard again and recorded that now she, this stranger, a woman, was turning to the hostess and ordering a drink. Oh my god. "Abort" messages and alarm bells were going off all over Frances's brain.

She needed to respond. Her brain was not working. "Reboot and find me some words!" Frances screamed inside her head. She was not completely sure she contained the scream. Now the stranger was sitting less than two feet from her. Frances wanted to turn away, but the woman across from her was so beautiful, with the most amazing complexion and fascinating light-brown eyes. Wait. No. That is not right. They are going to really pay for putting me in this position. I've been punked. This is all a joke. Frances started to rise and was going to go over and confront her three ex-friends when the woman spoke again.

"Frances? You are Frances, a.k.a. 'Irish Coffee'?" The woman leaned a little closer to Frances across the table, and Frances got a glimpse of the most beautiful black lace bra she had ever seen. The bra was a Unicorn. Frances thought that lingerie like that was only in the movies. The sight caused Frances to stand up so quickly—she tried to pull back from the view, this woman, and the whole bizarre situation—that she knocked over her chair. The crash of her chair caused the other conversations in the restaurant to cease. Her ears turned red-hot first as she thought of several different ways to kill her friends for such an extreme dating surprise.

"Yes. I mean, no. Sorry," Frances said as she tried to right her chair and then caught the faces of the conspirators, who were trying really hard not to laugh. It looked as though Winter had her phone out. A waiter came over and helped reseat her. She was now once again face-to-face with her date, a woman. The butterflies in her stomach were now fully engaged in combat flying maneuvers, and Frances was not sure she could keep them corralled. She wished that she had not taken a sip of the worst alcohol she had ever tasted.

"Yes. No? Can you help me understand who you are?" the woman asked again, this time crossing her arms and leaning away from the table.

"I am so sorry. I was set up on this date, by some 'friends.'"

"Your name is Frances. But not the Frances I have been emailing the past three weeks?"

"Three weeks…How many emails?" Frances now turned toward the bar, the heat from her ears burning across her face. Those three had kept this information from her. What did they tell this woman? What did this woman say? "This is going to be a much bigger discussion when I get them alone. I am so sorry. Might we start over?" Frances was trying to cover up the fact that she did not know this woman's name. "I am so nervous. I've never done this before."

"Done what? Eaten dinner in a restaurant? Been involved in catfishing? Been on a date?"

"I've been on a date before. I was even married." Frances felt her hackles coming up. She wondered if she needed to clarify that she had been married to a man. What was the etiquette on a date with a woman? She knew it was bad to mention her marriage and divorce in the first minutes of a date with a guy. Frances felt like she was sinking further and further below the surface of the water and had no clue which way to swim to get herself breathing again. The music in the restaurant started to pound into Frances's head. She was not sure how, but she continued to talk with this stranger across from her. Time seemed to be slowing down. What was happening? Colors were blending into slow-motion movement. Oh my god, have I been drugged? Frances tried to pull herself together. She gripped both sides of the table with her hands, knuckles going as white as the tablecloth. An odd heaviness was hitting her chest as she filtered through a few responses to the barrage of questions thrown across the table, pelting her non-stop.

"I was trying to get your name. I still don't know your name."

"Well, it appears that we were both left out of some crucial details about this meeting. I am Samantha Iverson, a.k.a. 'towel42.'" Samantha took her first sip of the drink she had ordered, and Frances had to stifle a giggle because the look on her face had to be close to what her own face had registered. The drinks in this place matched someone else's idea of what good tastes like.

"I hope the food is better than the drinks they offer," Frances said, trying to break the ice. "I love the work of Douglas Adams, all of it. Towel42—that is classic. I thought I was a *Hitchhiker's Guide to the Galaxy* geek." Frances watched the words leave her brain and then worried if she needed to stop and explain. She had started to relax a little, and the temperature of her face was starting to cool down until she had gone and called this beautiful woman sitting in front of her a geek. She had a small amount of hope that the makeup the two minions had applied hid some of her emotional blushing. The slow motion returned around Frances, and the music drowned out the rest of the sounds from around them. Frances had let go of the table and fumbled with her utensils.

"Well, your 'friends' hooked me with a couple of great quotes from the book. Glad that part is true. I'm wondering about the rest of what you—I mean, what they had said to me in the emails. I had all but given up on using the website to meet anyone. You can call me Sam or 42."

The mood shift was almost instantaneous as Frances floated on the effortless sound of Sam's soft laughter. It cut through the loud operatic-style music that had replaced the soft, soulful jazz. Holy cow, this was weird. It reminded her of something, but what that was eluded her grasp, receding far away into her memory. She knew it wasn't déjà vu because she had never been in the position of being on a formal date with a woman. An image of Olivia jumped into Frances's mind and she found herself wanting to be anywhere but here.

"Have you done this before, then? Been on a date with a woman?" Frances whispered the last word in the sentence. She wondered if she had done something wrong as Sam crossed her arms again and cocked her head a little.

"This isn't the 1950s. Although with the last election, people might believe they can go back to pushing us back in the closet. The words lesbian, gay, queer, etcetera are out of the closet, too. Not to mention, we are in San Francisco. It's not like this is even close to being a red state."

"Are you a professional?" Frances leaned in closer and knew that was not what she had meant to ask. Insert foot now. Sam's expression changed with that question. "Let me—"

Before Frances could finish an explanation, Sam stood, leaned across the tiny table, pulled Frances toward her by grabbing the lapels of the jacket she was wearing and kissed her directly on the lips. Stunned and caught in a flurry of feelings she could not identify, Frances let her lips linger and felt them part a little as Sam's tongue briefly brushed hers. Sam let go and sat back down, leaving Frances frozen in a half-standing, half-seated position. The world around Frances dissolved into stillness and silence. What was happening? Where were her ears, her eyes? What happened to the people? Where was she? When Frances's brain had rebooted, she stood completely up, pushed the chair back, and ran out of the restaurant.

"Uh-oh. We are in big trouble," Cheryl said to Winter and Dana, all three staring open-jawed at what had just happened.

CHAPTER NINETEEN
THIS IS NOT ART

NATHAN Steiner stood completely still, looking out the freshly washed window of his brand-new Union Square art gallery. It was a moment he wanted to savor. The photo-taking tourists, focused city workers, and noisy traffic fueled the energy of the square. He heard the sounds as if each one was personally calling to him. After twenty years of being an art broker for some of the most prestigious Silicon Valley art collectors and managing Olivia's gallery, Nathan finally had taken the leap and opened his own gallery. The first installation and grand opening were set for tonight. This beautiful, quiet moment was going to be lost soon to the phones, the catering crew, the artist, and his assistants.

The timing of opening this gallery did not make sense to him, but maybe this was the universe giving him the push he needed. Nathan knew that he needed to talk with Frances about her art and to caution her about Olivia. Life had gotten so mixed up in the opening of the gallery that he had not seen her since Olivia had stolen her off to lunch. What was going on in this frenzied world? He took a deep breath and told himself that Frances was an adult and could look after herself. No time to worry about her now.

A noise behind him made him turn to see his partner, Felipe Cruz, walking toward him with a small gold-rimmed porcelain cup of espresso. Nathan smiled and walked to meet Felipe in the center of the gallery. They stood for a moment and just looked at one another, no words. Nathan gently accepted the coffee with his right hand and touched his lover's face with his left.

"We did it. Can you believe this is our own gallery? No more fighting for our commissions with greedy gallery owners." Nathan kissed Felipe gently and walked back to the window with his morning pick-me-up.

"This is not art, you know. It's business. That buzz you are hearing through the window is what we need for this junk in here." Felipe came and stood next to Nathan, taking in the view of the square and the Macy's store that was almost directly across from their gallery.

"Filly, you are so rude. This is art. Remember, I sold out that last show of Ethan's, the one we hosted down in Los Gatos. Those people are chomping at the bit to see what else he has created." Nathan walked around the twelve sculptures that were arranged around the space. Something in them spoke of a wickedly gifted artist. They required one to look deeper than the twisted metal and rotting wood that Ethan used to create his cynical view of modern society. "The difference is that we will no longer have to deal with Olivia or her family. Olivia never appreciated that all those people that came to our hosted shows came because of us."

"Can we move past the wretched woman and everything we had to do, please? Time to move on. Don't invite that energy back into our lives. Are you sure the valet parking service is all set up and will be here early for the VIPs who are meeting with Ethan at six?"

"Yes. Relax. It's all going to be okay. But remember, Felipe, that woman brings money wherever she goes. I am not opposed to selling to her. Money is money."

Nathan took his empty cup back to the kitchen and called the valet service to triple check. He knew he could sell the show out tonight if everyone felt special and in a panic to buy. Ethan was going to be taking some time off from his art to travel the world and become inspired. Or that was the story they helped him come up with after hearing him talk about his inability to do anything except rebuild old cars.

Something was not sitting well with Nathan about the last conversation he had with Ethan. He struggled with whether to discuss it or keep it quiet from his Filly. He would need to fill him in about Ethan using their warehouse in Novato, but not tonight. Filly could get so easily wound up. The first time Nathan had seen Ethan's work, it was at a juried show over in Oakland. At that time, Ethan's paintings were so bold, raw, and dark that Nathan easily convinced a couple of his art collectors to purchase those pieces.

After such a successful start, Ethan stopped painting. He refused to create anything else for a while, saying it was against what his soul wanted him to do. Nathan hated working with artists who refused to see that art was also a business and that an artist needed to keep producing when people were lining up to buy what they produced. It did not matter if it was good or not; it often shocked Nathan what people bought in the name of "art." Most art was sold through a show of smoke and mirrors, and people with more money than they knew what to do with were so easily convinced to buy. Nathan shook his head as he scolded himself for the cynical turn he had taken right at the opening of his very own gallery.

"The magazines you had printed for the gallery just arrived. They look really great." Felipe came over and sat next to Nathan with a stack of the gallery guides.

"These aren't magazines, they're books." Nathan smiled as he flipped through the pages that showed what the gallery would be offering over the next six months. Six shows in six months was ambitious. After some careful planning, they had decided how to place the artists to optimize sales across the art-collecting spectrum. He had connections all over the world and knew that this book would help sell pieces internationally. What a world. All he had to do was make them feel the need to invest in the art. It was easy—a talent he had learned selling used cars on his father's lot in San Diego. "Thanks, Pop," Nathan said as he made the sign of the cross and kissed the Saint Cajetan's medal he wore on a chain around his neck, a superstition that he continued because it always seemed to bring him good fortune and luck.

CHAPTER TWENTY
WHAT IF?

F RANCES flipped through the channels on the hotel television as fast as she could. As the delay started to stack up, she put the remote down and watched the channels continue to cycle through without end. When the TV finally stopped on a station showing a group of people standing around smiling and holding up giant fish, she picked up the clicker again to make the image go away. After a few more channel flips, Frances turned the TV off and climbed out of bed, checking the minibar to see if there were any more overpriced snacks. She had pretty much cleaned it out while she watched *Harry Potter and the Deathly Hallows: Part 1* on Pay-Per-View.

Frances ruminated on how she had come to find herself staring at an empty minibar in a boutique hotel in Union Square in her home city. Oh yeah—it was due to her friends throwing her into a double-blind, surprise, computer-created date with a woman. It was okay until she felt herself respond to the kiss. The kiss from a stranger had more impact on her than any she had ever received before, and that included the experience she had with Olivia. When she had exited Meadows Bistro, she went straight to a cab and was gone. At first, she was going to go home, but instead she had the cabbie drive her around San Francisco. The lights seemed brighter than before. Streets were busy with

people and cars. It was a beautiful night in the City, and what had occurred at the table—she wanted more. Tired of being driven around
and noticing the taxi bill was now pushing close to sixty dollars, she
had the taxi driver take her to Union Square, where she decided to
hide herself in the boutique S Inn. The problem she realized after taking stock of the empty candy wrappers, small bottles of alcohol, and
empty chip bags was the fact she was trying to hide from herself. How
appropriate she was hiding in a place that if you said it too quickly
sounded like you were saying boutique *sin*.

Her trance broke when she remembered that they had amazing hot
chocolate and crème brûlée French toast, not to mention the softest
feather-top beds that she could disappear into and hide. Not wanting
to face anyone, not even herself, she had turned off her phone. Her
iPad and computer were back at her loft, and she didn't want to go
back there for fear that the threesome would be waiting for her, so she
was basically unplugged from her world. It was a new-found freedom
to be completely checked out from life with no one knowing where
she was now. A couple of times, she turned her phone on to check for
messages from her Irish Mafia. Other than that, she was not interested in responding to any of the avalanche of texts, voice messages, or
emails from the conspirators responsible for her current need to retreat from the world.

She was over it. Frances could not stop thinking about that kiss.
There was no way they could know what she felt. "Embarrassed" was
one word that kept popping up. She had left that ambush of a date in
such a crazy way. Restless, Frances counted her steps to the window.
She looked down on the ocean of people flooding the sidewalk and
decided that it was time for her to get outside and take a walk. What
kind of person was she, hiding from the whole thing? They were attempting to help her come out of the closet. She had been talking to
them about it hypothetically for longer than she could remember, to
the point that they were starting to tease her over her choice in music
and movies. She put on her new jeans and shirt, grabbed a fleece that
was still sporting its price tag—all of which she had had delivered to
her hotel via the ease of her smart phone—and headed out of the hotel room into the sea of anonymous people.

The city air helped dislodge a little piece of the anger she harbored over being set up on a blind date. Frances looked left and then right to get her bearings on the square and struck out toward Tiffany's. She loved to window shop at the jewelry store. A long line of people was blocking her passage along the sidewalk as they were waiting for the next cable car. This was all part of the experience of Union Square, and Frances counted four different languages being spoken as she maneuvered through the crowd up to the corner of Post and Powell. What does it all mean? She kept trolling through the memories from the date and the excitement she felt when she realized Samantha, the beautiful woman in the amazing suit, was her date. Why had she run away from a woman like that? Because she was in shock, she told herself. No, she hid because she was mad at how she had reacted.

Frances was swept into the middle of the crowd of walkers as the light changed. She crossed Post Street and worked her way to the square windows of Tiffany's. Her reflection in the clean window made her pause as she noticed a few curly strands of her wild hair had worked themselves free from her ponytail; the ringlets now framing her face softened her jawline. The overcast skies reflected off the windows made her eyes look blue-hazel today. All she was trying to learn for herself was where she stood.

It wasn't until she moved out west that she encountered what systematic cultural prejudices existed against gays. News often contained arguments against gay marriage countered by those supporting it. Where did she stand on the issue? She loved her neighbors, Russell and Simon, and had known many people in the gay community through the years. "What a jerk!" Frances screamed inside her head. They aren't different. They are people. Ellen had made the news and raised her curiosity with her comedy show. Look at what had happened when she announced she was gay. Even though everyone felt they knew, it devastated her career for several years. Shit. What are you doing, Frances? Frances stood staring into her reflection, thoughts about gay life flooding through her mind.

What did she really know? The *L Word* had kept her attention but could not have been close to reality. Most of the gay women she knew in real life worked for UPS or FedEx. Now she was stereotyping. Holy shit, she was prejudiced against gay people. Maybe it was good she ran out before she said anything else to the woman that would have revealed her as the prick she was. Now it seemed to be the thing to do for Hollywood actors to come out as gay or lesbian. In many respects, it felt like it was the latest fad. Was she jumping into a fad that would, in a few months, pass over her and be gone?

That wasn't fair for her to do to anyone else if they knew what they were. This was another issue she had with it—what someone is or isn't. Does it matter? She guessed it would if they were a serial killer or criminal, but who cares who you love? Love is love. Isn't it? What is so wrong with it? Was it because she felt physically attracted to that amazing woman, Sam? What about Olivia? Was it because she could help her sell her art that she felt anything for her? No. Her body responded. She enjoyed that time with Olivia. She looked down at her feet and felt like she was walking on wire over the Grand Canyon, and she was sure she was going to fall.

Frances had watched a comedy special in which Kate Clinton pointed out that keeping gay people from getting married was the thin barrier between keeping straight people from marrying their pets. That struck her as so funny. She never fully comprehended how gay people could not get married. After her marriage and divorce, though, she could not understand why people would want to. Frances knew she was acting like a straight, upper-middle-class jerk to the right of the middle. That comedian was brilliant at dispelling the flawed logic that gay people were the only barrier between straight people and weird marriages. Frances felt even worse when she replayed what her own divorce attorney claimed—about how she wanted to open civil marriage to anyone and everyone because that meant more business for her.

A large, broad-chested man wearing a blue coat, white shirt, and black tie approached Frances. "May I help you?" he asked.

"No. Those are beautiful earrings." Frances left, wondering when it became a crime to stand at a window display and debate social issues in one's mind. As she walked up Post Street, she noticed a piece of art in the window. Without warning, Frances stopped in the middle of the flow of walkers, almost causing a pileup of people and strollers. She quickly dashed to the window of the gallery and peered into the space, seeing more of the work she would recognize anywhere. Ethan was having a show. Why had he not told her? The piece in the window was one he had started when she was still renting studio space next to his. What gallery was this? She did not remember a gallery being here before. She dared not step back out into the rush of pedestrians to look for a sign. Frances inched along the window over to the glass door and tried to open it. No luck. To cut some of the glare, she pressed her hand to her forehead and leaned into the glass. It would be unusual that the gallery wouldn't be open at three in the afternoon.

Frances saw Nathan come into the gallery from a back room. Of course, Nathan would be representing Ethan's work. Frances knocked on the glass with one hand and waved with the other to get Nathan's attention. When he finally looked at the door, she jumped up and down. It was clear he did not completely recognize her as he slowly walked a few feet closer and then stopped. Frances put her hands on her hips and blew a piece of her hair off her face.

Nathan quickly crossed the floor and opened the door for her. "Frances, it is so amazing to see you. How are you?" He gave her a hug and kissed her on each cheek.

"Nathan, you didn't tell me you were doing a show for Ethan."

"My goodness, you must have heard me thinking about you. What a wonderful surprise."

"Good dodge. Explain this amazing space. Is this one of the galleries Olivia was talking about?" Frances asked as she walked around the piece that was anchoring the center of the room. The metal spiked out at sharp angles; in the center was a shopping cart that had been partially melted to resemble a human body of sorts. Random objects had been welded to the shopping cart, giving it a strange post-apocalyptic darkness.

"Ethan didn't tell you himself? He has you on his list of VIPs."

"I haven't seen him in a while. We don't see each other much since I moved out of the studio space. How are you, Nathan?"

"Brilliant and stressed. The opening is tonight, and the caterer has called saying they might be running a little late due to all of their servers calling in sick."

"Not good."

"How's your work?"

"I'm still doing that commissioned work for a bank in Santa Rosa. I've got some other paintings going too." Frances was still trying to get her bearings in this space and not pester Nathan about the three pieces she had left at the other gallery. What did all this change mean?

"You've got to come tonight. Any time after seven. Now, I must send you on your way so we can finish our opening prep," Nathan said.

"Love this gallery space. So cool."

"We need to see your art. Now that we own our own gallery we can show whomever we want. I get to decide and don't have to wait for approval."

"This is yours? But what about Olivia and her gallery?" Frances asked.

"Sweet woman. We need to talk. Now is not the place or the time. See you tonight."

Frances put her arms around Nathan's neck and kissed him on his cheek. She loved the fact he was so kind to her. Her world continued to tilt, and she was unable to get her bearings. She turned and looked at the art Ethan was showing and felt a little hurt that he hadn't called to let her know. Frances hoped it was because she had been away from her loft and that there would be an invitation waiting for her upon her return.

It was already late in the day, so she decided to stay in the hotel another night. She needed an outfit for the opening and headed across the square to Macy's. Frances contemplated her spending rate and knew that this could not continue. It had been a long time since she had purchased a fun evening-out dress and shoes. She probably could con someone in the makeup department to do a makeover for her. Off she went to spend money she knew she really did not have.

THE crowd in the gallery ebbed and flowed with a fluid essence around Ethan's art. Conversations about his brilliance, brutality, and truth pelted Frances as she stepped into the evidence of what would be a successful opening for both Nathan and Ethan. For the first time in a long time, Frances had allowed herself to embrace her own concept of going out on the town. The form-fitting, dark-green cocktail dress accentuated her curves in all the right places. She had splurged and dropped into a salon that specialized in doing blowouts. Her hair, freed from curls for the evening, fell around her shoulders with a beauty that turned heads as she walked toward the open bar.

"Who is this most lovely creature that stands before me?" Nathan asked.

"This is amazing, Nathan. You must be walking on air," Frances said.

"Actually, I am walking on American Express Platinum cards and the offer of a diamond. We might sell out the whole show tonight. A first for a brand-new gallery. Has Ethan seen you yet?"

"I don't think so—he is so busy chatting with the fans."

"Frances, go talk to him. Come, I will take you over right now. A beautiful woman like you always helps sell art just by her presence around the artist." Nathan held out his arm and Frances felt herself blush as she accepted with her free hand.

A flutter of nerves went through Frances when Ethan met her eyes. He held her gaze far longer than she wanted and she looked down at the glass of champagne in her hand. The crowd of four people who were asking him about his work dispersed with the help of Nathan.

"How did you know? I didn't invite you," Ethan said.

"Do you want me to leave? I wanted to tell you that your work is amazing. It has changed dramatically since the last time I saw any of it," Frances said as she tried to shake the nerves she was feeling. It wasn't attraction. There was something else, but she could not identify what it was. Ethan looked every bit the troubled artist dressed in black. He had pulled his hair back into a tight ponytail, which made his face even more angular and pale in the lights of the gallery.

"Don't leave. I'm sorry. What am I saying? Frances, please."

"Ethan, this show is strong…and who is this beautiful woman you are talking with?" A woman dressed in a dark-blue suit interrupted Ethan. Frances noticed the woman's winning smile as she extended her hand and introduced herself.

"Excuse us, but I need to talk with Frances about something," Ethan said.

Frances tried not to trip over her new three-inch heels as Ethan grabbed her by the elbow and pushed her to the back of the gallery and through to Nathan's office. The feeling of wanting to run was now rising higher in Frances, but she told herself to relax. This was Ethan. He was probably nervous over his opening. Why had he not told her about the show? Was she so involved in herself that she failed to know that he had been doing all this work?

"Ethan, have I done something to upset you?" Frances asked.

"I need you to not talk as I collect my thoughts," Ethan said.

He wrapped his long, slender arms around his own waist and started to vibrate like he was going to explode. Frances looked and noticed another door toward the back of the office. Ethan was blocking her exit back into the gallery. With the noise of the music and the people, she figured it would be hard to hear her scream. What was she doing here? What was going on with Ethan? Her father had warned her about men who were dangerous or off. But this wasn't what he was talking about—it was more a warning not to walk alone on city streets at night. The silence between them was jackhammering through her brain to run.

Frances turned and ran for the door and hoped it led back into the gallery. When she pushed through into the alley behind the gallery, she screamed. Ethan responded without hesitation and pulled her into him, placing a hand over her mouth.

"I need you to listen to me," Ethan said.

She wanted to bite his hand, but instead she decided to relax and see if he responded.

"Frances, I am in control here. I am an artist and you are my muse. Don't you see that? Don't you feel that?" Ethan took his hand away from her mouth and kissed her.

It was all she could do to stay standing. Her mind was exploding, and she felt the pain searing through her as Ethan grabbed both her arms and pushed her up against the brick wall of the building. He kissed her hard, and this time he took his hand off her arm and pulled at her dress. The ripping fabric filled Frances's ears as she tried to move.

"Stop!" Frances yelled.

"You want this. You dressed for me," Ethan said as he lifted her dress up.

Frances got her hand free and slapped Ethan as hard as she could.

"What is going on here?" Nathan asked, standing in the door. "I saw you go into my office and came in to get you. I sold the *Red Tears* piece, and the buyer wanted to talk with you, Ethan."

Frances went toward Nathan and tried to straighten her dress and fix her hair.

"Frances, you can't come in here looking like that—wait here. Ethan, you come with me."

The tears started to fall. What was going on with Nathan? "Ethan attacked me. I am not going to stay in this alley. This is—"

"I know you are upset. I am going to send Filly out to take you home. Stay put. You'll be safe." Nathan pushed Ethan through the door. The red hand print was still quite visible on Ethan's face.

CHAPTER TWENTY-ONE

A BURNING FAMILY PHONE TREE TURNS TO ASHES

T HEIR mother had a dream in which she saw Frances lying dead in her apartment, rotting away because she had failed to call anyone to tell them she had died. The impossibility of a dead Frances calling to let them know she was dead could not be explained to their mother. Theresa had to stifle her own morbid laughter; only their mother could make it the responsibility of the corpse to call and let everyone know they were now dead. How does one even…Theresa decided to stop trying to wrap her head around her mother's logic.

What the heck was going on with her? The family text messages had reached into the hundreds by this point. Theresa wondered if it fell to her to go out to San Francisco. She knew the family would say she had the spare time to do it; being unmarried with no kids equated to a life of unlimited free time.

Theresa reasoned that maybe Frances needed a break from the constant questions Mom wanted to get answered, especially in this family with the iron-fist-in-the-velvet-gloved rule of Mom Bridgette. None of this business about Frances leaving her corporate world job would be an issue if Edna and Beatrice had not thrown Frances under the bus by making it an issue. It was a trick learned early on: to get the wrath of Mom focused away from whatever was wrong in your world, you throw another sibling up for sacrifice. Sometimes it was real, and sometimes the facts were an alternative to the reality. Right now, it was easy to point out there was something terribly wrong with Frances as she was an unemployed divorcée living in scary San Francisco. Theresa's heart was heavy, knowing that she had fled from college for reasons that she had not chosen to reveal, and that no one in the Kavanagh Mafia had really said anything negative about her abrupt life change. Why had no one in her family questioned her quick exit from Notre Dame? This was peculiar to not be upset over her leaving the gold standard of Catholic universities.

"Honey, what are you doing? It's two in the morning." A soft sleepy voice came out of the pile of blankets on the other half of the queen-size futon that doubled as their couch during the day.

"Checking email again. Sorry, didn't want to wake you."

Theresa shut her computer screen and punched her pillow a few times before snuggling up. "No one has heard from Frances in days," Theresa said as she nuzzled the back of her lover's neck.

"I don't think anyone in my family would be worried if they never heard from me ever again."

"That's not a family. My god, I think my mom carries around a journal and records how many times we talk to her in a week," Theresa said. She moved her body even closer and pulled the blankets over them both.

"I think if she could, she would record every time you took a shit and said your prayers. I wonder if she has hired spies through an underground Catholic network. I think she's more wired into the Catholic network than the Pope," Kelly said.

"Now you understand why I don't come out to anyone."

Kelly pushed Theresa back and sat up in the darkness of their studio apartment. "I moved to this roach-infested studio apartment with the woman I love because she promised we were going to get married. What do I get? This reality of the Kavanagh Mafia keeping you scared shitless of being who you are and you not telling them who you love. Not sure I can hang on much longer in this family drama. Why are you in charge of finding your sister? Maybe she's gay and decided to come out, and that is why she isn't talking to any of you brainwashed, uptight penguin lovers."

"What's a penguin lover? I love penguins—what's wrong with them?" Theresa asked while trying to kiss Kelly, only to be blocked by an elbow to her jaw. "Ouch. No need to turn cage fighter."

"Sorry."

"I'm the only gay one in the family. They don't need to have that pressure. It's enough that I dropped out of Notre Dame and came to New York. Hey. What are you doing?"

"I'm calling your sister, Frances."

"Hello?" Theresa heard her sister's faint voice through the phone and reached for it, not knowing what Kelly would say.

"Shit. She answered," Kelly said.

"Hello? Theresa, are you okay? Why are you calling so late? It must be three in the morning in New York."

"Hi, Frances. It's only two in the morning." Theresa put the phone on mute. "Stop it. You are not going to kiss and caress me while I'm talking to my sister. She'll hear you."

"Frances, are you okay? Mom and the rest of the Irish Mafia are going crazy since you went silent. Mom wants to know who you think you are, tearing her apart like that—"

"Theresa—"

"Frances, what is it? Are you all right? What's happened?" Theresa asked.

Frances wanted to be with Theresa in this moment but she had no idea what to say. She sucked in a deep breath and talked through her pain. "Fine. I'm fine. Call Mom and tell her you talked with me and to call off the hounds."

"Hold up there. You don't get to disrupt my life and make me worry about you because Mom calls me, frantic that she had a dream you were dead. I know you're not at your place...I called your neighbors and checked."

"You called my neighbors? I'm an adult and older than you. What the heck, Theresa? What did they tell you?"

"Frances, what are you not telling me?"

"I don't know. Tell Mom I'm fine and not dead. I think she might kill me or wish I was dead," Frances said and hung up. She hoped the call ended before her sobbing had started.

"What did she say?" Kelly asked as she started to ply Theresa with a parade of kisses up her bare arm.

"That our mother would rather have her dead than alive. That quite possibly is a true statement as Frances has consistently challenged her and the family in ways that…I am too tired to go into it. Frances sounded so strange. I think she was crying."

Theresa gave into the kisses and fell into the arms of her lover, letting the strange call with Frances be kissed away.

CHAPTER TWENTY-TWO
CINNAMON ROLL SAND

F RANCES was watching the morning commuters stop in Specialty's for coffee when she felt a light bulb burst in her brain. She realized that there existed a "Twilight Zone" tilting of her world, and everything that she thought she had known about people was wrong. After what had happened with Ethan during his art opening at Nathan's gallery, she was shocked she had the power to slap Ethan. Not to mention how Nathan turned so cold. To top off the less-than-perfect evening, her sister Theresa had called to let her know their mother was focused on Frances. Note to self: call Mom when hiding from the world to pretend everything is normal.

Frances forced a smile upon her face as a person who was trying to decide where to sit gave her a smile and a nod. It was a total stranger, and she worried more about that stranger thinking she was a grouch than about being honest with herself. She did not feel like smiling, talking, or existing with other people, but she was too scared to be alone. What was wrong with her? She was trying to hide the turmoil and fear that was percolating inside her right below the surface. What Ethan did in the back alley of the gallery should have sent her straight to the police station. Should she go now? She mentioned it to Filly but he said that would cause all sorts of problems for Nathan. Shit. Nathan was helping her get her art out into the world.

Frances took another bite of her cinnamon roll. Her thoughts were already screwy and had propelled her into sleepless nights. With the sugar and fat rush, her mind flipped to the blind date and that kiss from Samantha. Why did she run from Sam and not from Olivia? The electricity eventually flowed through her body, at levels that felt almost dangerous, when Olivia touched her, kissed her, and introduced her to one of the most physically passionate sexual encounters she had ever had in her life. It took her a while to relax into the situation with Olivia. Was she forced into it? Frances bit her lower lip as she realized that what happened with Olivia was counter to how she normally responded and acted. She was not a woman who kissed on a first date. Was that a date with Olivia?

How did that fit into everything in her world? Frances traced her upper lip with her finger as she thought about the instant electricity she felt when Samantha had kissed her. It was soft and strong at the same time. She tasted a little salty, and Frances felt the kiss all the way down to her toes. It was a contrast to what she felt with Olivia at first. Holy crap…are you attracted to all women? How to test this theory without alienating her friends? Did they have a reason to worry? What were those knucklehead friends thinking? She needed them right now because Ethan really scared her, and she had thought for sure he was going to rape her had Nathan not come out into the alley. He looked like an animal ready to devour her. How was that different than what happened with Olivia? Frances's tears fell and she quickly tried to cover it up by fake sneezing into a napkin.

A shiver went down her spine as she thought about him. He was her friend. Ethan wouldn't hurt her on purpose, would he? But he did. She took another bite of the buttery, sweet, cream cheese–frosted drug called a cinnamon roll to numb herself. What the hell was Ethan thinking when he pushed her against the wall and ripped her dress? Was he drunk or high? Why was she looking for an out to explain his behavior? What, if anything, did this say about her? Nathan's reaction puzzled her even more. He stopped the action but he was not her friend in that moment.

She had gone and purchased a cocktail dress at Macy's for the opening. Her motive was purely to support Ethan and Nathan. She had gone, she thought, as a friend surprising and supporting another artist. The opening was beautifully styled. The place was filled, standing room only, and Nathan must have been selling because he looked so happy. It took a while for her to even get over to chat with Ethan because the prospective buyers constantly swarmed him. "Buzz, buzz, buzz" was all she wanted to say to him. He looked every bit the part of an up-and-coming artist. He was dressed in black jeans and a black T-shirt, with his hair pulled back into a stupid man bun. Frances wished she hadn't teased him about the man bun—yet another reason she thought he was quite possibly gay.

While Frances was lost to her thoughts as the scenes of last night replayed in a loop, a man dressed in an out-of-place, pale-green suit came over and pointed to a chair. It didn't make sense, and Frances looked around before responding with a head nod that he could take the chair. She did clash a little with the normal crowd because today she was wearing a brand-new pair of purple University of Washington sweatpants, a white hoodie, and a pair of UGG boots—clearly not a street person but quite possibly classified as a hoarder of empty chairs in the cafe.

The noise levels were rising in the cafe, and Frances considered getting a second cinnamon roll as she was down to the last few bites of her current one. Two in one morning would be a first for her. They were large rolls, and no one should ever consume that much sugar. Frances wiped the crumbs away from her lips and tried to hide from the shadows running through her brain of Ethan's forced kiss and his knee pushing to spread her legs. He told her it was the least she could do for him after all he had done for her. Had she led him on? Was the dress too revealing? She had lost some of her post-divorce weight and was feeling good about herself, good enough to buy a green velvet cocktail dress that made her look like she was a member of the "in" crowd and not stuck in 1999.

"Excuse me, can I use this chair?" A woman wearing an unimpressive black skirt and white blouse asked Frances.

"As hoarder of the chairs, I suppose you can have the chair," Frances responded, the joke falling flat on the floor by her feet. As she was not overly worried that the morning had given way to lunch, Frances finally took in the last bite of her roll. That last bite, void of frosting, quickly sucked all the moisture from her mouth. The once-trusted treat turned into a mouth full of sand that cut her air off. The bite made it impossible to chew, swallow, and breathe. Her brain, already writing her obit, started out with "cause of death: the last dry bite of a cinnamon roll." Tears started to collect in her eyes as her lizard brain went into overdrive trying to figure out a survival path. Frances sat paralyzed and cut off from air because there, in living color, less than three feet away, stood Samantha Iverson. Samantha was staring at Frances with a slight smile on her face. Frances felt a new sort of fear mixing inside her with an unknown level of excitement and a possibility of fainting due to lack of air. Her brain was sounding off a series of alarms from the lack of oxygen. Her tears started streaming down her flushed face, which was quite possibly changing through hues of red to purple to blue as it was now more than a minute since she stopped chewing, stopped breathing, and started choking.

The woman who had asked for the chair was now hitting Frances sharply square on her back, asking her if she was okay. A huge wad of cinnamon roll sand finally dislodged and flew out of Frances's mouth, landing in front of Samantha's amazing shoes.

"Are you okay? Can you breathe?" the woman shouted into Frances's ear.

Hoarse and wanting to hide, Frances responded in a whisper, "Fine."

Frances fell back into the black leather chair and put her face in her hands, afraid to do anything. Conversations had started again and she could feel the rush of a couple of employees coming her way. When was this train of weird going to stop? Why couldn't she have normal outings like other people?

"Frances, are you all right?" Samantha asked. She was dressed in a suit that draped so perfectly, it must have been tailored especially for her. She leaned down closer to Frances and placed a hand on her shoulder.

"Sam, you—?" A man dressed in an equally expensive suit now stood next to Samantha, blocking any quick escape route as Frances peeked through her fingers and saw only tall people with exquisite suit pants. Before he could finish, Frances watched as Sam took her spiked Prada heel and most deliberately stepped on his foot, effectively ending his line of questioning.

"I suspect that you have been caught by surprise," Sam said. She pulled a chair over and placed it directly in front of Frances.

Frances was frozen because Sam had gently placed her hand upon Frances's knee as she leaned in toward her.

"What...do...I?" Frances whispered her nonsense into silence. She was blinking hard, focused upon Sam's hand resting quietly on her knee.

"Now that we are here face-to-face and you are going to live, I am curious to know: why did you run out of the restaurant? Honestly, that has never happened to me before. I have had a few dates that I wanted to run out on myself but didn't."

Frances hid her face in her hands and shook her head from side to side, unsure of what to do or say. When Sam tightened her grip on Frances's knee, she felt a sudden shot of electricity run through her body. Humiliated by her own lack of ability to communicate, Frances could not say anything. Her brain would not let go of any of it, and she tried to focus to come up with something pithy to say to save face with this astonishingly beautiful woman who, as far as Frances could see, dressed nicely all the time. She laughed out loud as she wondered if this woman slept in a suit.

Sam sat back and crossed her legs. "Care to share what has made you laugh?"

With some effort and a last attempt to keep some dignity, Frances sat up and faced Sam. Frances was not prepared for Sam to break out in laughter, nor was she prepared for Sam to reach over with a manicured forefinger to wipe some cream cheese frosting off her cheek and then lick it off her finger. Completely on freaked-out overload, Frances jumped up and grabbed her purse, ready to bolt, but Sam reached out and caught Frances's wrist and gently pulled her back into her seat.

"You're not going to run away from me twice."

"Sorry," Frances sighed.

"You are not sure if you are into women or not? You're spooked like a horse spooks at a shadow. I get it. Grow up." Sam's words filled the space between them.

Frances wanted to stare into her eyes and her face but knew that would not happen. She was so anxious that she hoped she didn't lose the contents of her stomach in the moment. What could she say to this woman? What was it about her that made it okay for people to physically control her? When Sam took her wrist for a moment, Frances was back in the alley with Ethan pinning her bare arms to the cold brick wall.

"Listen. I have no clue. I'm sorry my friends did that to you, and that I ran out. It was rude."

"Was my kiss that bad?"

"Yes. I mean, no." Frances saw the light leave Samantha's face a little, and she knew she was blowing it again.

"You know, Frances, I wish you well. Maybe when you figure things out we can actually have a nice conversation." Samantha stood and went back to the table of business associates who were trying not to stare.

CHAPTER TWENTY-THREE
GHOSTS

FRANCES had carried her loot to the foot of her closet in the loft and set it down. It was good to be home. The act of unpacking the shopping bags gave her a needed break. Mindless work was good right now. Then she hesitated. The green dress laid at the bottom of the Macy's bag. Frances pulled it out and placed it over herself again. She rolled the dress into a ball and threw it toward the back of her closet as the tears continued to cascade down her cheeks. Her body started to twist and twitch in discomfort and she sank to the floor, resting her head on her knees. It did not take long for the cold cement floor to drain away her heat. The dark feelings continued to reach further into every part of her being. She rubbed her hands on her thighs as emotions ran over old scars that were threatening to reopen. Words from her family tore at the scarred wounds of past choices. Those words covered her in Technicolor detail, concerning her failed marriage, unemployment by choice, and the fact that she lived in California.

That last "problem" always made her laugh. What was it that her mother had against California? "Failure" and "self-absorbed" were the main catchphrases currently used by her parents. After her phone call with Theresa, she figured that "crazy" was now permanently part of her name. What would they say about assault and attempted rape?

It took every ounce of strength Frances had to pull herself off the floor in her closet and turn her mind away from the chatter that her family had placed in her head. She knew that her mother was going to tell her that she had to get right with the church. Not right with god, but right with the church. To disengage from the Kavanagh clan was not going to be easy. She really saw no way around excommunication from them. Her family not only installed the emotional buttons that controlled her, they also knew how and in what order to push them. She had tried to explain to Winter and Cheryl once about the debts extracted for giving one life by an Irish Catholic Mafia family. Dana understood because she grew up in an Italian Catholic family. They might have been real Mafia. The other two were still thinking that Frances came from the world's greatest family. It didn't help that the Weasleys of the Potter world elevated portrayal of red-haired families as supportive and fun-loving.

"Gall, I wish you were still here. You'd know what to do. Shut up, Frances! You know what to do. Call the police right now and report Ethan." But she had waited. Why didn't she do it that night? Frances screamed to the ceiling of her loft, her eyes focused beyond to the sky above. Gall had been her closest sibling, born just thirteen months after Frances. He often told people his family of saints was going for a world record of children. Poor Gall was born on the feast day of the Irish saint, Gall. Their mother had apparently argued fiercely with their father over naming her son after Gall, which could be mistaken to be gull, a shorebird. Dad had said the name is pronounced like "al" with a hard "k." Ultimately, Gall got exceptional at fighting through school as kids liked to call him "gal" or "call girl" or various other sissy names. Agatha, Edna, and Beatrice, all higher up in the birth order, took care of the bullies most of the time. Beatrice was built like a solid goalkeeper or football linebacker. She really did take after her namesake saint as she sported the most beautiful, straight, red-blonde hair and perfect unblemished skin. Unlike Agatha, Beatrice was also a sweet person to everyone—friend or foe—unless you did something to one of the Kavanaghs, and then look out because Beatrice would clobber you.

Frances let the tears fall as she walked through memory lane. No more mason jars of wine—she was going to be civilized and drink wine out of a real wine glass tonight. As she headed over to her sofa, she picked up the book her sister Theresa had put together as a Christmas gift for them a few years back. The pictures were both wonderful and horrid, and Frances stopped on a page that showed the whole family standing in front of Our Lady of the Holy Cross on the first day of school a million years ago. If anyone ever looked at the school from the outside, it seemed like a total horror movie. Much of the student body were light skinned, light haired, and wearing the same clothing, doing exactly what they were told. A note needed to be sent to Stephen King about a new horror story.

All the Kavanagh children were marched through the Holy Cross torture fun house run by a gang of nuns. Parochial school was not at all what Hollywood made it appear to be in the movies. Frances laughed nervously as she swallowed a sip of the red wine, remembering her very first sip of wine when she and Lori Brondster had taken a dare and snuck sips from the offerings before mass. This wine was a long way from that horrid red stuff.

Memories of the mandatory school masses during Lent came rushing back as she flipped through the pages. Those priests used an inordinate amount of incense on purpose. Most of the kids knew it was done to make them cough and make their eyes water to see if one of them would pass out from the sickly-sweet smoke they used to fill the church. Such torture at the hands of the priests and nuns cemented friendships because they all suffered and survived together. Father Pat had sent one class home in tears when he caught them pasting the Eucharist wafers to the back of the pew. He told them they were going to turn into hamburger meat for the worms when they died. Horrid does not describe Father Pat. It was rumored from the high school kids that he was the creator of the Spanish Inquisition. Since they were little and had no clue what the Spanish Inquisition was, they continued to spread the rumor. Eventually, it got the whole school in trouble and everyone had to say ten full rosaries during recess. They didn't get recess for two weeks. It takes a long time to say ten full rosaries. It was no surprise to anyone when, two decades later, Father Pat was one of the priests named in an abuse scandal. He was convicted and sent to prison. Maybe there was a god.

It wasn't all bad with the penguins that ran the school. There had been some talk that the nuns had run a military academy before coming to Our Lady of the Holy Cross Elementary. The nuns kept everything and everyone on a strict schedule. There was never any question about which the alpha dogs were in that school. Frances was always scared of the lot. To this day, if she saw the rare nun wearing a black habit, she crossed the street and avoided eye contact.

Frances's sister Agatha had reached legendary status with the student body in her senior year. Named for Saint Agatha of Sicily and not the British mystery writer, Agatha's antics were over the top. Unlike other schools, Our Lady of the Holy Cross did not allow students to dress in Halloween costumes. It made a dreadful walk to school when, as a kid, you were forced to wear the tell-tale white Peter Pan–collared blouse, blue plaid skirt, knee-high white socks, and ugly brown fake-leather loafers. The outfit screamed Catholic school and marked them as targets. Jealousy ran high during the days around Halloween for the Catholic kids stuck in uniforms while other kids, lucky enough to go to public school, were not subjected to the wrath of the nuns. They went to school on Halloween dressed as vampires, witches, heroes, princesses, Muppet characters, and, strangely, nuns.

The day after Halloween was even worse. All Souls' Day was celebrated in complete silence at Our Lady of the Holy Cross. The nuns were experts at torturing little kids. Everyone always had to attend classes, and if for some reason a student was absent, there had better be a good excuse or it was detention with Sister Mary Rose for a month. She was all thorn and no rose petal softness. Those tricky nuns sold the concept of a Day of Silence to the parents as a day of solid reflection over the sins committed by past sinners. What the heck was that? Gall had always said it was so the nuns got a day off work but were still allowed to keep on scaring kids.

The nuns were brilliant at spreading the fear of themselves and god into people, and so the nuns got their Day of Silence. Although the day that Gall was hit by a car, when he was the week's special student and crossing guard, the nuns didn't tell Frances to stop screaming. Gall loved his turn as hall monitor and crossing guard. He let kids keep their hall passes and never turned anyone in for walking as slowly as possible back to class. It was a day that Frances thought she would never forget, but as she looked at the pictures of Gall in the photo album, she no longer remembered the exact day in the fall that he had died. She remembered that Agatha had picked her up and tried to get her to calm her screaming and crying. She had held her so tightly as they waited for their parents to arrive. Gall had been taken to the hospital by ambulance, but the police proclaimed that he was already dead. It was the first time in her life that Frances had yelled at god and said a bad word. Sister Mary Peter, the head penguin, had ignored her rant against god and did not say a word. Sister MP, as the students called her, cried and held her hand. Frances remembered that she had stayed away from school for three months after Gall's funeral. No one said a word about it. Sister Mary Peter would come by and bring her school-work. She told Frances that she would know when it was right to return.

Maybe it was because Agatha thought the school needed a different focus, or maybe she was mad at Sister Mary Peter's number one hench nun, Sister Mary Rose, threatening to put Frances back a grade for not coming to school for three months.

When the prank was pulled off, Sister Mary Peter sprinted down the length of the elementary school wing in seconds. It had to be a mile long. Not really, but to a little kid, fifty yards could be a mile. The floorboards vibrated with each one of Sister's footfalls. It was the first time there was solid proof that Sister Mary Peter, a giant of a woman at six-foot-two and at least two hundred pounds, doubled as a linebacker for the Green Bay Packers. The silence of prayer hour was squashed that year with the screams of about a hundred kids. We all erupted into screams and tears of horror thanks to Agatha. She had masterminded the whole thing. For several months prior, Agatha laid the ground-work with us younger kids. It was quite possibly something that struck her with Gall's death. Morbid is what Bernard said when Agatha finally told them all how it went down years later.

First, she and her group of friends had to convince Sister Mary Patrick that they were really into wanting to become teachers. They were each placed in a younger grade and everyone knew that if you showed up, Sister Mary Patrick gave you an A. Agatha and her comrades spent their time in the classrooms laying down stories about the ghosts of kids killed by nuns roaming the halls. They knew that little tidbits would lodge so much better than giant stories. The crafting of this took so much strategic planning; it was amazing that Agatha was not running her own covert ops military force. Days passed, and they would say the ghosts were seen or they would talk about how something was moved in a classroom with no explanation. Then they advanced the stories to the one about a boy who was forgotten by his parents at the school and so the ghosts took over his body and he was never seen again.

We were freaked out and believed every word they fed us. Like lambs to slaughter, we listened and never questioned. No one said a word to our classroom teacher, Sister Mary Joseph, because if we did, we would have been the first kids to be ghost chow. The ghost kids hated snitches, according to Agatha. She claimed our brother Gall was helping her from the other side and, of course, he was an angel because that is what all the nuns had said.

Frances remembered how she stood up against the very loud know-it-all Todd DiMarco, who claimed ghosts did not exist and that the story was made up. It helped that a young priest trying to fit in with the students told them about a priest who performed an exorcism in St. Louis on a twelve-year-old little boy. This gave Agatha some leverage against the ghost non-believers, like little Todd DiMarco. Agatha could be so calculated and simply evil because she also weaved a rather bad demise for the tattletales like Becky Teelin.

With the stories planted in their minds helping them turn into their own ghost stories, Agatha and her gang rigged up fishing line on a few clothesline pulleys. They attached jackets, hats, gloves, and boots from the lost and found that had been collecting over the past fifty years. The targets—us elementary kids—were all quiet in our seats doing prayers when a fire drill practice was announced. The whole elementary school, grades first through sixth, were lined up, ready to exit the building. When Sister Mary Joseph opened the door, those coats, hats, and shoes were flying through the hallway like ghosts. Little Diane Bonniefisk was the first one to see them because she was the first in line. Her scream was so high it almost shattered the glass in the windows.

As the empty coats and various items flew through the hallway, no one noticed that the hats didn't fly with the jackets. The effect was all they needed. Even the nuns screamed at the empty, dancing, twirling jackets. With each turn of the ghosts, the screams grew in intensity and volume. Of course, Agatha had covered all her bases and knew we would run back into our classrooms. The screams evolved into a whole new level of terror as kids ran back toward their cloak closets looking for places to hide. Kids were diving under desks yelling for their mommies. Frances knew she had run toward the cloak room, or at least that was how she remembered that time. She didn't see the fishing line strung across the floor. She had triggered her class's jackets flying off their hooks and hanging before her friends in mid-air like magic. Her friend Lori Brondster had fainted. Timmy Cook had peed his pants. Frances was not proud of the fact that she froze and vaguely remembered screaming for her mommy.

Because of the noise, all the upper grades came running to our rescue, or more likely to see what exactly was going on and to tease us little kids. Frances was still not sure how Agatha had gotten to her in the chaos. She had picked her up and calmed her down by letting her know that Gall protected her. The strange thing about the whole prank that was talked about for years after was that no one ever got in trouble for it. How did she slip through life with so much luck? Agatha had confessed to the whole thing years later along with some other memorable days at the school.

Most of her friends from school were still in the St. Louis area, or if they moved, their families were still there. This meant a better part of Frances's trips home had been spent getting the gossip on her classmates. It also suggested that whatever Frances did would eventually make the rounds of the gossips. Would they talk to her if they ran into her in public? Now that she was no longer a CEO of a successful consulting firm, would they call her for favors? Since she had wiped herself off most social media, she had lost track of those childhood friends. Did they know she is an artist? She took in a deep breath and told herself none of the gossip mattered. She no longer lived in that world. But her parents did, and they let her know if something was said, they felt that it reflected poorly on the family.

Frances put the family photo album back on the lower shelf of her coffee table and stood up, stretching her body and looking toward her fresh white canvases. She stood and made her way over to her painting easel, touching the canvas that was waiting for her to make a mark. The walk down memory lane and her late brother Gall gave her some anchoring in her pain of loss and the knowledge that life continues after losing someone you love. It struck her how, as the years passed, she still really missed Gall, but the memories no longer tied her in knots. The empty canvas represented life in the present moment. It was full of prospects in this post-divorce era. No longer wanting to escape from the emotions, she walked to her iPad and picked a playlist that had Nine Inch Nails paired with a random grouping of music. She knew the boys were gone to Palm Springs, so she turned up the music and danced herself over to her shelves filled with paint.

Her eyes narrowed and her right nostril flared slightly as an image fixed into her mind, and she pulled out a large tube of ultramarine oil paint. With her left hand, she pulled out a clean paint palette and squeezed out almost half the large tube of blue paint onto the clear glass. The color pulled her into the moment, and she grabbed a dry, four-inch, angled brush and put it directly into the snake of paint. Frances pulled the butter-thick paint across the dry white canvas with an added force and power that silenced any taunting from the blank canvas.

The rough line of wet paint let white bits of the canvas show through the edges, while the ridges created by the stiff brush bristles held the motion of her stroke. Energy from a bottomless resource surged through her hand as she pushed the brush back into the paint on her palette. Focused like a predator on its prey, Frances pulled up the rest of the paint snake deep into the bristle talons of her brush. She stretched up on her tippy toes and placed the loaded brush on the upper right corner of the canvas. With an exhalation of air, she pulled it across the canvas through the other line of paint. Right before she reached the edge of the canvas, Frances turned the brush back into the center, forcing the color into another level of dynamic range. With the controlled hand of a surgeon, she took the brush into even heavier sections of laid paint. She pushed, stroked, and coaxed the paint on the canvas with the attention of a lover.

Frances strode back to the shelf and squeezed excitements of color from paint tubes labeled alizarin crimson, Payne's grey, and cadmium yellow medium. With a new tenderness, Frances took hints of the new colors and transferred slight strokes of paint onto the ghost skin of the ultramarine blue, blending them into the traces of the blue snake that started the energy. Frances squared off and faced the current state of the canvas. In silent motion, she pulled her favorite half-inch filbert brush out of her vase of paintbrushes. The brush rested easily in her hand, with its wooden handle covered in layers of paint nestling into the cradle of her thumb. This was the first truly professional paintbrush she had ever purchased. Frances loved how holding it was like talking with a great friend from another world. It always brought light, breath, and delicate proportion to her work with its fine lines. While the big bristle brushes wanted to close a painting in moments, the fineness of this brush let her slow down. She let the brush gently pull the crimson paint into the blue on the canvas, and the line that formed followed an inspired curve. The strokes on the canvas opened in the story forming deep inside, as her soul liquefied into the paint.

Lost in time, Frances stood back and smiled at the paint and brush strokes telling a story she had never trusted herself to tell before. Parts of the painting were delicate, holding the innocence of a child peeking around from behind the safety of a parent's leg, only to give way to that child growing into a questioning teenager as the bold brush strokes displayed raw power. Back to her shelf of paint, Frances pulled out a tube of indigo. While squeezing a huge rope of paint into the center of mixed colors on her palette, she smiled at the future. With a dry brush, Frances pushed the tips of the bristles into the darkness of the indigo blue. Then, with gentle confidence, she pulled the color across the centerline of the canvas. Red. Frances followed her inspiration and grabbed a tube of cadmium red. Bypassing the palette and the brush, she squeezed several dots of red on the canvas. With a fan brush, she quickly twirled the paint with the touch of a soft breeze. Her phone rang several times only to roll into voicemail. Sirens sounded out the window. A knock on the door had come and gone. Frances kept her drive long past the moment when the streetlights had become her only source of light.

Finally, Frances pulled back. In that moment, she stood, shocked, as the painting looked back at her. Was it challenging her? What answers did it hold for her? Frances stared at her paint-caked hands, forming them into fists triumphant with their power and courage to paint. She had a strange feeling that the woman in the painting, the one that questioned her, seemed curious and was asking her how far she was ready to go with the life energy she was tapping into. The minutes ticked loudly from the clock on the wall, and Frances started to reach out to the woman's hand in the painting. She stopped. Frances recognized that what she had painted was everything she had been hiding about herself. It revealed the scary thoughts hidden from the lights of understanding. There they stood, gathered in color, brush strokes, and captured light held tightly to the surface of the canvas. The more Frances watched, the more it appeared to her that the woman in the painting had reached her hand out to pull Frances into her and into the painting. The dark and the light had finally balanced into Frances's true dynamic range.

The figure stood alive on the canvas, swirling in the colors of her body and torn clothing. She held out Frances's fears, failures, what-ifs, dreams, and hopes. Frances sat down in front of the painting on the cold concrete floor, her body sore from the hours of painting, and watched herself drying in the paint. Her hot tears fell silently as she registered the peace of her loft. The power of the primal woman made of her emotions and paint was standing strong in front of her. There no longer was fear in the release of all her emotions. The painting, so balanced and ugly in its beauty, stood before her in power, screaming out that she, Frances, was her own solution to her life. The early morning light started to fill her loft with the soft gray haze of a foggy San Francisco morning. Frances rose from the floor and flopped into her unmade feather bed, falling into a deep sleep.

CHAPTER TWENTY-FOUR
NATHAN IS AWOL

N ATHAN had been on Frances's mind, and she could not shake the need to confront him over what happened with Ethan at his gallery. She had not gone back to the gallery because she did not want to run into Ethan. It was strange that she had not heard from her Nathan or Felipe at all, not even a call to see if she is okay. She had not called him either, and she knew it was because she was going to yell at Nathan. Dana would tell her that she was only acting out due to her own lack of action. Frances reasoned with herself that she needed to clarify with him that her paintings were still at the other gallery. She had not seen or heard from Olivia either. What were the chances that she would create fantasies over two different women, both of whom battled in the high-end world? Or at least they were dressed like they were in the top 0.0001 percent of the population. She knew she had expensive taste, but this was beyond champagne taste.

Dana told her the universe was responding to her, finally following the consciousness of her life path. Of course, she needed to clarify whether it leaned toward the creation of art or her personal attraction toward women. To Dana, lust was the downfall for most of humanity. Frances had left that conversation with Dana feeling like she might have been manipulated in the situation by Olivia. It was all so confusing to her. She was lost to her thoughts, making the bus ride to the gallery seem short, as traffic was unusually light through the City. "Have I missed a holiday?" she wondered as she stepped off the bus.

As she got closer to the gallery, Frances realized the art piece in the window was a new sculpture. She had hoped it was a sculpture and not a real corpse. It looked like a person with their skin removed. Now directly in front of the piece in the window, she could make out that it was a human form completely sculpted out of processed meat products. It lacked imagination. The balls were meatballs, and a small breakfast sausage was used to depict a penis. She giggled at this depiction, which she imagined would cause most men some discomfort. Unlike Michelangelo's marble sculpture of David, the hands of this meat creation were also unusually small.

Frances walked through the doors of the gallery and controlled her sudden urge to gag at the overwhelming smell of rotting meat. It was not quite the smell of a dead animal left on the road, but very close. She wondered if this exhibit was going to last long outside a meat locker. She walked around a couple of other works depicting various stereotypes of people. There was a large person built out of nothing but baked goods. It was both grotesque and insulting, even though she was not in the obese category. Who was this artist? More importantly, who bought this crap, and where would one display decaying food sculptures of people?

Frances saw no sign of Nathan as she walked around the gallery. There was no sign or sound of anyone, making this installation of art all the creepier. The artist had used fake glass eyes, making the sculptures appear almost human. What if she painted with decaying foodstuffs? Would that make her art sell at the level of these pieces? An urge to take a baseball bat to Nathan's gallery crossed her mind. This anger had to be controlled. But why? What is wrong with her? Ethan and Nathan caused her to feel shame when she had done nothing wrong, and then their silence made her question if she was in the wrong. Frances let the stench of the rotting meat distract her.

"Hello? Anyone here? Nathan ..." Frances shouted into the empty spaces of the gallery. When she heard no answer, she walked over to a glass table that was acting as a desk and set her bag down. It was odd that no one was there and the door was left open. What if a person walking past was hungry and decided to come in and help themselves to some meat or a pastry? Stranger things have happened in this city, although serving people from human food sculpted into the form of people would take performance art to a whole new level. But with the popularity of shows like *The Walking Dead* and *Santa Clarita Diet*, people might pay a lot of money for the "cannibal" experience. The whole concept made Frances sick.

"Gross," she said to the sculpture sitting at a table eating from a bowl of what looked like noodles from his gut.

Curious about the installation, she decided to sit in one of the swanky new low-profile white leather chairs and started reading the brochure on the artist. It would probably require a helping hand to get her out of the chair. This was a problem. Nathan was no help the night Ethan attacked her. Is he so oblivious that he did not see what was going on and is denying to himself that anything was wrong? She wondered if Nathan had sold Ethan's show out. The contrast of this ultra-modern glass, concrete, and white space compared to the gallery owned by Olivia was telling. Frances felt the coldness of the sharp hard surfaces of concrete and glass fit the Nathan that left her standing in an alley. Is this what the rich tech kids of the Bay Area wanted? It must be. Nathan was all over the details.

"May I help you?" Felipe asked, coming out from a back room.

"Felipe. I'm here to see Nathan. Where is he?" Frances stood up with some effort to face Felipe. Frances noticed that Felipe matched the gallery dressed in a stark white suit accented with a burgundy-colored silk square in his breast pocket. He looked striking amid the rotting meat.

"Frances, so sorry sweetie, Nathan isn't here right now. Can I get you a coffee? We have fine Italian espresso capabilities now. How are you? I was so worried about you when I walked you back to your hotel that night."

"What time is Nathan going to be back?" Frances tried to keep her composure. She had words to shout at Nathan.

"Nathan didn't tell you about the trip he's doing for the gallery? He's traveling and gathering items to sell."

"What? I knew I needed to call him, but I was so shocked and trying to figure things out."

"Why are you so hard on yourself? Did Nathan call you? He said he was going to. Cream, sugar, or both?" Felipe smiled and showed his dazzling white teeth.

"Both. No. Nathan never called." Frances went back and sat down on the chair. She wasn't sure if she should bring up her work in the other gallery.

Felipe carried a cup filled to the rim with espresso over to Frances. The beautiful smell of rich coffee temporarily replaced the odor of rotting garbage.

"Frances, I am so sorry. What happened to you was wrong. Nathan told me that he saw you and Ethan in some sort of a situation," Felipe said seeing Frances sitting there in the gallery. "Nathan was under such pressure that night. I know he regrets how he acted." The strength of Felipe's voice startled Frances. She flinched and hit the cup, causing the coffee to spill down Felipe's white linen suit.

"I am so sorry. I—"

"Frances. Relax. It's okay." Felipe took both of Frances's hands and got her to settle down before she caused any more havoc in the gallery. "I had heard about your ability to pretty much turn into an accident on roller skates. You are a reminder that I have been a very bad man. I forgot to get you a check for your paintings that sold over at Olivia's gallery. The new gallery manager she hired is a complete fuck-up and sent the check to Nathan. Amid everything going on, I was to get the funds to you. I am so sorry," Felipe said and let go of her hands.

"Seriously? You aren't pulling my leg? My paintings sold? All three of them?" Frances's face went wax-paper white, and she struggled with her balance as the gallery of meat started spinning on both its vertical and horizontal axis.

"Hang on there, Frances," Felipe said, fanning her face. "Let me get you something to eat. You sit right here and do not move." He ran to the back to search.

"I could just have a pastry from the guy over there," she called after him as she regained some of her equilibrium.

"Do not eat the art!" Felipe said from the back room.

Frances couldn't believe that her paintings had sold. She had gone past that gallery last week and saw through the window that her paintings were still hanging where they had been placed. It was cool to see her work at that high-end gallery, but she was unsure that anyone would ever buy it. Now she knew they had sold and the money went to Nathan. She would have to ask Felipe if she owed Nathan a commission for putting her work there. Why didn't Nathan ever call to check on her? He had to know that what happened was an attack.

When Felipe came back around the corner and walked toward Frances, she had to stifle an urge to break out in tears. The coffee stain really had ruined most of his suit. Maybe with the sale of her art, she could buy him a new one. He and Nathan always dressed like they were on the cover of *GQ*.

"Do I pay Nathan a commission for the sale?" she asked as he handed her a box of chocolates.

"Nope. The other gallery took their commission for the sale. Nathan deposited the money into an escrow account for you. You know him, by the book. I'll get the check personally delivered to your loft."

"That's okay. I can come back."

"Frances, this is a must. Nathan will be upset with me because I was to do this transaction without being prompted by seeing you. I am in trouble with a capital B."

"Capital B?"

"As in Big Trouble." Felipe laughed and sat down behind a computer on the glass table.

"Send me a bill for the suit. I think I'll be on my way. Good luck with the most unappetizing food sale."

"Frances, you don't have to leave, but isn't this the...wurst? Get it—as in bratwurst and liverwurst. The sickest thing about all this rotting art...people bought pieces from this collection. I told Nathan that when this show came in, we might get shut down by the city health inspector."

"How does this art last?"

"It doesn't. It is part of this new fad called the decaying art movement."

"The what?"

"Decaying art is all the latest rage. Blah, blah, blah. Frances, why don't you help yourself to another chocolate? I'm in double deep doo-doo now."

CHAPTER TWENTY-FOUR

"Okay. These chocolates are so yummy. What else did you forget?"

"Well, as I'm on the computer, I see there are several messages for you from Olivia. I have no clue why they weren't forwarded to you. I swear, the two people we have working here part-time are costing me more of a headache than is justified. Let me print these out for you."

CHAPTER TWENTY-FIVE
WTF!

C HERYL was getting more than annoyed over the fact that her closest friend, Frances, had not responded to any of her offerings for a truce. The way Cheryl saw the whole blind date situation, Frances was going to get a free dinner at the newest, swankest restaurant in San Francisco. All she had to do was act like a decent human. The yenta minions felt they vetted the date well. Samantha practiced law in the City, was in the right age bracket, and liked that sci-fi comedic *Hitchhiker's Guide to the Galaxy* book. Frances could at least have sent a text response to the deluxe box of the most amazing chocolate caramels made in the City. Granted, Cheryl had paid a courier to do all the legwork, but she still came up with the thought of sending him to four different artisan chocolate shops that had sprung up around the City like a Starbucks virus. She thought for sure the caramels would melt her nutcase of a friend. Why was she sending her gifts anyway? It was Frances who had acted like a complete jerk. Who runs out of a place knocking over chairs? Frances.

A couple of twirls in her desk chair had Cheryl mumbling about how all her friends were certifiably insane and whether this reflected on her own state of sanity. The caramels got no response, so Cheryl persuaded Dana and Winter to join her in finding the maker of the

Woolbuddies and ordered enough wool to create little wool creatures for an entire zoo. What type of person makes no contact after receiving such gifts? No texts. No emails. Nada. Cheryl clicked open her email folder one more time. Still no message from the missing Frances. There were two emails from Dana and one from Winter saying the silence continued with them. Honestly, this was stupid, and she was going to tell that to her friend as soon as she got a hold of her.

Cheryl turned her chair to watch the view out her window. She had finally made it to an outside office, one with a window. This feat took some wrangling and was hard fought. Cheryl sighed deeply because all they were trying to do was help. Frances had racked up a few bad dates with men and started talking more and more about going out with women. Her actions said otherwise though as she ran so fast when Samantha had kissed her, you would have thought the building was on fire. Was it that Frances was embarrassed that she ran out of the restaurant? Maybe Cheryl and her co-conspirators should not have stayed in the restaurant. "Crap, Frances, pick up the damn phone and let one of us know you are okay because I am getting ready to kill you myself."

It was the three of them who went and apologized to Samantha for Frances bolting. It was more than awkward, and they did stay and eat dinner with Sam. Cheryl shook her head because Sam really was an amazing person and Frances screwed up something that could have been great.

Was this temper tantrum by Frances justified? Cheryl realized as she looked up at the ceiling tiles covered with small toy animals that she missed her friend and wanted the gang back together. And she wanted to know exactly what had made Frances run so quickly. The little zoo dancing across her office ceiling was something that Frances and Winter had done without her knowledge. It started with just one and then another on her desk. But when they came to pick her up for lunch shortly after she had been promoted and moved from cubicle to office, the zoo on the ceiling was hatched. It was amazing that most people did not notice it until around animal number thirty, quite possibly because it was a giraffe that had been glued to the ceiling. The four-inch-tall giraffe stuck out above the rest of the little critters. It made her smile, and she gave no explanation when asked about the parade of plastic animals on her ceiling.

"Call me now, Frances!"

Screw this waiting crap. Cheryl called Dana and then Winter to see if they were available. This was going to end. They had started it; they might as well end it. The phone tree was employed with the first and most important call being made.

"Hello," Russell said, clearing his throat.

"Good morning. Russell? This is Cheryl, and I have not heard from Frances since the date."

"Seriously? I just spoke with her yesterday. She called us about the papers outside our door."

"You aren't home?"

"Not until this afternoon. We're in Monterey; it's Simon's birthday celebration."

"Happy birthday to Simon! Sorry for the interruption. I need to ask a favor. Would you let us into the building this evening, so Dana, Winter, and I can put an end to the silent temper tantrum Frances has been waging against us?"

"Absolutely. Sounds like fun. We will be in sometime after six. See you tonight."

With the logistics of how they were going to surprise Frances figured out, provided Frances was at home, Cheryl turned to her email and sent the plan of attack out to the girls. It was not right that they would be forced to suffer after trying to do something unique and nice for her. Who was she processing any of this with? The boys had been gone and she had not contacted any of the girls. Not to mention one of the Kavanagh tribe had left a message for Cheryl on her phone. But Cheryl, not being able to keep anything exactly private, did not want to chat with the spokesperson for the family. However, the message told her that Frances had cut everyone off. After the call with Russell, Cheryl was no longer holding her breath over the safety of her friend. They had their way in and were going to go to Frances's loft and clear this whole mess up.

CHAPTER TWENTY-SIX
EXPLORATIONS

D ANA Miller loved her mid-afternoons when she would shelter herself in her backyard garden, tending to her vegetables and flowers, and checking on her growing bee colony. Last year she started with one white boxed hive, and soon a colony buzzed around her hillside of lavender that sloped down to the beach and the bay. No one bothered her in the garden. She ignored the house phone and left her mobile on the counter inside. This, the flat hours of the afternoon between lunch and 3:00 p.m., was her magic time. Doris Day and Lulu would follow her out into the garden. Lulu would find a warm, comfortable place to stretch out and take a nap, while Doris would scratch and peck up bugs and snails, helping to keep the garden in impeccable shape.

This day, the sun was particularly warm in Marin County. Dana surveyed the patch of dark-brown earth she had picked clean of unwanted weeds and then decided she had done enough work for today. Now it was time for pure indulgence—a special Nespresso coffee, a few slices of salami and cheese, and wandering through the internet on her iPad. She picked up her little picnic and a beach chair, and she clucked to Lulu to follow her out the door and down the street to the point about fifty feet away from her house. From the base of a coastal pine that had been shaped into a seahorse by the wind, Dana set up her chair and used the old stump of a tree as a table for her coffee. She settled in for a most relaxing afternoon overlooking the San Rafael and Bay Bridges, contrasting with the undeveloped beauty of Strawberry Hill across the water.

Dana had been coming to this spot since she was a little girl, no higher than an elephant's ankle, she would often say. The little isolated village of San Quentin was protected in its peace by the California state prison that took its name and was built directly west of the village. Dana would tell people to squint when looking at the prison. There existed a beauty in the old architecture, and squinting took away all the razor wire and fences. The east gate to the prison was less than twenty yards from Dana's house, but she never worried about it. As she would point out, the prisoners were not the problem; it was all the protestors who caused the problems. They would come and camp outside the prison's east gate, blocking the road, creating noise, and tromping through her yard. Today though, it was quiet. There was only the normal traffic of the guards and deliveries to the prison. It made for a beautiful, peaceful afternoon.

The paradoxes of life were not lost to Dana, who turned her iPad on and went to her email. Lulu stood and looked for a different place to nap in the long soft grasses. The breeze brought the brine and salt mix of the bay up the hill to where she was sitting, and she inhaled deeply as her email loaded. She saw the email from Cheryl and her hand shook slightly as her pointer finger touched the cold glass to open the message.

Dana and Winter,

We are going to put an end to Frances's silent treatment. The boys are going to let us into the building, and I know Dana has an emergency key since Frances has most likely removed her hide-a-key. Pick up something good to eat and quite possibly a bottle or two of wine. This is a must. If you have other plans for tonight—cancel.

All for one,
Cheryl

DANA pulled in another deep breath and held it. She was over all of this and was not sure she wanted to confront anyone. The breeze softly moved her bangs across her forehead as she looked at the sun reflecting off the ripples on the water, wondering why she would leave her little slice of heaven on earth to go confront an angry Frances.

"I'm too old for this crap, Lulu." Dana smiled as Lulu raised her sleepy head up to acknowledge something had been said to her.

A few black-capped night herons stood on the sea rocks that had once been part of the land Dana had parked herself upon. They looked like a group of hunchbacks gathered for a meeting. They were strange, beautiful birds with red eyes and black feathers on their heads that tapered down their backs, making it appear like they wore a cape. These birds flew to this area of the bay the same time every year, right as the fall started to cool into winter. They would spend the next few months building nests in the shore trees, diving for fish in the bay, and then in the spring, they would hatch the next generation. When the babies learned how to fly, the whole flock would vanish right before the heat of the summer. It never stopped surprising her when she was in her garden glancing at her acacia tree and see one. A few minutes later, she would glance back and see more than thirty standing sentry still, all looking at her with their beady red eyes.

She reread the email from Cheryl. It confirmed for Dana that she was out of the yenta business after the Frances experiment. She pondered whether there was a word in the Catholic world that equaled the Yiddish word for matchmakers. One did not quickly come to mind other than the word "meddler." She did not care that she made a pact with her conspirators. The whole ordeal was more than her retired heart wanted to endure. She was ready to leave it to the younger ones. Even though Dana outranked the crew in the number of birthdays celebrated and collected, she still loved hanging with them most of the time.

In retirement, all she wanted was to tend to her garden, sit by her sea horse pine tree, go to yoga, and enjoy a carefree life. Heck, she felt she had already put up with enough hormonal psychotic behavior from the thousands of teenagers who had passed through her advanced placement biology classes. More than thirty years of raging hormones in teenagers was enough for anyone.

Dana had been avoiding her phone in case Frances called and did a number on her for the blind date business. Even though Frances claimed she was mostly Irish, she could display the hot temper of Dana's Italian and Spanish mother when provoked. Dana took a long, slow drink of her special dark Nespresso. It was a treat she loved; the smooth velvet flavor of coffee rolled over her tongue. Her iPad started to alert her to a phone call. Darn it. Dana realized that she had left her phone at home and had forgotten to disconnect it from the network.

"Good day," Dana said as lightly as she could, feeling somewhat self-conscious about talking to the screen of her iPad. Even though she had adapted to the new world of technology and FaceTimed with her grandsons all the time, it still unnerved her a little.

Warm sun, soft breeze, and the smell of sweet grass accentuated the nirvana that was San Quentin Village's peaceful bubble—one that Frances knew she missed as she hiked up the small hill to reach Dana.

"I see you. I'm on my way up." Frances hung up as she walked up the twenty or so uneven stairs cut into the side of the short hill leading up to the point where Dana had set up for her private afternoon. The point was protected from much of the village and from the prying eyes of drivers headed westbound on the Richmond–San Rafael Bridge due to the curve of the land. Frances wished that she still lived next door to Dana. It was a great rental, minus the days the fierce winter storms rolled through the bay. The house itself felt like it would blow over in a brisk breeze and had several critters, from mice and carpenter bees to squirrels, that also called it home at various times.

"I know I'm interrupting," Frances said as she bent down and gave Lulu lots of attention. Lulu took all the pats in and rolled onto her back, asking for more. Frances loved all dogs, but Lulu was special due to her friendship with Dana's chicken. "Where's Doris Day?"

"Dorris Day is most likely making a nest in my Swiss chard."

"Did you bring Winston?" Dana asked.

"Winston is off with the boys on some short vacation to celebrate Simon's twenty-ninth birthday for the tenth time. Do you think there is something genetically wrong with me?" Frances placed a beach chair next to Lulu so she could continue with her job of spoiling Lulu with attention.

"What the heck are you talking about? Frances, you don't have webbed fingers and you appear to have above-average intelligence most of the time."

"Seriously, Dana. Why would I go from being married to Dickhead to suddenly being attracted to women? What were you all thinking?" Frances sat back in her chair and sighed.

"If you continue to lie to yourself, you will continue to be miserable and deserve all the crap that comes your way. Knock it off with your stupid self-delusions. Don't be your own Woody Allen *Blue Jasmine*. You are clearly attracted to women, or at least more than curious about it," Dana said.

Frances took another deep breath as she took in the beauty of the view and the peace of the point. She was still a little miffed about the whole thing, but she knew she was more upset with how she reacted. She couldn't stop thinking about the kiss and now, the touch. That, combined with the darkness from Ethan, made her continue to stumble over herself. Frances respected Dana and her perspectives on life because she had quite the collection of experiences, from when she was married and divorced twice, to her assorted stories of when she taught inner city school kids biology.

"Jesus H. Christ in the mountains, Frances. Why not be attracted to women? You know men are the ones genetically screwed up and not playing with a full deck. The lack of two X chromosomes makes them much more susceptible to diseases and stupidity. Proof in fact: more men are color-blind than women. Men run most world nations and start wars. Not to mention, you never go on and on about them like those other two knuckleheads. And quite frankly, you're very intelligent and might be over dealing with the stupid simplicity of men." Dana took the last sip of her coffee, draining her cup. She smacked her lips. "I wished I had done a double."

"Why isn't Doris up here today?" Frances asked again.

"You didn't come out here to discuss the comings and goings of my chicken, and if you did, you really are a nutter."

"That woman you all set me up with—well, I asked her if she was a professional. By the look on her face, I think she thought I had asked her if she was a prostitute."

Dana snorted as she started laughing. "Frances Olar Kavanagh, we love you, but none of us are going to pay that much for you to get your jollies off with any one man or woman. She is a wonderful woman and handled being running out on with grace. We all sat and ate dinner with her after you ran off like the village idiot." Dana lacked a napkin, so she used her sleeve to wipe her nose.

"I am so confused because of the kiss she gave me. Well, it felt like the world stopped and I had stepped into a time warp. That kiss reached every part of my body. Was it because it was a woman? Was it that particular person?"

"No clue. One theory states that we are meant to meet a match. Maybe she is your match and you screwed it up on the first outing. You said something that made that very smart woman take the risk. As to the underlying question you are not asking, sexuality is said to be a spectrum. Some people are only attracted to the opposite sex and not ever in question, while others are only into the same sex and could not ever imagine being attracted to the opposite sex. Then there are those that fall into the middle, and they are open to the best person, same sex or opposite. You, Frances, are most likely somewhere in that middle of this spectrum."

Frances leaned back on her elbows and stretched her legs out as she tried to let what Dana said sink into her frazzled brain. A couple of kayakers paddled past the point, riding over the wake waves caused by the afternoon commuter ferry headed to Larkspur. Frances wanted to stop time and stay in this quiet for as long as she could.

"My dear young Frances, I am working hard not to be too irritated over the fact that you invaded my me-time. You know I love you. It appears that you are currently on a road that is going to force you to grow as you struggle through a curtain of culture, religion, family, and most of all, your own questions about what directions your life is going to go. Why limit yourself, Frances? Does it really matter anyway? Heck, life is nothing but brutal trial and error. What makes you think that any of us has any answers? We live, we die. Look at me. I've been married and divorced twice. I am not struck down by a bolt of lightning if I step foot in a Catholic church."

"Alex Trebek has all the answers. Plus, you've never dated a woman." Frances pulled her knees up to her chin and played with the duct tape that was keeping the sole of her boot intact.

"Grow up. Who cares if you are attracted to women? Your family is so big that I suspect you are not the only one. Winter, Cheryl, and I acted upon your own request to help you get out into the dating world.

Maybe we could have eased you in rather than throwing you into the deep end. Figure it out and have some fun."

"I saw her two mornings ago," Frances said.

"Saw who?" Dana sat up, a little more interested.

"The woman you all hoodwinked into a blind date. Or was it a cat-fish? Not sure I understand that concept, but anyway, I was at Spe-cialty's down in the Financial District, hiding, and she was in there with a group of beautiful people all dressed as expensively as she was." Frances picked up a stick and tried to detect if Dana was interested in hearing more or not.

"Did you talk with her?"

"Well—it didn't go any better than the blind date. I basically choked on a cinnamon roll, had some stranger pound my back, shot the chewed dough out of my mouth, and it practically landed on Samantha's shoe."

Dana burst into laughter. "Frances, you're a wreck around this woman, aren't you? Maybe it is more than the fact that she is a woman. You might have a spark for her. Another explanation is that you are completely inept at communicating with beautiful women." Dana lost herself to rolling spurts of laughter.

"Thanks." Frances focused on the marina across the bay from where they sat. The masts of the docked boats danced with the rolling motion of the water.

"Frances, you need to be an adult. Man up and go figure this out."

"Did you tell me to man up? Seriously?"

"You know what I mean. Get out there and continue to make mis-takes. The important thing is to remember to laugh. Call Cheryl and Winter and apologize for being a donkey's behind." Dana stood and picked up her chair. Lulu stretched and slowly walked over to Dana's side, knowing that it was time to go. "Ta ta," Dana said and was halfway back to her backyard gate before Frances moved her legs out in front of her, laying back and soaking in the sun. What did she want? Was it the kiss? Was it the fact that she was finally being faced with the reali-ty of what she had been trying to suppress without consciously know-ing that was it. Would she go to hell for what she desired? Would her family disown her? Frances sighed as the family separation had started over her openly declaring she was now a painter and not the kind that paints the exterior of houses.

Another hour had passed with Frances sitting on the point watching the traffic build to a crawl on the San Rafael Bridge. A couple of crew boats from the Marin rowing club were making their way toward the open water of the bay. Pelicans were flying in formation inches above the undulating surface of the bay. Her thoughts came and went like the breeze. She wondered why she didn't tell Dana about the painting she had completed. Or what had happened with Ethan.

Why does one's sexuality matter? Her friends were clearly fine with it. They set her up on an amazing date with a woman. Poor woman. The news spewed the rhetoric of those who, for some reason, were fascinated with the love of the same sex. Why? How did her loving a woman impact anyone else? Her aunt had married a man from Ethiopia and her family had ex-communicated her. Why? Because his skin was the darkest brown and her aunt was pale and blonde. Her cousins were gorgeous people, and they dealt with prejudice from every direction.

Frances took off her boots and socks, allowing her toes to sink into the soft grass. Cheryl had commented on more than one occasion that the music and tea selection that Frances harbored screamed "lesbian." Why? Today, people all over the world were out and open about whom they loved. States were even allowing gay marriages. That words have more than one meaning made her giggle because "gay" was used in place of "happy" by her Grangran. Yes, marriage should be gay. Does that mean straight people aren't happy when they marry? Frances knew she wasn't exactly happy at her own wedding.

Taken out of her thoughts by her phone, Frances was surprised to see that Dana was calling.

"Get yourself home. We are showing up to confront you about your silly little silent treatment."

Frances tucked her phone in her pocket because Dana had said her words and hung up. Frances slowly picked up her socks and got her feet corralled back into her boots. A deep breath and Frances was doing what she was told. Then her phone rang again. She almost missed the call trying to get the phone back out of her pocket.

"Hang on, and you can give me a ride. We have to stop at Mollie Stone's so I can pick a couple items up," Dana said.

CHAPTER TWENTY-SEVEN
THE WATCH

T HE fog was starting to digest the top floors of the office buildings Ethan could see from the front seat of his latest junkyard car zombie creation. He had been parked on a side street a block away from Frances's loft since three in the morning. He clicked from camera to camera in her loft, frustrated that he had fallen asleep and not seen her leave. Where had she gone? Why did she sit on the floor of her closet for so long? Ethan felt an ache at the back of his throat that would not go away. His phone rang, pulling at his attention. It stopped, and he went back to flicking through the camera feeds. The phone broke the silence again. He looked at the phone and saw that it was Emily; he knew she wouldn't stop this calling pattern until he answered. He would not put it past her to try and hack his phone to find out where he was and decided it was better to deal with her now.

"What?" he asked, unable to control his voice.

"Hello to you too. Where did you go? I was at your art opening and guess what? The artist was not to be found," Emily said, giving him her best fuck-you voice.

"You owe me. I went on a date with Frances."

"Noooooooo. You did? Why didn't you call and tell me or at least text a picture?"

"It didn't end well."

"What do you mean?"

"Talk later. I'm busy."

"Sure."

Ethan turned his phone off and focused back on his camera feed from the inside of Frances's loft. He studied the painting that she had on her easel. When she had first started, he thought she seemed so directionless and was drifting with a mess across the canvas. He had hoped he was the instigator of that energy she demonstrated as she painted. Ethan felt her in his soul, knowing she was his, a gift from his mother. He was so thirsty to taste Frances. There was something familiar about the way she laughed and talked when they were together. He had thought it would only be an issue of her working through the time of her divorce. After that, she would come running into his arms and be all his. Like the others though, he knew his mother would not want him to get stale. The visions in his head showed him that Frances would be spectacular in film.

Only, Frances had not come running to him. She talked about being set up on a date with a woman, and that she was hiding from her family. He didn't invite her to his show on purpose, and it worked. She was a little angry that she had not gotten an invitation. Did that mean she cared? Did she miss seeing him? He closed his eyes and let his mind swim through the memory of touching her arm, of catching the smell of her shampoo as they walked through Nathan's gallery. The way her breath felt as she whispered into his ear about a person she found attractive at the art opening. It wasn't him.

"Frances, you need to know that I would've killed for you. Now you make me hunt you," Ethan said.

What happened to being the hunter who calmly waited for his prey? It was something that he had rehearsed and found worked best when he let the prey come into his trap before he struck for the eternity he craved. Ethan paused, recalling how Frances's eyes shone at the shock of his strength. It had made him excited, and he felt his erection growing harder as he thought back over the course of that night. I am your guardian angel. I am going to save you from this life. She was his. Her eyes were the color of his sea, and her body the shape of the sand dunes that he was seeking for comfort.

His computer pinged as Frances and Dana entered the loft. Ethan gripped his steering wheel and unzipped his pants as he watched his Frances unpack some groceries. It was all he could do not to jump out of the car and take her, driving himself deep inside her, letting her discover his world.

CHAPTER TWENTY-EIGHT
BUENA VISTA IRISH COFFEE CLUB

C HERYL, Winter, Russell, and Simon sat at the very last large round table at the back of the Buena Vista. The crew was working on their second Irish coffee of the early afternoon. The Buena Vista had become the normal standing room–only tourist destination, making conversation difficult.

"I'm so happy the gang is all back together, and crazy Frances is up to her usual strangeness," Winter said, hugging Simon around his neck before sitting in the empty chair next to him.

"It was touch and go. Thank god Dana played mediator and decided to make her way to the City. Dana called Frances on her shit and told her to apologize. Nothing like a high school teacher to crack the whip," Cheryl said.

"Where is she? She set the time for this Saturday's meetup and she's late," Simon asked, checking his watch again. Fortunately, they had snagged a table on the window side. From the window, they had prime viewing of the cable car line that now snaked around the barriers set up to contain the masses who had to do the San Francisco Rice-A-Roni trip. This table also had a good view of the Buena Vista crowd and the long, ornate bar that ran almost the whole length of the narrow restaurant. They loved adding strangers to the mix and learning about the myths of the city those visitors carried with them. It was a good spot for locals and tourists to mingle.

"Do you think she survived last night?" Cheryl asked as she ordered a third round of Irish coffees for the table.

"She has more guts than I do, doing that speed dating thing again," Simon said as he eyed a tall man with a well-groomed beard standing alone at the bar. Simon quickly held up his fork and pointed in the direction of a couple wearing matching Golden Gate Bridge sweatshirts in an obnoxious 1970s orange color. Winter followed with a knife, putting an end to this round of Darwin Pool. Cheryl thought the game was rather cruel, but she soon joined when Winter and Russell came up with the game in order to openly fawn over an Adonis they deemed eye candy one Saturday.

Their scoring system was easy and hid from anyone what they were doing. A lifted spoon casually pointed in the direction of a person meant that person was someone you wanted to spoon in bed and more. It was the highest compliment. A knife meant that the person, or in some cases, groups of people, had to be cut out directly. A fork required a vote of the group. If the person or group was to be saved, everyone drank a sip. Should a tie happen, the deciding factors were the salt and pepper shakers. Salt directed that they were to be tossed. Pepper meant the person was saved to the gene pool but kicked out of the silverware drawer. The worst possible thing would be to have anyone notice them playing the game. If that happened, the offending player must cover the tab for the morning. No one had been caught yet.

"How many dates has she gone on now?" Winter asked, picking up a spoon and pointing to a cyclist out the window.

"Who knew you unleashed a monster? I think she said there were going to be forty people at the speed dating thing last night."

"Does that mean she can say she's been out on about thirty-nine dates?" Simon, always the logical and pragmatic thinker when it came to dates, asked.

"No. I did not go out on thirty-nine dates, and they need to rename speed dating 'torture dating,'" Frances said as she sat down.

"Thanks for finally showing up—you set this meeting of the BVICC. And where is your shirt? If I'm wearing this tent of a shirt, you had better wears yours, missy." Simon pointed to his chest when he saw that Frances was wearing a rather wrinkled suit jacket.

"You didn't wear a suit to the speed dating event, did you?" Winter asked, looking rather horrified over Frances's latest fashion don't. "You would wear black stockings and sandals on vacation, wouldn't you?" The table burst into laughter, mostly because they knew that Winter was likely correct.

"Walk of shame?" Cheryl asked with her eyebrows reaching the top of her forehead. "Spill the beans."

It was no use for Frances to try and make up a story. Her face instantly flushed with Cheryl's question. "Let me order an Irish coffee first."

"Ohhhhh—you got some, didn't you, girlfriend?" Russell snapped his fingers in the air and high-fived Winter.

"Relax, everyone. I—"

"She did it! Was it with a woman?" Winter asked.

"Her face is practically the color of a steamed lobster," Cheryl said as she picked up a menu looking for food.

"I spent time with someone—" Frances said but was cut off before she could say another word.

"Nailed it. Our work here is done. The student has morphed into a dating adult." Winter stood and tried to get the others to leave with her.

"Sit down. I want details now. Dish it up, sister." Russell leaned forward, ready for the juicy details of what they all believed to be Frances's first real triple-X date with a woman.

"Well, after the torture of speed dating where a whole host of characters picked straight from the freaks and geeks catalogue—"

"You know, you were there too, Franny, so don't be so quick to judge," Simon said.

"Understood. I was walking to the Hyatt to catch a cab home because my phone was out of juice and I couldn't get Uber. You know, it is so much easier to get a cab from a hotel in this city."

"Not important. This person? A man or woman was not one of the freaks or geeks from the speed dating?" Winter asked.

"I ran into her trying to get through the revolving door at the Hyatt."

"Oh no. Not another F.O.K. point of gracefulness. And a woman. Yup. Nailed it." Winter shook her head and laughed at the image and high-fived with Russell.

"A high five? Seriously...this is not a sporting event. Continue, Franny," Simon said.

"She was coming back from a long work day and was carrying a banker's box while I was trying to dodge the glass panels of the rather fast revolving door. I backed into her, causing her to drop her box of papers. Our eyes met over me trying to help her pick up the freed paper birds. Those things fluttered all over the place. I have no clue if we recaptured all of them."

"How does one back into a person going through a revolving door?" Cheryl asked.

"Again. Useless boring details—get to the good stuff," Russell said.

"Take a breath, Russell. I am getting to the good stuff. I asked her if I could buy her a drink for the trouble I caused. And she said—"

"Yes. We got that much. How did you jump the canyon of moral mixed-up shit that had you running from one woman who was well-vetted by your friends when she kisses you on the lips in a restaurant, to asking a stranger out for a drink, to the walk of shame today?" Cheryl asked.

"Rough crowd. We went to the bar and we ordered a drink and talked. I lost track of time and realized that there were some sparks. She asked me if I wanted a night cap in her room, and the rest is history."

"Nope. That is not history. We are going to get you at least three or four Irish coffees and some food and you are going to go through it step-by-step. Was it everything you imagined?" Russell stood and went to the bar before Frances could raise any objections.

"Was it different?" Winter asked.

"Yes. And this time confirmed what I had already known," Frances said.

"Oh my god, you are not going to make us pry it out of you. You have been holding out on us, F.O.K. How could I have missed this? Not going to let you leave here until you tell us everything," Cheryl said.

Before Frances could answer, all the color drained out of her face as her eyes locked upon one person she did not want to see—Ethan. Winter followed her gaze and, not understanding, waved Ethan over to the table. Behind Ethan trailed a young, beautiful, very fit woman. Frances saw the flirter recently buried inside Winter reawaken as she flipped her hair over her shoulder when Ethan approached. Winter had always said she had a crush on Ethan, with his tall stature and anti-establishment look.

Frances swallowed hard and took the last gulp of her Irish coffee. She had so many emotions running around in her brain that she did not know how to tackle them herself. No one at the table knew that Ethan had tried to rape her. Was it really that bad? Shit. Was she now downgrading it to have only been a misunderstanding between friends? It shook her to her core, and the voice in her head was yelling to get up and run. Frances vaguely recognized the woman but couldn't remember her name. Who was she? She remembered noticing her at Ethan's studio space. Why was she with him, and why did he decide to join the BVICC today? He had always sworn it off as stupid before. Frances came around when Winter kicked her under the table after everyone else had finished with their own introductions to Ethan's friend.

"Hey, Frances, you've met my best buddy from high school before—do you remember? Everyone else met Emily while you were off mind-surfing again," Ethan said.

Frances's ears went numb as Ethan's lips moved. Emily stood awkwardly behind Ethan and looked like she was ready to leave as quickly as possible. The conversations were happening at the table, and Frances sat mute. Frances noticed that Emily had stopped her fidgeting and was staring unabashedly directly at her. Did she know? Had Ethan told her what had happened? How did he know she was here? God, Frances, you are so egocentric. Maybe they happened in on their own and this was only a matter of coincidence. Something deep in her gut told her it was not.

"Ethan, come join us. Frances was just telling us about her first but not her first one-night stand with a woman," Winter said and patted the empty chair next to her.

Frances was screaming in her head that it wasn't her first sexual experience with a woman, but her fear of Ethan and the fact that he was clenching his jaw over the news that Frances was out with a woman continued to keep her silent.

"Wouldn't want to impose on the group here. Emily and I were stopping in for an Irish coffee ourselves, and then we'll be off to watch the sailboats in the bay."

It was all she could do to stay seated. Frances tried to smile and rejoin the conversation. "Emily, are you into sailing?" she asked, trying to mask her shaking voice.

"Yup. I arrived to sailing late. I took a class when I first started at the Farm. I needed something to balance my toiling away in a windowless computer lab," Emily said.

The afternoon limped into the evening and the setting of the sun. The group had lost count of how many rounds they had downed. Winter and Cheryl had decided to share a ride back to the loft with Frances and the boys. Frances was relieved that she wouldn't be alone, and it wasn't until she stood outside in the cool air that she breathed again. She dared not turn to look at the restaurant. She already knew the answer. Ethan was watching her every move.

"Wow, Emily is a hottie," Winter said as Russell and Simon argued over who was going to ride in back with the girls. "What did you think, Frances? And don't think you are off the hook over your one-night stand."

"I don't need to report anything right now," Frances said.

Frances watched the cityscape as the ride took them past the quieting streets of the Financial District and into the land of lofts and rebuilding that had struck the City over the past year south of the Giants ballpark. What was she going to do? Ethan was going to keep popping up in her life. She felt that he was playing with her, much like a cat plays with a mouse. A shiver ran down her spine, and she pulled her messenger bag closer to her as she tried to hide her fears from herself.

CHAPTER TWENTY-NINE
ETHAN ON THE HUNT

A new reserve of energy pumped through Frances as she power walked the path along the bay at Fort Mason. It was a perfect morning. The Golden Gate Bridge looked like it was illuminated from within in the early morning sun. A couple of dogs ran, chasing tennis balls hit almost the full length of the green grass by a man using a tennis racket. Smart way to tire a dog, Frances thought to herself. Something she must remember when taking a wild Winston out for a play date.

Frances stopped to watch a golden Lab and a pup that looked to be a mixed mutt on the run, tongues hanging out, competing for the round yellow ball. The Lab made it to the ball first and skidded to a stop. She pounced on the ball, snatching it up in her mouth. A couple of steps later, the Lab stopped and the mutt took hold of the ball easily from the Lab's mouth, running it back to the man twirling the tennis racket. The play started all over again.

Frances returned to her walk and felt a twinge of sadness as she remembered her walks with Riley. They fully explored the best parks of San Francisco and what the surrounding places had to offer—hiking, running in fields, and playing on beaches. It was during a walk with Riley when a woman walking her dog along the beach first approached her. Frances thought about how the conversation had evolved from the dogs to how beautiful the beach was to how the woman had noticed both Riley and Frances before. When she asked Frances if she wanted to get coffee, Frances thought the woman was being friendly. Then, when the woman saw her wedding ring, she came up with an excuse as to why she had to leave. At the time, Frances thought it was weird. Now she understood.

Today, it felt like the world stood still as she soaked up the beauty of the bay. It spread out in front of her, the water a dark steel-blue gray reflecting the last of the pink sunrise. Whitecaps on the bay showed the wind was coming from the south as they curled over and were re-absorbed into the inky darkness of the cold waters that swirled around Alcatraz Island. She was on the lookout for seals playing in the bay but was not lucky spotting one yet. A young couple stopped to take pictures with their mobile phones of the Golden Gate Bridge. Frances smiled as she passed them, thinking it was a very dramatic picture-taking type of day.

Her sweatshirt pocket started to simultaneously sing and vibrate with a call. She was excited for the excuse to take a seat and chat—maybe it was Brice calling her back with the latest comedy caused by her nephews. Frances quickly pulled out her phone and stopped as she saw the caller ID. Ethan's face filled her screen. The sight of his dark eyes made her cringe. He had acted so strange trying to act so normal at the Buena Vista. Frances's hair stood up on the back of her neck. The prickles crawling across her skin were warning her but she decided to ignore them. She could handle herself. He was on the phone, not here in person. She bit her lower lip and answered.

"Hi, Ethan."

"Frances, I am so glad you answered. Listen, don't say anything—this is not easy."

Frances shivered as she continued to watch the surface of the bay. Something inside her told that Ethan was close. Frances quieted the voice and told herself that she was being paranoid. There would be no way that Ethan could be watching her. It was more of her Frances-centric self-delusion, Dana would say.

"I don't know what to say," Frances said.

"The night of my art opening, I thought you were ready for me. I get it. You want to play around and figure some things out."

As Ethan spoke, Frances had an image cross her mind of him standing right behind her. She turned around slowly and breathed a sigh of relief when she saw only the trio still chasing the tennis ball. Her gaze went past them to the now crowded parking lot and glanced over the cars. She did not see Ethan sitting in the passenger seat of his Frankenstein Cadillac watching her through a high-powered rifle scope.

"Ethan—"

"I know you are dating women now. That was made completely clear at the Buena Vista."

Frances wanted to hang up on him as the quiet, smooth tones in Ethan's voice made her skin scream out in pain with sharp needle pricks. This was not what she wanted from him at all. How could she solve this? She knew him as a friend. Not anything more. "Ethan, you need to listen."

"You are not listening to me. You need to listen. This is your fault but I will forgive you. To prove it, and hopefully make it up to you, I'm going to help you out. I have set you up on a date with a good friend of mine. This woman is special, and I know you both would hit it off. She runs a little cafe close to Chestnut and Fillmore. I set the date up for a late lunch at one o'clock on Thursday."

Frances put the phone down in her lap. She was not sure what to do. Ethan's voice sounded strange, and she felt him tossing her about, blaming her for what happened the night of his opening. He was trying to control her. Hang up on him now.

"Why are you silent? I said I was forgiving you," Ethan said.

Frances still held the phone down in her lap, letting the distance and his voice stay away from her for the moment as she tried to think through what was going on in this relationship. There was an agenda behind all of this, his showing up with Emily at the Buena Vista and being overly charming to everyone. And now he was setting her up on a blind date?

"Ethan, I am not going on any more blind dates. You heard about what happened to me at Meadow when the girls did the blind date thing. I did nothing to you to blame me for you pushing me up against the wall and ripping my dress. If Nathan had not come out, what were you going to do?" Frances gripped her phone so hard, she was worried she was going to crush it with her hand as it started to shake.

"Frances, you clearly don't understand how you've used me. If you'd stop pulling your phone away from your ear and listen, you would see. The last thing I want to do is scare you. This is an offer of truce and apology, and it isn't a blind date. You met her at the opening. She was the woman in the blue suit. She's interested in you."

"You totally freaked me out, and then when you showed up at the Buena, I was floored. You showed up there after you assaulted me. I don't understand you." Frances sat up straighter. She started to look around the park again and at the people on the walkway. The voice inside her was telling her to get up and run to the nearest police officer.

"I wanted to apologize, but it was strange with Winter and everyone else there."

"What did you think? I would go there alone? Ethan, you're more than screwed up and need to get some help. I am—"

"Frances, don't punish Beth. Please go meet her." Ethan continued to watch Frances as she sat on the bench.

Frances felt boxed in by this conversation. Ethan was twisting her mind and trying to get her to say she would do what he wanted. Maybe it would be better if she said she was going to do what he wanted. It would give her time. Her instincts were telling her that he was at the park and she needed to get away from there.

"Text me the address. I haven't told anyone about what happened, in case you're wondering." Frances was trying to end the call and not incite any suspicion in Ethan.

"I figured you hadn't because Simon and Russell probably would have pummeled me. They are very protective of you—same for their dog. He sure barks a lot when people come over."

Frances pulled the phone away from her ear again and stared at it. Had she said something about Winston to Ethan? She couldn't remember. She must have talked about him, but this was the third comment that struck her silent.

"Gotta go—" Frances didn't wait for a response and ended the call.

She didn't know that Ethan continued to watch her as she sat on the bench with her arms crossed. Her body started to shake. She was unsure of what to do next. She knew that she had to leave the park.

Would the police even understand what was going on here? A fear gripped her and tears fell, her emotions bundling into a dark space she had never known before. Ethan was so much stronger than she had realized. She rubbed her bicep where his fingers had temporarily tattooed their imprints into the surface of her skin.

CHAPTER THIRTY
PROCRASTINATION POTLUCK

T ONIGHT, Frances thought, was going to be a way to relax and let off some steam with her closest friends. She was thrilled that Dana was going to be joining them tonight. It was one of the disadvantages of having moved away from San Quentin Village that she didn't get to hang out with her as much. Frances walked around her loft and realized that Winter had done it again. She had decided that it was time for a procrastination potluck and had chosen Frances's loft. What a bunch of bull about it being Frances's turn. The last two potlucks were held at the loft. Frances turned in a slow circle as she took in the current state of mess in her place, and it was a level four on a five-level scale. Five required shutting the door and setting the place on fire because it was so messy.

The piles of paint tubes, brushes, and wadded-up oil rags took up much of her working space. In the center of the loft stood the piano that normally had nothing on it as Frances loved to play with the top open. Right now, it supported two piles of clean but unfolded laundry. The kitchen was the only place that appeared somewhat clean. Newspapers, blankets, a sweatshirt tower, and magazines took over the main sitting area.

The group had all jumped on this procrastination potluck concept when Winter had proposed it. She got the rest of the group to buy in easily on her idea to fight the work fatigue. She had created the rules of freedom for the night, where they scheduled a no phones, no electronics, and no expectations meetup. The rules were intense as it forced them to give up whatever plans, if they weren't tickets to something, to get together and eat, unplug, and revolt against the "dream." Basically, Winter was burned out and needed some social time away from the firm.

Frances sat at her piano and started playing some Broadway show tunes from her big book of Gilbert and Sullivan hits. She knew that the notes filtered into the boys' loft like hurricane winds and would blow two handy maids over to her place shortly. A wicked smile crossed Frances's face as she knew exactly what she was doing; she was being the siren at the piano. It was probably good the two loads of laundry muffled the sound a little because she could have more gay men than she wanted to show up for the Broadway tunes sing-along.

As she started into a very loud rendition of "I Am the Very Model of a Modern Major-General," she heard the knocking and then a key turning in her door as Russell burst through in full voice.

"I love this musical. It's one of my all-time favorites," Russell said as he shut the door behind Simon and Winston.

"She knew that, Russell—I think I'll unleash the hounds for this snaring of us," Simon said and took his hand off Winston's collar. Free from the boys, he took three large loping steps over to Frances and licked her face like she had covered it in bacon.

"Welcome, boys. I was wondering if you wanted to waste some time helping me straighten up before tonight's potluck?" Frances tried to keep the smile off her face while she watched them gauge the amount of work it would require. She managed to get Winston to settle down next to her as she wiped his slobber off her face.

"On one condition," Russell said as he started to pick up the newspapers that had covered her table. "You play the score from *Into the Woods.*"

That was all Frances needed to hear. She replaced her big book of Broadway with the full sheet music for the movie version of *Into the Woods* and started at the beginning. It really didn't matter that she cut some corners on the notes—she followed the music well enough to get them humming along. Frances let herself focus on the music and tried not to watch the cleaning fairies turn her place from offensive to comfortable. The playing took her back to her days in college and graduate school when she would pick up gigs playing everything from weddings to late night lounge lizard hours at various bars. As she worked her way through "Agony," both Simon and Russell joined her at the piano and belted out the lyrics like they were on stage themselves. Fortunately, both had amazing voices that matched their well-sculpted male bodies. Frances exhaled, grateful that she had really hit the gay neighbor jackpot with these two.

"What if we broke up this little sing-along with some *Les Miserables*?" Frances said as she seamlessly transitioned into one of her favorite numbers from *Les Mis*. Russell stopped cleaning and focused on "A Little Fall of Rain." Her tears were falling as the last note was struck and the damper pedal allowed the piano wire to match the softening tone of Russell's voice.

"Okay, you two mushy Queens—and that is with a capital Q—we need to get some upbeat music going in here. Tears in the eyes make it hard to clean. Find something fun to play. I know, Ms. Franny, play something from my all-time favorite musical." Simon grabbed a stack of papers and took them over to an empty spot he found on a shelf.

Frances started to play around with some notes on her piano, trying to jog loose the score for "Gravity" from *Wicked*. Simon came to her rescue by finding it on her iPad and setting the electronic sheet music in front of her. She dove into the song with gusto, and the boys sang while they cleaned. The end of the song morphed into "It's a Hard Knock Life" from *Annie*.

"Enough. You are not going to play that wretched song. It will have us all—"

"Don't even say the word, Russell—let it go. Uh-oh." Simon knew he had done it. They all had gone to the early showing of *Frozen*, where the little three-foot-tall miniature people screamed the songs at the top of their lungs. It was too late; Frances was already into the song, and Russell was screaming it in his best imitation of a five-year-old child with no volume control.

"Oh, now that was fun. But I need to decide what I'm going to contribute to the feast tonight. Time for the canned tunes," Frances announced as she walked over and hit play on her now ancient iPod. Frances opened her pantry, an old armoire she had rehabbed in the loft. It had worked and she liked the fact that she did not have to bend over to get into a low kitchen shelf. Plus, it was a unique piece she had found at an estate sale for thirty-five dollars and—once it was sanded, repaired, and stained a dark black walnut color—it looked handsome to her.

Her fridge held the perfect answer: a dish she knew she could easily whip up. A roasted veggie frittata would do the trick nicely. She had the makings for brilliant chocolate ice cream. Perfect, she said to herself, and she started to gather the ingredients for the ice cream first: eggs, heavy cream, sugar, and the most amazing Belgium semisweet baking chocolate. Frances found herself humming along with the music as Simon and Russell moved through her loft putting finishing touches on their cleaning creation.

"You know, the difference between your style of cleaning and mine means no overstuffed drawers, and my bed is not higher due to the number of items I've tried to hide under it. Everything is in order and it smells so fresh, like a field of flowers."

"Frances, we've been over this. You know what our secret is about everything having a place. I'm done lecturing you. You have the same cleaning products that we do. I know because we gifted them to you. Use them and you too can always have this spring rain field smell. Oh, and Russell brought over our Lampe Berger and lit a candle in your bathroom."

"Come on, Simon, we need to feed Winston and run to the store. You are on your own, Franny."

"Thank you," Frances responded as she stirred her ice cream custard base on the stove. She was looking for it to coat the back of her wooden spoon, a critical point in the timing of it all. A quick glance at her clock let her know that she had at least an hour before the brave souls of procrastination potluck would descend. Before she got to another thought, her door burst open and in walked Cheryl carrying a cheesecake from Harvest Eddie's and some Philly cheesesteaks from Jay's on 23rd. The smell of Jay's original sauce was mouthwatering.

"I have got to change the lock on my door. It appears that everyone has anytime access. Whatever happened to knocking and waiting to be invited in? Guess none of you are vampires. At first, I was going to say you're early, but you are forgiven because of the Philly cheesesteaks. Did you bring fries too?"

"Of course. I came early to help you clean up and to make sure there are places to sit down this time that are paint free. However, I see you are either an alien impersonating my friend or you have turned over a new leaf and are now overly neat." Frances watched as Cheryl walked around the loft and sniffed the air, much the way a hound would try to ferret out a squirrel. "The air smells...this is familiar...Russell and Simon the cleaning elves were here."

The two burst into laughter, and Frances went and retrieved the ice from the freezer so Cheryl could get to work on making her famous on-the-rocks margaritas. As they worked in the kitchen, focused on their tasks at hand, Frances felt strange. She looked at Cheryl, but Cheryl was busy juicing the limes she had brought with her. Frances shook her head to try and shake the feelings and went back to chopping vegetables for her egg creation. She needed to tell someone about Ethan, the gallery, the call, and her fears.

"Music stopped—I'm going to pick something a little more "dinner party." Enough of this female alternative contemporary angst music."

"Hey, I love Adele and so does the rest of the world," Frances said as she defended her playlist. "No electronic house music either. This is a classy loft, not a night club or rave."

Frances was at the stove with her back to the door, and Cheryl had picked out a jazz playlist that filled the loft with the sounds of trumpets, Ella, and warmth. With the music and sounds of ice being crushed for margaritas, Frances did not hear Dana and Winter enter the apartment. It was a game among them, scaring Frances, as it was so easy. Dana and Winter softly walked over and stood directly behind Frances, waiting. Frances, focused on sautéing onions and garlic, did not hear the two frozen statues standing behind her. When she turned to get the mushrooms from her chopping board, she screamed and threw her stirring spoon into the air.

Three of them burst into laughter. Frances tried to cover up that they had scared the crap out of her and pushed her tears back. Overly freaked out due to the new Ethan she was getting to know, she tried to shake the creepy feelings off with forced laughter. Maybe she should ask Cheryl what she thought about it. Before she could though, the festivities had started for the procrastination potluck.

"Time for a toast." Cheryl handed out her famous margaritas to each one of them and they held their glasses together, clinking in time to the current song filling the loft. "One for all and all for the SF Giants!" Cheryl took a sip and looked pleased with this batch of her signature drink. The doorbell rang and Frances looked at the clock.

"Did someone forget to tell me this was arrive early day? I would like to point out that they are using the doorbell. Hey, Winter, get the door."

Frances returned to her work at the stove, and it looked like she had grown two more hands as she chopped, whisked, and mixed everything into a beautiful blue pan, a pan that she had fallen in love with at first sight. It made a good story so she ran with it. The pan came from what had become one of her favorite kitchen stores hidden out in the hills east of Sacramento. When she walked into The Big Little Kitchen store one hot summer afternoon after wine tasting in the gold country region, she knew that this pan fell into her hands—due to Frances running into the display. Frances, focused on getting the frittata into the oven, did not catch who had arrived until she stood up and turned directly into Ethan, causing her to scream so loudly it silenced all conversation in the loft.

"I didn't mean to scare you," Ethan said.

"It's okay. She's been jumpy tonight and you are not the first one to get that response," Cheryl said as she started pouring a few more drinks for the new arrivals.

"Frances, I hope it is okay that I brought Emily and a friend of hers from her lab." Ethan took a drink from Cheryl.

"Ethan, you never show up to these. Why are you here?"

"Frances, you know the rules, the more the merrier or something like that," Winter said, a little surprised by Frances's coldness toward Ethan.

"Excuse me a moment—I need to get a spice and ice from next door." Frances grabbed Cheryl's wrist and pulled her with her as she practically sprinted out the door, slamming it behind them.

"What gives? That was rude," Cheryl said as she rubbed her wrist.

"I need to tell someone before I explode. You have got to keep this private. There is a feeling I get about Ethan that is not—I think he thinks I am his."

"What? There is something going on between you two but I think that is an odd statement." Cheryl stood with her arms crossed.

"I went to his art opening, and—"

"Hey, ladies," Russell said as he came up and hugged them both at the same time. Frances shot Cheryl a look that silenced any follow-up questions as the three of them walked into the loft.

"Cool, Ethan, I like the eyeliner," Russell said as he came in and took a sip out of Winter's drink. "Who brought the fresh meat?"

"Stop it, Russell, or I am going to send you home. Those are friends of Ethan's. Emily and Vanessa," Dana said as she ate another handful of fries.

"Welcome to procrastination potluck where we eat and play games. I get dibs on Emily; I understand she is in grad school at Stanford," Russell said while he stole another sip of Winter's drink.

"Go get your own drink. Is that true? You're really at Stanford?" Winter asked. "I thought you all were pulling my leg at the Buena Vista."

"Yes. So is Vanessa—she works in my lab helping me crunch the numbers," Emily said as she opened a can of Guinness and poured it into a glass she had helped herself to from the cupboard. The action was not lost on Frances. She could not stop watching Emily. It was a distraction from trying not to notice Ethan.

"Winter, you can be such a snob. I can smell my creation cooking, and it's almost time to feast. Anyone late to the party will have to fend for themselves," Frances said and helped Dana and Cheryl finish getting the mishmash of food, plates, and everything else they would need for a night of feasting. As she moved around her loft, making sure the guests were finding what they needed and avoiding Ethan, Frances could not shake a couple of things that were causing her to worry. First, was Ethan stalking her? She knew the answer to her own question. And second, how come she could not stop blatantly staring at Emily? Her short hallway chat with Cheryl added to the bizarre evening because Cheryl kept trying to corner Frances as she ran around playing hostess in a way no one had witnessed before.

"Winter, didn't you go to Stanford once upon a time?" Ethan asked as he took his first few bites of food from his filled plate.

"Stuff it, Ethan. No one wants to talk school. What game are we starting with tonight?" Winter asked. She usually never ate much, but tonight she was plowing through her plate like it was the first time she had eaten in days. Frances found herself laughing a little too easily as the conversations finally flowed into an effortless cadence. She made sure to sit on the couch next to Emily and away from Ethan. The evening went into its third hour, and people were filled with food, drink, and decadent desserts. Winston was brought over to join the fun and to keep him from barking and annoying the senior couple who lived below the boys. He had taken over the chaise lounge. Vanessa had found a fondness for the dog and tried to make him share it with her. Frances figured that Ethan had brought Vanessa to try and make her jealous. He had been giving her a lot of attention, but from Vanessa's reaction, it was not wanted. Dana was talking with Russell and Cheryl about the latest developments in her garden.

The music had stopped, and Frances needed to change things up; she went to the piano and started to play whatever came to mind. It was one of her own creations because she did not want the boys to break into song. She relaxed a little but still felt some uncomfortable energies rolling off Ethan toward her. She would have to follow up with Cheryl. She couldn't talk to Winter about it because she knew that Winter, for whatever reason, had a hot crush on Ethan and would most likely defend him.

Frances had seen Simon exit the loft and figured he wanted privacy at home to use his own restroom. He did that type of thing often, leaving to go use his own toilet. She appreciated him being so weird that way. She wondered what he did if they were far from home. As she was finishing up with the melody, she felt Emily touch her shoulder first and then slide in next to her on the piano bench.

"Don't stop playing. Your music is beautiful. I don't recognize it. What's it from?" Emily asked Frances, who was having a hard time comprehending what she heard. When it finally clicked in her mind, Frances was unable to form words and turned back to the piano keys, starting something new. She felt Emily's leg touching hers and the soft smell of her perfume. It reminded her of sandalwood, cinnamon, and vanilla. The aroma was yummy and Frances wanted more. She knew that from this vantage point, Emily could see into the area of her loft where she painted. One of the things Frances had done was move her paintings and cover them to keep as private as she could. Emily got up and went straight to the revealing painting that Frances had just completed.

The cat was out of the bag when Russell had followed Emily into the land the boys knew they could not enter. Frances felt her heart rate increase as both Russell and Emily stood silent, held captivated by the woman on the canvas looking back at them.

"Simon, you need to see this," Russell said, almost choking over his own words.

Frances stopped playing and went over to the three of them, as she was trying to pull the sheet back in place to cover her painting and herself. Emily stopped her by touching her hand, and their eyes locked.

"Frances, that is …" Simon couldn't speak anymore.

"What do you call it?" Emily asked in a whisper, placing her hands on Frances's shoulders.

"Me," Frances said.

"Enough!" Ethan shouted from the kitchen. The anger in his voice silenced all conversation in the loft for a second time that night. Winston raised his head from his snooze on the chaise lounge. Emily could feel Frances shiver as Ethan approached.

"I am not going to let this happen. You have a date with a woman your own age next week," Ethan continued to shout as he grabbed Emily and pulled her away from Frances.

"Ethan, what are you talking about?" Frances said, surprised at her own force.

Cheryl had come to stand next to Frances, and the boys were ready to pounce. At this point, Frances was ready to let everyone in the loft know about Ethan's violent behavior toward her at his art opening. The hair on the back of her neck was on edge as Ethan's face took on a demonic darkness, his eyes looking like they were completely black.

The field of tension eased when Emily hauled off and hit Ethan with an open-handed blow to his chest, which caused him to fall back and let go of her arm. Simon and Russell did not lose a second and had Ethan up on his feet, hauling him toward the door.

"I'm sorry. I didn't mean—Frances, I am here to protect you," Ethan stammered as he twisted against the iron-clad grip that both Simon and Russell had on him. Frances watched and was relieved that their muscles were real and not only for show. She felt herself wanting to hide from the group. Emily came over and put her arm around a very shaken Frances.

"Leave. If you come back here, I will call the police," Russell said between clenched teeth.

"Relax. Cool down, man. I'm not going to do anything." Ethan smiled and left.

CHAPTER THIRTY-ONE
PARTY DEATH

SILENCE continued over the group of the once lively loft party. Frances retreated to the one area of privacy in her loft, the bathroom, shutting herself away from the stunned astonishment going on in her loft. Emily sat down on the couch and let Winston try to crawl into her lap. He had gotten his head and chest on her before Simon made him get down. It gave everyone in the room something else to focus upon, as the air was heavy with uncertainty. Winter poured herself a fresh glass of wine and surveyed the drama that rested on the faces of the once merry crowd.

"Ethan was totally out of control. What do you think that was about?" Winter asked. The group all focused their gaze upon Emily. Frances heard the question through the bathroom door and wanted to rush out. It was unfair to focus on the young woman because none of them knew that Ethan was staking a claim on her. None of them knew the calculated moves he was making with showing up tonight. Frances placed her head against the back of the bathroom door and tried to find the courage to let them know.

"You know she isn't looking for a lover," Winter said as she sat down across from Emily.

"Oh, really? That is news to me. Haven't we created a little dating machine?" Russell responded as he was looking over the counter filled with delectable desserts.

"Apparently, Ethan is wanting something else from Frances," Cheryl said.

"You all have no idea," Frances said as she came out of the bathroom, her face freshly scrubbed. She wanted to break her silence and tell them all about the night of the art opening. None of this was what she wanted. It was all because she was trying so hard to stop her confusion. She saw so much in the woman sitting on her couch now cross-examined by a worried Winter. She had been married to a man and part of the "establishment" but had been so unhappy in that situation. Was it her? Other people seemed to work it out.

"Are you okay? That whole thing was scary," Simon said, quickly jumping up and offering his seat to Frances.

"Where do I start? Ethan is not what he appears to be." Frances took the glass of wine from Winter's hand and took a long, slow sip. She let her gaze find Emily, who was looking down at Winston and avoiding eye contact with anyone at that moment.

"Emily, aren't you Ethan's bestie? What's the story?" Cheryl was now standing behind Frances and appeared ready to pounce on the thread that Winter had started. "You know, it was strange that you and Ethan showed up here tonight."

"Cheryl, it is not. Would you lay off Emily? She is not responsible for Ethan's behavior. He—"

"Frances, what is it you are not telling us?" Winter was now locking her friend under her laser-truth focus.

Frances rose from her chair and walked over to Emily, putting her hand out. Emily accepted and rose to stand, accepting the embrace of Frances's open arms.

"I'm sorry about all of this, Frances," Emily quietly whispered.

"Would you mind staying tonight?" Frances asked. Emily embraced her and hugged Frances a little tighter, and Frances knew the answer was yes.

"Hello? Frances? Did you forget we're all here?" Winter stood facing Frances with the look of a perturbed parent.

"I've had enough. I'm calling the party dead. Now, if you all would please go, that would be much appreciated," Frances said, looking only at Emily.

"This is not what this night is about. You have no right to kick—"

"Russell, time to go—get Winston," Simon said as he went and took the cheesecake and a bottle of wine off the counter. "The party will continue at our place next door for anyone who wants to join us."

"This is so wrong. I'm going with the boys." Cheryl grabbed her purse and was out the door.

Frances felt a twinge of guilt, as all she wanted was to be alone with Emily—to talk with her about everything that had happened and, more than anything, to taste her lips. It was something she could not get out of her mind. She was almost obsessed with wanting to kiss this woman. More self-delusion to avoid facing the monster that had left the scene.

With the loft empty, Frances let go of Emily's hand and walked over to her piano. It was one way for her to reconnect her body and her feelings. To play music was a way for Frances to open her feminine voice in her masculine-dominated world of searching for a perfection that no human could ever truly achieve. That was the joke, she thought to herself. We are all the same when it comes down to it. She could sense Emily watching her and was a little unsure of what to do next. She had asked her to stay. She knew what she wanted to do. The energy Frances felt from her suggested that something was going to happen soon.

"Again, the music you're playing is unknown to me," Emily said as she lightly placed a hand on Frances's shoulder.

Frances didn't answer; she just let the music pour out of her fingers. It was soft and captured a melancholy feeling as the sound left the strings. A melody soon repeated, and Emily leaned into Frances and softly bent to caress her neck. With each soft kiss along her neck, Frances let the music explode out of her and the tempo increase. Her heart was beating faster. Emily let her hands gently comb through the soft red hair that had plagued Frances as a child. The tenderness in Emily's touch was pulsing so loudly through Frances's body that it was all she could do to continue playing the piano—this felt so good she didn't want Emily to stop.

Frances stood, taking Emily into her arms. Then she pressed her soft lips against Emily's with a desire that came from deep within. Emily didn't object, and the two fell into the dance of their first kiss that held all the violence and softness of the evening. The flicker of car lights from the street silhouetted the shadow of their embrace on the ceiling. Frances broke the embrace to breathe in oxygen and to look at the woman she held in her arms.

"Is it okay? I know you're not looking for a relationship right now," Emily said and took Frances by the hand over to the bed.

"What are you talking about? I have no clue what I'm looking for, but right now, I want to learn to play your body like I play the piano." Frances kissed Emily again and they both fell into the cloud of her down comforter. She marveled at how touching Emily made her senses shimmer and blend into the strength and softness of Emily's body against her own. Emily sat up and took off her shirt, revealing a sheer, black lace bra that brought Frances to her, lightly caressing Emily's nipples through the lace. Frances wanted to slow the unwrapping of this most amazing package, so she pulled Emily onto her body, holding her close. She took in the warmth of her skin, the roughness of her jeans, the light smells of spice.

Emily pushed Frances down and started to unbutton her blouse with a care that took Frances's breath away. It was the slight brush of her fingertips against her skin, the glint of something in her beautiful eyes. Frances craved Emily's experiences and time spent making love with women. It was both exciting and comforting. How quickly Emily revealed her heart to Frances as she felt her lips touch her neck and move down ever so slowly to the top curve of her breast. Frances was so glad she had taken Winter's advice and invested in some new lingerie; she was wearing a new bra tonight. As Emily reached behind and undid her bra with a quick twist with her left hand, Frances worried that she would not know enough to please this woman.

"Relax, Frances. I know you are still counting your encounters with women on one hand. Enjoy the newest flavor." Emily kissed Frances hard and deep, not letting her respond with words; she had worked her hand inside Frances's pants. Frances gave into the night and let Emily teach her more than she could have ever anticipated.

CHAPTER THIRTY-TWO
FRESH AIR

WINTER Keller checked her calendar again to make sure she had the place correct. Even though it did confirm she was where her schedule said she should be, she was not trusting. Her latest admin had not messed up, yet there was always a first time, and usually it was with a court hearing, not with a lunch date with friends. Winter thought about the fact that she went through admins almost as fast as she went through relationships. Could it be her? No. The revolving secretarial door had more to do with the idiots the office manager kept hiring. The previous three missed some rather important events for her and the firm. One was with the California Supreme Court. She wanted to complain to her friends but knew they would not understand and call her heartless. Winter did not want a lunch where she got lectured on her lack of feminist ideals for not supporting female idiots in the workplace.

Winter had wondered if her one admin that had opened the letter for the hearing only to promptly file it in the trash had been a spy, planted to throw the case off the rails, from the other side. Life had become so busy with trying to juggle her career, her boyfriend, and her social life with the crew now that Frances was back in full force. It was the core group of the crew that was standing her up now.

She was looking forward to lunch at Jay's Cheesesteak. Jay's, a tiny hole-in-the-wall place, was just far away enough from the Financial District and the rest of the dark-suited, ashen workers running on their respective hamster wheels. Was she here for the food or the company? Winter checked the time on her phone and decided that seven past the hour was enough time. She was going to place her order and eat before she was out of time. This was one of the few places that Winter, the mostly on-again vegan, could eat something that would fool any meat-eating human. The seitan Philly was out of this world. Maybe it was the bread or the sauce; it didn't matter. She ordered her vegan Philly and took her iced tea to the empty table next to a mural so busy and bright one could see spots for days if they looked at it too long.

"Hey, lady? Mind if we join you?" Frances asked, startling a Winter lost in the colors of the mural.

"Jesus H. Christ, Frances ..." Winter said as she caught her tea from hitting the floor.

"An impression of Dana? I wonder, what impressions do you do of me?" Cheryl asked as she stood in the line that had materialized out of nowhere. "Frances, what's your order?" Cheryl stood fast, elbow blocking the two construction workers who tried to do an end run around her to the order counter.

"Now that lunch is figured out...details. Have you heard anything from that freak, Ethan?" Winter asked as she crossed her arms and leaned back in her chair.

Frances bit her lower lip and thought about the word "subterfuge." What a strange and perfect word. She wanted to figure this Ethan crap out, but at the same time, she was feeling like she needed input from anyone else. She was also feeling like it was her fault. Her shame was yelling to keep it quiet.

"Earth to Frances." Cheryl was snapping her fingers.

"That is so rude. Honestly, I'm not sure what to say," Frances said as she picked up a French fry from Winter's basket, studying it for salt and ketchup ratios before taking a bite.

"Frances, I have got to talk about this issue or I am going to explode. Work is driving me up the wall, across the ceiling, and down the other wall," Cheryl said as she now stole a couple of fries from Winter's basket.

"You two are going to owe me fries. Speak, Cheryl. With a windup like that you have got to share," Winter said and chomped down on her sandwich with fries thrown inside for added flavor and to keep them from the two sets of sticky fingers sitting at the table.

"They moved back into a fucking 'open office' floor plan. I lost my office with a window and odor control. I am back in the sewer with fart boy and the rest of the unwashed IT nerds."

"That sounds promising. No cubicle fabric to soak up the smells," Frances said.

"Careful what you ask for—they relocated my desk to the area that is right outside the door to the lady's restroom on the fourth floor."

"Cheryl, you got prime real estate, not having to walk miles or go to a different floor for the bathroom. How great," Winter said between bites.

"Not great."

Winter continued to eat her sandwich and winked at Frances over how serious Cheryl was looking as she talked about her desk location at work.

"Trust me when I say it is not the prime spot at all. Each day I am treated to the disgusting smells of rotten eggs, dirty gym socks, and methane gases."

"When did you move your desk to a third world country? Seriously. Cheryl, you are exaggerating." Winter was getting bored with the conversation.

"Wait. It gets more interesting. First, the soundproofing for the bathroom is zero. I hear everything. I mean everything. Second, the bathroom is shared by two other floors, and the sixth floor has decided to do a green smoothie cleanse. I am now the gate watcher to a smelly dairy farm."

"Burn a candle. Light some incense—the stuff those priests used in elementary school masses could choke out any other odor," Frances said between bites.

"I'm not asking you to solve my problems, Frances. I happen to work for a 'fragrance free' company. I am not allowed to burn or have any open flames at my desk. I tried that back with fart boy and got written up."

"What? Cheryl, you burned incense at your desk? I'm thinking. Granted, I do not normally discuss bathrooms over lunch but this is different. There might be a case. Not to mention the fact you described your area of the office smelling like a dairy farm. Could it be considered a hostile work environment when your job is coding computer software and not plumbing or mucking out cow stalls?" Winter took another bite as she processed the possibilities.

"Hostile air environment. My brain cells are dying from the lack of clean oxygen. There are two offenders who are the worst. One woman walks by my desk farting all the way. It's like her jet propulsion. Most people try to be discreet. Not this woman. She hits that area right by my desk and lets it rip the last few yards to the bathroom."

Winter and Frances were now laughing hysterically.

"I finished my required HR training on fragrance issues in the workplace only to be stuck at the sewer desk."

"You had to go to fragrance issue training? What the hell is that? Now why didn't I hear about any of this?" Winter asked.

"I knew you never listened when I talked. This has been a topic of conversation at several Saturday BVICCs. HR came up with six hours of training to torture me for putting air freshener stick-ups everywhere. They don't really work. I had put up about twenty or so, and all it did was enhance the smell of the sewer with a sickly-sweet air smell.

"Anyway, this one woman kept coming by my desk, and she would go into the bathroom and be in there for a serious amount of time. I wondered if she was in there sleeping. One day, last week, I decided to find out."

"Cheryl is a bathroom stalker," Winter said.

Frances almost lost her sip of water to Winter's classification of Cheryl.

"No, Winter, it is worse—she is the bathroom police," Frances said once she got control over not spitting water across the table.

"Wait until you hear what I uncovered. She always has this huge purse—"

"Maybe it is her sleeping stall bathroom hammock? How does someone sleep in a bathroom stall at work?" Winter said.

"Do they have those? Maybe we could make some money. I bet we could get some people to buy bathroom hammocks for those poor Joes who don't work for a Google-type company that has nap pods."

"We could call them the iPoohangers."

"That sounds like a hanger you put your poo on. Winter, that is gross." Frances faked a gag.

"No, it's a hammock that you can hang in a standard bathroom stall. You would use the toilet as a stepping stool to get into it. Then you could nap away."

"Winter, it would need a gas mask or alternate air supply. Trust me, there is no one sleeping in our company bathroom. It stinks."

Frances glanced around the tiny sandwich haven and noticed that people had stopped talking. She took a couple more fries and dipped them in a mustard and ketchup concoction she loved, wondering if there was something to the bathroom hammock idea. It would make a funny painting. She looked at Winter in her suit and Cheryl in her blouse with her corporate leash around her neck and wondered exactly how the three of them really got along so well. Differences do attract. Could she be attracted sexually to either of them? The thought made her choke on her fries as she realized the answer was a resounding "no." Should she tell them? Would that be offensive? How do people deal with changing their sexual preference with friends? Will they wonder if she was attracted to them in that way, or will they be fine? They did set her up with a woman and seemed fine with that—shit, Frances you are so self-centered.

"Earth to Frances?" Winter tapped Frances on her shoulder to bring her back to the conversation.

"Sorry, what were you saying, Cheryl?"

"You are a wonder sometimes, Frances. I was asking if you two are done making fun of this situation." Cheryl was not smiling. "I explained, this woman carries in this big bag. She is one of those women who always wears expensive heels. I was careful and let another woman enter the restroom. Then, I followed and went in an empty stall. I looked for the red pumps that the bathroom loitering woman was wearing, and they weren't there. Instead, I saw these ugly maroon bell-bottoms and Birkenstocks. The other woman that I had followed in was in the far stall. No one else had entered, and the bathroom had been empty before the three of us had entered."

"Are you telling me that you are now keeping track of who goes into the bathroom and how long they are in there? How much work is getting done on your project? And people wonder why companies hire employment attorneys," Winter said as she finished the last bites of her sandwich and licked the spicy sauce off her fingers. "I think I need to reevaluate who my client is in this case."

Frances was trying to sit still and not erupt into knee-slapping laughter over this whole conversation. "Basically, you are saying the woman puts on a disguise to go poop in the office bathroom," Frances summarized and let her laughter out, not caring that she had snorted loudly.

"You all would not be laughing if you had to endure the smells that go wafting past my desk, even with the bathroom door that automatically closes." Cheryl sat back playing with the last bit of her lunch. She could tell she was not getting the understanding over the issue that she needed.

"I'm being held hostage by HR and it isn't fair."

"To quote Dana, Jesus H. Christ in the mountains, Cheryl, have you lost your mind?" Frances was now gasping for air and moaning because her stomach hurt from laughing so much.

"I wish I could lose my sense of smell. I started working from home because it's getting so bad with the green smoothie cleanse stampede dumping their crud. Not to mention, there are a couple of women who flush the toilet every time they do something or drop a log. The backdrop music to my code writing is flushing toilets."

Winter was now resting on Frances's shoulder crying from the laughter. "Why don't you wear those cute little Hello Kitty ear muffs we got you for your birthday and a swimmer's nose plug?"

"I still smuggle in air fresheners and place them in hard-to-find places."

"Cheryl, you don't put them—"

"Funny. I think I need to get back to work. Thanks, girls, for your empathy."

"Wait, Cheryl," Frances said, catching her breath. "Have you seen those ads for this stuff you can spray into the toilet bowl that traps the smell and keeps it from 'wafting' out?"

"Great. Like I have time to run into the bathroom before anyone uses a stall and spray the stuff," Cheryl said and acted like she was ready to leave.

"Cheryl, you can't leave yet, we haven't heard about Frances's fun with Emily and that other one…the revolving door woman. JHC, I have forgotten her name."

"I'm in the office today—so this keeps me in better smelling air longer. Hang on, I'm going to go order another basket of fries. I deserve it," Cheryl said.

"You must give us the details, woman. I'm still with Jason and feel I must live vicariously through you. Plus, we both know Cheryl is stuck on her own strange on-again, off-again man."

"Winter, you know I am not a girl who kisses and tells," Frances said.

"Bullshit. You can't wait to tell us about your latest exploits," Cheryl added as she sat back down. "Start with Emily because she is a little hottie."

"We had a great time. She picked me up and we went to her computer lab at Stanford."

"I hate showoffs."

"She wasn't showing off—Cheryl, I had asked her what she does all day and night when she isn't teaching me something new about the lesbian culture."

"Culture. Is that what the young people are calling sex? Different," Winter said and stole a hot fry from Cheryl's basket.

Ignoring the banter from her friends, Frances toyed with how much to share of the time she spent with Emily. Was it feeding too much energy into a relationship she knew was not going to last? "We then went to this Greek place for lunch and took a drive to the beach. It was late and we decided to get a hotel room in Santa Cruz for the night."

"You are a marathon dater," Cheryl said.

"Either that or it takes two women forever to get down to the fantasy and friction part because they talk so damn much about everything and anything. With a man, it doesn't take much, and you can be on your way to get on with life. I know I couldn't be a lesbian; it takes up too much time. Although that woman we set you up with was beautiful. Emily is like a piece of new fruit that is young, sweet, and perfect," Winter said.

"You are making me sound like a cougar. I am not a cougar, nor am I old. I understand that this is a fling and not that serious."

"Are you still holding out for that art woman from the East Coast?" Cheryl asked.

"What art woman? What am I missing? Shoot I need to get back to work but this is now getting more interesting," Winter asked.

"I bet she is actually married and has three-point-two kids, a dog, a house with a white picket fence, and a husband who pays for it all," Cheryl added.

"Thanks. I will remember you when I prove you are wrong on all accounts. I am not 'holding out'—if I were, would I be dating other people? Winter, you know you claim you're a listener, but this is not the first time you displayed a lack of either listening or a memory of previously hashed-out issues. In addition to Emily and art dealer woman, I spent time with the revolving door woman. We have spent more than one night together, but I have not heard from her in a while."

"Now I really have lost count. I thought you were only with two women. I guess the count is three. The Hyatt woman you tackled in the revolving door, Olivia, and Emily," Cheryl said counting the names off on her right hand.

"Cheryl, don't forget that guy she took home after we finally went out again after the Meadow's debacle."

"Oh yeah. I had completely forgotten about that poor guy. What did you call him, Frances? I think it was 'tic-tac' or something like that."

"Cheryl, you are so crass sometimes. I don't even remember his name other than I did refer to his member as 'light switch.'"

"For a woman saying she's thinking about going for women, don't you think you should give the male population another chance and go out with someone who is more endowed than 'light switch' man? You know, there are some excellent male lovers too. Frances, you are not serious with these other people. It seems like you're playing with them. If anyone should get a second date, it is the woman we found for you." Winter said this between shoving a couple more fries into her mouth. "At least she could read and had a really nice wardrobe. I even told Cheryl I would consider a woman like that if I lost interest in men. Not going to happen, but she was hot." Winter started to gather up her mess of crumpled, sauce-filled napkins.

"No kidding. But that's not our Frances. Nope. She needs to find the baby-dyke at Stanford or the unavailable bisexual from the East Coast. To throw us off, she dates these other poor unsuspecting souls with—what's the plural for penis?" Cheryl asked.

"Men. That is the plural for dickheads. Are you done? I find it interesting that you're lecturing me about dating, Winter. You declared yourself the queen of one-night stands and continue to carry around a collection of straight single men. When are you going to give Jason the heave?" Frances asked.

"Ouch. Someone got personal. I am not giving Jason the heave anytime soon. If you would accept an invitation to spend time with us outside of our cloistered group, you would get to know what a great guy he is. He isn't a trophy or one of my conquests. He is a person and he has a name."

"I think we need to move this lunch up the street to the chocolate sundae place."

"Cheryl, that's almost on the waterfront," Winter said.

"Exactly. I am talking it is time to share a sundae at Houston's. This conversation needs a gravy boat of warm melted chocolate fudge."

CHAPTER THIRTY-THREE
SHADES OF BROWN

FRANCES had decided to take a break. Her body was starting to cramp from painting for the last several hours. It never occurred to her that keeping her head tilted to the right for hours on end would cause her neck to refuse to support her head normally. As she tried to force herself past the pain, she wondered if this was like making a face and having your face freeze that way—she had believed that as a kid. Now she would be permanently walking around with her head tilted to the right like she needed a V8. She dipped her paintbrush into the bucket of mineral spirits and swished the bristles over the wire coil set on the bottom to help remove extra paint. The color of the cleaner was an ugly red-brown gray. With all the vibrant colors she was using, it always amazed her that this ugly brown was usually the result when the paints blended together.

She looked at the three canvases she was working on now and knew they were not meeting her standards or the direction of the project she was hired to deliver. She had heard a story about Picasso slashing multiple canvases with a knife, in front of a gallery owner who sold much of the work. The gallery owner was thrilled with them, but Picasso wasn't and he destroyed them all. The thought of this made Frances feel better. If Picasso could destroy masterpieces, she could most certainly grow past three baby-poop brown figures.

The past frenzied days of painting had resulted in three very different canvases; however, they all appeared to be sporting the same shade of baby poo. Not one of the images resonated with her now, and they looked about as interesting as dirt. Frances dropped the paintbrush, letting it continue to dance in the mineral spirits as the current started dissipating.

One by one, she moved the canvases to their own empty space. There was nothing more she would rather do at that moment than trash each one of these paintings. The lines, the color, and the lack of attachment were screaming at her as the time ticked away. Frances bit her tongue and asked for creative fairies, or god, or muse energy to come back to her. She was desperate. She bit her tongue as she walked past the canvases. That was it. Even separated, the three canvases conveyed the same damn message.

"Baby shit. I have painted three variations of crap." She wasted no more time and walked over to her shelf of supplies, pulling out a large tube of titanium white and the widest brush she had. The three canvases had no clue they were going to be set back to pristine white in moments. A reset had to happen because the cost of these linen canvases was a higher priority than preserving her mistakes. She thought about the luxury of an artist she met in Berkeley. He claimed to keep everything he painted. That way, he would show others how his art evolved through his life. "Yeah—my painting has evolved to the level of shit," Frances muttered as brush stroke after brush stroke of white paint on the first poo-colored canvas restored the possibility of something better. Each stroke took her further and further from the reality of the painting she was covering and into a new form. A crude outline of a human figure walking started to emerge out of the thick white paint.

Frances hesitated and sat back on her feet, cocking her head once again to the right. She knew that she had to stop the hypnotic voice of the future creeping in and lulling her into inaction. This was the voice of procrastination and maybes. The only way she knew to get a painting that was inspired was to do the work. Frances straightened her head this time, ignoring the pain in her neck, and stood. She took the canvas in both hands and put it back on her easel. Something wicked and wonderful was forming under the wet strokes of white paint. Instead of submitting and disappearing, the painting she had tried to conceal under the white coat of paint shouted out its power.

Immediately, the figure made her think of Felipe and the beautiful linen suit she had accidentally spilled her coffee all over. Frances ran to her shelf and grabbed a tube of red paint to match the red silk scarf that she had so delicately blown her nose into that horrid morning. "Gotcha," Frances said as her fingers grabbed two tubes of paint, one an iridescent silver and the other alizarin crimson. She stopped at her mixing table and found a clean piece of glass, then squeezed out two blobs of color. A half-inch filbert brush in hand, she walked to the image that she was thinking of calling "Felipe" and dipped her brush into the paints, pulling the colors into a puddle on the glass.

Promises of beauty and excitement arose with the bright-red color waiting on the tip of her brush. The first few strokes of red on the canvas provided hints of silver and hushed tones of the red as it embedded into the white. With quick, delicate precision, Frances painted a triangle of color for the handkerchief and used more of the silver to further define the human form. She was careful to erase any suggestion of pink. The strength of the red had to hold the eye of the observer. It had to grab you and pull you into the painting. It was the hook.

Before her eyes, this painting was turning into twists of fate and intrigue. For the next several hours, she built upon the canvas the scene of her meeting with Felipe. Delicate lines merged into another world that screamed of modernist art. The brown color was brought back with the scraping of a palette knife where she remembered the coffee landing. Frances was in the marathon of painting as her mind, body, and soul focused all her energies into her work. Inspiration from another source was pulling the brushes through the paint. She was captive and continued to dance with the energy. Time continued to slip for her, and she phased everything else out.

"What the hell is that buzzing sound?" Frances asked aloud, annoyed. It had not registered that the sound had been going on for about thirty minutes. It took her another five minutes before she realized it was the buzzer to her intercom from the front entrance. It continued to scream into her space, and Frances threw her brush down on the table as she walked over to give the impatient buzzer pusher a piece of her mind.

"Did you think that I might not want to chat with anyone after the first five minutes of buzzing? Buzz off, you annoying buzzer pusher," Frances said into the intercom.

"Hey, no need to shoot the messenger, lady. I was told to stay here until I got this envelope in your hands. I don't give a rat's ass except for the tip I get when I prove I got this to you."

Frances bit her lower lip, realizing that she should always look at the video monitor before mouthing off. Shoot. It was probably the check from the gallery. In the video monitor, she saw the angel face of a young bicycle courier who had a strong look that screamed he had no fear of the San Francisco streets, hills, or traffic. In one hand he held an envelope, and in the other he held his bike, which probably had no brakes. Brakes are for toddlers, she was once told by a bicycle courier.

"Sorry. I'm in loft C on the top floor," she said sheepishly and buzzed him into the building. Frances looked down to make sure she had enough clothing on to answer the door. She dared not look in the mirror for fear that her current state screamed hoarder, not painter. Embarrassed by her outburst against an everyday person doing his job—"What is wrong with you, Frances?"—a knock on her door got her out of her mother-implanted, self-scolding recording.

"Hello, stranger," Russell said as he walked through the open door into Frances's loft.

"Do you have any cash?" Frances asked.

"An intriguing hello. Are you thinking about a new line of work? Bank robber perhaps—"

"A courier is on his way up and I thought you were him, but I have no clue where my wallet is and I need to tip him. I might have yelled at him for interrupting my painting session."

Russell took out his wallet and handed her a five-dollar bill. Frances let his stare hang in the air as she heard the elevator door open at the end of the hall.

"What is it you're getting hand delivered?" Russell asked as he cleared a half-read newspaper and a blanket off the couch so he could sit.

"Frances Kavanagh?" the courier asked.

"Yes. Yes. I'm Frances Kavanagh."

"I'll vouch for her. Trust me, no one would admit to being Frances," Russell shouted from the couch.

"Sign here." The courier backed up a few steps as Frances took the clipboard with more energy than she realized.

"Here you go." She grabbed the envelope with the excitement of a little girl opening a birthday present. Frances missed the courier shaking his head as he crumpled up the bill and shoved it into his pocket.

Frances plopped down next to Russell on the couch, not bothering to move any of the mess out of the way. She caught the expression of horror running across his face as he registered that her loft was in a rather large amount of messy chaos.

"What's in the envelope?"

"My first real check as an artist."

"You've sold work before."

"These paintings sold for more than all those other pieces added together times ten. It's serious art now," Frances said as she held the envelope in her lap and looked at it.

"While you open it, I'll go get some bubbly. This calls for a celebration. The perfect reason to pop open the champagne." Russell hopped up and exited the apartment before Frances could respond. She slid her pinky finger into the small opening that allowed her to open the length of the envelope and peer inside. Her heart was beating into her throat as she slowly took out a portfolio. On the outside was a taped and folded piece of light lavender paper scented ever so lightly with a perfume Frances instantly recognized.

"Holy shit in the tabernacle," Frances whispered, falling back into her couch and letting herself stare up at the ceiling.

Russell, Simon, and Winston were standing in her open door, silent.

"Should we see if she's alive? How big was this check?" Simon asked Russell.

Russell walked over to Frances and sat beside her, then picked up the portfolio, opening it as Frances continued to stare off into space. "Honey, this is no check—it's a first-class airplane ticket to Honolulu with your name on it."

"What have you been keeping from us?" Simon asked as he poured sparkling wine into three flute glasses he had brought over with the wine. "Time to spill your secrets."

"Felipe was supposed to send me a check. This is from out of the blue. They all said that I must have been her one-night stand. Well—one-night-and-a-weekend stand."

"Keep us in suspense. Who? What? Come on, sister. Enough with the tension," Russell said, taking a flute of champagne from Simon.

"No secrets. I'm not exactly sure, but I believe that this is from Olivia. It's scented in the perfume she wore when we met and I have never, ever smelled it on anyone else. Her perfume was so perfect it was like jasmine flowers were blooming all around her. This note smells just like her." Frances inhaled deeply.

"Seriously? You're going to get into the floral notes of the perfume."

"Calm down, Simon. She is a little in shock. You think it's a big fat check, and then it turns out to be a first-class airplane ticket. That's a lot for a little girl from St. Louie to take in and accept. She's been clanged by one heck of a trolley."

"Russell, no one from St. Louis says 'Louie,'" Frances said. "The note reads 'Trust. Meet me at the white hotel by Paradise Cove at 92-1001 Omani Street, Kapolei.'" Frances reread the note about forty times, after which she finally looked up at the two silent faces of her neighbors. They had both knocked back the bubbly in their glasses.

"Are you sure you know this is from this woman, Olivia?" Simon asked, concern creeping into his voice.

"Yes. I think—nope, I know. It has got to be Olivia. Unless…no, Sam wouldn't do this after I ran out on her twice." Frances picked up the ticket and saw that it was for a flight leaving from San Francisco International Airport tomorrow. "Oh shit, I have so much to do before I leave. What am I going to wear? What do I pack?"

Russell took the handwritten note and smiled. "Not much because this is one heck of a booty call."

"Slow down. Are you sure you want to go? Why didn't she sign her name? Who starts a note with the word 'trust'?" Simon started pacing around the loft. He couldn't help himself, and he automatically began picking up the land of disarray and chaos.

"Simon, I know this is her—we talked all night about trust. She did sign it."

"There is no way I could be lesbian. All you women do is talk. Is that the same as sex for you? Is it like hot foreplay, or is the very act of talking more of an orgasm? Are we having sex right now? Is that why you talk with us so much?" Russell asked as he laughed over his own joke.

"Funny. I am not going to answer that—"

The buzzer to Frances's loft broke into their conversation, making all three of them jump.

This time, Frances looked at the video monitor before she pushed the button and said anything. Staring up at her through the video feed was another angel-faced courier. This one sported a nose ring and a shaved head. Where was his helmet? Frances immediately buzzed this courier into the building. She was not going to be a jerk again. As an afterthought, she yelled through the speaker, "Loft C, top floor."

"Wow. Another courier. Aren't we the important one today," Simon said as he refilled his glass.

"Do either of you have any money?"

"There she goes again." Russell retrieved another fiver out of his wallet and handed it to her. "Hey, Simon, did you notice she didn't protest when I used the word 'lesbian' when talking about her?"

"Right. It must mean something?"

"You two need to stop being so title-centric." Frances went and opened her door to wait for the courier. As the courier walked toward her, she realized that this was not a guy.

"Frances Kavanagh?" the courier asked.

"Yes. This is from Felipe. He's sorry for the delay, but the bank took longer than they needed to cut the check." Frances signed for the envelope and handed the courier the tip, shutting the door without saying a word.

"Rude comes to mind," Simon said as he ran to the door and yelled out a thank you.

"I am a real artist." Frances sat down and opened the envelope that contained a cashier's check.

"No, sweet woman. You were a real artist the day you quit everything else to paint. That was the day you became a real artist. The money, fame, or whatever has nothing to do with your art. It is a nice side effect, but don't ever forget what gets you to shut yourself off from everything else in the world and do what you do." Simon stood and walked over to the painting on her easel and pointed at her current rendering.

CHAPTER THIRTY-FOUR
THIN LINE TO CRAZY

C ALL it a woman's intuition, or maybe it was the fact that Frances had been missing in action for more than a few days. Both Winter and Cheryl called Frances within minutes of one another. Cheryl's call came in first. Frances had to turn the shower off to be sure she had heard her cell phone. Of course, she had left it somewhere other than where she was in the bathroom. She decided to finish her shower. Whoever was trying to reach her could leave a message. The warm water refreshed her tired and sore muscles. She let the hot water pound the soreness out of her upper back and shoulders as she thought about the words that the boys, Russell and Simon, had said.

It wasn't the money that validated her as an artist. That was her family's marker of success. No. She felt she understood the craving for paint, brush, and canvas that would flood through her when she fell into timeless creative sessions, the moments where she really was unable to explain what exactly she had done. She could point to a finished painting, but to explain every step that it took to create—that was impossible. People thought she was hiding her talent and her secrets by not recounting exactly what prompted her to do X or Y. The water was starting to cool, so Frances turned off the faucet and stood in the last steam of her shower.

Her phone was ringing again. She decided to try and find the noise machine as she stepped out of the shower and wrapped a towel around her wet body. The concrete floor of the loft was cold as her bare feet quickly took her to the counter in her kitchen to retrieve her ringing silence breaker.

"Hello," Frances said quickly, hoping it was not too late. The number came in unknown, and she thought it could be Olivia.

"Frances, I haven't heard from you in a couple days. What's up?" Winter asked. Frances could not exactly place the sound of strange enthusiasm in Winter's voice.

"Oh. It's you. Not much," Frances answered as she walked over to her pile of unfolded clean laundry and grabbed another towel to wrap up her wet hair.

"Nice. You sound so excited. The last time I got a response like that was when I was calling a client who failed to pay his legal invoice for five months," Winter said.

"Sorry. This day has been rather strange, and I was in the shower. I thought you were someone else."

"Clearly."

"Sorry, I'm getting another call. Hang on." Frances checked her phone and saw Cheryl's mug appear on the screen. "I'm going to merge the call."

"Hey, Cheryl, welcome to chit-chat with Winter and Frances." Frances giggled as she said this, having a hard time not spilling the beans of her excitement.

"Two for one. I need to go buy a lottery ticket," Cheryl said.

"At least she was sounding nice to you. When Frances figured out it was me on the other end of the line, she was less than enthused," Winter said.

"Winter, you could easily win gold at the Olympics for first-class pouting," Frances said. "I'm putting this call on speaker phone so I can get dressed."

"As long as we aren't on FaceTime. I don't need to see any more of Frances than I already do." Cheryl laugh-snorted on the call.

"Funny. Well, I have been busy painting and lost track of time—sorry about the absence."

"Phew. I thought you had entered into another marriage and we had been tossed, cast off once again, like yesterday's emoji." Winter gave the message a little more seriousness than she had meant when it was met with complete silence. "Kidding. I was only kidding. Mostly kidding."

"I get it. Sorry. I promise I won't ditch you anytime soon. Today I received a—well, two very interesting courier packages. One was a check for those paintings I sold through Olivia's gallery, and the other was a first-class plane ticket to Honolulu that leaves tomorrow. It has been quite a day. I have no clue what I'm going to wear, let alone pack."

"Slow down, woman. I need time to digest what I think I heard. You got paid for those three paintings that you claimed could have been painted by a dead dog?" Cheryl was overly slow in her delivery, which made Frances stop dressing and come back to her phone.

"What do you mean a first-class ticket to Hawaii? Who sent that to you?" Winter asked in her lawyerly "I know you are guilty" voice and in full command.

"Not sure how else to explain it. I believe that Olivia sent me a first-class ticket and we will be meeting up in Hawaii."

"Frances! What do you mean you believe Olivia sent you a ticket? Do you know who sent you this ticket?" Winter was zeroing in with her interrogation, and Frances knew it would be difficult to shake her from this line of questioning.

"This call is over—we are on our way over to your place. Cheryl, I will pick you up on the way," Winter said.

"I'll be ready. Frances, stay put," Cheryl said.

Frances finished dressing and picked up the ticket, looking for anything that would reinforce what she felt she knew. Who else would send her such a gift? Is it a gift? Oh crap, this is so weird, even for her. Frances dialed the airline phone number printed on the back of the ticket to find out more about the mysterious gift. After going through what felt like sixty different automated promptings to press any chorus of numbers on her phone, Frances finally heard another human on the other end of the line.

"Hi. Thank you for calling Hawaiian World Airlines. I'm here to help you. Can I please have the reservation number from your ticket?"

"JZH2QR6B"

"This is a new one. I have never seen a ticket quite like this. Whom am I speaking with, please?"

"Frances Kavanagh, and I was hoping you could tell me who purchased this ticket for me. What do you mean, you've never seen a ticket like this one?" Frances asked. She was not going to get any more nervous than she already was, but it was taking her last ounce of one class of yoga training to keep herself breathing.

"Well. I can't tell you who purchased it—it was paid for in cash."

"How much cash?" She felt guilty about asking because she was taught never to ask how much someone spent on a gift. Her mother's voice was ricocheting through her brain, announcing how rude she was being.

"This is why I've never seen a ticket like this before. It's an open-ended first-class ticket that will fly you from Honolulu to Sydney, Australia, and New York. No order of events is required. The only set date is the one for tomorrow's flight."

"What do you mean, a ticket to Australia and New York?" Frances sat down slowly as this was all starting to sink in. She was now 99.9999 percent sure that Olivia had sent her the ticket. It was one of her dreams to go to Sydney, and the New York part—well that was where she had said she lived.

"Is there anything else I can help you with?" The kind voice on the other end of the phone asked a Frances who had been stunned mute.

"Um. The price of this ticket?" Frances quietly asked.

"Twenty-seven thousand. It is a special ticket that makes sure you get the flight you want. Like I said, never seen anything like this."

"That was paid in cash?"

"Yes. Is there anything else I can help you with?"

"No. Thank you." Frances ended the call and tried to get her mind around the ticket and the cost. Who spends money like that? Who has money like that to spend on someone they met for a brief tryst in San Francisco? "Air, Frances, keep breathing," was all she could say to herself. She pulled the blanket over her as she curled her feet under her on the couch and felt the thin line finally breaking, leading her into the world of crazy.

CHAPTER THIRTY-FIVE
FRIENDS OF THE BUENA VISTA IRISH COFFEE CLUB ROUND TABLE

WINTER let herself and Cheryl into the loft with her extra key that she had demanded from Frances as a safety measure so she wouldn't do some artist trick and chop an ear off or worse. It took Winter a moment to locate the lump of Frances under the blanket on the couch. The loft was in a bigger state of chaos and entropy than Winter had expected. It made it easy for one to hide in plain sight though.

"Oh man, Cheryl, we need to open some windows and get some fresh air in here or we will all be accused of huffing." The two of them walked over and opened a couple of windows to let in some fresh air and avoid making the first contact with the hidden Frances. Winter looked at Cheryl when they walked back to the couch and stood before the rather large lump with feet that was under the blanket.

"You poke it," Winter said.

"I don't want to disturb the sleeping Frances. She might bite," Cheryl said.

"Hello. Where's Frances?" Winter asked as she dumped a stack of magazines on the floor, clearing herself a place to sit.

The noise of the magazines made Frances stir as she pulled the blanket down and blinked her eyes against the light.

"That's a look," Cheryl said.

"Careful, Cheryl, that woman has a good right hook if spooked."

"The ticket cost twenty-seven thousand ones in cash," Frances said.

"What?" Winter asked, sitting a little taller.

"I think she said the airplane ticket cost twenty-seven thousand dollars," Cheryl said.

"Yup. It was paid for in cash. Who does that? Who goes to an airline counter with twenty-seven thousand dollars?" Frances pulled the blanket back over her head.

"How much did you say your painting—"

"What has that got to do with the ticket, Cheryl? Sometimes I know why you—"

"Be nice, Winter. I think I remember that Olivia took the paintings to her gallery. Or something like that—I don't know, this is all so crazy," Cheryl said.

"Have you heard from Olivia?" Winter asked.

"Not until this note and ticket. When I went to talk with Nathan at his gallery, Felipe said there were some messages for me from her, but they only said that Olivia called for me. I never received those messages. Felipe blamed his workers."

"Jesus, woman, you cannot put Emily in the same theater as you put Olivia if she is dropping such a hefty chunk of change in your direction," Winter said.

"What do I do?" Frances asked and looked first at Winter and then at Cheryl. Neither one of them responded in any intelligible way.

"I need Dana," Frances said, burying her face into her blanket. Winter stood and went to the fridge to hunt for something to eat, leaving it to Cheryl to phone Dana. This was a call to the highest order. Their friend was going off the deep end, and someone with money was pulling her there.

"Dana, this is Cheryl. No time to chat. We are at the loft and we need your help. Frances got a huge gift and she isn't exactly sure who it's from. She is hiding under a blanket."

"Jesus H. Christ in the mountains, Cheryl, what are you talking about? It's nearly rush hour. I'm not going to come into the City. You know I don't like to drive in the City, let alone in rush hour mayhem."

"Dana, the traffic is going out of the City now. You should be fine. What if I order you a car service? I will. You are needed. This is a Round Table, and you are needed." Cheryl knew better than to let Dana answer and hung up to dial the car service.

"I've got Dana on her way—crossing my fingers, I hope the traffic really is moving," Cheryl said and sat down at the piano.

"Oh look, she moves," Winter said through a mouthful of cold noodle salad she scavenged from the fridge.

Frances went to Cheryl and tapped her on the shoulder. It had worked. Cheryl had annoyed Frances enough that it got her to sit at her piano and start playing as they waited for Dana to join them.

Frances let the music flow and experienced a sense of relief knowing that Dana was on her way. She was not exactly sure how she felt. Excited. Scared. If she could only talk to Olivia. But like an idiot, she had not pressed Felipe for her number. She really needed to get up and call him and track this down. But would that violate the trust? Was she going to take this distraction from her work? She glanced at the painting on her easel and let her gaze fixate on the triangle of red. It looked like a flower opening her eyes to the painting, and she let it trap her in the risk that she was willing to take for love.

Her phone ringing snapped her back into the moment. Frances picked up the phone, surprised to see Emily's name.

"What the fuck, Frances?" Emily yelled before Frances had a chance to say a word. "How dare you send the police to my lab, telling them that I'm in danger from Ethan. Take your melodramatic ass and go jump off the bridge."

"What are you screaming about?" Frances asked.

"Knock that shit off. The police said you lodged a report saying that you were afraid of Ethan and worried that he was going to do something to me because he was jealous of our relationship."

"I didn't call the police. Emily, I really don't know what you're talking about." Frances walked over to the window of the loft trying to figure out what the heck was going on and why she was getting this from Emily. Sure, they had slept together and Frances had enjoyed it, but she hadn't hung anything on the relationship beyond the fun they had together.

"Fuck off, Frances, and I don't ever want to hear from you again."

As Frances was taking the abuse through her phone, she glanced out the window and stopped. She had to do a double take.

"Emily, are the police still with you?"

"No, you bitch. Do you think I would talk to you like this in front of a crowd? Fuck."

"Emily, shut up for a minute. I'm at my loft, and I am looking at Ethan standing in front of my building holding what looks like an automatic rifle."

"You take the cake, Frances. You are a fucking freak."

"Emily, listen to me. I am not making this up. Ethan is out front, right now, with a gun. I didn't tell you this, but the night of his art opening…Emily, this is real," Frances said, her voice cracking as she tried to control her fear.

"Fuck. Frances, if anything happens to Ethan, I am holding you responsible. What the fuck did you do to him? I am on my way now."

"I don't think that's a good idea." Frances hung up the phone. Winter and Cheryl were standing stone still as they couldn't help but overhear the conversation.

Winter didn't hesitate. She dialed 911 on her phone.

Cheryl went straight to the door and made sure it was locked.

"Should I call the boys next door?" Cheryl whispered.

"Yes. We need to warn them," Frances answered as they waited to hear when the police would be there. "Can you call them?" No sooner had Frances uttered those words than a pounding on her loft door caused all three to jump and scream.

"It's Russell, Simon, and Winston. Let us in—it's an emergency."

"Frances, is Ethan still in the street?" Cheryl asked.

Frances nodded her head yes and decided to get on the floor and crawl under her piano, hating the fact that she had a wall of windows.

Cheryl opened the door, letting Russell, Simon, and Winston in and screamed when she saw that Simon had a black pistol in his hand. She quickly shut the door and locked it again. Russell and Simon pushed a huge wooden desk in front of the door and turned off the lights in the loft.

As they worked, Simon told them, "Winston had started barking and running the length of the window wall. When I went to see what was causing him to bark like a dog chasing a postman, I saw Ethan in the street with the gun staring up at the building. Winston always acted uneasy around Ethan. Kids and dogs know."

"Not helping, Simon. Are you all okay?" Russell asked, looking around the room.

"I'm talking with 911 right now," Winter said. The first sirens could be heard in the distance. They were responding, and everything felt like it was in slow motion to Frances as she looked at the pale faces of her friends. What had she done?

Winston came under the piano and curled up next to Frances, licking her face. She buried her face into his furry shoulder. She had no clue what she was doing or where she was going. Here, sitting on the floor under her grand piano, she hugged all her doubts and pain into Winston. "I want this to stop. Ethan ..."

"Mind if I join the party?" Russell asked, lying on his stomach.

"Come on in." Frances snuffled up her response, trying to stop the tears from falling. Russell put his arm around her and held her.

Sirens were coming closer, and Winter had crab-walked to the furthest window to peer out and give information to the police.

"He is still standing in the middle of the street staring at the front door of the building. I can't tell what kind of gun it is. He is wearing a black leather jacket, black pants, and black boots of some kind. His hair is black. No," Winter said.

Simon pushed the couch in front of the desk that was barricading the door and sat down on it. He patted the cushion next to him and got Cheryl to come sit down with him.

"There are three females, two males, and one dog in the loft," Winter answered.

"I really don't want to die today," Cheryl said out loud.

"No one is going to die in here today," Simon said and put his arm around her.

"I didn't know you owned a gun?" Frances's voice rose from under the piano.

"There are lots of things you don't know. I am a man of mystery," Simon said, trying to lighten the mood in the loft.

The sirens sounded like they were right outside now, and there were a lot of them. Simon couldn't help it; he crawled over to where Winter was and peeked out to see Ethan, statue still, standing in the middle of the street and holding the gun at his waist. Police cars were blocking both ends of the street.

"Holy shit. It looks like he has something strapped to his waist. He looks like he either gained fifty pounds or he plans on blowing this building sky high," Simon said aloud.

Winter tapped Simon on his shoulder and handed him the phone.

"They want to talk to you," Winter said. "I can't look away from him. I know this is fucked, but he looks so hot. Why did he always ignore me?" Winter asked.

"Seriously? I really don't understand women. This brings dangerously sexy to a whole different level," Simon said as he took the phone.

CHAPTER THIRTY-SIX
AN UNKNOWN FORCE

FRANCES tried to separate herself from the rest of the crowd that was now taking over her loft, making her start to feel claustrophobic. The police had sent Russell, Simon, and Winston back to their loft with a couple of officers. There was nothing more that Frances felt she could tell them about her relationship with Ethan. An officer came rushing in saying that the possible offender's longtime friend, Emily, had arrived. Frances watched and took it in, knowing that this whole thing was all so messed up and strange. She let herself sink to the floor and rested her head against the cold brick wall. She hugged her knees into her chest and wanted to close her eyes and have all of this go away. Before she could drift into some fantasyland far away from this moment, her phone vibrated in her pocket.

"Oh my god. I forgot about Dana." Frances quickly answered her phone. "Dana, are you here?"

"Yes. Holy crap of feathers in a goose factory, Frances. Are you okay? They won't let me through the police barricade. What the heck is going on?"

"I am fine. I think. Hang on, let me go find someone to let you come up," Frances said as she stood. She went up to the closest uniformed officer in the sea of people and guns. "Who do I need to talk with to get my friend Dana up here?"

"Detective in charge. She's over there." The officer pointed to a slender but strong-looking woman talking with a group of plainclothes officers. They all had their badges hanging around their necks.

"Excuse me, but I have a friend who I need to see. Can she come up?" Frances asked the group collectively.

"No one allowed coming in or out. Tell her to go home. We have a lot to figure out right now," a short, bald man, wearing a suit that was two sizes two big, said to Frances.

"You don't understand—I am not sending Dana home because she would be worried sick. I was told she is in charge." Frances dropped all manners as she pointed directly at the detective. "Please. I had called Dana before any of this unfolded, and she came all the way in from San Quentin to help with another matter," Frances said.

"Is this a prison matter?" the short bald man asked.

Frances ignored him and put the softest look she could on her face without looking completely and utterly desperate.

"I need to talk to the detective in charge," Frances said. She crossed her arms as the bald, vertically challenged man looked her up and down and then turned to confer with the detective in charge. They used foreign words like "possible active shooter," "unknown explosives," and "not breaking the perimeter." Frances figured it was a lost cause and started to hold her breath. How was she going to tell Dana she couldn't come up? Were they going to survive this night?

"Are you talking to your friend on the phone right now?" The woman had stepped around the short, bald officer and was standing directly in front of Frances.

"Yes." Frances handed her phone, unprompted, over to the detective in charge and waited.

"Hi. This is Detective Woods. I want you to go to the first uniformed officer you see and hand that person your phone." Dana did as she was instructed. It took less than five minutes, and Frances finally released her tears, crying full throttle, in Dana's arms.

"This was some welcoming committee," Dana said as she guided Frances over to the couch. Two officers were sitting on the couch, and Dana shooed them off so she could sit and get some answers out of Frances.

"Your life is definitely brilliant, my girl. What brought half the SF police force and SWAT team out to your building?" Dana asked, trying not to spook Frances into another set of tears.

"Ethan—I have no clue."

"Okay. Frances, you win the award for attracting first-class freaky," Winter said as she joined them on the couch, munching on a can of mixed nuts she had uncovered in the boys' pantry next door.

"Basically, you were called here, Dana, before Ethan decided to go postal, because little Miss Freaky had received a first-class, open-ended ticket that will whisk her off to Hawaii tomorrow. Only to be followed by trips to Sydney and New York." Winter summed it up as she tossed another cashew into her mouth.

"Slow down. I can't seem to digest any of this. Ethan is here threatening you with a gun and bombs because of an airplane ticket?" Dana stopped moving and closed her eyes for a moment.

"Sorry." Winter laughed. "Nope. I think Ethan is here because he has a mad crush on Frances. You missed the strange potluck when Ethan got weird. Then, Frances hooked up with his best friend, Emily. Not sure why this is all happening right now. The airplane ticket is unrelated to Ethan—at least Frances thinks it is unrelated. The police are here because I called 911 when we noticed Ethan standing in the middle of the street holding an automatic rifle."

"No shit." Dana sat back, the color draining from her face as the information finally registered.

"I couldn't see over the throng of police out there—what was going on? And Winter is right, you have attracted some strange crap."

"You are all safe. Our negotiator is talking with Ethan, and he appears to be backing down from doing anything with the weapons he has brought. He has put down the rifle but claims he has a knife. No explosives. The first pass-through of the building with our bomb sniffing dogs did not show any explosives. You are safe," Detective Woods said as she stood over the group, holding a small pad of paper and a pen. "Would you mind if I asked you some questions, Frances?"

"Weapons? You mean more than one?" Frances asked.

She watched as Dana stood and moved away from her as the severity of the scene continued to register. Frances counted six men standing at the window in full SWAT armor with guns pointed out the open windows. She wanted to go hold Dana close as she saw that Dana's body visibly shook.

"Let me help you. I am Captain Todd Gruggs." A young man held out a hand to Dana and guided her away so Detective Woods could chat with Frances somewhat alone.

"How are you doing?" Detective Woods asked Frances. "I want you to know that we have the situation contained, and you and your friends are safe." Detective Woods held out her business card to Frances.

Something about the business card struck Frances as so surreal and strange. She couldn't help it as laughter spontaneously erupted out of her. The outburst caused the rest of the conversations in the loft to halt momentarily.

"F—okay?" Cheryl asked.

"Yup, that's my name, don't wear it out." Frances started laughing harder. "I'm sorry, Detective. I guess I didn't know detectives would have business cards."

"Thanks to TV shows, we had to start carrying them and solving murders in fifty minutes."

"A sense of humor or sarcasm?" Frances asked as she tried to stifle any other braying laughter.

"What can you tell me about Ethan?"

"Well, not any more than I told the other officer. We met in a weekend refresher class on color and light in oils. He helped me a lot through my divorce."

"When were you divorced?"

"Recently or not—guess it depends on how you value time. Ethan helped me move into the loft. I used to have studio space next to his."

"Were you dating him?" Detective Woods was all business as she went through her list of questions. Frances realized that the woman was quite attractive. Was it the strength in the way she handled herself or her blue, almost gray, eyes? No makeup, but she did have mascara on and that had Frances curious. "Seriously, Frances, you need to focus" was screaming through her head.

"Frances, are you okay? Do you need something?" The detective put her pen down and waited to see if Frances could continue with her questions. "Did you ever date Ethan?" Detective Woods asked again.

"Sorry. No. We never dated. But ..." Frances stopped and stared at her shaking hands. She knew the detective probably saw her hands shaking, so it was too late to make up a story, nor did she really want to make anything up. Who was she going to protect? Ethan? Nathan? She felt her face flush as she knew that all of this was really twisted, and she had not shared the story with any of her friends. She felt herself walking on a wire that was going to break, and there was no way she could stop it.

"Detective Woods, the bomb squad has cleared the area, but there is a question about what he might be concealing around his waist and they want to know if they need to get the robot here?"

"Excuse me, Frances. I need to go handle this." Detective Woods left, and Frances felt the laughter exploding out of her again as she glanced at the business card in her hand. The detective's name was Molly Woods. God, what if her parents had named her Holly? A few of the officers searching her place stared at her, and she quickly silenced her laughter. She could not stop watching the detective; she had an accent, one that Frances couldn't quite place. Was it Irish or was it Scottish? Are they even close? Was it real? Of course, it was a real accent. "Shit, I've lost it. I'm answering myself in my head," Frances said aloud as she buried her face in her hands.

"Frances, do you mind if I ask you a few more questions?"

"Detective Woods, do realize that you got off lucky?" Frances responded.

"What?"

"Your parents could have named you Holly. You know, Hollywood?" The joke fell flat on its face between the two women.

Frances reached out to Dana who had made her way back to the couch. There was comfort in grasping onto Dana's hand. It felt like she was going to be okay with Dana's reassurances.

"Jesus H. Christ in the mountains, Frances, you truly are a nutter. There are thousands of XY chromosomes with guns running around here and you are making lame jokes." Dana let go of Frances's hand. "I need some coffee or tea and probably should make it decaf."

CHAPTER THIRTY-SIX

"Did you ever date Ethan?" Detective Woods asked.

"No. I am not lying about that. Have you heard something else? If so, it's not true," Frances said, wishing this whole thing would disappear.

"Who is Emily?" Frances's head snapped up when she heard the name. Okay, it figured that they already knew about that whole sordid affair.

"I did not send the police to her lab."

"Did you date Emily?"

"Not really. We went out a couple of times. I found out later from her that she had challenged Ethan to see who could get me to go on a date first. She won. At least, I think she did."

"Are you still seeing Emily?" Woods asked.

"No. She thinks I'm the one who caused Ethan to snap. Seriously, I have nothing to do with this. The night of Ethan's art opening at Nathan's gallery, Ethan tried to make me—and I basically fought him off. I have barely talked to him since his art opening." Frances looked down at her shaking hands and balled them into fists trying to quiet them.

"What's this? Why didn't you say anything? What do you mean you had to fight him off? What did he do to you Frances?" Winter was now standing next to Detective Woods.

"Please, I need some—Captain Gruggs, could you please come and take her statement?" Detective Woods turned toward Winter. While Winter was distracting Woods, Frances noticed the detective was wearing a very light but spicy perfume. Her skin was tan and her neck had the lightest freckles. Frances looked down quickly when Detective Woods turned back to her, ready with her pencil and small tablet.

"Frances, did you report the incident to the police?" Woods asked.

"No. I thought he was high on his art opening and wine. Felipe took me back to the hotel. Ethan had ripped the dress I was wearing and, well, I had to break away from him by slapping him hard. He was stronger than I realized he could be and he bruised my arms. Nathan had walked out when Ethan had me up against the wall and saw me slap him. I…It was the look from Nathan. I didn't tell anyone." Frances unconsciously rubbed her upper arms where the bruises were still visible—the main reason Frances had not been wearing any short-sleeved shirts.

"Why did you not share any of this with your friends?" Woods asked.

"Shame. Guilt. I don't know. I was so confused about everything. It was Nathan's new gallery. I thought maybe it was my fault."

"Detective, we have that information for you." The short, bald detective playing dress-up handed Woods some papers.

"Excuse me one more time, Frances. I'm sorry."

It was all surreal, Frances thought to herself, that she could not stop watching the detective. To pull herself away, she decided to go play the piano. It would help her calm down. Her hands were shaking as she sat down on her piano bench and placed them on the black and white keys. She did not want to call any attention to herself, and she knew as soon as the notes sounded, people would watch her. She shut it all out and started to play as lightly as she could. Eyes closed, Frances let the music out and felt the shakes start to leave her hands. Conversations stopped in the loft, and Detective Woods watched, as did everyone else except the sharp shooters stationed at her windows. The music was soft and delicate, in direct contrast to the situation.

Suddenly, a sound like a firecracker was heard, followed quickly by breaking glass and almost everyone hit the floor in the loft. A volley of sound broke the millisecond of silence, and the smell of steel and something else filled the air. It was over in a hail of bullets all focused on one point. Then silence. Frances stood and walked to a window, her nostrils flaring with the burn of the unknown odor. In the street, under the light of several spotlights, was Ethan. He was lying on his back in a pool of his own blood. A pistol was in his right hand. His eyes were open.

CHAPTER THIRTY-SEVEN
ETHAN ENDS HIS BORROWED TIME

"How are you feeling?" Detective Woods was leaning against a counter in a garishly lit, mint-green room. Frances felt a sting in her hand and lifted it to see that an IV had been placed there. She hated needles. Did she faint when they put in the IV?

"You passed out and hit your head pretty hard. When you didn't come back right away, we decided we needed to get you in to have your head checked out." Detective Woods was the only one talking. Frances could see the back of a uniformed officer standing on the other side of the hospital curtain. Then a short boxy shadow showed up next to the officer pushing a cart. This was not going to be good, Frances thought to herself and started to fidget. Detective Woods reached out and touched Frances's hand and quickly withdrew it as the nurse pushing the cart approached her in the bed.

"Hi there. I'm Valerie, your nurse. Can you tell me your name? Do you know what the date is? Who is the president?" Frances ran through the questions and decided to answer them without making any jokes. Her head hurt like it was in a vice grip, and she was not liking the whole hospital thing. Quite frankly, the smell of this hospital was wreaking havoc on her gag reflexes.

"Ethan?" Frances asked Detective Woods.

"Yes. He fired a shot through your window. He yelled, 'good-bye means forever' right before he did it. Do you know what that meant?"

"It meant he wanted you to kill him. He was unstable and knew that he could never have me." Frances wasn't going to cry. She was tired and those words made her head hurt even more. Ethan was not coming back, and she could not get the answers she needed.

"Frances, did you know that Ethan had been recording you at your home?"

"What?"

"We swept your place and the building. There were hidden cameras and audio bugs throughout the building and in your neighbors' apartment too."

Frances closed her eyes and tried hard to keep herself conscious. Had she heard Detective Woods correctly? Ethan had been watching her in her apartment? The tears streamed down her face and into her ears as the happenings of the night choked her.

"How could you ask me that question?" Frances said through her tears. "Why do you think I would know anything about it? What the hell? Are you really a detective? What kind of questioning is this?" Frances could feel her anger exploding through her vocal chords. She wanted to be alone. She wanted to stay afloat, but she was drowning. Frances had not noticed a man wearing superhero scrubs enter the room until he handed her a Kleenex.

"Looks like you are having a fun day. Hi. I'm Rodney, everyone's favorite CT tech. I need to get her to CT for a head scan." Rodney went to work attaching her IV bag to the bed and winked at Detective Woods as he wheeled Frances off to the scanner.

"I will have some follow up questions, Frances," Detective Woods called after her as Rodney wheeled her away.

"Sounds like you get to spend more time with the sexiest detective on the force," Rodney said as he stopped pushing Frances and the hospital gurney to wait for the elevator.

"My friend was killed tonight," Frances said.

"I am so sorry. Quite a night. I figured something was up with all the police protection you have right now."

"What do you mean?" Frances asked.

"There are cops stationed in the ER lobby and outside your room. Not to mention the one that is following us to the CT room."

Frances tried to turn her head to see what Rodney was talking about, but it hurt too much. She cringed and closed her eyes as the pain drove another nail into her head. The image of Ethan staring up into the night sky was all she could see when she closed her eyes. He looked so close to her when she looked down on him from her window.

"Hang tight, Frances, I am moving you onto the elevator," Rodney said.

"No worries. I am not sure why I get all the police attention. I am not in any more danger since they shot and killed Ethan."

"I guess I will need to watch the news. Let's talk about something else to help you get through this day."

"Rodney, would it be okay if I don't talk? My head feels like I have a whole pre-school of toddlers playing with hammers in my head right now."

"Understood. You know it could be worse?"

"What? How would you know?" Frances asked.

"You could have been assigned one of those asshole white Republican male cops that see any woman as a hysterical victim that caused the man to snap."

"You sound like a feminist, and you are making my head hurt worse."

"But I have you focused on something else," Rodney said.

CHAPTER THIRTY-EIGHT
NEWS TRAVELS FASTER THAN LIGHT

THERESA Kavanagh was walking home past a bar when she glanced in the window and noticed her sister Frances on a giant TV screen. She had to do a double take and walk back to the window. There, on about a fifteen-foot screen, were images of her sister Frances being loaded into an ambulance. Theresa put her hands on the window as she tried to figure out what was going on as she watched the twenty-second video replay. Theresa ran into the bar asked a waiter to turn up the volume.

"What are you drinking?" he asked.

"That's my sister," Theresa said. She tried to focus on what she was hearing. None of it made any sense. She took out her cell phone and dialed Frances, only to have it roll into Frances's voicemail. "What the hell? Frances, please pick up the phone."

"Hey, Arty, this girl here says that woman on TV is her sister."

"Really? Did you know your sister was killed by a terrorist?"

Theresa pushed through the two men and back out to the street. She saw the images, and Frances was not moving. Her eyes were closed. Theresa was shaking as she turned in first left and then right. Where could she go? Who could she call? Theresa called her parent's home number. It was going onto its third ring, causing Theresa to break out into a run. She had to get to Kelly.

"Hello, Kavanagh residence."

"Mom. Turn on the TV to CNN," Theresa said.

"Who is this? I am too busy right now."

"It's Theresa, Mom. Something has happened to Frances and she's on CNN. Well, an image of her being loaded into an ambulance is on CNN. San Francisco had a terrorist attack."

"What? Stop these jokes. It isn't April first. You're pulling my leg. I have the local news on in the kitchen, and I can hear that they are talking about the Rams moving to Los Angeles. I say good riddance. You think if an attack happened in San Francisco they would be talking about a football team? I have so much to get done before church on Sunday. I don't know where your father is right now—I asked him to go pick up some quilting supplies. He knows how badly I need those. Sometimes I think he ignores me."

"Mom…listen, I saw Frances. It is not good. Turn the TV on and find out for yourself. I tried calling her—"

"Theresa, I am making a memory quilt for a little girl who lost her father. I promised to get it done before mass on Sunday. I am laying out all the different pieces of clothing that the mother had given me. You know I can't be interrupted when doing this project. I should not have answered the phone."

Theresa stopped running, not wanting to believe what she was hearing from their mother. She had heard Frances talk about the fact that their mother did not know how to have a conversation, but this was the first time Theresa finally understood what that meant.

"The little O'Brian girl really needs this quilt, and I promised her mother when she gave me a bag of clothing. I had told her not to wash it, but she didn't listen. I guess she heard that some of the other quilt makers I have given the patterns to wanted the clothing laundered. That takes the purpose away for the kids. It is comforting because it smells like the person."

"Mom, listen to me. I said that Frances was in some sort of big thing that happened in San Francisco, and she was being loaded into the back of an ambulance. I don't know if she is alive."

"Theresa, I don't have time for this right now. I'm getting another call. Hang on a minute."

A click and she was holding on a silent phone line. The street where Theresa stood waiting for her Mom to come back on the phone was packed with people. To get out of the main crush, Theresa worked her way over to a lamp post, using it to shield her from the stampede of people headed home after work. Theresa's tears were falling and she didn't bother to wipe them away. Her sister was possibly dead and Theresa had never felt so alone. She didn't want to lose the call, so she decided to text Kelly.

911 it is about Frances. Can you come get me I'm on the corner of LaGuardia Place and W 3rd street. On phone with my mom.

"Hello. Theresa? Are you still there? Edna called and told me that Frances was on the news. I am going to tell you what I told her. It was not Frances. I know because I am her mother and no one has contacted us. If something so bad happened, we would have been notified."

"Mom, it is Frances. I'm hanging up now and am going to call Edna."

Theresa found hanging up on her mother caused her to cry harder. She hit Edna's number and waited for her sister to answer.

"Hello. Theresa. I'm sorry, I can't stop crying," Edna said.

"It's true, isn't it? That was Frances on the news?" Theresa asked.

"They gave her name. It is, and I tried calling different hospitals in San Francisco and I am not finding her. The San Francisco police main number got me nowhere. What if she is dead?"

"I know. Edna, do you think Mom is crazy?"

"She is definitely something, but I don't think she is crazy. Where are you? It sounds really busy."

"I am outside the school. I am waiting for a friend to come and pick me up."

"Theresa, can you go out to San Francisco? We'll buy your ticket. Someone from the family needs to go out there and find out if she is okay."

"Yes."

"I'll make your reservations and send you an email. Get packed."

"Edna, I love you."

"Love you too."

Theresa spun around when she felt a hand on her shoulder. She was ready to fight.

"Sweetheart, what is going on? I got here as fast as I could. Class was running late," Kelly said.

Theresa fell into Kelly's arms, crying and scared of all the unknowns. The world faded away around them as she cried, gulping for air. There was no explanation for the reaction of her mother.

"I was walking past a bar that had CNN on and saw Frances. She was being loaded into the back of an ambulance. Something happened in San Francisco. A terrorist attack or something. I called my Mom and she was—"

"Baby, I'm here now. Let's go home. We can find out more online."

"What if she is dead? Edna is buying me a plane ticket so I can go out there."

Theresa stopped her crying and tried to wipe the snot from her nose with her jacket. She looked at Kelly and wished to be anywhere but standing on the street in New York.

"Kelly, I am so scared."

"I'm with you," Kelly said.

"Don't you see? My mom is treating Frances like she is no longer part of the family. She doesn't care and wasn't willing to listen. All because Frances got divorced and quit her job. What do you think they are going to do when I tell them I am marrying a woman?"

"One thing at a time. Don't tell them anything right now. We need to go home and locate Frances. You need to get some food and try to find some answers. I don't care about your family. I care about you. They can go fuck themselves."

Theresa stopped walking and looked at Kelly. What was happening? She took Kelly's hand and started walking again. Her cell phone vibrated and Theresa looked down to see who was calling.

"Bernard," Theresa said.

"I just got over to Mom and Dad's. Did you see the news? Frances was involved in some sort of terrorist thing."

"Bernard, I called Mom and so did Edna."

"You need to come home now, Theresa. Stop your play acting or whatever you are doing in New York and come home," Bernard said.

"Edna is getting me a ticket to go to San Francisco. I need to go find Frances."

"God damn it! I told her not to do that. I just got off the phone with her. You are coming home to St. Louis. We need to meet as a family. I'm tired of all this bullshit that Frances is putting the family through. Did you see that she was involved in some sordid love triangle with a man and a woman?"

"Theresa, hang up," Kelly said.

"Who is that? Theresa, who are you with?" Bernard asked.

"I am not coming home—I am going to go find Frances," Theresa said.

"With what money?" Bernard asked.

Theresa hung up the phone and turned to Kelly.

"The family wants me to come back to St. Louis. I need to go find Frances. It sounds like Bernard told Edna not to buy the ticket for me," Theresa said.

"We have the emergency credit card. Let's go get you a ticket. I am sorry I can't come with you. I will hold down our place here. I love you. Go find Frances," Kelly said.

Theresa took Kelly in her arms and kissed her. The two women hugged and then started walking the ten blocks to their studio apartment. Theresa tried to quiet her mind and focus on the sounds of the city around her, the smell of the concrete, and the light scent of Kelly's Bond No. 9 Peace perfume.

CHAPTER THIRTY-NINE
HOW DOES ONE SCAN A CAT?

"ARE the rumors about what happened true? I heard you had a rather abrupt ending to a love triangle—rough day," Rodney said as he helped Frances get situated on the less than comfortable sliding table for the CT scan.

"Not sure exactly what happened. It wasn't a love triangle. Is that what people are saying? Oh my god…I'm so far under, I'm gasping for air." Frances tried to keep from screaming out in pain as she laid her head back into the foam cradle that another tech was helping Rodney get her head placed into. At least the pain was keeping her focused on not completely freaking out in front of these total strangers. A love triangle? With Ethan and Emily? Who thought it was a triangle? Ethan? why? Frances blinked hard to try and clear the tears out of her eyes.

"This is going to keep your head still so we can take these pictures and get you out of here." Rodney smiled, which showed off his adorable dimples. His expression was so open and friendly, Frances found herself drifting into a strange comfort. What was it about gay men that could so easily disarm her and put her at ease?

"Have you ever scanned a cat?"

"Not the first time I have heard that one; however, I heard about you teasing Detective Woods about her name. Girl, I would chalk it up to hitting your head. The reason we shortened computerized axial tomographic to CAT and finally just CT is to stop horrid jokes about scanning cats."

"What is it with you? Are you like central control on gaining all the latest gossip?" Frances said. She tried to turn her head but couldn't because of the harness they had her locked into. "That name thing happened before I hit my head. It was all so strange—a friend was standing outside my loft with a gun, and someone said explosives, but the dogs didn't find any bombs. When I heard her name, it was a release valve. That's the story I am going with right now."

"That is some messed-up shit," Rodney said as he checked something on the giant machine that Frances was trying to ignore. "Detective Woods and I are friends. She gets all the crazy cases and they always bring them here."

"Ouch. I thought you said you were the favorite or nicest tech? Could you do me a favor and call my friends for me and let them know I'm okay?" Frances asked Rodney as he was walking out of the room to get the scan started.

"Sure thing. What's the number?"

"Oh crap. I don't know. I have them all on speed dial. Technology is making me stupid. I used to know all my friends' numbers by heart before mobile phones."

"No worries—we will get you out of here in minutes and you can call them from your phone. Now, take a good breath for me and let it out. Take another, okay—breathe slowly and be as still as you can."

Frances listened to the machine whirr and click into action as the table moved her ever so slightly. She didn't know if she could blink her eyes or not and decided to keep them closed. The image of Ethan lying in the road was vivid, and tears started to roll down the side of her face and into her ears.

"Are you okay?" Rodney asked over the intercom.

"Sorry. Did I move?"

"You are doing fine, Frances. Take a deep breath; we have two more to do and then you'll be done. With this super machine, less than thirty seconds."

Before she could count to ten, Rodney was helping her sit up and transfer back to the hospital gurney. "You're shivering—honey, you should have let me know you were cold. I have heated blankets." With that, Rodney grabbed one out of a warming cupboard and tucked it around her on the gurney. Frances felt small and safe for the first time in a long time. She wanted Rodney to slow the ride down back to the emergency room. This was the first time she felt peace.

"Do I have to go back? The detective is going to barrage me with more questions. My friend killed himself tonight. I think he committed suicide."

The two were quiet as Rodney pushed the button for the elevator. The hallway was quiet, and Frances closed her eyes, trying not to see what her brain was showing on its big screen. Ethan was lying on his back in a pool of blood. But his face—his face was so clean, and his eyes were open. Frances couldn't stop it, and fortunately for her, Rodney had a barf tray in front of her before she knew it was coming. The elevator door opened, and Rodney pushed the hospital gurney into the elevator like nothing had happened. Frances lay back and hoped that was the last of her vomiting for a while because it added a whole new layer of hurt to her pounding head.

"Detective Woods is a good one. You are lucky because there are some real winners on the force. Tell her you're tired, and she'll talk to you later," Rodney said as he gently took the barf tray from Frances's hand.

"I'm headed to Hawaii tomorrow. I think I am anyway. I don't know anymore." Frances offered the statement to escape her current situation.

"You know, I keep telling my husband he needs to take me to Hawaii. I want to go. Can you talk to him for me?"

"The Hawaii trip was a surprise for me. But today turned into—hell."

Frances focused on counting the light fixtures on the hallway ceiling as Rodney pushed her back toward the ER bay she woke up in. With each passing light, one more shadow fell, revealing a replay of the scenes from earlier in her mind—the shards of shattered glass, explosions of sound, and the gathering of police around Ethan's body as the bullets found their mark and held his body down against the asphalt. Frances felt her throat tighten and coughed hard, trying to reclaim her breathing. She was still here. She was still alive. Rodney stopped and banked a hard left, angling Frances back into the bay.

"We're back. Lucky you, as it appears there are no detectives to interrogate you right now. I'll go hunt down your mobile for you so you can make that call." Rodney gave Frances a pat on her shoulder and was out the door.

Frances shut her eyes and took another deep breath, knowing that she couldn't wish any of this away. It had happened. The result? Ethan was dead. A deep breath in—even though it physically hurt to breath so deeply—reaffirmed she was alive. Did he really want to kill her? Or did he want her to see him die? Her tears were leaking again and her head was pounding. What did she want? She wanted love, her art, and her friends. Had she blown it all? Maybe her parents were right to worry about her throwing it all away to chase a stupid dream. What dream?

A swirl of noise and activity suddenly surrounded her, which snapped Frances out of her silent thoughts and jolted her into the present moment. People dressed in scrubs carried items in and out of the area. No one stopped or said anything until a nurse who towered over her put a blood pressure cuff on her left arm and pumped it up with such quickness and velocity, Frances was worried her arm was going to be amputated. A short little man waited quietly as another person in a white lab coat put a rubber tourniquet on her bicep and tapped the inside of her elbow. The blood draw was coming, and Frances closed her eyes. Why didn't anyone ask her if she fainted easily? She was lying down, so it probably didn't matter. Frances opened her eyes just in time to see the phlebotomist push a needle into her vein. The blood filled the vial quickly.

Through all the commotion, Frances's eyes focused on Detective Woods, who was silently watching the circus with a quiet face and arms lightly crossed. Who was this woman? Why was the uniformed police officer still standing guard outside her door? Was she under arrest?

"Hi, Frances. I'm Doctor Ned. They tell me you hit your head," said the quiet, short, little man who had waited until the blood draw was done.

He shined a light into her eyes and for a moment she saw nothing but polka dots. "Can you tell me your full name?"

"Frances Olar Kavanagh. F.O.K. for short."

"F.O.K.—now that is funny. I knew a general surgeon whose initials were W.T.F.," Dr. Ned said. "I want you to take my two fingers and squeeze them with your hands." Dr. Ned held his hands out in front of her with two fingers together on each hand. Frances thought all of this was odd. "Tell me what kind of pain, if any, you are feeling."

"A rather intense throbbing in my head. Will I be able to get on a plane tomorrow?" Frances asked. With that question, she noticed that Detective Woods stood and had unfolded her arms.

"Sure. You hit your head, but everything looks clear on the scan, and you are having normal responses to a good head bang. I am going to run through a series of exercises to make sure we rule out concussion. You pass those and you are good to go skydiving if you want."

"Will those tests tell you if I'm crazy? I did not hit my head for fun. I'm not crazy. At least I don't think I am." Frances stopped talking and stared at the clock, counting the number of hours before she could escape.

"Frances, do you think you can answer some more questions—"

"Now, Detective, you will have plenty of time with the patient. Right now, it's my time. You can stay, but don't be a distraction."

"Too late," Frances said. "I said that out loud, didn't I?" Frances felt her face flush several shades of red.

"Play poker much?" Dr. Ned said as he laughed.

Detective Woods started to walk out of the room. "Wait. Detective, did they have to kill him?" Frances asked.

"Yes. He set the ball rolling when he fired that shot. Now we're going to try and get to some answers if we can." Detective Woods flipped her notebook closed and chatted with the police officer standing watch.

CHAPTER FORTY
CRAZY WORDS

"Do you think she's still at the hospital?" Winter asked between bites of her Patxi's pizza. For some reason, the past couple of weeks Winter could not satisfy her need to eat. She was still working out the same, and Jason, her longest-term boyfriend, was better than ever. Maybe it was the stress from work and her new client. Maybe this uncontrolled need to eat had everything to do with crazy Frances. Would the others who were not eating notice she was chowing through it like there was no tomorrow? Winter considered having herself checked for a tapeworm because she was eating so much food lately. Winter looked down at her tummy. It all looked normal. Her suits were fitting fine. Then something clicked in her mind. Holy shit, her period was a couple weeks or so late. Of course, something like this would happen in the middle of a Frances crisis. Winter finished chewing and reached for the water instead of the beer.

"We could call the detective and maybe find out what's going on or head back to the loft. Do you think she's going to use that ticket and go to Hawaii?" Cheryl asked as she took another long sip from her cold beer.

"No. There is no way she can go anywhere. Ethan was shot and killed on the street in front of her loft. If Frances wasn't a nutcase before, this will surely put her into that realm." Dana offered her opinion as she hunted for another anchovy to put on top of her salad.

"Did you know that Ethan had attacked her?" Winter asked the crew.

"Nope. She hasn't said anything to me," Simon responded and took stock of the rest of the group.

"I think she should go to Hawaii. We need to help her get a suitcase together," Russell said, downing the last of his Coke.

"Crazy words, Russell. It has been a long day. We can't get into her place. The police are still all over it worse than sugar ants—our building is suffering from an SFPD infestation," Simon said.

"Let's go and work our way in and get something ready for her. I highly doubt she has anything appropriate, anyway."

"Russell, I will drink to that. I wonder if she even owns a bathing suit?"

"Winter, don't you know someone who could help us better than the boys?" Cheryl asked. "I think that Frances was trying to tell me about the Ethan thing the night of the potluck. She was acting so strange and had pulled me out of her loft right after Ethan had arrived. It was so not Frances."

"The whole thing is sick. But Cheryl, you are brilliant. You're right—I know who can help us. Let me call her—she's always around. Plan on a field trip. We are going on a shopping spree at Catharine's on Second. She owes me some huge favors," Winter said as she listened for her friend, Tran, to pick up the phone.

The crew crammed themselves into a cab on their way to do the impossible: get Frances a wardrobe that didn't scream "I am a woman, but I would rather dress like a Mormon boy on a mission or a crazed artist."

CHAPTER FORTY-ONE
MUSIC WHISPERS

THE black-and-white squad car pulled up to the back door of Frances's building where she could see straight through the windows of the lobby. Police were still swarming in the front of the building, and they still had the street closed. The darkness of the night was wiped out with large bright lights, giving the whole area the eerie look of opening night for a club or theatre. Frances walked slowly through the door being held open by a faceless uniformed officer. She kept her focus on the ground and her feet. Frances knew where she was by the changes in the concrete flooring. How could a place be both so familiar and so foreign? Frances knew where she was walking and felt the elevator button give way as she pushed it with her knuckle. Her usual way to hit the button.

"Ethan," Frances said aloud. She pressed her hand against the bump on the back of her head and was relieved that it shot a quick stab of pain through her body. The ER doctor had determined she was fine and gave her something to stop the pounding headache. Now that she was back in her building, she thought this was all a hoax. This was some elaborate, sick joke. Frances walked through the hallway and stopped briefly at the open door to the boys' loft. She could see some policemen working in there, like they were rewiring the electricity of the apartment. She decided to skip seeing if the boys were home. There was something she needed to see again.

Frances did not want to look down on the street in front of her loft, but her mind put her on autopilot. She felt an immense weight of gravity bearing down on her when she walked through her door, held open by another unknown police officer. All around her, despite the activity of people, Frances felt a heavy suffocating stillness in the air. All this commotion would eventually go away, and then what?

There were still several officers collecting items and going through her loft. Frances slowly walked to her windows facing out to the street. What did she hope to see? Did she want Ethan to still be there? Detective Woods entered the room, too late to stop Frances from going over to the window. The broken glass was still all over the floor from the window that had been shattered by the bullet that Ethan fired. Frances stopped and held her hands flat on the glass as she looked down at the top of a white canopy that had been erected over Ethan's body. The bomb squad was using a robot to take pictures of his body. Frances could see Ethan's black boots with yellow stitching. There was no movement in those boots. She turned from the scene and looked around her loft, not registering anything. She wanted to separate from this world and fall into bed and sleep forever. The doctor was right. His drug had worked and the major throbbing in her head had finally stopped, leaving a very light drumbeat tapping at her nerves again.

Had her troubles ended tonight? Was this a blessing instead of a tragedy? Ethan had been watching her. Frances shivered again. She sat at her piano, her brain recalling almost instantly the moment everything exploded. She watched her hands, now steady, lightly touch the keys. Frances kept her eyes open because she did not want to see the image that was the main feature in her brain. Her fingers floated over the keys and the music was barely whispering to her above the silence. The grand piano had never sounded so quiet. Frances felt herself turning inside out as the music poured from a place she did not recognize.

Each note sounded out another whisper that surrounded her building with a web of comfort in that moment. The music danced around her, each note creating another layer to her cocoon. Frances glanced up and noticed Detective Woods standing motionless in her open doorway. With each chord progression, Frances felt the attention of

Detective Woods focused upon her as tears formed in Frances's eyes. She stopped playing and turned to the still Detective Woods. Their eyes caught for a moment, and Frances felt the emotion change from a softness to something else. Detective Woods turned and walked down the hallway toward the elevator.

"SEE? I told you that she would be here," Winter said, pointing in the direction of Detective Woods.

Woods turned when she heard the voices and watched as the group was quickly silenced by the piano music floating down the hallway. Frances was home and at her piano. The music cried and produced such a feeling of melancholy that it quickly silenced the group that detoured into Simon and Russell's place. Woods walked toward the open door to the boys' loft. She hoped that they would be too distracted to recognize her. Woods remembered meeting the boys at a fundraiser with her ex-girlfriend. Woods took a deep breath and exhaled out in the hallway.

"Even Winston is impacted by all this crazy and has decided to stay in his bed," Winter commented as she set the load of bags she was carrying down.

"What should we do with all this stuff? There is no way Frances is going to Hawaii," Russell said as he walked to the fridge to get a drink of water.

"I think we pack it up for her and give her the option," Dana offered, reaching into a bag and folding the items to be packed. "Life is too short to let a freak of nature stop us from living. Besides, it would be good to get her out of here."

"You forget that we don't really know who sent her that invitation," Winter said as she joined Russell at the fridge. "Got anything cold to drink in there?"

"Knock, knock. May I come in?" Detective Woods asked at the open door to the boys' loft.

"Of course, Detective. Would you like anything to drink?"

"Whiskey neat is what I want, but I'll take a coffee if you have it. Could any of you tell me more about this trip to Hawaii?"

"We have both—maybe an Irish coffee?" Russell tried a smile as he made his brilliant suggestion. "I know the secret of the Buena Vista and could make us all one."

"Sounds wonderful, but I'm on duty and would love a coffee with a little milk or cream."

I'll take an Irish coffee since you are offering," Cheryl said, sitting on the white leather sofa that only worked in a house with no children. "Detective, where did you grow up?" Cheryl asked.

"You picked up on my accent. Astute," Detective Woods said.

Dana turned to the detective. "Not sure we can help you out much. We know that Frances believes the ticket came from this woman, an art dealer out of New York, who she met through Nathan Steiner and spent some time with here in San Francisco."

"Dana, your description of the crazy that is Frances is so flat," Cheryl said. "Frances swore this woman quite possibly might be the love of her life. The heavens opened, and she knew that this was her soul mate. She must have some kind of faith or otherwise is way off on judging how other people view the relationship."

"Cheryl, you are highlighting the obvious about Frances being unable to accurately judge people's intentions. Look at Ethan—Frances had no clue that guy was so insane," Winter said. She placed several glass coffee cups on the counter and was gathering the whiskey for the Irish coffees.

Detective Woods went to the counter and sat on a bar stool as she listened to the bantering of the tight-knit group.

"Detective, where are you from again? Your accent is so cool. It makes me think I'm watching the BBC," Simon said as he sat next to Cheryl on the pristine white couch.

"I had not said where I come from yet. You didn't miss it, Simon. You display an interesting flavor of the English accent too. I was raised in London for most of my life. Spent time in Dublin and Glasgow. Went to college here in the States. I guess you can say I take after my father, who is Scottish. My mother and her family were raised in Maine, but she migrated to San Francisco. Enough about me—is there anything else you can share about Frances, Ethan, and the day's events?"

"Not that you probably don't already know at this point, Detective. Here's that coffee for you." Russell handed her a cup of freshly pressed coffee.

Woods closed her eyes and inhaled deeply. "This makes me wish to be home, and that isn't going to happen anytime soon as we need to sort all this out. Forgive me for this lapse."

No one said a word as they watched Detective Woods walk toward the door. Piano music was still making its way down the hall. Detective Woods turned to the group and took another sip of the coffee.

"There's my cue. The music has stopped. I need to go see if Frances can add anything else to the narrative. May I take this?" Detective Woods didn't wait for an answer. The coffee was rich and gave her some much-needed energy. As she walked toward the open door of Frances's loft, she watched Frances at her piano, just sitting. "Frances is both beautiful and sad," the detective whispered out loud. She had to shake her head to get her thoughts in order so she could get this job done professionally.

CHAPTER FORTY-TWO
HOW MUCH DO YOU KNOW?

FRANCES, from her perch on the piano bench, watched Detective Woods as she gave instructions to a couple of policeman carrying some items out of the loft. Had this been any other happening, she would have moved immediately, but right now all she wanted to do was sit—sit and not do anything. The hustle and bustle in her loft had quieted since she had started playing. Maybe she used the music to suck the energy out of the room. She wanted her place back to herself. She wanted to paint. Frances stood from the piano and went to the kitchen sink, splashing some cold water on her face.

With her back to the door, she heard Detective Woods's distinctive voice give even more directions to the uniformed officers who were stationed throughout the building. It was clear they were going to be here for a while. She let the water drip off her face and didn't reach for a towel. It felt real. It felt good. The cold water turned warm from the heat of her skin. Frances went back for another splash of cold water, this time getting more on her shirt than her face.

"Frances, I'm glad to see you are back in one piece from the hospital." Detective Woods came in and shut the door to the loft. A uniformed officer sat in a chair close to the door. Frances continued to let the water drip off her face and didn't turn around.

"Detective, I don't think there is anything else I can talk to you about right now," Frances said as she reached for a dishtowel off her drain board.

"What can you tell me about Nathan and Olivia?"

Frances turned around so quickly she lost her balance. "Why? What have they got to do with any of this? Ethan was clearly a pervert. What can you tell me about the extent of his spying? Is there a website out there with my private life splashed all over so a world of sickos can jack off? What can you tell me?"

"We know that he was recording you. There doesn't appear to be a web outlet of the information he collected, but it is early in the investigation. The story went national, and we were contacted by two other police agencies about unsolved murders." Detective Woods studied Frances and wondered if she was giving her too much to handle now.

"Are you sure you guys found all of the cameras and the microphones? The tracking devices in my bags and on my truck?" Frances was physically shaking, and she wasn't quite sure if it was from anger or fear.

"We will do another sweep in the daylight tomorrow. What I need to know is if you are going on this trip to Hawaii."

"I haven't thought about it. I really had no thought of leaving. Before all of this, I was excited to be headed for Hawaii. Now, I'm exhausted and unsure of so much."

"Understood. When was the last time you spoke with Nathan?"

"I don't know. I haven't really counted the time since we last spoke, really. Ethan's gallery show was when I last saw him in person. That was at least a month ago, if not more. There was a phone conversation about a week after that—wow, it has been awhile."

"How would you describe your relationship with Nathan?"

"It has been great. He is a mentor type to my art and to me. He has helped a lot of us newly declared artists. It's his specialty, to find the next 'artistic genius.'"

"How often did you speak with Nathan before your painting sold?"

"I sold three paintings at the gallery he used to work for before opening his own."

Frances bit her lip as she walked to her favorite leather chair and sat down, contemplating what her relationship with Nathan really was.

"I talked with him any number of times over the phone, but I don't know how many calls exactly. Sometimes we'd meet for a coffee. I think I was his excuse to splurge at the Nespresso bistro," Frances said. The questions had her retreating into her memories and trying to remember the last time she had a real conversation with Nathan. Had she been that distracted with dating women in her own crazy world that she had dropped Nathan? Or had he dropped her? How does that happen? "He never told me anything about his extended trip. I went to the gallery looking for him, and that was when Felipe filled me in on Nathan being gone."

Frances stood as she rifled through the mountain of paper on her coffee table, looking for the check and the airline ticket. In all the commotion, both were lost to the entropy of her creative crazy.

"Relax, Frances. I have the check and the ticket in a folder. I might have to keep them as evidence," Detective Woods said.

"But you can't. Those have nothing to do with Ethan. That is my money and my ticket."

"We don't know if they do or don't have anything to do with today. We are trying to track down exactly where the ticket was purchased and who had access to that kind of cash."

Frances sat back down, shaking her head. "That's gross. Nathan is an old man and quite possibly might be a woman hater. He has his husband, Felipe."

"A woman hater? What makes you say that?"

"It was the look on his face when he found Ethan and me in the alley. He looked right through me like he wanted me to disappear," Frances said.

"Frances, a lot has been going on for you. I am asking you these questions to find the pieces that you aren't able to see because you are in the middle of it all," Detective Woods said.

"What do you think? You seem to be pulling at something here, and I give up. It's three a.m. I want to go to bed and have all this gone when I wake up."

"I'm gathering as much information as I can. You must admit that all of this is rather disjointed and bizarre."

"Detective Woods, are you judging me and my life?" Frances stood, ready to show her the door.

CHAPTER FORTY-TWO

"You can drop the 'Detective' and call me Woods."

"Now that's friendly."

A police officer knocked at the slightly opened door and poked his head into the loft.

"Excuse me, there is a group of people demanding to see Frances." The officer was pushed aside by Winston who came bounding over to Frances, licking her face before she could defend herself.

"We are done here for now." Detective Woods turned to Frances and handed her a piece of paper that she had written a couple of phone numbers on. "There are police officers posted throughout the building and crime scene. They will be primarily located at the entry doors to the building, and a squad car is in the parking lot. The crew out front will be there for the next several hours. If you need anything, you call one of those numbers. They will get it to me. I know this is difficult. If you decide to go out of town, please let us know how we can contact you." Detective Woods handed Frances the folder containing both the airplane ticket and the check from the sale of her paintings. Frances watched as Detective Woods exited. There was something she wanted to say, but with everyone else in the loft, she took a deep breath and turned to Winter and Dana.

"Wow. I feel like I was watching a crime show. That was amazing," Winter said as she came in and dropped two packed suitcases in front of Frances.

"What are these?"

"Well, Frances, we, the duty-bound knights of Buena Vista Round Table, took it upon ourselves to get you a decent wardrobe, should you decide to get on that plane in a few hours." Winter took a seat on the couch.

"I am so lost, I can't decide if I should go or stay. I'm drowning and I—"

"Oh, sweet girl. I can call you 'girl' since I'm older than all of you in this room by two or three decades. But I'm not measuring? Age is all up to attitude and luck. The trip might be what you need to find that you really aren't lost." Dana held Frances tightly.

"What if I'm wrong and my instincts are screwed up? What if this has nothing to do with love or soul mates?" Frances was talking herself out of getting on that plane.

CHAPTER FORTY-THREE
TRUST

THE plane had pulled away from the gate right on time and was ready to taxi across the tarmac when Frances accidentally hit her recline button. Her first-class seat almost went completely flat. Frances frantically tried to right the seat and ignore the scowling faces of her fellow first-class passengers. She pulled herself up and out of the seat, desperate to fix the situation or magically fade into the thin air. Still fumbling with the controls, Frances could tell the seat was not doing anything and felt the panicked sweat beading across her forehead and trickling down her back. After pushing a combination of buttons on the armrest of the space-age leather seat, she made it worse when she popped up the foot rest with a loud creaking noise.

"Sorry," Frances tried to apologize as two flight attendants rushed toward her, attempting to stifle their laughter.

"Trust me, you're not the first to have a fight with this seat. We keep telling maintenance it's defective." With a few quick button presses and a swift kick to the footrest, the seat folded back into an upright position. Frances was scared to sit back down for fear that the seat would decide to completely break, ejecting her from the plane. Maybe the first-class seats knew when they had an imposter. The plane was still moving and was turned onto the runway. When the plane stopped,

Frances let out a little scream, worried that the pilots were going to taxi back to the gate and remove her in handcuffs from the plane. It was a different world, and maybe someone dialed 911 saying a strange red-headed woman was sabotaging the plane because her seat back was not in its most upright and uncomfortable position.

"Okay, take your seat now and try not to push any buttons until after takeoff," the female flight attendant said, rushing back to her jump seat and strapping in as the engines roared with the power to push this jumbo jet filled with thousands of pounds up into the air. The jet rolled down the runway, pushing Frances back into her seat. She made sure to keep her hands, elbows, and legs away from the control panel of the seat of terror. A sigh of relief left her lips when she knew the plane was not headed back to the gate.

Her heart missed a few beats as the plane hurtled into the air. The wheels were off the ground, pulling them further away from the planet in a defiant act against gravity. Was she acting against the force of the gods by leaving the mess behind? There were no answers, only more questions. All this crazy thinking made her heart rate jump up. In about five hours, she would at least get confirmation of one answer she knew was right. She quickly glanced around the cabin and was relieved no one cared about her as their phones or electronic tablets distracted them.

Was she trying to run away from the whole mess? Yes. "There you go again, Frances. You know you should not be talking to yourself." She closed her eyes and let her body relax a little into the leather seat. The staleness of recycled airplane air was already starting to dry out her sinuses. Maybe sleep would be a good idea. But she was too excited and decided to study the controls on the armrest carefully.

After some trepidation, Frances touched two buttons and safely reclined her seat, raising the footrest without harming herself or anyone else. Seated next to her was a very tall, tan, twenty-something, with sandy blonde hair and the whitest teeth she had ever seen. When he smiled, his teeth glowed so brightly in the darkened light of the plane that she felt she could read her magazine by their light. He wore headphones almost as big as his head. His eyes were closed, and he was clearly off in his own world. His Tag Heuer watch hung loosely around his wrist and went well with his Sex Wax T-shirt. His jeans probably cost around the same amount as her monthly mortgage payment, but then, who was she to comment? Her airplane ticket could pay her mortgage for half a year. Why did she pick such an expensive city to live in again? She might have to revisit that choice.

She was now studying her center console armrest, trying to figure out how to make a video screen materialize for herself. She had not been trying long when a swift hand from the flight attendant who had saved her from the seat fiasco reached over and pushed the top of the console down, causing a video screen to magically pop up. With the other hand, the flight attendant handed Frances a headset.

"This way you can watch and listen, or maybe you like filling in your own dialogue. Some do."

Frances settled into her seat and started to scroll through different screens, looking for a movie to pass the time on the flight. After all the tragedy of the last twenty-four hours, a comedy was the focus of her search. She was torn between the latest Muppet movie starring her favorites, the Muppets along with Tina Fey, or a more adult comedy. A glance at her traveling partner, who still had his eyes closed, made her feel a little more comfortable in choosing a kid's movie. This was so cool, she thought to herself as she pushed play. Her guava mimosa and some warmed trail mix filled with cashews, candied pineapple, almonds, and some yummy crunchy thing rolled in sesame seeds, rounded out her flight. She could get used to this style of travel.

The movie took her mind away from the world as she became completely engrossed in the singing and dancing Muppets. She started counting the number of times Tina Fey, playing a Russian prison guard, changed her Russian accent. It was almost every scene. Was that part of the joke? It made the film even funnier. Try to do that, Meryl Streep, Frances mused to herself. Meryl Streep was a favorite of hers too, although the movies Meryl chose to appear in were usually so intense she could watch them only once. *Sophie's Choice* brought Ethan front and center in her mind again. They had talked about that movie for hours one night at the studio. Holy shit. What the fuck, Ethan? She looked around her again and no one was watching her as the tears fell. What was she thinking? Leaving her friends for an unknown rendezvous across the Pacific Ocean.

She took the napkin from the nuts and tried to blow her nose. The result was that she blew nut dust across herself and her sleeping seatmate. It took her a few minutes to try and compose herself. Should she wake him? Should she try to wipe off the snack dust? The flight attendant came over with a small box of tissues and a warm, wet towel. Frances had no words as she sat back in her seat and tried to clean herself off. The flight attendant made a motion to not worry about the young kid who was sleeping next to her. In a smooth motion, the very attentive flight attendant restarted the movie for Frances. It took her some time to relax enough to allow some giggles out.

Thirty minutes later, a tap on Frances's shoulder had her jump so high out of her seat that she almost hit her head on the overhead compartment.

"Sorry. Didn't mean to startle you," a flight attendant said to Frances, who was trying to push her racing heart back down into her chest. With her headphones now barely hanging on for dear life, Frances turned her attention to the person standing over her.

"So, glad you are enjoying your movie. Your laughter—"

"I am so sorry. Was it that loud? People heard me laughing over the sounds of the engines? I will keep it under 110 decibels. Really, I'm sorry." Frances felt that red tone hit her cheeks again as she quickly glanced around, looking for the passenger she had offended with her laughter that was apparently louder than jet engines.

"No worries. I love that movie too." Frances glanced over at her seatmate and saw that he was awake and no longer wearing his headphones.

"Sorry. I didn't mean to wake you," Frances said to him.

"You didn't but your scream did." He smiled, flashing those glowing white teeth again. Frances could not stop staring at his teeth.

"Are you staring at my teeth?" he asked, laughing. "Before you ask—yes, they are naturally this white, and no, I don't use any whitening product, nor do I work for a toothpaste company."

"So, you've been dealing with this issue for a while?" Frances responded.

"Since I can remember."

Still in disbelief that his teeth were not altered in any way, she watched as he put his headphones back on, closed his eyes, and went back to whatever state he was in before her scream. His teeth were heaven white. What is that? Heaven white? Frances, you are off your rocker, she thought. She didn't bother him anymore. She understood that headphones and closed eyes were a strong sign that he was not interested in talking.

Frances shuddered a little, thinking about how she might come across. She was sitting in a new V-neck T-shirt and a pair of linen shorts that her friends found at some boutique Winter had forced the owner into opening in the middle of the night. What kind of lawyer was Winter? Now this was a follow-up question for her friend. Frances glanced down at her exposed skin, which was on the whiter shade of pasty white. When was the last time it had seen the sun? Vampires had more color in their skin than she did.

Frances decided not to finish the movie and turned to some Hawaiian music, hoping it would let her grab an hour of sleep. The music worked. Her eyelids felt remarkably heavy. She had enjoyed a most delicious brunch at the start of the movie, and the alcohol was also kicking in to help her relax. At last, she let the last of the resistance against sleep go and fell into a deep, snoring, and drool-producing sleep.

For the second time in the flight, Frances screamed. This time the scream was produced when her seatmate, the boy-man with sparkling white teeth, started shaking her arm.

"Time to wake up. We're ten minutes out. Fill out your form. Be sure to declare all those snakes and exotic animals you're smuggling into the islands."

Awkward did not begin to explain how Frances felt as she tried to wipe the string of drool away from the corner of her mouth without drawing any attention to the pool of wet on her shirt. A couple of hard blinks brought her back to her senses, and she focused on the red-and-white form that had been placed on her seat table.

"Ladies and gentlemen, please check your seatbelts. We are cleared for landing. All seat backs and tray tables stowed ..."

The intercom distracted Frances, but thankfully the flight attendant who had taken care of her from the start was at her side getting her ready for landing. She felt like a toddler. This was crazy. In less than an hour, would she know who had done this? Who had given her such a great gift? Now Frances felt the butterflies flying around in her stomach and she worried she was going to take flight from all their activity. She was now so close to finding out who had whisked her away on an open-ended first-class ticket; it was like Christmas morning. This was better than anything she could have dreamt herself. Frances walked off the plane into the humid tropical warmth and let it completely wrap around her. Through the windows, she saw the beautiful blue sky, swaying palm trees, and the sparkling green-blue waters that made this an enchanted vacation destination for the world.

Frances scanned the people as she made her way to baggage claim. She did not recognize anyone. There were a couple of different tour groups that held up signs with arms heavily covered with various types of floral leis. A young man stood toward the front of the baggage claim area holding a single rose. This made Frances smile. He watched the crowd coming through the security doors from the terminal with anticipation and focus. She wanted to see the reunion. What was his story? His hair was sporting a military-close shave. Her inner mind narrative decided that he was a young Navy officer who had been stationed on a carrier in the South Pacific. He had been on an extra-long deployment. His young wife was flying to Hawaii for the first time from a small town in Iowa. They were probably going to make a baby on this reunion.

Frances scoped out the best spot to stand where she could watch for both the young lovers' reunion and her bags. She did not want to show up with a ton of baggage, but her friends insisted she needed everything they packed for her. Not to mention the emotional baggage of what had transpired over the past day. What the heck was she thinking? Frances turned back to watch some luggage start to come out on the conveyer belt. When Frances traveled for business, she always envied those people who had two small bags; maybe they sported a sleek shoulder bag for their tiny laptop, and a small suitcase that easily fit in the overhead. She never traveled that light, toting at least one suitcase and three or four banker boxes with materials she needed for client presentations. It was always a long way from baggage claim to the rental car counters for her.

The man with the single rose was now on his tippy toes. He must have seen his love. Frances clasped her hands together, anticipating the embrace. It took her a moment to focus. The man was now in a full-on embrace with another person, this one a little taller and with a similar haircut and in uniform. The two men kissed. Frances realized that she was not the only one staring at the two men now. The male lovers turned and walked arm-in-arm toward the bags that were coming out on the conveyer belt. Frances shook her head and realized that her made-up story was rather old-fashioned and stupid. What did this mean about her life? Because she did not see her name on any of the signs held by strangers, Frances breathed a heavy sigh. No one was there to greet her. She was relieved that she was not put into a strange uncomfortable situation. Would she willingly kiss a woman passionately in public? All of this was still so new to Frances. She felt like she was just learning how to crawl, let alone go retrieve her two heavy bags off the baggage carousel.

No one was here to greet her. The address in the note was for a luxury hotel. She had looked the address up online and had fallen in love with the beautiful white towers and blue lagoon that were less than fifty yards away from the hotel. Many of the rooms looked like they had amazing views of the ocean. Frances would know soon.

CHAPTER FORTY-FOUR
DON'T FORGET

"WHAT did we all say to her before she went through the TSA line?" Cheryl whispered into her headset. She hated being back in the open spaces of the "shared office." It was so difficult to make a private call. At least Cheryl had some cover as her placement in the desk herd was on the outer edge.

"I know. Think about all that she must handle once she gets there. Relax. You know she made it. The flight tracker says the plane arrived. She'll call," Winter said. Cheryl could tell by the tone of Winter's voice that she was trying not to be annoyed with this conversation. Cheryl wondered how Winter was processing Ethan's death. She had not really said anything to anyone about it. In all the winds that are Frances, no one else really said anything about Ethan, and it most likely came down to being in shock. It was like a calculated suicide. But why did he want to die?

Pacing around her desk, Cheryl was trying not to be worried sick about Frances. Who was she fooling? There was no way she was going to get any work done today. The past twenty-four hours had brought no sleep and a whole host of tragic weirdness.

"Did we send Frances off to a serial killer?" Cheryl finally sat down in her desk chair, tired of her nervous walking.

"Well, if we did, they sure spent a hell of a lot of money. What is that banging sound?"

"My head. I'm banging my head against my desk."

"Stop it. Go home. What are you doing at work, anyway? I'm at home in bed. I'm sure Dana has her phone shut off, and the boys…well, they are probably scoping out the police force running around the lofts right now."

"You're probably right. Sleep. Home. Fresh air, as this office floor stinks. I want to force those 'con-slut-ants' to come down here and work at my desk. Some great idea to foster creativity."

"Cheryl, calm down. You mean con-sult-ants."

"No. They are business sluts ruining my life. I'm going to chat later. When I got promoted and finally made it to a real office away from the open sewer of the floor, I celebrated too quickly. Now I have a fancy title, and I am back downwind from a swampy dairy farm. Lesson. Life can be shitty."

Cheryl started to lightly knock her forehead against her desk again, the word "crazy" being repeated over and over in the process. There were lots of crazy things along the past fifteen or so years that the two of them had called each other. Frances's whole exploring her sexuality with women thing didn't really surprise Cheryl that much. To have Frances get on a plane after Ethan pulled his life-ending stunt—now that made her wonder. So much information found about him—his stalking her and proclaiming his love in such a weird way, and then to have it all end so violently. Cheryl sat back in her chair, barely balancing, and stared at the ugly ceiling tiles that made up much of business office ceilings across the US. She missed her little plastic animal zoo that had been glued to her office ceiling tiles.

Cheryl thought about Russell and Simon talking about the fact that the police had swept through their apartment too and had found several listening devices. It had freaked them out. Why would Ethan bug their apartment? Was he, like Frances thought, a gay man? Or was he bi? Cheryl thought it was all overly creepy, and she was exhausted.

What was it that Russell kept talking about? Cheryl thought about how Russell kept saying that he had to have done it when Winston was out of the loft because the dog had never liked Ethan. Not that Winston would do anything to him, but still, he would get a very low growl stuck in his big doggie throat whenever Ethan was around. Cheryl reminded them all during the late-night pizza splurge that animals and kids were the divining rods for good and evil, only to have Winter shoot that theory to hell by bringing up all the evil children who kill their families.

The business card that Detective Woods had given her was still in her pocket. She pulled it out and thought about calling her. There was something good about that person. Frances needed stable and strong in her life. What did she know? Detective Woods was probably married with children. Cheryl threw the card on her desk and let her gaze wander over the desks of her peers. What a mistake. The open office concept was great at reducing productivity. There were thirty coders on the floor and no one was touching a computer keyboard.

Time to call her crazy friend and leave a message. The phone rang and rang with no rollover to voicemail. That was odd. Cheryl hung up and tried again. Same result. This made her more than a little nervous. Cheryl did not like the nerves that her friend was bringing up in her. Life was supposed to be on autopilot right now. Make money, save money, remodel home, and maybe date a nice guy. This was not to be a time of worrying about people stalking your best friend. Or worse, your best friend on a plane, flying to be with a crazy person, on an island.

With voicemail not working, Cheryl decided to text her friend. She spent the next few minutes trying to compose her thoughts and editing what she really wanted to type. She finally texted *Aloha!!!!! Give me a ring and let me know you're there enjoying a tropical drink.* Now she had assumed the role of a protective mother. The hotel was a five-star hotel. Who gives the victim they are going to kill a first-class, open-ended ticket? She watched too much *CSI* and *Law & Order*.

Whatever happened, this was going to cause her to get gray hair prematurely. Frances was going to have to pay for her hair appointments to cover her prematurely graying hair. She wondered how Frances's Irish Catholic family had handled the whole divorce and, now, foray into the world of lesbian exploration? The news reports were great at talking about the Ethan, Emily, and Frances triangle.

When Cheryl decided that business school was not for her and left, it was Frances who gave her the courage to do what she wanted. They used to spend a lot of time talking about what it was like for Cheryl to grow up the daughter of immigrants in the United States. Cheryl had to get over how easily Frances would laugh over some of the issues she dealt with. Although once Frances found out that people would often approach Cheryl and ask her if she spoke English, it gave her all sorts of fun.

Cheryl did use a few of Frances's one-liner suggestions. Cheryl was born and raised in New Jersey. Her parents did not teach her their native language when she was young to reinforce that they wanted her to learn English. Cheryl and her brother, Charlie, had other theories on the language barriers their parents kept with them. The dreams her parents had for her were long gone, and Cheryl had tried to help Frances understand why that was so difficult to reconcile. All these random thoughts were bouncing around like popcorn in a hot kettle. She was sleep-deprived and worried sick about her friend who definitely lived every ounce of life.

No response on her phone. Cheryl felt stupid and decided to head home, unplug from the world, and sleep until she woke up on her own. She checked her notes on her computer where she kept track of her own PTO. The fact that she had accrued more than forty-two vacation days made her realize how pathetic her concept of work–life balance really was. There had to be a knight in shining armor in her own life. Maybe he wouldn't get her a first-class ticket to Hawaii, but there had to be someone, anyone, maybe a guy with a moped who could take her for a slice of real New York pizza or just a bowl of chowder.

CHAPTER FORTY-FIVE

ALOHA

FRANCES gathered her overly stuffed suitcases and contemplated her transportation choices. A bus would be most economical if one went out that far. Who arrives first class and then takes a bus? No car was here to meet her that she could readily see, as her name had not appeared on any signs being held in the baggage claim area. This was a rather peculiar situation. Who would go to through the trouble of a first-class, open-ended ticket and then not send a car? Knock it off, Frances. She could get herself the last seventeen or so miles.

A taxi would work because it was easy and was something she knew she could splurge on this once. Bags in hand, Frances set off for the line of taxis outside baggage claim. When she stepped out of the air-conditioned terminal into the tropical mugginess, it took her breath away for a moment. The air was moist and warm. The smell of cigarette smoke was not what she wanted for her first impression, but she got a lungful as she recovered from her first shock of the humidity.

The butterflies were all up and flapping about her stomach again, and this time it felt like they had advanced from roller derby to cage fighting. Frances took a few shallow breaths, trying to avoid the cloud of cigarette smoke, and headed to the taxi stand. She rummaged through her shoulder bag and found the note with the address. This was all so amazing to her as she thought about how she was never asked to dance in middle school or high school because she towered above most of the boys. Or maybe they knew what she didn't. Here she was in Hawaii. And she wasn't here to meet a boy. At least, as she bit her lower lip, she hoped she was not here to meet a boy. She didn't know any that would do this type of thing anyway.

A spry brown man with snow-white hair hopped out of his bright-green Prius cab and swooped her bags up like they were filled with clouds and marshmallows. Frances settled herself into the back seat, relieved that the cab was clean and did not smell of the stale grossness that often accompanied one's cab ride in San Francisco. Frances often thought that scientists should study the strange growths in the cabs. Who knew what species might lurk there? There might be a mold that could be the cure or the demise for humanity.

"Headed to the big white hotel in Kapolei. Here is the address," Frances said, handing the Post-it note to the driver, who was smiling and not speaking at her from the front seat. He nodded his head several times, and they were off in a flash. The acceleration was so fast, it shocked Frances and she decided to put her seatbelt on and hang on to the door. Traffic wasn't too bad as they were out of the airport and on H-1 headed west. So far, Frances thought to herself, Honolulu looked an awful lot like a southern California city as it was filled with concrete and palm trees. Graffiti art adorned many of the buildings as they zoomed along the highway. Frances was glad the cabby was not a talker. She was taking in everything. The further from the airport and the Honolulu area, the more the land opened and she could see the sparkling blue water of the Pacific.

She turned the note over and over in her hands and felt the excitement building over what lay in front of her. It was such a quick surprise, and with all the crazy from Ethan, Frances really did not have time to process exactly what she was getting into. Maybe that is why everything turned out the way it had. She would continue to focus on the positive side. A dark shadow started to crowd into her brain as her last image of Ethan began flooding her view. It was all she could do to push it out of her mind. She had never led him on directly.

Frances refocused on the drive as it took her out of the Honolulu mess of traffic. Soon, the buildings were starting to give way to more open fields that she could see in the distance as the highway went past places like Pearl City and signs for a place called Ewa Beach. There was a serious amount of building going on, and Frances tried to picture what this all had looked like before the eruption of houses and neighborhoods. From the freeway, it was a gentle slope down to the edge of the island and the beautiful blue-green water. She imagined one could see whales breaching from here and quite possibly the green flash. That was a myth or a legend as far as she could tell. Her parents claimed they saw it once on a trip to Mexico. The horizon had to be completely clear and, as the sun passed below the horizon line, a green flash of light would be created. Her parents? This was the first trip she had ever taken without telling her parents. Holy shit.

What was going to happen? That question kept churning through her mind. Was it Olivia? It had to be Olivia. How was this all going to play out? Had Frances been waiting her whole life to find that person she could share her life with, love, laugh, and explore the passions that come with such intimacy? Something unsettling was sticking in her thoughts. She really wanted to be in love—but why? Her painting was starting to become her substance. The fact that she was on her way to meet a woman was a surprise to her, even though Cheryl and Winter said they had seen this coming and were not at all surprised. What took her so long? Frances sat back and realized that she needed to stop placing any expectations on this whole thing. Follow this path into the blue of the ocean and the person who is waiting.

The cab driver took an exit off the highway. They were now headed into a beautiful place right on the oceanfront. The rough grasses and ungroomed volcanic rock gave way to beautiful manicured tropical gardens and tall palm trees. The trees stood as gentle greeters along the roadway that led up to a guardhouse. The bright fuchsia-pink and purple flowers clung to the dark-black cut lava stones that lined the road. The colors of the flowers were made more vibrant against the darkness of the rock. In the distance, a pristine golf course green was hosting several players. Frances had to close her mouth as her jaw was stuck open. The beauty was beyond anything she could have imagined. The pictures she viewed online did not do this resort justice. Beyond the guardhouse stood a majestic white hotel that had such stoic beauty. It added to the surroundings like both were created at the same moment.

Asian architectural accents had been borrowed to soften the exterior. Flowers and ferns grew from balcony planter boxes as if they were suspended in air. It was all so perfect.

A security guard wearing a bright aloha shirt waved the cab through, and the driver waved back with his pinky and thumb raised. The cabby, speaking in his peculiar own language—English mixed with something else—explained to Frances that the hand gesture was the local's "hang loose" or "all is good" greeting. It was one she knew she would quickly adopt. The road curved slightly past a beautiful place called Paradise Cove. The driver took a right onto the main driveway leading up to the front entrance. Frances failed to notice that he had stopped the taxi. She jumped when a valet opened her door and offered her hand to help her out of the back. When she couldn't get out, he gently pointed to the fact that she had not undone her seatbelt yet. Frances timidly took his hand once she freed herself from the seatbelt.

The entrance to the hotel was so grand as the archway towered a good twenty-five feet above the marbled entrance. On either side of the walk were sparkling ponds filled with large koi fish and graceful black swans. Frances stepped out of the cab and into the world of beauty, wondering what exactly she had done to be in this spot at this moment. She glanced at the few people wandering through the lobby but did not recognize anyone. A woman was sitting on a gorgeous chaise lounge reading a book and paying no attention to anyone else in the area.

In the center of the open lobby stood the largest round wooden table that Frances had ever seen. It was magnificent and supported a tropical floral arrangement so elegant that she could not resist walking over to study it. The flowers were a mix of red, white, and yellow hibiscus, birds of paradise, and red ginger. Frances tried to figure out exactly how large the arrangement was because it towered over her head. It had to be at least five feet wide and at least that tall. The vase itself looked like a sculpted bathtub.

"Beautiful, isn't it?" asked a young man wearing a white mandarin-collared shirt, dark pressed slacks, and a kukui nut necklace as he greeted Frances.

"It's unlike anything I have ever seen. Do they use a crane to lift it onto the table?"

"Close. It is rather huge. They use a forklift. The plants in the middle are potted and the surrounding vases are filled with fresh cut flowers each week. So, it changes weekly. I am Juan-Jules, or JJ. May I take your luggage? They can help you check in at the reception desk." JJ pointed in the direction of the front desk, which had amazing woodcarvings of the island life depicted in its base. "What is your last name for the reservation?"

"I'm not sure." Frances spoke the words and felt the roller derby butterflies try to punch through her stomach wall. She didn't know the name the reservation was under, and she really had no clue if her hunch was right. How would she answer this question? The letter with the ticket had given this hotel's address; she had assumed that she was going to be staying here. Sweat droplets began appearing on her forehead, and she could feel her palms turn clammy. The lobby tilted suddenly and she reached out and placed her hands on the table, trying to stop the ride she was on. The last thing she wanted to do was faint.

"Are you okay? Do you need a chair?" JJ asked. Before Frances could answer, two other men dressed in similar attire had produced a chair and a bottle of water. Frances gratefully sat down and took a sip of water. The concern on the faces around her was more attention than she really wanted. What if the person she was going to meet was watching all of this? What type of first impression would she give? This was not a movie star entrance, F.O.K., but then, you aren't a movie star either.

"Thank you. I am not sure what happened. It might be under my name, Kavanagh."

"Oh yes. Ms. Frances Kavanagh. My apologies—there was a mix-up and our car was not able to meet you at the airport. We will get you to your villa immediately." JJ whispered to one of the young men, who took her suitcases and was gone in seconds. An older man with light-gray hair framing his face walked up with a folder.

"Aloha, Ms. Kavanagh, and welcome to the Ihilani. I am Kevin Gabriel, general manager of the Ihilani Paradise Cove. Please consider this your home while you are with us. If there is anything at all that we can do, please do not hesitate to ask. This is a welcome package we have put together for you."

Frances shut her eyes hard and opened them again. Was she dreaming? Were these people all treating her like she was someone? Who? And why? The tan face of Kevin smiled at her as she looked around. Off to the left of the general manager stood a young woman who was holding the most beautiful flower lei that Frances had ever seen.

"Are you feeling all right? We have a traditional gift for you. But should we wait and deliver it to your room?" Kevin asked.

"I am fine. Honestly. It must have just been the travel. That never happens." Frances stood and held out her hand to try and cover the fact that she was barely holding herself together. A line of sweat had just run down her back, and she was relieved the T-shirt she was wearing was a dark blue, which hopefully would hide her body's overly productive sweat glands.

The general manager waved the young woman over, and she placed the lei over Frances's head and kissed both her cheeks, welcoming her to the islands. Frances took in the amazing aroma of the beautiful full-flowered lei. She recognized the small tuberoses that produced the strong wonderful smell. The lei was a mix of plumeria flowers, tuberoses, and purple orchids. As Frances studied the beauty of the lei, she realized that the general manager was silently standing there, watching her with a very relaxed smile. "Sorry. I know you don't have all day to stand here and watch me. If you would point me to the room, I will get out of your hair."

"Time to transition to 'Hawaiian time,' Ms. Kavanagh. I'm here to take you to your villa and answer any questions you might have about it. Please." Kevin extended a hand, pointing the direction toward the ocean. Frances took the lead and felt like the dream kept getting better and better.

A warm, gentle, tropical breeze traveled through the lobby like an old friend greeting her, and she knew exactly where it was going. As they crossed the white marble floor, the lobby opened into a manicured park-like setting with white walkways, comfy soft chairs, and more chaise lounges set in out-of-the-way places. A couple of empty hammocks were calling to her as she passed. It had always been one of her dreams to relax in a hammock between two palm trees. Cliché as it was, she knew that she just might get to fulfill that simple little dream. When they walked down a couple steps into a different level of the hotel, an elegant restaurant and most inviting pristine round pool sparkled in the sun. A few people were sunning themselves on cushy blue lounge chairs. It was so quiet and relaxing, Frances could barely wait to recharge there. Kevin pointed out various pieces of art and was talking about the history of the hotel itself. Frances tried to pay attention and felt she had covered her tracks well. A white walkway took them past display ponds that held a variety of the native species of fish.

"Are those sharks?" Frances almost shrieked, a little worried about what would happen should someone fall off the walkway.

"Yes, we have a couple resident nurse and baby hammerhead sharks. They are quite amazing. If you would like, we can arrange to have you meet them." Before he could say anything else, a young man appeared out of nowhere and was standing next to the general manager with several message slips.

"It appears these messages are for you, Ms. Kavanagh. I am so sorry you were not given these right away." He handed her about seven different messages.

Frances tried to hide the shake in her hands as she accepted the pieces of paper. Could this be her lover? Then she saw the messages were from Cheryl, Winter, Russell, and Detective Woods. Cheryl had more than one. A little miffed at herself for not texting, she hid her disappointment that none of the messages were from Olivia.

"Thanks for the notes. I will take care of these soon. That sounds amazing, meeting the sharks. Do they have names? One gets to meet them from a distance, right?"

"We have a program here where you go into the water with a trainer and feed them. The guests who do that activity rave about getting up close and personal with sharks. Gets a person's blood pumping."

"Seriously? Have you talked to a lawyer about that?"

"We don't allow land sharks here. No worries."

"Your parents must be really proud. Not only are you a general manager of an amazing property, you're a comedian too." Frances laughed at her own comeback and was starting to feel a little more relaxed.

"It usually takes a couple days before people find that they can let go of the rest of their worries and relax. Right this way." Kevin opened a door with a key card that let them into an atrium area. From there, Frances counted six different units. The flowers and garden continued to amaze her. Palm trees provided shadow designs on the flagstone walkway and patio.

"Here you are." Kevin opened the door into a marble entrance. A glass wall of windows opposite the entrance showcased the brilliant sparkling blue of the ocean. It hit Frances that it was framed with no obstruction, like a painting or a building. It was breathtaking. The sleek, modern lines of the furniture kept the focus on the view out the window. A gentle breeze perfumed with the scent of gardenia and plumeria caressed the air. Frances walked into the center of the living room, mesmerized by all of it from the attention of the general manager and the lei to the ocean calling to her through the window.

She closed her eyes and took a deep breath, filling her lungs fully, feeling like she could burst from all this life that was exploding in beauty all around her. What a contrast from the night before. "I woke up on the other side of the rainbow." Frances walked to the window and saw the private infinity pool and Jacuzzi hot tub that were only steps from the sliding glass door. A hammock with a cushy pillow was softly rocking in the breeze, and a white stone walkway disappeared between manicured bushes and reappeared on the beach below.

"Again, if you have any desires, questions, or needs, we are here to serve. It is a pleasure, Ms. Frances." Kevin set the packet and key on a table where at least three dozen roses waited alongside a note.

"Oh my gosh. I totally missed those flowers. Wow." Frances watched the door shut and found herself twirling and dancing like a small child bursting at the seams with energy and excitement. She bent down and breathed deeply, pulling in the aroma of the red, orange, and white roses. There must have been more than forty roses in that one arrangement. She plucked the card from the holder in the center of the arrangement. Seeing her name written in fluid calligraphy on the envelope had her giddy. It surprised her that her hands were shaking as she tried to carefully slip her pinky into the slight gap on the back of the envelope. The heavy cotton paper inside was smooth to the touch. She pulled out the note from her purse to compare the writing styles. They were remarkably similar. This made her stop breathing.

Dear Frances,

It pains me that I am not there in person to welcome you to the island myself. Enjoy.

Frances turned the notecard over, looking for more. That was it? She walked into the pristine gourmet kitchen and opened a fridge that was stocked with an array of fruits, meats, cheeses, beers, wine, and champagne. On the counter was a basket filled with various Hawaiian coffees and chocolates, which included toffee-covered macadamia nuts. She picked up a couple chocolates, went back to the fridge, and pulled out a sparkling water, pouring herself a glass with ice. This was all so confusing. Why did the handwriting look like it was a close match? Was the woman here on the island already? Those toffee- covered macadamia nuts called her back, and she happily helped herself to a small handful.

She walked into the master bedroom and saw that her suitcases had been set neatly on top of a small bench. There were no other cases or clothing in the closet. The master bath off to the right of the bed was done in white marble, glass, and brushed nickel faucets. It was stunning. The tub looked like a small pool itself. She stood in the center of the bathroom and calculated that it was larger than most apartments in San Francisco. Frances took herself through the rest of the villa, which boasted two more bedrooms, both a little smaller than the master. They shared another huge bathroom between them, and both were empty of any personal items. How many people were going to be staying here?

A soft breeze brought her to the open wall and she walked out, deciding to complete her simple desire and wait in the hammock. Frances set her drink down on a teak table beside the hammock. She stopped. The last time she was in a hammock, it didn't work out so well. She turned and studied the webbed hammock and wondered. Would this be a good hammock or a bad hammock? Would it release her with grace, or would she end up flipping over, falling flat on her face underneath it like the hammock at Winter's? They had all agreed that Winter's demonic, dangerous hammock was a reincarnated bucking bronco. It did not matter how one tried, even with help, to get out of that hammock. It always won. It would twist and turn until you were face down on the ground underneath it, afraid to move for fear that it might smack you down again.

"I doubt they would have a bucking hammock ride here. This place is really amazing," Frances said aloud to the flowers and trees around her own little secret garden view of the Pacific Ocean.

"Now, that is a new one on me," a woman said, standing on the path leading up to the villa from the beach. Before Frances could stop herself, she had flopped onto the hammock and was out of balance from the voice. She had done a complete 360 and was lying face up under the hammock. Her face flushed beet red as she knew she was stuck under the hammock. "I am so sorry. I didn't mean to frighten you. The meeting was done early, and so I thought I would see if you had arrived," Olivia said as she came over and held out her hand to a stunned Frances.

"I knew it was you." Frances took her hand and, with some help, stood face-to-face with the woman she had fallen for months ago. She closed her eyes and went in for a kiss.

The kiss held more emotion and excitement than Frances thought her body could handle. Her brain was going crazy as she enjoyed the way her lips felt against Olivia's soft and somewhat sweet-tasting lips.

"Now, that is one heck of an aloha." Olivia took Frances's hand and together they dared to sit on the hammock. The brilliant blue sky held soft billowy clouds above them. The two women silently rocked in the beauty of the afternoon. Frances was lost in the beauty of Olivia's green-blue eyes. Her smile was soft and sweet, and she knew that she was exactly where she wanted to be, holding hands and staring at this most beautiful woman.

"Olivia. I. This is all so…you wouldn't believe what happened in San Francisco—" Frances was tripping over her words. She really did not know what to say. It had been several months since she had seen or even talked to Olivia directly. She knew that Nathan had given Olivia a lot of information about her, but still. This was amazing.

"Shhhh. This is to enjoy. I am so sorry I did not get in touch with you directly, but Nathan can be such a flake sometimes. He kind of left me without notice. We can talk about business later." Olivia stretched and put her arm under Frances's shoulders, pulling her into her for another kiss. "I saw the paper. You are safe now. You are with me. Let that other life go."

CHAPTER FORTY-SIX
DETECTIVE WOODS

DETECTIVE Woods, flanked by two uniformed officers, walked through the owners' parking lot at Frances's building. Russell and Simon had called her in a panic when they had found an envelope hanging from the oversized side mirror on Frances's truck. They didn't dare touch it because the outside of the envelope looked like it had dried blood on it. Detective Woods was not ready to share what they had uncovered from the first part of their investigation. There were more pieces that had to fall into place. It was not going to be easy; her team had discovered that Ethan had possibly much darker plans for Frances.

It had taken them less than a day to figure out that Ethan had developed a sick obsession with creating his own snuff films. He parlayed his skill set in sculpture into creating some of the most sought after films in that sick market. He must have decided that killing the women he was collecting would bring too much attention to him. Or maybe it took him away from what he called his masterpiece works. Frances was at the top of his list of his current collection of women.

After Detective Woods had learned about the picture of the billboard on Ethan's phone, she reached out to the New York police. Her blood ran cold when she received the information from a detective in

New York. They identified Annette as one of Ethan's victims in a snuff film. One of the officers that had to go through the videos found in Ethan's place became visibly sick watching how Ethan had taken days to kill her.

The way Ethan filmed his crimes took murder to the darkest level Detective Woods had ever experienced. It brought a new form of terror to the police officers and detectives assigned to the case. Most in the force tried to help her and her team relax, knowing this guy was dead. She knew there was a lot more to learn, and she was not looking forward to it. Now they had the gruesome task of viewing his tapes and identifying the women he tortured. They could bring closure to some missing person cases. He had quite the web of women.

But what was Frances? Was she one of Ethan's special collections? He had the most tape on her. Or did he stalk all his victims for years? Woods had called for additional backup along with another crime scene investigation unit when she saw the braided ponytail that had been used to attach the bloody envelope to the truck's mirror. The envelope was not flat, and there was no telling what was in it. There was something in the way it was attached to the car window that made Detective Woods's stomach turn.

"How was this done? When had it been done?" Woods silently asked herself as she stood in the center of the parking lot and looked at the posted positions of the uniformed officers. This package appeared after the team had finished its sweep of the truck and found the tracking device, video cameras, and bugs. How was she going to explain this to her boss? Someone got into an active crime scene and made it more complicated? Was Frances the target, or was it because this part of the truck was hidden from the view of the officers posted here to keep everything safe? Shit—this was getting them no closer to any answers.

The new crime scene unit pulled up and got busy blocking the area off and getting pictures. Detective Woods decided to go up and interview Russell and Simon. She was going to let her partner yell at the uniformed officers. They would be replaced in the hour. Detective Woods had met both Russell and Simon three years ago at an AIDS fundraiser sponsored by a local theatre group. A woman whom she was dating at the time was a co-chair of the event with Russell. Woods was glad to be over that relationship. It had ended with a rather nasty break-up period. Woods let her ex-lover take the dogs with her. She had never felt good about that choice, but she had needed to get out of there; it was breaking her down. People found it hard to believe that Sara, her ex, was hooked on drugs. God, she hoped that Russell had not put two and two together yet and realized that she was Sara's ex-partner.

Woods rode the elevator up, lost in her thoughts about the year it took to get completely out of her last relationship. She shook her head, thinking about all the crazy in the world. Why couldn't she have met Frances in a normal way? Not in the middle of a bizarre case. There was no way that she was even in that woman's league. Hell, why would she even consider it? Talk about some mixed-up shit. Frances was a woman who had completed graduate school and held talents in the arts that were amazing. How does a person like that come to live in the world? It all was so unreal. Woods never ever had any attraction to any victim she had helped. Why? Why could she not get the image of Frances playing the piano out of her mind?

"Hey, Detective Woods. Didn't hear you knock," Russell said, trying to hide the fact that the sight of her standing at their door had startled him. "I've got to take Winston out. He's crossing his paws—he has to go so badly." Winston didn't wait for anyone and rushed to the elevator doors, barking.

"I just arrived. You beat me to the knock. Hey, Winston." Woods smiled at Winston. "Better go tend to that—the back is blocked off with a new crime scene crew."

"Sorry about him."

"No problem, Russell. I love dogs. Mind if I ask you and Simon some questions?"

"Go on in. I need to take Winston out or we'll be experiencing a flood." Unlike Frances's loft, the boys had completely refinished and modernized their space. There was no exposed brick anywhere. Soft edges and stained wood made you forget you were in a converted industrial building. They had installed a beautiful bamboo floor. Everything had a purpose and place in this home. The only part of the loft that was in any sort of disorder was Winston's corner. A toy box possibly had more than a hundred dog toys in various levels of disassembly in and around it. Next to that lay a giant memory-foam dog bed that was buried under many soft blankets and even more toys.

"Can I get you a coffee or tea, Detective?" Simon asked as he came from the direction of their master suite. They had basically put up walls to make a maze of small rooms in their loft. Despite the maze of walls, Woods found it all to be softly beautiful.

"Coffee with cream and two sugars, if you have it."

"Of course we do. We only have real food in this house. What have you learned about that freak, Ethan?"

"Still gathering information. Thanks for calling. How did you find that thing on her truck?" Detective Woods took out her notebook. Part of her really liked the old-fashioned pen and paper when she was stumped. This case posed a mystery to her both personally and professionally. She felt herself falling, and she was worried that she could not help herself.

"It wasn't us. Winston was walking by and started barking and growling at the car. Then Russell saw the envelope. Totally gross." Simon set a cup of coffee in front of the detective. "We came up here and found your card so we could call you right away, hence the reason poor Winston's eyeballs were swimming in pee."

She was trying not to betray her thoughts and took a sip of the coffee as she was wondering what exactly was in that note or, worse yet, in the truck. Her mind wandered into dangerous territory again. Her friends had told her to stop protecting her heart so much after Sara. She wanted to be head of the department and so threw herself into her career, broken heart and all. Right now, she had a puzzle that was causing her to question her ability to focus and get to the truth. This whole situation was surreal and was turning her mind inside out.

"Do you know where Frances keeps the keys?"

"Yeah. We have a spare set." Simon went to a rather peculiar item that looked out of place in their overly spotless loft—a Cookie Monster cookie jar—and reached inside and pulled out a set of keys.

"Cute. Is that how you store all your extra keys?" Detective Woods laughed and took another long sip of the rich dark coffee. The sweet coffee rolled over her tongue, and she wished she was there on a casual visit instead of police business. Some shadow thought was haunting her, and she could not get the shadow to be still long enough to figure out what it had to do with this investigation. Winston bounding over the couch to get to her at the dining room table broke the silence.

"I am so sorry, Detective. He can't keep himself away from you." Russell was trying to get Winston to detach himself from her.

"It's okay. I love dogs, and he is quickly becoming a favorite. Who wouldn't melt with this kind of attention? Mind if we get some questions out of the way?"

"Ask away. We will try to help. This is all so unsettling," Simon said as he sat down at the glass dining table opposite Woods and Winston. Russell joined them, taking a seat on the other side of Winston to try and keep their dog from climbing into Detective Woods's lap.

"Did you notice anything out of place in your own loft? Any strange issues with your computers, TV, or phones?"

"Not really. We thought the dropped calls were because of our poor cell phone reception in the building. Now I'm thinking it was from all the crap Ethan put in our lofts."

"Simon, you are so dramatic. I'm still freaked out about the fact that Ethan had all that stuff in our place. What a creep." Russell got up and retrieved a box of Thin Mints from the freezer. "I eat when I'm stressed. Every year, we support Simon's niece and buy way too many of these deadly yummy little cookies. Would you like one?"

"Of course. Thank you. Brilliant, you freeze them. Did Frances ever express any feelings about Ethan?"

"Not really. She saw him only as a friend. The night he went ape shit over Emily and Frances flirting was strange. Emily hit him so hard in the chest he fell to the floor. We carried him out of the loft. That caused her to stop and examine their whole friendship. But she never really said anything negative about him. Hard to believe how he came to his end. After all of this surfaced, I wasn't surprised he attacked her. But why didn't she say anything to us? What was that about? I did see the dress. I hung it up. It was a mess."

"Holy crap, you realize that nutcase watched his friend, Emily, and Frances—oh, that is beyond creepy. It might end up as a reality TV show." Russell and Simon looked at one another and watched the color drain from their faces. "Did your boys find any hidden cameras in our place?" Russell asked softly.

"No. Just the listening devices. We can check again, but they are very good when they sweep a place. If it makes you feel any better, I haven't seen any footage of your place, only audio on the hard drives. Do you know if there is anyone else out there who would have an issue with Frances?"

Simon looked away from Detective Woods. She watched them both and was stunned by their silence. This was not what she expected. Russell shifted his weight a few times in his chair. Why were they so nervous?

"You know, I just love your Scottish accent. It is Scottish, isn't it?" Russell asked.

"Damn it all. Can it, Muffin. Hold up, I do like your accent, too. It's just that we promised Frances we would never talk about this with anyone," Simon said quietly, not taking his eyes off the window.

"I think we need to. I'm going to break the promise because there is some serious shit going down and I'm scared for all of us." Russell got up and went to a bookshelf, then touched some part of the side panel that caused the shelf to slide to the right, revealing a wall safe.

"Well, that's a surprise. I did not expect that—this day keeps getting stranger," Woods said as she watched Russell pull out four CDs or DVDs—she couldn't quite tell how many and exactly what they were. He also took out a binder and placed them all in front of Detective Woods.

"Can we be arrested for holding someone else's evidence?" Simon asked, his face white and expression flat.

"It depends. What is all of this?" she asked.

"I guess we should have called a lawyer," Russell said, trying to laugh.

"Can't—they are the problem. Plus, the real owner of all of this is in Hawaii, and who knows what she is going to get herself into now? Life was so easy B.F."

"B.F.?"

"Before Frances," Simon said flatly.

"She worked for some pretty big-wig clients. One of her clients was, well, she was a consultant to an elite few. She blames her husband for leaving her work, but there is more to that story and the girl is not talking."

"Still find it hard to believe she was married to a man," Detective Woods said as she took another sip of her coffee and eyed the materials set down in front of her.

"I said the same thing when I first met her, Detective."

"Call me Molly or Woods—'Detective' is starting to wear on me right now."

"When she moved in here, she found out about our wall safe and asked if we could hold these items. Once we found out they weren't the heisted royal jewels and just some papers and data, we said sure. She started getting into them more often recently."

"That might have been our mistake, but Russell is such a softie for those pretty girls."

"Did you ever ask her what this information contained? How well do you know Frances?" Detective Woods started thumbing through the binder, but nothing really registered. She closed it, deciding to leave the grunt work to her research guy back at the department. The DVDs were not marked with anything other than a series of numbers.

"I'm going to take these into evidence. I will call and talk with Frances. We are impounding her truck, and I think we might want to go back through her loft."

"Can you do that? She isn't here, and she hasn't done anything wrong. At least, I don't think she has. Has she?" Simon asked.

Russell stood and started to pace around the table. His agitation got Winston to join him. It was a rather interesting scene—a giant wolfhound matching Russell step for step.

"Is that how you walk, Winston?" Woods asked, laughing and trying to lighten the mood.

"Oh. Sorry. I'm feeling so off about all of this and quite frightened. If it was just Ethan, it wouldn't seem so bad." Russell continued his pacing and Winston continued to match him.

"Do you have anything you can share with us to make us feel any better?" Simon asked.

"What I can tell you is that there are several highly-trained agents working on this along with myself and a couple of other very good detectives. I admit, this all looks wretched right now. The patrol cars and officers assigned to watch over the crime scene will be here a while longer."

"Thanks. I think the rest of the building will be glad to hear that until we get some answers. I'll type up the letter. After all, we are co-chairs of the homeowner's association." Simon got up and went to the computer.

"I know I already asked this, but is there anyone you can think of who would be after Frances?" Woods asked.

"Maybe you'll find out by going through those materials. I hope she'll still speak to us. I feel like a yellow-coated Benedict Arnold," Russell said through his teeth as he bit his fist.

CHAPTER FORTY-SEVEN
PACIFIC HIGH

FRANCES opened her eyes to the early morning light that streamed in through the open window. She stretched the last of the deep sleep out of her body and watched the white silk window sheers dance lightly in the wind.

"I didn't want to wake you. You were so sound asleep," Olivia said, sitting down next to her and holding out a cup of coffee.

"Good morning. I must look a mess. You are already showered and dressed?"

Olivia sat the coffee on the nightstand and bent down, kissing Frances gently on her lips. Then, following the line of her chin, she covered her with gentle kisses down her neck. Frances loved this but also worried about the fact that Olivia's kiss was a mixture of coffee and mint and Frances could tell she had morning breath.

"Olivia, you are—"

Before Frances could finish her sentence, Olivia had pushed Frances back into her pillow and had climbed on top of her naked body, finding a much stronger and more passionate kiss parting her lips.

"I can't get enough of you. I want all of you," Olivia said as she pulled the sheets down, exposing Frances's naked body to the light of the morning and the soft breeze coming in from the ocean.

Frances tried to unbutton Olivia's shirt, only to have her hands gently but forcefully pushed away. As Olivia straddled Frances, a wild feeling of freedom accompanied the deeper kissing. Olivia, with a quiet husky whisper, tickled Frances's ear with the words "Don't try so hard. Please, let go into this wildest moment."

Frances responded by pushing her tongue into Olivia's mouth, causing her whole body to tingle. The weight of her lover's body had her craving the feeling of her butter-soft skin against hers. The linen suit Olivia wore kept a thin layer of mystery between them. Frances pulled Olivia in closer and felt her breasts firm on hers. The impact was electric to Frances.

Olivia moved her body to lie beside Frances on the bed. She lightly caressed the smooth inside of Frances's right thigh, causing them to both softly moan under the passionate kissing. Frances wanted Olivia to feel the juices of passion flowing from her touch. She wanted her to know how much this woman turned her on and what it meant to be together and sharing so intimately; it meant that trust was back in her life.

To Frances, this meant she was saying yes to life, to love, and to herself, and what she knew to be true for her life. Olivia's fingers gently parted her wetness, discovering how open Frances was to receive the pleasure that Olivia was unleashing first thing in the morning. The surprise now had Frances wanting to rip through the clothing that clung to Olivia's tight, muscular body. Frances loved the feeling of running her hands over Olivia's hips and onto the small of her back.

Olivia pressed her body into Frances as they moved together in one motion. It was a wake up that Frances found beyond words as she felt the tremors of an orgasm approaching like waves forming on the surface of the ocean outside. The feeling was reaching ever-higher heights as Olivia went from kissing Frances's left breast to gently biting her nipple.

Frances let out a gasp of air as her body trembled under the soft aggression of her lover. Olivia knew to increase the pressure upon her by pushing her hand hard against her. Frances shuddered into the orgasm and quickly placed her hand upon Olivia's hand to keep it from moving.

As the waves pulsed through Frances's body, she let go and rode the feelings of intimacy and the fact that she could feel the intensity with this person.

"Wow."

"Shhh, Frances, ride the waves and enjoy." Olivia removed her hand and pulled a sheet up to cover Frances. "I have to go, but I will be back later this afternoon. Enjoy."

"Wait—"

"No questions. Sleep. Relax. I will be back around four."

Olivia went into the bathroom, and Frances closed her eyes, capturing what just happened. She didn't know what to do. Right now, she felt amazing. After their lovemaking last night, she had no clue that her body could respond so quickly.

"I'm afraid you're going to smell like me."

"What's wrong with that?" Olivia asked as she leaned against the doorway to the bathroom. She was drying her hands. It was amazing to Frances how orderly she looked. Did she press her suit while she was in there? How does one look so good after such passionate horsing around in bed? Frances knew there was no way she could pull something like this off. Not in her DNA.

Olivia blew her a kiss and was out the front door to the villa before Frances could get another question or even a thank you out to her lover. "That is what she is, right?" she asked herself. Frances took a sip of the coffee that Olivia had set on the nightstand. The rich dark coffee warmed her throat and made her feel completely safe. This woman was good for keeps. How is it that it felt so right? What she experienced with Olivia went way beyond anything she imagined when she was watching all those movies and reading books. This was a memory of lovemaking that she would hold on to forever. It was pure passion and more.

Frances stood and let the sun hit her pale skin. It felt amazing, and she walked out to the hammock knowing that she was playing with fire. Would the fire consume her or would it ignite a new Frances, a bold Frances? Who spends money like this with no explanation? Since her arrival, Frances had mastered the hammock with Olivia's instruction.

She stretched out and was glad that the shade was starting to cover her. Sunburn would put a real damper on the action happening between her and Olivia. Frances sipped the coffee and watched the waves breaking on a reef about fifty yards from the shore. The scene was magical, and she never wanted to leave this paradise.

CHAPTER FORTY-EIGHT
EVERYTHING IS BETTER WITH IRISH COFFEE

THE Buena Vista was quiet this morning as it opened its doors up at 8:00 a.m. Russell and Simon were on the steps and were the first through the door. It felt like a year had passed since everything had happened on Tuesday and Wednesday. They had not heard from Frances since she left and had no clue if Detective Woods had told her about their violation of trust.

To survive, the boys decided to convene the group and see what they could come up with in the way of answers. None were coming from the police. Frances was silent. The world was tilting, and they wanted to know how not to fall off and survive this whole mess.

"Hey, early risers," Winter said as she kissed Russell and then Simon on the cheek. "You know, some people use the weekend to sleep in and catch up."

"We wanted to get the back table. Thank god it is quiet this morning. One never knows with this place. Sometimes they drop people off by the busloads."

"The busloads don't start until the afternoon. Are you eating or drinking this morning?" Mary asked her regulars that morning.

"Food and drink today, Mary," Russell responded while gently taking a menu off her tray. "We have a couple more people joining us this morning."

"I saw the news. Is Frances okay?" Mary asked.

"Yes. She's fine and off in Hawaii," Winter said with more scorn than she had planned.

"Jealous much?" Simon responded.

"Good for her. Irish Coffee for the round?"

"Yup. Thanks, Mary."

"Not for me today, Mary. Right now, a Sprite would be perfect." Winter hoped it didn't sound too obvious that she was not drinking alcohol or caffeine.

"Here comes Cheryl. She isn't looking exactly chipper this morning. Did anyone contact Dana?" Winter asked as she took off her coat, revealing an Alcatraz sweatshirt.

"Want people to think you're a tourist? Great disguise, Winter."

"Dana isn't coming. She said she doesn't think she will venture into the City anytime soon. If we want to see her, we need to give her at least forty-eight hours' notice so she can get her doomsday cellar ready."

"She's our sage. I'm missing her one-offs. At this point, I think she might be on to something when talking about Frances. Has anyone heard from our runaway?" Winter was ready for her Sprite. If heaven had a drink, she felt it would be the Irish coffee, but she was not going to put her little bundle at any more of a disadvantage. A glance out the window at the few healthy people jogging and the real crazies swimming in the bay made her feel like the world was getting back to normal.

"I got a lame text message stating she had arrived and that the villa was beautiful."

"Did she tell you if it was Olivia? Oh my god, I can't believe the suspense."

"I confirmed that it was Olivia that met her there and that was basically it. Not a word more." Cheryl gratefully put her hands around her glass of Irish coffee sporting the perfect white cream collar floating on top of the dark rich goodness of coffee, Irish whiskey, and sugar.

"Since the gang that is sane is here, we need to talk to you all about something that happened Wednesday after we got back from the airport." Simon took a deep breath. "Someone left a rather scary-looking envelope attached to the side mirror of Frances's truck."

"Holy shitty, shitty, bang, bang, batman!" Winter laughed.

"The envelope looked like it had blood seeping through it from the inside. It wasn't flat, and it was attached with a rope that looked like human hair," Russell said.

"Thanks for the visual—I thought we agreed to let me do the talking this morning. Winston was the one who found it, he started madly barking at Frances's truck," Simon said.

"It was so weird because he loves everything about Frances," Russell said.

"Who's telling the story?" Simon asked.

"Okay...you get the microphone. I'll be quiet," Russell said and sat back in his chair and acted like he was dropping a microphone on the floor. Winter and Cheryl were frozen. Neither one of them liked this story.

"We called Detective Woods because the uniformed idiots at the back door clearly had missed the person or persons that put the thing on her truck."

"Detective Woods was there in minutes. It was strange, almost like she was hoping someone would call."

"Really, Russell? Are we going to get your editorial through all of this? I'm done. You tell the girls." Simon crossed his arms and took on stone statue stillness.

"Knock it off, ya old married couple. You both need to tell us what is going on because Ethan is dead, Frances is in Hawaii, and it sounds like the weird is going sideways. By the way, did anyone else catch the way that Woods and Frances were interacting?" Winter asked.

"I thought I was reading something into it because that Detective Woods has me reconsidering women." Russell kicked Simon under the table for the comment.

"There is something there from both sides, but I doubt either one of them will act on it, especially now with Frances back in the arms of her 'soul mate.'" Cheryl's emphasis with air quotes on the word "soul mate" had them all burst into laughter.

"Back to the story. Simon and I had been holding some papers and DVDs for Frances in our safe," Russell said.

"You guys have a safe? That is so cool. What do you keep in it?" Winter asked and was now leaning forward, anticipating something extraordinary and fun.

"Who doesn't have a safe? This is the City, you know. Anyway, we had promised Frances that we would not tell anyone about what we had and didn't think anything about the items until Detective Woods asked us if we knew anyone who would be after Frances," Simon said.

"What did you do? Did you spill the beans? Now the cops have all they need to put Frances in the clink and throw away the key."

"Hi, Mary. I guess we should place our order. How long were you standing there?"

"Long enough to know that you are telling a pretty good story. So, what'll you have this morning?"

Orders were placed, and the table unanimously agreed to another round of Irish coffees and one Sprite. The tables and bar were starting to fill with people here to sample the fame of the Buena Vista. They continued to talk and speculate long into the morning. It was all they could do to finally pull themselves away from the giant round table at the back of the restaurant and move into their own days.

CHAPTER FORTY-NINE
THERESA GOES BICOASTAL

THERESA parked her rental car in the visitor space after she had explained to the uniformed officer that she was Frances Kavanagh's sister, pulling out her driver's license to confirm. Theresa had tried over the past several days to get in touch with Frances after seeing her sister's face and story splashed across the news. It had made the national news, which made sense; after all, the guy had explosives strapped to his body. That elevated the story to one of a possible terrorist plot. Not to mention, he had dark hair and a darker complexion, like that of a Middle Eastern person. Lost in the story was the fact he was a third-generation Jewish American. The art world could harbor a terrorist, but Theresa highly doubted that to be the case. What had her sister gotten involved in, and why couldn't she seem to find her?

Theresa walked to the back door of the building, not knowing what to do next. She had briefly talked with Simon on the phone. He refused to answer any of her questions. The Kavanagh clan was in a civil war over the national news stories and Theresa's outburst on the phone. Theresa didn't tell anyone in the clan that she had caught the first flight she could from New York to San Francisco.

"Can I help you?" Detective Woods held the glass door open for her. "I'm taking a break from the meeting happening in the common area of the building with the rest of the building's owners."

"I don't know. I'm looking for Russell and Simon," Theresa said.

"Come, follow me inside. We're wrapping things up. Who can I tell them is waiting for them?"

"Theresa. Theresa Kavanagh."

"Right. Frances's sister—I can see the resemblance. I'm Detective Woods. I'm running the case for the SF Police Department." Woods held out her hand. "Firm shake."

"Sorry. I get that way when I'm nervous."

"I'll let them know you're here," Detective Woods said. Theresa watched her as she stepped back through the double glass doors into the common room of the building, which boasted a large-screen TV, a pool table, a ping-pong table, several comfortable lounge chairs, and a huge gas fireplace. Theresa could sort of hear a person addressing the group about what had been found in the parking lot.

Theresa walked around the hall looking at the art the building had on display. It was all black-and-white photography. Something about it made her think of her sister. She knew it wasn't Frances's, but still she figured her sister would find a hip building to call home. Theresa decided to call her girlfriend, Kelly, and let her know that she was safe and at the loft. Before she could get the call started, a big dog came up to Theresa and put his front paws on her shoulders, cleaning her face with his tongue.

"Winston, down! Are you okay?" Russell asked as he grabbed for Winston's collar.

"You must be Theresa. Welcome to your home away from home. We put you up in the guest suite. I hope that's okay. We figured it would give you more privacy than your sister's place right now. It's infested with police and detectives and other such people." Simon closed by giving her a big bear hug.

"Where is Frances?" Theresa asked.

Russell and Simon looked at one another and then back at Theresa.

"No. Please, god." Theresa started to shake and couldn't control her tears. "She's dead, isn't she?"

"Frances is off the hook—clearly drama runs in the DNA of her family," Russell said as he put his arm out to steady Theresa. "No, sweet girl. Your sister is on a trip right now." He wasn't sure how much to share with Frances's family member.

"Damn it! I feel like such a...I haven't spoken to Frances. A trip? I saw her being loaded into the back of an ambulance on CNN."

Theresa accepted the Kleenex that Detective Woods held out to her. "When was the last time you spoke to your sister?" Woods asked.

"I would have to think about that...we don't talk that much as it is, but we do send emails regularly. I'm a student at NYU, and she didn't want to interrupt my studies."

"Well, I know you've had a long trip, so you take some time to relax and get settled. You are very safe staying here. If you need anything, you can call me. Here's my direct mobile number. Russell and Simon have it too."

CHAPTER FIFTY
THAT'S HOW EVIDENCE FALLS

DETECTIVE Woods got a message from her main investigator and evidence expert that she needed to get to the office immediately. Aaron, her investigator, was a good guy, but he often exaggerated the need to be somewhere "immediately." She would need to talk with him again about the exactness of his language. Right now, everything was an ASAP need. The world did not work like that in the field. One had to learn how to prioritize things. With the finding of the strange package left on Frances's truck, she decided to head back to the station. The other issue with Aaron circled around the fact he had left messages with "immediate" action requested, but he would never answer his desk phone, his cell phone, or pager when he was called at the central desk.

Woods figured that part of his difficulty in responding came with the fact that he loved his deskwork. Those who hated their deskwork answered their phones. Aaron was brilliant; he worked on what he wanted to work on and ignored the pressure because he knew others would not hoof it to his world until the last possible moment. Woods laughed. She had witnessed Aaron's daughter, a toddler with a voice, get Aaron to do whatever she wanted. He had no backbone and kids knew it. What he lacked in field skills, he more than made up for in figuring things out.

She had turned over the stack of items she got from the boys that had belonged to Frances. With everything that was happening so quickly, Woods still had not been able to contact Frances to let her know they had those items in evidence. With the item that was found hanging from her truck, that stack would need to take a back seat to figuring out if there was a new killer on the loose. It had to be a very well-schooled killer, copying the tactics of a serial killer who found his way to the electric chair about thirty years ago. Back then, that guy held the City hostage through the long months of an entire summer.

It was a case that had made Detective Woods think twice about entering police work. Her uncle had worked that case, and even with her studying it at the academy, he could not bring himself to talk about it. The killer had started to alert the police to his killing spree by leaving pieces of his victims at other crime scenes around the City. Many suspected the killer had to be a cop because he had infiltrated some well-protected crime scenes. It was a fluke that he had been caught at all. Thank god he was, but still it made her skin cold thinking about that whole ordeal. Thank god it wasn't a policeman. The details of that killer were recently explored through a documentary. Why anyone would want to relive that terror was beyond her.

The elevated excitement level in Aaron's message had her anticipating something big on the envelope. As she walked down the hall where they kept their active evidence investigation, she could hear a lot of talking coming from the viewing room. It struck her as odd that there were shouts of laughter too. She double-timed it to the door.

"Here she is, the finder of the most amazing pieces of evidence we have seen to date," Aaron said with a flourish she did not know he had. Woods was caught off guard by a standing ovation of her fellow detectives and police officers. The fact that many were wiping away tears from their eyes and their red faces had her nervous.

"What?"

"Detective Woods, come in and have a seat. You've got to see this the way everyone else has."

Aaron made a motion toward what looked to be a young kid running the electronics. He was in uniform, so he had to be at least twenty something. When a movie voiceover announced this to be the greatest clips reel, she knew she was in for something she probably would not live down for years. The screen faded to a woman holding a platter that was barely large enough to hold the huge cooked turkey. The woman, looking so proud, walked around what probably was the whole house, parading the turkey. There was no sound, and it looked like it was circa 1970-something, most likely filmed with a handheld eight-millimeter camera. The turkey was carried on a platter from the kitchen and then through a den, a living room, and a dining room, which housed a large family, all of them clapping. "Wait for it," Aaron said. Some others were already laughing. The woman placed the turkey in the center of a beautifully set table. Everyone on the screen stood at one end of the table, probably a move directed by the filmmaker as the scene was awkward. Then, as if by magic, the turkey fell through the table. Thankfully, the filmmaker kept filming. People scattered. The woman who had paraded the turkey fainted into the arms of several members of the crowd. A couple of people tried to take charge, and the mayhem got worse. A dog came running into the room and took off with a part of the turkey. Four kids, all sporting wild red hair, kept running around the adults with small axes made of paper. The laughter of the police detectives watching this went through the roof.

"This is better than the funny video of the day on YouTube," someone said between breaths.

A couple of detectives had spent the time to figure out how the turkey had fallen through the table. This conversation generated even more laughter. They pointed out that the huge table was two pieces of plywood put together to handle the giant family for Thanksgiving. Only, no one told Mom, the turkey maker, not to place the giant bird on the crack.

Woods covered her face with her hands. She knew she was not going to live this one down. "Aaron, you spent time making a favorites reel? Seriously, you have absolutely no other pressing business?"

"Molly, wait until you see this next one—might be child abuse or neglect on this next one," Aaron said, laughing through his nose.

Molly removed her hands and saw a red-headed toddler running around in nothing more than a loosely hanging cloth diaper. Several other red-headed children surrounded her. The video quality had improved, and this one came with sound. The narrator sounded very much like a young teenage boy.

"Potty training Franny, take twenty-seven?"

You could hear the laughter of several people on the video as the camera heard the small cries of a child.

"Mom, Bernard left the toilet seat up again. Mommy! Help, Mommy!" The video panned the interior of a bathroom and revealed the feet, hands, and red curls poking up from inside the toilet. The little toddler had clearly fallen into the toilet and was unable to get herself out. Molly was horrified. But the crew gathered in the room was already into hysterics again.

"Remember, we told you that you were supposed to sit on the edge and not crawl in the toilet?" said a boy off camera. The toddler smiled and shook her head up and down in the video.

The older boy promptly flushed the toilet, and the little red-headed kid splashing in the toilet water was laughing and shrieking with glee.

"Shit, where are the parents? That is child abuse." Only the toddler in the video was laughing and saying "Again, again."

"You uncovered the unknown vault of *America's Funniest Home Videos*. It appears this family had quite the propensity to not only pull jokes but also film them. Granted, the turkey video was probably not planned. That was too good."

"How many hours of this—?"

"Molly, you really made my day with this request. It appears that the little red-haired toilet diver grew to adulthood and was doing this project for some big family anniversary party."

"More likely, she was hiding these from the family."

"One more. You need to watch this next one. It is truly priceless." Aaron lost his composure and was laughing so hard that Woods started to laugh by default.

"All right, one more," she agreed.

"Roll it," Aaron said and left the room, laughing hysterically.

Detective Woods watched as two boys dressed in powder-blue tuxedos walked up to a front door and knocked. It appeared to be a prom or high school formal. The boys appeared nervous but proud of their powder-blue tuxedos and dark-blue bow ties. This had to be a parent filming the event. Poor kids, Molly thought, and then the crew, knowing what was going to happen, started snickering. The door opened and instead of two young teenage girls, there stood an older man wearing a wife beater T-shirt and holding a shotgun. Before the boys could run, the bushes reached out and held them in place. The poor boys screamed, and it looked like one had peed his pants. Those poor kids clearly did not see their dates standing in the background yelling at their father and brothers. She couldn't help it. Molly laughed out loud too.

Molly Woods stood up and took a bow for the audience, which was now standing and clapping. With her own face flushing red, she decided to exit the room. She also knew that she wanted to watch the rest of those DVDs. Humiliating as that was, she walked away shaking her head and laughing. The laughter continued as the crew that was in there continued to watch a few more Frances videos.

"Detective, hang on a minute." Aaron came half-trotting down the hallway after her. "I've got some information on that envelope that was found on the truck."

"Now you're going to tell me about some real evidence?"

"Come on, that was funny. How often do we get to do anything that causes serious pee-producing laughter in the evidence research department?"

"True. Okay, Aaron, what did you come up with on that rather grisly find?"

"You were right—the ponytail and the contents of the envelope are human. They don't come from the same human, though. We could not identify any fingerprints on any portion of the evidence or the truck. It was strange. The truck had been wiped completely clean inside and out. We found no fingerprints anywhere. I had a list of all the detectives who collected evidence from the truck. There was nothing, not even the owner's fingerprints. We did a bio swipe, and the only thing we found was the blood that splattered on the outside of the truck."

Detective Woods leaned against the hallway wall and felt her heart skip several beats. This was not good. She knew she had to get the report and have a chat with the Captain. "Aaron, is your report ready?"

"Emailing it now." Aaron typed a few things into his smartphone and then turned away to go back to the laughing crowd.

"Hey Aaron, thanks for the laughter."

"No worries, Woods, you bring 'em and I tag 'em. This batch was fun."

CHAPTER FIFTY-ONE
SPA CAVE

FRANCES awoke with a start. She sat up in bed and listened for the sounds of Olivia. All she heard were the waves crashing on the beach and the soft rustling of the breeze through the palm trees. Frances felt a little guilty taking a nap. "Why was Olivia... Stop it," she said to herself.

Frances pulled the hotel robe from the chaise lounge at the foot of the bed and wrapped herself up in its softness. How is it that this robe could be so soft? How were they able to capture the feeling of soft kittens in the cotton? Hungry and desperately wanting some coffee, Frances went into the kitchen and found a complete breakfast laid out on the table for her.

A plate of fresh pineapple, papaya with limes, strawberries, mangoes, and blueberries started the beautiful table buffet. Banana bread, bagels, and Danishes filled another plate. Beyond that sat a bowl of yummy-looking granola. It was amazing. The carafe of coffee was the first thing Frances touched, pouring herself a large cup.

She picked up a piece of pineapple and savored the sweet, luscious flavor. As she was trying to decide what to eat next, she saw the handwritten note at the other end of the table.

Hello Beautiful,

You looked so peaceful, and I know that after the week you've had, sleep was what you needed most. Please don't be angry that I slipped out without waking you. I arranged for you to have a massage and facial. Call Jamie at the spa when you are ready for your spa retreat.

I am afraid I won't be back until very late tonight. Thank you for a most wonderful yesterday. Can't wait to be back in your embrace this evening.

Olivia

FRANCES sat down at the table and filled her plate with fruit and banana bread, a favorite of hers. She read the note over a couple more times, unsure of how to feel exactly. They talked so much the first time they were together. This time was so different. Because she really had nothing to compare this situation to, Frances decided to go with the flow. She would eat a snack, shower, and head to the spa. What a day. No one had ever given her a spa day.

As she enjoyed the moist and most addictive banana bread, Frances felt her heart growing and swelling with a feeling she did not recognize. Olivia had taken Frances snorkeling at the most amazing fish-filled waters she had ever been in. That was followed by more love making that had Frances floating. This was a fairytale dream. When was the clock going to strike midnight?

The breeze was softly blowing through the window sheers and into the villa when Frances jumped, thinking she saw someone standing on the lanai. The wind moved the sheers again. There was no one there. Frances walked out onto the lanai, a little shaken. The gate to the beach was closed. As it required the villa room key to enter, Frances felt a sense of reassurance as she turned to the hammock and thought about taking it up on its invitation but decided to shower instead and get herself to the spa.

"Ms. Kavanagh, how nice of you to join us today." A smiling young woman was holding the front door to the spa open for Frances. This took her a little by surprise. "Hi, my name is Jamie, and my job is to make sure you have a wonderful time in our spa."

"Please, call me Frances." Frances watched as Jamie took a position behind a computer and quickly typed in some information. The whole time she was smiling.

"Frances, it looks like you are scheduled for a massage and a rejuvenation facial today. Would you prefer the massage or facial first?"

"I will defer to you. Honestly, I have never done this before."

"Well, I'm glad that we are your first spa experience. I would start with the massage and then enjoy the spa facilities, have some lunch, and finish with the facial. I will get you situated in a moment."

Jamie's easygoing manner put Frances at ease instantly. "That sounds like a great plan. Massage first," Frances said as Jamie came around the counter and opened a door into another world for her.

The walk to the spa was through a beautiful garden that was built below the street level of the hotel. Jamie held the ten-foot tall etched-glass door open to the women's spa, and Frances walked into a space where everything had been coordinated to put one into a great state of relaxation. "This is breathtaking," Frances said, almost in a whisper.

The front room was gently lit, and the light gold hues made everyone in there look younger. Frances chalked that up to spa magic. Off to the right of the room was a reading room with cushy chaise lounges and any major magazine or newspaper one could think of. Frances knew that Jamie was telling her about the amenities, but she was in awe. One woman was sipping spa tea and reclining in a lounge chair out on the private sun deck.

It was so peaceful. The sounds of a waterfall and soft music greeted Frances as they entered the changing room area. Each person had their own full-sized locker assigned for their time at the spa. There was a Roman soaking tub with suits optional, Jamie told her as she showed her the special shower, dry sauna, wet sauna, and cold pool.

"Where is everyone?" Frances asked.

"Nice, isn't it? We are full today and you feel like you practically have this place to yourself. Sue here is the ladies' attendant. If there is anything you need, see her. She will order your lunch for you when you're ready. Enjoy."

Jamie might have been a fairy sprite. She was so easygoing and tiny. Frances didn't appreciate how tiny Jamie was until she gave Frances a hug before leaving her in the capable care of Sue.

"Sue, I'm ready to live the adventure of the spa," Frances said and was off for her day of pampering. "My friends are not going to believe this one."

CHAPTER FIFTY-TWO
OUT OF TIME

"WHAT do you mean Ethan is dead?" Nathan asked.

"Listen to me. Ethan flipped out and went to Frances's loft with an automatic rifle. It has been all over the news," Felipe said.

Nathan took a long, deep breath. This was desperately wrong. He knew he shouldn't have trusted Ethan.

"Is Frances okay? Have you talked with her?"

"Nathan, I have not talked to anyone. What if they link us to moving his other art? The news is reporting that those films were real—that those women were actually killed."

Nathan heard Felipe try to control his emotions as he coughed several times. What was he thinking when he agreed to let Ethan store his DVDs in his warehouse? It didn't mean he was guilty. He had nothing to do with what Ethan was doing. It gave him the win on one of the hottest and most collected artists in the country. Ethan agreeing to show his work exclusively with Nathan finally gave him the resources to get out from under Olivia.

"Filly, you are to say nothing to anyone about this—"

"Nathan, the news crews have been parked outside the gallery. They know we sold his show out. They want a statement."

"Don't give them one. Say we are in the business of art and do not know what our represented artists do in their private lives. Take this down. Let them know the gallery is going to donate the profits from Ethan's work to a women's shelter in the City."

"Nathan, we can't do that...you have us stretched beyond our monthly budget as it is, and I used most of that money to pay off the contractors who built out our gallery. They were getting ready to file a suit against us."

He knew that Filly was right, but he also was far from the situation and not returning anytime soon. Nathan had so much to get in order and felt like the more he tried, the more things exploded into chaos. He paced around the small hotel room and thought about never returning. Life would be so much easier if he could disappear.

"Are you still there? Hello?" Felipe asked.

"Still here. If you want them to go away, tell them that we are preparing a statement and our hearts and prayers go out to all touched by the events of the past couple of days."

"I can do that. How are you?"

"I don't know. All this is a lot. I guess we celebrated leaving the witch, Olivia, prematurely," Nathan said.

"Honey, nothing is premature about you. Olivia was sucking our lives away. You know what they say—'the show must go on.'"

"Speaking of that, how did the decaying art sculptures do?"

"Back to business. We sold all but two. I'm thankful the news media has kept me from opening the gallery. The place stinks."

"Contact the buyers and arrange to deliver the pieces in the next couple of days. I've got to go now. Sorry you are alone dealing with this."

"Love you, N."

"Love you, F."

Nathan set his cell phone on the small hotel desk. He sat down on the side of the bed and took a couple of deep breaths. He wanted to call Frances and explain why he had done what he did the night Ethan had attacked her. It was all so much to process. He had viewed only a few minutes of a DVD clip that Ethan had said he accidentally sent him earlier that afternoon. The clip was awful. When Nathan questioned Ethan about it, he had told him that was only a movie and had meant to send the trailer to a marketer. Nathan had never seen anything so violent or horrifying. How could he have acted so cold to Frances? He knew in his soul that she was in danger with Ethan. It all happened so quickly. Was it accident or was Ethan trying to let someone know what he was doing?

Nathan got up and went to his computer. He looked up the San Francisco Police Department phone number. He knew he had to do this for Frances. It was the least he could do because he knew that if Ethan had not been killed that he most likely would have killed Frances.

CHAPTER FIFTY-THREE
KAVANAGH FAMILY DIVIDES

THERESA stood in the center of Frances's loft and felt like she wanted to run and hide. Detective Woods was working with a couple of other officers as they were going through the hard drive of Frances's computer. Theresa had fought with her own girlfriend, Kelly, over the phone this morning because she was not sure what she would tell the rest of the family.

Theresa took a deep breath and dialed her parents' number.

"Hello. Theresa, is that you, honey?" Bridgette's voice was trembling as she answered. "Have you talked with Frances?"

"No, Mom. I told Bernard when I first called that she is on a trip." Theresa decided not to tell them anymore than the bare minimum.

"Mom, is Dad home?"

"Yes. We are all right here. I'm putting you on speakerphone. Edna and Bernard are ready to come out there and help you pack her place up and bring her back home."

"Mom, we are not packing her place up. Listen to me. Frances is fine. Some guy has been spying on her for about three months. That was the guy who was shot and killed in front of her building."

"Theresa, this is Bernard. Where is Frances? Why didn't you listen to me and come home to St. Louis? I ordered you to come home."

"Bernard, if you want me to answer any questions, you had better change your tone with me. You do not order me to do anything. Frances is on a trip. She is okay. They took her to the hospital because she had fainted and hit her head."

"What do you mean, she's on a trip? Who is she on a trip with? Who takes a fucking vacation at a time like this?"

"Bernard, watch your language. You know we do not talk like that in this house." Bridgette never failed to correct her children.

"I don't have all the answers. She went on a trip to meet a friend—my guess is to get away from the craziness here. That guy did take a shot at her through the window."

"Theresa, you're not answering the question. Who is this friend? The news is reporting that Frances...Frances is a lesbian," Bernard said.

"Bernard, who fucking cares if she is a lesbian. The news is out for ratings." Theresa looked around the loft to see if anyone was listening to her conversation. They pretended to be busy, but she figured they were all listening.

"Watch your language, young lady. I will still wash your mouth out with soap. Honestly, I didn't raise you kids to speak like a bunch of thugs," Bridgette said.

"Mom, is that all you are going to say when Bernard is being so ..." Theresa was shocked into silence. She could not believe the conversation she was having with her family.

"If she is sinning against the church, I'm not going to spend one more minute worrying about Frances," Bernard said.

"Now, Bernard, that is extreme. Calm down. You are not the judge of your sister," Patrick Kavanagh said, causing silence to hit the conversation. It was not usual for him to speak up, but clearly this situation was far from normal.

Theresa could hear their father in the background continue trying to restore some order to the conversation. It had to be her sister crying because Bridgette could be heard throwing some pots on the stove. No one else would be throwing pots around because no one could touch anything in the kitchen.

"Edna, shut up and stop crying. Look at what she has done to Mom and Dad. Has she called any of us? No. Why not? Because she knows she's going to hell. Everyone has seen the news reports," Bernard said.

"I have had enough of this bullshit, Bernard. You are not speaking for everyone in this family. Give me the damn phone," Brice said.

"Brice?"

"Hey, T. Things are a little out of control here right now with the ultra-right idiot," Brice said.

"Can you get him to calm down. It sounds like he is whipping Mom and Dad into a frenzy. I haven't seen Frances yet."

"Brice, I am taking that phone back. You get the fuck out of here. No one asked you to come over here. Go home and drink yourself into a stupor because that is what you are good at doing. Theresa, you get yourself back here now!" Bernard shouted into the phone. Theresa pulled her phone away as a yelling fight broke out between her brothers.

Theresa watched the police and crime scene detectives work as she listened to her family fight over the issues of Frances. The way Bernard had said the word lesbian made Theresa feel like he was driving nails into her own heart. His voice had such hate and venom. The more she listened, the madder she became. This was Frances, their sister, and some terrible things had happened to her over the past days. Where was the compassion for her? Theresa gripped the phone and felt her other hand turn into a fist. She knew if she was standing in the same room with Bernard, she probably would have punched him in the stomach. He had always terrified her when they were growing up. Bernard was the type of kid who had no problem pulling wings off flies or burning ants with a magnifying glass.

"Bernard, are you done? What has she done to Mom and Dad?" Theresa asked.

"They can't go anywhere. Have you seen the news stories coming out about her being in a love triangle with that freak and another woman? Father Ben won't even talk to them on the phone. Mom tried to go to the church and she was told to go home," Bernard said.

"You know, I don't think that's such a bad thing. Didn't you always say Father Ben was—"

"Shut up, Theresa! I am over this. Why are you protecting her?" Bernard asked.

"When did this become a witch hunt?" Theresa asked. Like her sister's face tended to react, Theresa's face flushed red.

"Mom, Dad, this is a rather serious situation out here, and it is much bigger than this speculated love triangle that Bernard is concerned over. Frances might be in some real danger."

"Theresa, I don't believe she's in any danger. I think she is trying to create a bunch of drama to hide the fact that she...I can't ..." Their father went silent and did not finish his thought.

"Dad? What are you saying? I can guarantee that after talking with the police that Frances did not create this, and you know what? You can all think about this. I'm a real lesbian. I live with my partner, Kelly. We have been together as lovers for two years now. We are getting married, and that is why we moved to New York, where it's legal."

Theresa had anticipated the silence on the other end of the phone. She now realized that no one in the loft was pretending to be working anymore. They were all watching her.

"Someone say something," Theresa said with much less volume than her angered shouting.

"Theresa—I know you are not that way. I am your mother. What has that school done to you? You are not a lesbian. This is only a phase."

"Mom, this is all part of a plot by Frances to discredit this family. You and Frances can rot in hell together," Bernard yelled and hung up the phone.

Detective Woods walked over and put her arms around Theresa, who made no objection. She cried on Detective Woods's shoulder. Theresa couldn't believe what had happened. What would she tell Frances? What was she going to do now? Their parents would come around—but what if they did not? Her tears turned into sobs and she held onto Detective Woods like she was the only thing keeping her attached to the planet.

CHAPTER FIFTY-FOUR
A SIDE OF ANSWERS, PLEASE

WINTER had decided she needed to get some answers about the past week's events. She was tired of being left in the dark. No one had heard from Frances for a couple days. Work was not getting done. Winter found her focus was on finding out what had put Ethan in the street with explosives and an automatic rifle.

She rifled through her study desk, looking for the business card that Detective Woods had given her. No one had called her to ask her any more questions. It made sense that Russell and Simon were still very much involved because their loft was part of the investigation. It was not right that she be considered a second-class citizen. Frances was still silent, and that was not okay.

Not finding the business card in her mess, she decided to call Russell and get his help in collecting some answers.

"Hi, Russell—Winter here."

"I know who's calling. Remember caller ID? Invented to keep us from prank calling people and trying to get them to go chase their fridges?"

"Funny. That was a fun time, wasn't it? Kids have no clue what they are missing today. So innocent."

"Speak for yourself, sweetie. My prank calls were not innocent. What's up?" Russell asked.

"I lost Detective Woods's business card. I want some answers."

"You and us too. Hey, you're a bitchy lawyer. Do you want to come over? She's here. She was talking with Theresa, and they were trying to put Frances's loft back together after pulling out all of Ethan's surveillance equipment."

"You keep her there; I'm on my way. I'll see if Cheryl can join us."

"What about Dana?" Russell asked.

"We can fill Dana in later. You and I both know she was serious when she said she isn't coming back into the City."

Russell, following orders, decided it would be good to get out and away from the work he wasn't doing anyway. He kept his computer online and ran a little program to make his coworkers think he was busy working away. He thought about the tragedy of having to use such a program to live. The group he worked for basically expected people to work around the clock.

"Come, Winston, we are going next door." Winston lifted his head from the couch less than an inch and plopped it back down. "Guess I'm going next door."

Russell texted Simon to let him know that he was going to be attending an impromptu meeting with Winter, possibly Cheryl, and Detective Woods. Russell walked through the open door and stopped.

"Hey, Theresa. What is going on?" Russell asked as he pointed toward Detective Woods. With the new person in the loft, Theresa took a couple of hiccupping gulps of air and pushed herself away from Detective Woods.

"Hiya, Russell. I came out to my family, and my brother Bernard said Frances and I would go to hell and hung up the phone."

"Honey, this calls for a celebration. You are free. You no longer are living under the burden of a lie. You know you gave them all an opportunity to grow. Now that you are going to hell, it's high time you meet your people and start the party now," Russell said as he gave Theresa a big hug.

"Yeah. But my family—at least I think I still have a few members of my family who love me—maybe I don't."

"They might have birthed you, raised you, and brainwashed you, but it doesn't mean you are banished to solitude and your life is over." Russell took Theresa by the hand and led her to Frances's couch.

"We all have our own coming-out stories. Your sister Frances has not completely come out yet, but she will thank you for helping her."

Theresa sat back and covered her face with her hands, trying not to burst into tears again. She wanted to call and talk to Kelly, but she had to get herself under control.

"Detective Woods, I'm here on some unofficial, official business. Winter, most possibly Cheryl, Simon, and myself would like a side of answers to go with this story, please."

"Fine. I will be here until the guys are done putting things back together. Did they finish in your loft?"

"Yup, everything is smooth, white, and tidy."

"Why is it that whenever a gay man speaks, it always sounds like he's referencing sex?" Winter asked as she entered the loft.

"That was fast. You must have beamed yourself through the portal."

"Funny. Nope. Got green lights all the way through," Cheryl said.

"Winter and Cheryl, it's nice to see you both looking better rested than at our last meeting," Detective Woods said and sat down at the large wooden table that Frances had made from reclaimed barn wood. "Come have a seat, and I will answer what I can."

"Russell, you get a gold star," Cheryl said.

"Cheryl, Winter, let me introduce you both to Theresa, one of Frances's sisters," Russell said and then, like a traffic director, moved Cheryl and Winter to seats at the table, leaving Theresa alone to recover from her shock. "Theresa is going to take a few moments before joining us."

"Should we wait for Simon?" Cheryl asked.

"No. I can fill him in. He's trying to catch up on everything at once, so he is a crazy worker man."

"Detective, you can start from the top. What brought all this about?" Winter asked this very open-ended question on purpose.

"Honestly, I wish I could tell you what started all of this, but I have no clue. I don't want to rehash what you already know. So, I'll get to the thorns that sprouted after we last spoke. Ethan will be most likely classified as serial killer. We are finding some rather disturbing footage that he created using women that he stalked. He had very detailed ideas on what type of 'art,' as he called it, he had planned for Frances. His art was killing women in snuff films. That was where he was making most of his money. We are working with some other police departments around the country as we try to identify his victims."

"He was making money on snuff films? I didn't even know those were real. I thought that was an urban myth," Russell said.

"Was Frances his next victim?" Winter asked, jumping to a conclusion that would surprise her more than Frances dating a woman.

"Still trying to figure that out. The package that was left hanging on her truck mirror the next afternoon speaks of another layer to this whole ordeal, and we are trying to sort it all out. Our crimes lab is still trying to figure out exactly what was left in that envelope," Woods said.

"It was hung on her truck by what looked like a braided ponytail of human hair."

"Thanks, Russell. I don't think all the gory details need to be shared." Detective Woods tried not to smile over the excitement Russell seemed to have in being able to share his part of the story. "We have a crew going through the hundreds of hours of video and audio recordings that Ethan had, along with quite a bit of other items in his place. It appears the art thing was an easy way for him to meet women. What still doesn't make sense is that Ethan had called the Stanford campus police and reported himself."

"Does Emily know the truth? That little woman was cursing up a storm—Frances was getting blamed for something she didn't do."

"That is her cross to carry in this life—it happened to her all the time at home," Theresa chimed in and came and sat at the table, still blotting her eyes with an overused Kleenex.

"Yes. Emily is aware and dealing with the fact that she too was most likely going to be one of Ethan's victims."

"That gives me the creeps. I never liked that guy," Cheryl said as she got up to go see if there was any coffee left in the place.

"What about this thing that was hung on her truck?" Theresa asked. "You hadn't mentioned that earlier."

"We really don't know how or if it is related. Although it really looks like it might be connected in some way, we are not ruling anything out right now." Detective Woods was looking through an iPad as the crew gathered around the table, staying unusually quiet.

A knock on the loft door took the attention away from the silence as a uniformed officer opened the door to reveal Winston and Simon.

"No one ever expects the Spanish Inquisition or an Irish wolfhound," Simon said as he walked in and took a place at the table. "Cheryl, might you be making a pot of fresh coffee?"

"I might be…would you like a cup? I will brew it, but you all can serve yourselves."

"Deal. Did I miss much? Has she talked about what was on those DVDs and stuff we had hidden for Frances?"

"Great, Simon. You are so good at keeping secrets once they're out of the bag," Russell said.

"Relax, Russell. It's okay. I haven't been able to get in touch with Frances about those materials yet. She isn't responding to my texts or emails." Detective Woods was still reading through information on her iPad.

"I can share this with you all, thanks to Simon. The information that she had is not in any way connected to Ethan's work, but we did find a group that appears to be cropping up. Does the name Triple Crown Peak Investments mean anything to any of you?"

"Wait. Why would an investment banking firm be tied into this?" Winter asked, sitting a little straighter.

"Winter, you have heard of Triple Crown Peak Investments?" Detective Woods asked.

"Out of Denver, Colorado?" Winter was up and out of her chair. "I need to talk to you alone, Detective Woods."

"Winter, you are such a bitch, you can't do that to us. Why can't you talk in front of all of us?"

"Attorney–client privilege, and I'm not sure I should be saying anything, but I might be able to put this to rest. First, I need to make a phone call. In private."

"You can use our loft." Simon tossed her the key, and she was out the door.

"The plot thickens. Where is Agatha Christie when you need her?" Russell turned around and saw the crossed arms of Detective Woods.

"Sorry. It was only a turn of phrase. We don't need Agatha because we have our own British crime solver."

"What is the strangest case you ever worked on, Detective?" Simon asked.

"Well—this one is quickly gaining speed to the top of the list. It's the first one I have had the pleasure of working on with other agencies. Most of my crimes are local, so we get to keep them all to ourselves."

"How about the funniest thing that you've come across?" Russell asked.

"I'm not sure cop humor works well in the general population. What I might find amusing, you all might think is completely dark and twisted," Detective Woods said.

Before she had to give up any stories to the crew, Winter burst back into the loft. "Detective, you and I need to go to my law office now. The head partners are going to meet us there. You might want to call some reinforcements on your side for this."

"Wait, we were going to get some answers. Here you are the one that called this little powwow." Russell said.

"Sorry. Gotta go. Do you want to drive?" Winter wasn't dumb. She knew that if she got Detective Woods to drive, she would need to return to her car at the loft. Winter winked at Cheryl as they left.

"Well, what are we going to do now?" Simon asked, frustrated over leaving work.

"We can share stories with Theresa about coming out, and I think we need to concentrate on getting ahold of Frances. These two sisters need to talk."

CHAPTER FIFTY-FIVE
A WINTER STORM IS COMING

THE ride from Frances's loft to Winter's law office was stiff. Winter kept tapping her fingers on the armrest of the unmarked police car. She was glad that her office was not that far from the loft. It was in a cool brick building on Jackson Street, a few blocks from the Embarcadero; Detective Woods took some side streets to get them there in no time.

"Detective, I am going to share something with you and I need you to not react. I have been doing my own research."

"Winter, I'm a cop. If you are going to tell me about illegal activity, I'm obligated to act upon it." Detective Woods slowed the speed of her car.

"I know this client, the one you brought up, has been doing some business deals...let me say, they push the interpretation of the law right to the edge."

"Are you trying to tell me your clients are white collar criminals using you to figure out exactly where the line lies?"

"Something like that, Detective. If I uncovered something else that I know is criminal, who would you suggest I talk to in the District Attorney's office?"

"You could tell me and I could bring it in for you?"

"Thanks, Detective. I need to figure out how to talk without going to jail. I am not responsible for what they are doing."

"Are you sure?" Detective Woods asked. They pulled up in front of Winter's office.

"Did you want to wait for your people?" Winter asked as Detective Woods parked in a no-parking zone. Winter fished her keys out of her purse and let them into the elevator lobby of the building. "Stairs or elevator?"

"Elevator. I already did my run this morning," Detective Woods said as she pushed the button to call the elevator.

"Where do you like to run? I love running through the Legion of Honor grounds myself."

"I usually try to run the Embarcadero over to Fort Mason and back to the office."

"Holy shit, that's a lot of running. Yeah. I barely make my two miles. At least most of it requires running up a hill," Winter said.

Before the elevator opened and deposited them into the open lobby of the law firm, Winter turned to Detective Woods. "These guys can be real jerks. I was hoping your team would be here to help keep them in line."

"Lawyers who are jerks? No."

When the doors opened, the lobby was already lit up. She knew that they would be waiting for them in the conference room. Unlike most law offices, this one was cramped and almost every space was filled with a file cabinet or bankers boxes. It was a mess once you got past the lobby. The hallway had barely enough room for them to walk through as the boxes lined both walls two rows deep.

"The fire inspector needs to see this place," Detective Woods said under her breath.

"Tim and Robert, this is Detective Woods. She is investigating a case that looks like it involves our largest client," Winter said as she sat down on the side of the table that Tim and Robert were occupying.

"Detective Woods, we were not aware there was an active investigation concerning Triple Crown Peak Investments. Can you enlighten us as to what the San Francisco Police Department is doing?"

"Before we start sharing any information, I need to get your names and numbers." Detective Woods sat in a chair that was quite a bit lower than the other chairs around the table. These guys are good, she thought to herself. Such sophomoric crap made her salivate.

Winter had retrieved a couple of business cards off a credenza and passed them over to her.

"I appreciate that you have attorney–client privilege and do not expect you to answer any questions. The person in charge of this part of the investigation should be here in about five minutes."

"Well then, we will see you when that person arrives." The men stood and Winter followed as they exited the office.

Detective Woods shook her head at the game play these people were into. She was going to enjoy this one more than she thought. She checked her phone and had no messages. The crazy thing was that none of this really had much to do with Frances. She was in the free and clear. Poor Russell and Simon were sure she was holding some top-secret information. The DVDs turned out to be nothing more than forty-plus years of Kavanagh family movies. Frances was unfortunately a target of a serial killer. What was more troubling was the package left on her truck after the fact. Was there an accomplice working with Ethan?

What were the odds that one of her closest friends was the attorney for one heck of a shady and very powerful firm? The same firm that Ethan was using to do his sales and laundering of money earned off his snuff film industry. The psychologists working the case were getting a profile together on Ethan, and he displayed the signs of one calculated, cold killer. Frances was not his usual type physically. That she was his last target was raising some questions because she did not fit his pattern.

"Woods here, what is your ETA?"

"Parking behind your car now, and I hope that SFPD will extend hospitality and take care of any parking tickets?"

"Put a note on your dashboard that says you're working with Detective Woods. Can't promise you that will keep them from ticketing you."

Of course, Woods had the smile of the Cheshire cat now. The FBI and Tobacco and Fire Arms had been looking for the main head of the Medusa. The law firm was the start of the end. She knew that this group was one of many firms working for this crew, but because it was not on their radar before tonight, it was going to be good.

Woods decided to go down to the street and meet her supposed backup. "Winter, I'm going down to the car for a second," she shouted through the overly cluttered hallway, listening for the sounds of paper being shredded. This law firm looked like it was stuck in the paper chase era.

"Here's the key to the front door. You are good to get in from there." Winter handed her the keys and noticed the look on Detective Woods's face.

"I hope this turns out okay for you, Winter. Right now, you are the Trojan Horse."

WINTER watched as Woods practically skipped out of the building. Then she went back to Tim's office, located on the corner of the building. They could see the street below and the two very conspicuous unmarked police cars. Neither Tim nor Robert seemed at all alarmed by the situation.

"Did you call Anthony?" Winter asked.

"No need. We have this under control. There isn't any way the SF-PD has anything that's really linked to our client. But you did the right thing in alerting us to this nonsense. You can leave if you would like."

"Do you mind if I stick around? I would like to see how you handle the cops." Winter knew she was stroking the egos of the narcissistic jerks that she worked for, and she also knew it would work. The chances that an organization much bigger than the SFPD would be walking into this office were growing exponentially. Winter looked out the window and saw the street was now clogged with about ten large, unmarked, nondescript sedans. Ants wearing the FBI windbreakers and Tobacco and Firearms identification were securing the street. A couple of large vans were being positioned in place. This was a raid that was happening on her law office, and she had brought it. "Oh, shit!"

Winter felt her face go white, and a few points of spotted bright lights were crossing her vision. She raced back to her office and downed two headache pills as quickly as she could. This was no time for a migraine. She debated if she should say anything to her partners, but it was too late.

"Hello?" Detective Woods called from the front entrance.

"Detective, come on back to the conference room." Tim's voice could be heard but not seen. Detective Woods turned to her two counterparts and smiled. "Bring the hammer down on these guys," Woods said.

Tim and Robert sat casually as Winter entered, blocking the view of the two agents behind her. Winter figured they wanted to surprise her law partners because they all took their agency jackets off. Winter reached out and steadied herself as she felt her hands sweat and her breathing get shallow. This was probably not going to end well for her. She led the police and the feds to her law firm.

"Winter, do you need to take a seat?" Detective Woods asked.

"I'm okay. This is bad," Winter said.

Winter focused on the two men who sat in chairs that were set to make them taller than anyone else at the table. Winter had filled Woods in on the chair trick and she had passed that along to the other two men about the little parlor trick. Winter smiled as the three of them adjusted the chairs before they took seats directly across the well-polished, high-gloss, wood conference room table. Woods knew her counterparts were salivating at the treasure trove of paper that this office seemed to hold. Most firms today had gone electronic, and it was a pain in the ass to fight through the courts to get the encrypted files opened. This was going to be something different.

"Tim and Robert, I would like you to clarify for me exactly who you work with at Triple Crown Peak Investments. Is it the firm itself or a specific individual?"

Tim took control by sitting up straighter and looking directly at each one of the officers. He said, "I don't have to answer anything you ask. As I am sure you are aware, attorney–client privileges extend to the identity of the client." He smiled and folded his hands together as he placed them on the table. "Would you like a cup of coffee or water,

Detective Woods? We can give you a to-go cup," Robert said, smirking as he did so.

"Coffee would be great. I take about two ounces of cream if you have it."

Robert pointed at Winter. She was already on her way to get the coffee. Detective Woods hated situations like this and decided to turn the knife a little more before plunging it into the firm.

"I am aware of attorney–client privilege. I am also aware that you already acknowledged that this firm does have Triple Crown Peak Investments as a client. That's not a violation of attorney–client privilege. What we need clarification about is your own involvement. You can answer questions about your own investment strategies; those do not fall under attorney–client privilege."

"I don't know what you and your two reinforcements think you have or don't have. This question and answer session is over now," Tim said in an even tone as he stood, pointing toward the door.

"I'm sorry, I neglected to introduce you to my reinforcements. Tim, Robert, on my left is Agent Jaime Juarez with the FBI, and on my right, is Agent Mark Sanders with the ATF."

Agent Jaime Juarez stood and presented to Tim and Robert a warrant out of a folder he was holding to seize all property in the office and in the homes of the partners, and to take them into immediate custody.

"This is absurd. You have no right to do this," Tim stammered.

"Yes, this piece of paper signed by a federal judge says we do." Jaime gave Mark a nod, and Mark radioed the troops who were flooding into the office in seconds.

"You are so dead, you bitch," Robert said to Detective Woods as an FBI agent tried to read him his rights.

"What about the female attorney?" an agent asked Jaime.

"She is free to go, but make sure she leaves us all the information we need on how to get ahold of her."

Jaime, Mark, and Detective Woods stood in the front of the office and watched as the crew of FBI and ATF agents went to work emptying everything out of the office.

"We got word that the other two law firm partners were arrested at their homes. We have agents going through all four houses now looking for materials. I wonder if they will turn up anything as hot as that turkey video?" Jaime laughed out loud as he shared the information.

"What is he talking about?" Mark asked.

"Later. I can't believe it's already out of the SFPD."

"I have my sources. Remember, I am an agent in the FBI."

"Funny. I loved the expression on their faces as you arrested them."

"Detective Woods, are you in need of protection? I heard him make a threat on your life?" Jaime asked.

"Thanks. I will let you know. I think I can handle this one. Glad to help you guys out though on this little matter. Remember, I need the information on how they paid Ethan and what exactly they were having him do. There was something so odd and creepy about how this all went down."

"No kidding. It is a bizarre case. We have been following this law firm for the past three years. Only to have the pieces finally fall into place over a nutcase that filmed women. Bizarre."

"Jaime, you get to buy the beers when this is all over," Detective Woods said as she exited the law firm's office.

CHAPTER FIFTY-SIX
EXCOMMUNICATED

THE past couple days had been a dream. Frances had to keep pinching herself as she walked through the low-breaking waves along the lagoon. With each step, her toes sunk into the wet sand, almost disappearing as she let her foot get completely covered before taking her next step. She wondered if this was what quicksand was like. She studied how quickly the sand covered her toes.

Small, silver fish darted this way and that in the shallow water of the shore. Every once in a while, Frances would see a fish fly out of the water. Somewhere in the back of her mind, she remembered a factoid. Did that mean the fish was trying to get something or keep away from something? She giggled as she looked out into the deeper blue-green of the lagoon and imagined a whole host of sea creatures. Maybe a shark was in there deciding if it was going to dine on fish or human today. A few other vacationers were busy splashing about in the lagoon.

Right now, Frances was content walking along the edge of the lagoon, letting her feet get a pedicure with the sand. She reasoned that the sand had to take off some of her dry skin, making her feet soft and smooth again. If not, she might have to go back to the spa and have a mani-pedi done. That sounded like a great plan.

Two people, who obviously liked to punish themselves, emerged from the lagoon and immediately started doing push-ups on the sandy beach. The first time Frances saw this, she was startled. It wasn't until about twenty people had done this same drill that Frances figured it must be one of those fitness classes. Only, it had to be an extreme one because then they would morph from doing push-ups to a stand, jump, squat routine, followed by running to the next lagoon. She had to follow them. It was so curious that anyone would do this to themselves. They would run into the water of the next lagoon, swim across it, and repeat the torture on the other side. Then they would come back through and do it again.

A lounge chair on the beach, stranded and alone, was calling her name. "Hello, lounge chair," Frances said as she moved it a little to face the hotel and the ocean. "Would you mind terribly much if I sat my bottom upon your lattice work?" Frances swirled her head around hoping no one heard her talking out loud to a chair.

Frances lay back and marveled at the beauty before her. The white of the hotel dotted with brilliant specks of pink, purple, red, and green from the tropical vegetation, to the green of the manicured lawns that gently sloped down to the sand and the lagoons. The brilliance of the Pacific Ocean blue wrapped up the whole scene. Frances was in awe of it all. She had heard that the ocean had color like this, but she really found it hard to believe.

Her life growing up in a landlocked state did not exactly give her the experience of the ocean. When she did see the ocean off the California coast, it was beautiful. But it did not hold the deep blue and light greens she was seeing now. Most of the time, the ocean in San Francisco was a steel-gray color. All of it was better than the mud-brown color of the Mississippi River in St. Louis.

Frances closed her eyes and thought about how much she was enjoying her time with Olivia. It was so different than anything else she had ever done. Then, shouldn't it be like this? Easy. Olivia was so easy to talk with. She was light on the answers as to what she was off doing. She made her absence up with amazing spa visits, and when they were together, it was magical.

Frances was starting to relax into a spontaneous nap on the beach when her cell phone vibrated. She was going to ignore it, but then thought that maybe it was Olivia. When she pulled it out and saw Theresa's face, she hesitated, but then she answered. She had not talked to anyone in her family for days.

"Hello?" Frances said, almost timidly.

"Fuck, Frances." Theresa couldn't get any more words out before she broke down in tears.

"Theresa? Theresa, please talk to me. What is it?"

"Frances."

"Russell?"

"Yes. Theresa is…well she has something she—"

"Frances, you are a fucking cunt."

"Theresa, that's…Why are you with Russell?"

"Maybe if you had stayed home, you would know why. You know, I thought you were dead. Your picture was on the fucking news. Then they show you not moving, being loaded into the back of an ambulance because a terrorist is blown up outside your house."

"Take a deep breath, Theresa. I am fine. Russell and Simon and the gang all know where I am."

"Yeah? Did you think that your family might like to know you're okay? What is wrong with you? Are you that fucking selfish? Well, they don't care anymore if we live or die." Theresa started sobbing again.

"Theresa, you aren't making sense. What's going on?" Frances was now sitting up, digging her toes into the sand as the shadows of a world she had tried to forget crept across the Pacific Ocean, causing the light and brightness of her day to dim greatly. "Would someone please talk to me?" Frances yelled into her phone, not caring if she upset anyone else on the beach.

"Hi Franny, it's me, Simon. We didn't tell Theresa exactly where you are or what you are doing because, well, it isn't our place at this point. You and your sister have got to talk. Russell is working on getting Theresa calmed down enough so she can talk. How's it going?"

"It was going great until about a minute ago. Olivia is amazing and everything I thought she would be and more."

"Awesome. Are you going to kiss and tell?" Simon was sounding lighter on the phone, and Frances could no longer hear Theresa loudly sobbing in the background.

"Simon, you know you will get an appropriate account when I return. The breakfast we had on our own private lanai this morning was better than Condé Nast could ever describe. Fresh pineapple, papaya, and berries to start, and the coffee was exquisite and fresh from Kona. They have a baker on site who is magical. Her pastry is so light—it's like biting into a luscious cloud of butter and flour with lilikoi jam. For an entrée, I had lox. I don't know if I could ever eat lox again this was so darn good."

"Yeah. I get the picture. You are being spoiled rotten and probably will never return to the real world. Hey, before I turn this call back over, did Detective Woods ever call and talk to you about some stuff?"

"No. What would she need to talk to me about?"

"Oh, here's Theresa. Now you be a good listener and don't fall into your family's pattern of yelling. You two girls need one another now. Ta ta, Franny."

"Wait, Simon—"

"Hi Frances, I am so sorry I couldn't control myself."

"Theresa?"

"Yes. I better get this out before I start blubbering again."

"Get what out? Why are you crying so much?"

"Frances, I told Mom, Dad, and, well, the rest of the family that I'm gay. I got so mad at Bernard saying that you're going to hell because you are a lesbian that it just came out."

Frances had stood up and had started to walk back toward her villa, but this news set her bottom directly onto the sandy beach with a thud. Frances did not know what to say. All this time, she had been so focused on her own foray into the world of women, and her sister Theresa had already been there.

"Theresa, I love you. You have so much courage and grace," Frances said into the phone as her mind traveled a million different places at once. "How long have you been with your partner?" Frances marveled at the fact that she sounded so official.

"Almost three years now. I met Kelly at freshman orientation and knew immediately. Frances, it has been so hard not talking to anyone about my life. I feel like I've been lying, and that's a sin too."

"None of it is a sin. I believe that god made us the way we are, and god does not make mistakes. So, going back to you telling the whole family—"

"I had come to San Francisco and everyone else had gathered at Mom and Dad's in St. Louis. The bastards. I think Agatha wanted to come out here and check on you too, but you know her husband. Bernard has taken over being the head of the family for some reason. It's like Mom and Dad are no longer capable of being mean, so he has to do it for them."

"Calm down, Theresa. Bernard is only being the bastard he is because he claims he doesn't drink, but we all know he does. I would not be surprised if he likes dick since he has so much hate."

That comment caused them both to laugh out loud. Frances was now digging in the sand with her feet. This was not what she had planned on, but then her past days had already been so strange, to say the least.

"Frances, I am sorry. I wanted to make sure you were okay. Can you tell me where you are?"

"Here is the bottom line. I don't know if I am gay or not but I really do like playing with the fire right now. I am on the island of Oahu staying with a woman who has stolen my heart."

"That sounds pretty sure to me. What's her name?"

"Olivia. She lives in New York City somewhere. She runs an art gallery—I think called Olivia's Gallery."

"That is sounding like, wait, I think I know who you are talking about," Theresa said.

"No. How would you know her? Trust me, I don't think you two would run into one another."

"Frances, are you with her right now? What is her full name?"

"No. Olivia Porter-Stevens?"

"Everyone who pays attention to the rich and famous in New York City knows her name. Her family owns most of the world in Soho. Shit, Frances, she is married with four kids."

"What? No. We are not talking about the same person."

"Frances, we are if she claims she owns Olivia's Gallery. Did you know who you are with? Who did she say she was? Did she tell you she was married? Married to a man?"

Frances felt her world ripping away and could not control the feeling of nausea that overtook her as Theresa gave her the news. She survived going through what it was like to be burned in a relationship by her ex-husband and another woman. Right now, she wanted to puke as she understood that she, with Olivia, was the other woman. Why had Olivia not told her she was married? Why was she so stupid?

"No. Theresa, this is not…how could she be on a trip with me and—"

"Frances, have you gone out in public with her?"

"Well, not really. She's here working on a business deal that takes up a lot of time."

"I'm sending you a story from the *Post* right now. You'll see a picture of Olivia Porter-Stevens. Then you'll know. Maybe we aren't talking about the same person."

Frances did not want to open the link her sister texted her, but she did. Now she was the one who was trying not to cry like a baby. There in the picture was the woman she had been sharing her deepest desires and intimacy with the past few days. Everything about trust and love came bubbling up to the surface. There in black and white was an article about Olivia and her family spending time doing an art education cultural exchange project with the University of Hawaii and elementary schools. Olivia's family had funded the whole thing.

"Theresa, I am coming home. I'll see you tonight."

"Frances, wait—Simon wants to talk to you."

"Ok."

"Franny, you pick yourself up and smile. There is something we need to tell you, but we can wait."

"Tell me what?"

"Detective Woods is the person you need to talk to. They had to impound your truck."

"They took Snow White? Why?"

"Part of the evidence thing they were collecting."

"But they already went over her with a fine-tooth comb. I'll give Detective Woods a call when I get home."

"You give us your flight number when you get it and we will be there to pick you up."

"Nah. I'll take an Uber."

"No. We will be there to pick you up, so text us your flight number now. Chop, chop." Simon hung up the call.

Russell stood with his arm around Theresa, shaking his head.

"You didn't tell her about the other evidence."

"Russell, she can chat with Detective Woods and get the story. Right now she is reeling from the fact that she has been dating a married woman with children."

"Ouch."

"I hate the internet," Theresa said. "She sounded so happy, and then, what do I do? I crush it all like a little bug. I stomp it and grind my heel into the bug, making sure it's dead."

"Nah. Girls aren't violent at all." Russell laughed as he took a seat on the couch.

"Hey. Her bubble was going to pop at some point. We all warned her about this being too good to be true. You know what they say—the fireworks are beautiful, but then they go out. Look at us—Russell is my burning ember, and sometimes it glows bright, and other times it might be a little cooler, but I tell you, it is always burning, smoldering. I will take the ember over the firework anytime."

"Thanks honey-pie, but we get to deal with another blubbering redhead in about six hours or so. We better get reinforcements."

CHAPTER FIFTY-SEVEN
TRUST HERSELF

FRANCES could not remember the exact words she used on her note. She was surprised at how easy it was to get a flight so quickly back to San Francisco. As she sat at Gate Twenty-two a few hours before her flight was to depart, she began to doubt her actions. What was she supposed to do? Olivia had lied to her and controlled her. Frances thought she had the ability to filter people better, only to find she had been fooled again, and this time by a woman. Frances knew that she had another truth to face, and that was the one her family had dictated to her. Is that why Frances was nothing more to Olivia than a plaything, an oddity, a person to play with and then toss aside when she was done? There was no concept of permanence here—the only one talking about the future was Frances.

"I have got to stop doing that," Frances said to herself. "I am such a moron. There was so much I wanted out of this whole thing, and maybe that was why I didn't see the writing on the wall. Could I have at least given her a chance? A chance to lie to me some more?" Frances dug into her bag of hurricane popcorn and ate without tasting, her mind working through all her time with Olivia.

She knew it was all way too much because this type of love story does not happen to people like her. She was far from being a beauty queen. A tear started to form at the corner of her eye, and Frances looked around the empty terminal and let the tear fall. Why not? Her mind started to wander into the information about her parents and the rest of the Kavanagh clan. What would be the damage control there? Bernard did not speak for the whole family now. She knew her mother was not happy. Their dad would support his wife, but he would say his own thoughts. A man of very few words, he always spoke for himself.

"Okay." Frances realized she had to go back to the real world and deal—deal with the aftermath of Ethan and the family. She had not called her family. She was aware that the news media had broadcasted the story for all of five seconds, but then lost interest when the police were sure that Ethan was not a terrorist. Who was the fool? She was the total fool. Frances's hand had reached the salty end of her popcorn bag. She looked down to see nothing more than a few corn kernels and seasoning.

I was so mad, she thought, as I wrote that note. Frances had printed out the story at the business center in the lobby of the hotel. She felt that she had handled herself well; the staff all greeted her by name and wished her well. What a place this was. The word "luxury" did not come close to capturing what she had experienced with the staff, the villa, and Olivia. Frances let out a deep sigh. She had wondered what it was like to have money, and now she had received the tiniest taste of that life. Why didn't Nathan say anything to her about Olivia having a husband?

Frances sat up and realized that maybe Nathan was trying to protect her by not getting her the messages. Of course, he had known exactly what Olivia was going to do with her. The little devil that Frances hated acknowledging came out and was looking rather smug. "No, Frances," said her little devil, "Nathan is part of that world, and he most likely has a family and kids stashed away somewhere too."

"But he is so flamboyantly gay."

"Frances, you are talking to the creature of sin—Nathan is flamboyant in San Francisco, but you know he is smart and capable."

Frances tried to stomp her foot on her little devil and stood up to stretch. Only three minutes had passed since she last checked the time. This was going to be a long wait and an even longer flight home. At least she was in first class going home. That was what the ticket had paid for; only, she thought she would be going to Australia. Had she acted too hastily?

Stop it. You know you wouldn't be happy knowing that you were with someone who was married and had children. That is not the kind of person you are or ever were. Frances wanted to call and talk with Cheryl or Winter, but felt that was wrong. She had not spoken with them at all since she had arrived. A few vague texts scattered over the course of her dreamland stupor made her feel even more stupid. Seriously—she thought to herself—things like this do not happen to people like her.

She wondered how long the ride would have lasted. It didn't matter now. Frances felt sick to her stomach. The tears were on their way, but she was not going to spend the next several hours crying. No. She was angry and felt totally betrayed. Was she angry because Winter and Cheryl were right? That was not it. She had fallen hard for Olivia. Why? She had not come close to this emotional well with her husband. What was it about Olivia that got her to ignore any red flags and not dig too deeply? Was it the gifts and the luxury?

It was the whirlwind, and to Frances, the exotic mystery of the whole romance. Frances looked back at their first meeting and how that had all unfolded. Olivia had captivated her in a way that was so different and exciting. She was beautiful and easygoing but direct and funny. Also, she was very practiced in the art of seduction. Frances wanted to be seduced, and Olivia had taken hold of her and had played her all the way to Hawaii. How does one who gets her picture taken for newspapers keep her other conquests secret? Frances thought to herself about this and realized that she had captured a few pictures of them on her phone when Olivia was sleeping.

Olivia had been against pictures. It was believable the story she had given her about why she didn't want any pictures taken. Frances didn't think the pictures she took would be a problem, but she was glad she had never told Olivia. On her phone was proof, along with a couple of rather compromising positions, that Frances indeed had had an intimate affair with one of the wealthiest women in New York. As she looked at Olivia's sleeping face on her phone, she felt her heart melt. She wanted to run back to the hotel and say she was sorry. But why?

She had not been the one lying. She had been available and thought Olivia was too.

How does one talk about the future when they know they will not really be part of that future? That is twisted, almost as twisted as—Frances's phone rang before she could complete that thought.

"Heard you are coming home. Told ya so, lady!"

"Winter! I wanted to call you but I was—"

"I told you so. I told you so. I told you so."

"Okay. You told me and you were right."

"But man, did you pick a good one. Russell sent me a text and a link. Damn, girl! I am going to pick you up. Russell and Simon got invited out to a party and they are taking your sister with them."

"I'm coming back to reality, and I don't know if I want to. It hurts."

"Buck up, Frances. You need your big girl pants on. There is a lot of shit going on around here and, oh yeah, your detective arrested all four of my law firm's partners."

"What?"

"Text the flight number—I told you so. We can chat when you get back here to the real world. Winter drops the mic!"

Frances stared at her phone with a confused look. Winter really had hung up on her. The hang-up was understood, and so she texted her flight number and projected arrival time before she forgot. In this bizarre limbo of falling in and out of love, she wasn't sure which way was up. To eat up some of her angry energy, Frances decided to walk around a little to see if the sickness she was feeling would go away. These emotions needed to do something because what was currently happening inside was not pleasant.

She was passing a kiosk that had several helium balloons softly flowing in the tropical breezes coming in off the ocean. The red, yellow, and orange balloons looked so happy as they danced on the end of the matching colored ribbons anchoring their light energy to the kiosk. Frances approached the balloons and got an idea. She bit her lower lip and counted to ten. The idea was still in her head. She had said goodbye to the woman who she had felt was going to be her soul mate for the rest of her life. It was crazy. She took the risk and got burned badly. No one seems to take promises as sacred anymore.

"Excuse me?" Frances asked the young man sleeping under his hat who was tending the kiosk. He stirred with her words and sat up. "Can I buy these balloons?" she asked.

"I don't know. I have never sold balloons before. Don't you want to buy some pineapple candies?"

"If I buy some pineapple candies, can I have these balloons?"

"Don't know about that—they're part of the display. They work. They brought you over here."

"I need them."

"Why? Do you have kids?" The young attendant stood up and stretched his arms. This section of the airport was quiet right now, and clearly sales were not exactly high for this candy kiosk. Frances thought about lying. She did not have kids, but often balloons were purchased for kids.

"No. I had a really bad day and the balloons would help me feel better."

"Okay, lady. You buy a pound of my pineapple candies and you can have the balloons."

"Do you have a marker—like a Sharpie?"

"I'm not an office supply store, but let me look around." As he dug around a drawer filled with a few odds and ends, Frances freed the balloons from the kiosk and took out a twenty-dollar bill for the candy. She didn't worry about what she would do with a pound of pineapple hard candy. A possible gift for the boys? "Found one."

"Thank you so much." Frances grabbed the marking pen and the bag with the candy and took off toward the garden space outside of the terminal. She knew it was for smokers, but it looked empty right now and she was willing to risk the polluted air for her little project. She was already feeling better.

"Lady, you need your change?" the attendant called after her.

"It's a tip. Enjoy," Frances said as she hit the doors to the stairs that led down to the outdoor space. The air was free of smoke, and she thought she had the whole garden space to herself. She sat down on a bench, and the first word she wrote on the red balloon was "love." The letters curved around the belly of the balloon. Was one word enough? No. She wrote the word "promise" and followed that with "marriage" and "my heart." Frances sat holding the balloons and listened to the low, thumping sound as they hit one another. Was this really going to help her? It was, silly.

On the orange balloon, she drew a face and gave it some hair. She saved a section on the back of the balloon to write the name "Olivia." The yellow balloon looked so plain, and she quickly let her hand scribble any image that guided it. The balloon was now almost completely eclipsed under black marker ink. Her fingers were covered in the ink and she noticed that if a balloon touched her, it would come off quite easily.

Before she acted, she quickly looked around again to make sure she was alone. Then she took out an earring, and using the sharp end of the post, she poked it into the red balloon. It all happened in slow motion. At first, the wall of the balloon pushed out the other side from the pressure, and then the pop sounded, echoing off the terminal walls.

"What the fuck?" a voice from behind a bush yelled.

Frances jumped up, shocked. She thought she was the only person in the garden. She didn't walk around and look to be sure there was no one else in the area.

"Sorry, it was only a balloon. Didn't mean to disturb you."

"Knock it off. Are you crazy?" the voice asked, and silence filled the garden again.

With a deep breath and a slight smile, Frances popped the next two balloons quickly. She jumped up, discarding the broken balloon bits into the trash can, and then ran up the stairs. The voice that was hidden by the bush was now yelling some obscenities behind her as she double-timed her steps.

She felt better; she had channeled some of her anger and disappointment into the balloons and felt herself becoming lighter with each pop. When she was sure the person she had surprised in the garden was not following her, she slowed her gait and realized that popping balloons at an airport might not have been the brightest idea. Frances looked around to see if security or TSA were descending on the area. No one seemed to be moving any faster than a snail, so she allowed herself to gear down and meander slowly back to the gate of the flight that would take her out of her dream romance.

As she checked the time, she wondered if Olivia had found her note. Would she come after her or would she be glad it was over?

Someone else had spilled the beans, and Frances, being of some moral character and holding a whole lot of built-up Catholic guilt, would do what she did—leave.

CHAPTER FIFTY-EIGHT
A SISTER'S LOVE

T HERESA was as close to the terminal exit leading into the baggage claim as she could get. Tears were already rolling down her face when the flight tracker announced that Hawaiian Air flight twenty-six had touched down at San Francisco International Airport. Inside Theresa, a storm of epic proportions had been unleashed. She knew she looked as horrid as she felt, but all she wanted to do was throw her arms around her older sister and know that they were okay.

Simon had walked up behind Theresa holding a hand-delivered letter that had arrived for Frances as they were all leaving for the airport. It looked so important that he felt he needed to bring it with them. As he continued to watch Theresa flood the area with her sobbing, he decided this was not the time to give Frances a letter. It could wait. He saw Nathan Steiner's name as the sender. This could be another payment for Frances. Hopefully it was good news. Simon folded the letter and stuck it in his shirt pocket as he went over to wait for Frances's luggage at baggage claim. The sisters needed to see one another first. There was too much going on to fully understand this brand of crazy.

People started to give Theresa some distance as her tears were now building into sobs. The first few sunburnt passengers in obnoxious Hawaiian shirts were making their way to baggage claim. Theresa didn't know who saw the other one first, but it didn't matter. Frances was hugging her so hard that it forced her to stop crying and start to fight for air.

"Oh my god, I can't believe ..." Theresa let her tears overtake her voice, and Frances didn't say a word. She kept her hold on her sister, and the two of them stood there, crying together. A flow of passengers went around them, some annoyed, others curious, and most oblivious to the two red-headed women crying in the middle of the terminal exit.

"It's okay. I am so glad you are here," Frances said as she blew her nose into the top of her T-shirt.

"Here, use this, Frances." Simon handed her a handkerchief as he walked up to the heap of tear-melting Kavanaghs. "If you two don't stop this blubbering, you are going to make my tears come out, and that is so not pretty."

Frances let go of Theresa with one arm and pulled Simon into a hug. "Sorry. I—"

"Frances, it's okay. Let's get your luggage and get out of here." Simon maneuvered the two toward the baggage claim, able to see the bags that he had had a hand in packing. "You two stay here and wait."

Simon was gone in a flash and returned with two very overstuffed bags. "This way, ladies. Out to the curb."

"Is Russell in the car?" Frances asked as she was starting to gain her composure.

"Nope. He decided to stay with Winston at the loft. We have something better." Simon went out the sliding glass doors to the waiting unmarked police car.

Frances stopped walking when she saw Detective Woods standing and talking with an airport security guard.

"Come on, Frances, you get first-class pick-up service with Molly," Theresa said.

"You are calling her Molly? This is so not right."

"What?" Theresa stopped and looked at her paralyzed sister. "Oh my goodness. You like her?"

"I liked it better when you were crying. I don't have time for this, and you, sister, need to keep your big mouth shut. The reality of what I left came flooding back and I'm already drowning."

"Not nice. You still have some things to learn about, and they're still providing police protection at the loft. She offered. It made sense because she can park where she wants."

Frances watched Theresa walk out and hug Detective Woods. The whole action made Frances turn a lighter shade of red, and she felt the slightest flutter of nervous energy in her chest.

"Welcome home. Don't be upset that we crashed the sister reunion?" Simon said.

"Winter, you and Simon count as sisters too."

Frances wanted to run into the arms of Detective Molly Woods. She looked rather smashing leaning against the front of her car chatting up the airport police officer. The heat was rising in Frances's face, and she tried to sneak a look at Detective Woods as she turned from Winter's hug to put her in a better viewing position. It was one of her wildest moments as the world started to tilt for her. She was worried she was going to pass out.

"Are you okay?" Winter asked, giving her friend some stability.

"I am so clumsy. Still have my air legs I guess from sitting for five hours."

"Nice to see you again. How about we move the party from the airport?" Detective Woods had uncrossed her arms and was standing with the back door to her unmarked police cruiser open. Frances obeyed without objection and climbed into the center of the seat. Winter and Theresa caged her in on either side, and Simon hopped in front.

"Oh, can we put the light on? Please?" Simon pleaded.

Detective Woods got in behind the wheel. Her eyes caught Frances's for the briefest second. Then she switched on both the lights and the siren.

Thank you for spending time with Frances and the Buena Vista Coffee Club Crew. I hope you laughed, pondered, and enjoyed the mixed-up fun and some nail biting drama. These characters are back in book two with some new people added to the mix. Check out announcements on my author website, www.sheilamsullivan.com.

SHORT QUESTIONS & ANSWERS
WITH THE AUTHOR

Q: How often do you write and why?

A: I write daily. Sometimes it might be a grocery list but I do write something down. I write down the grocery list so I don't forget any items. Oh…you want to know about the stories I am writing. I write daily because if I don't I can be rather ornery. An idea will hit me in the head and if I want to plant that seed I need to get those words down. The characters can be very demanding at times.

Q: You hear voices?

A: That makes me sound a little crazy. My characters have their own minds and I try to capture their antics in words.

Q: What is your favorite book?

A: Frances, Samantha, and I have that in common. Douglas Adams, *Hitchhiker's Guide to the Galaxy*.

Q: You are serious about that being your favorite book?

A: 42.

Q: What was your favorite book as a child?

A: Not sure I have grown up but I loved *The Secret Garden*, *Winnie-the-Pooh*, *Wind in the Willows*, *The Hobbit*, *Nancy Drew*, *The Black Stallion*, *The Adventures of Tom Sawyer*, *To Kill a Mockingbird*… (*This list went on and on and on*).

Q: If you could meet any author living or dead?

A: Good question. Would the dead author be able to talk? Would this be like a zombie thing?

I am rather scared of zombie types because I do need my brains to work. That is a hard one because there are so many.... Ray Bradbury and Beverly Cleary.

Q: Not Douglas Adams?

A: Ray Bradbury has some explaining to do about a short story. Beverly Cleary is a UW Husky alumnus and I loved her stories too.

ABOUT THE AUTHOR

Sheila M. Sullivan grew up in Northern California enjoying adventures with her siblings deep in the heart of the redwoods. The love of books was instilled by both her parents who enjoyed a lifetime of reading and book collecting.

Today Sheila spends her time traveling with her wife, writing daily, and playing with their adorable Cardigan Welsh Corgi.

Drop me a note at: info@sheilamsullivan.com